BROOKLYN SUPREME

BROOKLYN SUPREME

ROBERT REULAND

THE OVERLOOK PRESS, NEW YORK

This edition first published in hardcover in 2021 by
The Overlook Press, an imprint of ABRAMS
195 Broadway, 9th floor
New York, NY 10007
www.overlookpress.com

Abrams books are available at special discounts when purchased in quantity
for premiums and promotions as well as fundraising or educational use.
Special editions can also be created to specification. For details,
contact specialsales@abramsbooks.com or the address above.

Library of Congress Control Number: 2021934844

Printed and bound in the U.S.A.

1 3 5 7 9 10 8 6 4 2
ISBN: 978-1-4197-5065-6
eISBN: 978-1-64700-118-6

ABRAMS The Art of Books
195 Broadway, New York, NY 10007
abramsbooks.com

This book is for my daughter Emma, with love

GEORGINA

ONE

Police Officer Georgina Reed killed a man. A boy, really. She gave me her story in a stationhouse basement. She really didn't know who I was or why she had to tell me, so she lied. She was scared. She had just seen her future rearranged in the time it took a single nine-millimeter hollowpoint bullet to find its target on a Brooklyn street corner, so the best she could do was to make it all sound perfectly reasonable.

After, I was still in Bushwick, idling at a green light and not realizing it was green until behind me came the first car horn, then the second and the third, each of them sounding indifferently urgent and far away with my windows closed and my mind stuck in the 83 basement, where Georgina Reed—too young for this, barely a cop—told me her story on a metal folding chair. She lied, of course, but by the time I learned the truth I no longer cared so much and just wanted to sleep. On the night of, however, idling at the green light, I wanted to know. I wanted to know what had gone down on that street corner because it was my job to know the truth and if necessary to hide it.

Across the street, traffic moved in the opposite direction, a blur of light in my periphery, and I heard the car horns. In my mirror I could see nothing definite. The rain on the glass broke the headlights and taillights behind me into a thousand pieces colored brilliant red and white. I wound down my window and all the noise sounded closer but still empty. I made a gesture with my hand and the cars pulled around and I was alone again and it was quiet.

This is where it happened, Broadway and Putnam, the scene of the crime. Maybe. Not my call. I'm not in the finger-pointing business. And who knows, I told myself, maybe it did go down just like she said—that she had to drop the kid, that she had no choice, but I didn't think so. Ask me, Georgina Reed was too quick on the draw. Besides, I was thinking, something's fucked with her whole story. There was an earnestness about her, in her need to be believed, and nothing betrays a lie like the urgency to make it credible. So, I was at Putnam Avenue and Broadway after leaving Georgina Reed in the basement of the stationhouse a few short blocks north after she'd said what she wanted to say, shaking my hand goodbye with her short cold fingers, her moist dark eyes suggesting hope that I could help her, if only I might believe her.

Already after midnight when I walked out of the stationhouse into the rain, I should've just gone home. Home anyway was not home but a few rooms in an apartment building, more hotel than home. I left the 83 and started my car and stayed there with the engine running thinking, now what? The possibilities were endless. I could've called Garrity and awaked him, given him the news, ruined his night. I could also have gone to see Kat. She might have been awake, I thought, and even if she wasn't she wouldn't have minded. She would've sat up in bed and held me and smelled like sleep. Or I could have gone somewhere quiet and pretended to drink it all away, doing a halfway decent imitation of my former self on an anonymous barstool.

Instead I ended up here, at the scene of the whatever. I wanted to know. Funny now to think there was a time when I wanted the truth. Even then I knew there were no answers for me on this street corner, yet I wanted to know anyway. I drove down these familiar Bushwick streets from the 83 house. I was thinking about Georgina's story and what I should do with it. I was thinking of that when I found myself idling at a green light on the corner where it happened. I double-parked and killed the engine. The wipers made the scene intermittently clear, then obscure, then clear. It was like her story.

Police Officer Georgina Reed told me the most plausible lie one could imagine. She was on patrol, she said between carefully measured breaths, working an four-by-twelve, in uniform, in a radio marked patrol car, with her regular partner, Police Officer Gordon Holtz. Holtz I knew from my time in uniform when I was assigned to this same command. Reed, however, was a new face. Not a rookie, she was nevertheless altogether new. Everything about her was newly issued: the black leather of her work belt, her holster, still a shiny black, not yet worn dull from years of getting into patrol cars, of getting out again, of running up unlit stairways of housing projects. The polyester material of her navy-blue uniform, too, was still fresh, still factory-creased, buttoned tight over her Kevlar vest, tight against a small body that was not fat exactly but full. Under the vest and uniform and whatever feminine thing Georgina Reed wore beneath it all I imagined she smelled of fear and scented deodorant.

Eight hours later Kat would ask me about Georgina Reed in the bright light of morning. By then the television had it, but only enough to fill thirty seconds before commercials. Things hadn't gotten warm yet. For now there were no signs, no marches, no flowers, no patrol cars overturned and burned, no impromptu assassinations, no lives thrown onto the pyre, no microwave ovens looted through the broken windows of discount appliance stores on Atlantic Avenue. That would all come later. For now Georgina Reed was interesting only because Georgina was not George, and the lede began, *Last night in Brooklyn a policewoman shot and killed.* . . . Later they would broadcast her service picture, Georgina against a green background, her skin bleached light in the flash. She might have been anything in that photograph, even a police officer. "What's she look like?" Kat would ask before that, meaning *Is she black or is she white?* because Americans can't talk about race even when they talk about race.

"Look like?" I would say.

"You know—pretty?" Kat would respond, still unable to pose the question.

Is Georgina Reed pretty? I hadn't noticed, so—no, she wasn't—at least she wasn't pretty under the scalding fluorescent lights of a stationhouse basement, trying to explain in very precise language how she may have killed a boy but didn't murder him. In another context Georgina Reed might've been pretty, who knows. I just listened. On the job I'm cool as a priest, receiving confessions with bland indifference. Authority is a great disguise. You can hide all of yourself inside.

But yeah, I suppose Georgina Reed was black, or black enough to make a difference. In person Georgina Reed was the color of coffee, two milks, her dark hair pinned flat, her nose somewhat aquiline yet narrow as an Episcopalian's. When later I wanted to know the answer for certain, I pulled her service record—a very thin service record—in the captain's office upstairs. She was twenty-three, I found, a Navy veteran, born in Pennsylvania, five feet five inches tall, one hundred fifty-three pounds, and the box Georgina Reed had checked was "Afro-American," not "White," not "Non-White Hispanic," nor yet "Other." None of that mattered when we sat on metal folding chairs in the 83 basement, the two of us facing each other, our bodies in the same arrangement of parts, feet spread, knees splayed, both of us leaning in. She told me her story as if she were on the stand, duly making eye contact to prove the truth was in her, pausing occasionally to take my temperature, waiting for me to call bullshit or just tell her to go on.

"Go on," I'd said.

"We were in the car, Donny—Police Officer Holtz—and me."

"When did the call come over?"

"Like six thirty—wait, um," she answered, rolling slightly to pull a pristine leather-bound memo book from her right rear pocket. Short, I noted, her femur half the length of mine. She'd been seated when I came down, waiting for me, and hadn't stood when I told her I was her union trustee. While she accepted me as friendly her face showed she didn't believe I was the cavalry. I had insisted no one talk to her before me, so she'd been sitting in the basement an hour alone before I arrived. An hour is a hell of a long time to be alone at such a moment so, cavalry or no, her eyes showed that for the moment I'd do.

"Ah, eighteen thirty-seven," she continued, military time, copspeak, favoring me as a member of the tribe, no matter what else she may have thought. "Radio run over central, ten-thirty, robbery of a bodega, corner of Broadway and Gates. We got a description, two male blacks, teens or early twenties, one real big, the other light skin and small."

"I see that a minute?" I asked her, leaning over her memo book, which she had on her knee, the stiff unblemished leather cover turned back on itself. As I moved in, however, she stiffened and nearly pulled it away. In the same instant she said, in a compliant tone, "Sure." She was all divided up that way inside, wanting to share what she wanted to hide. Her handwriting on the ruled oblong page was like a letter from your high school girlfriend, looping, overlegible, so unlike the indecipherable scratchings in the book I kept myself when I wore this same uniform, when I walked these same streets as Georgina Reed. There, I read verbatim what she had just told me, so her apprehension was not about what I might see written in purple pen but some altogether different, unmemorialized fear. I handed it back. In that moment our fingers brushed and the human contact seemed to loosen her somewhat. She sank slightly. "Let's get to the gun," I said. She started to ask who, then instead asked when. "I mean the job came over as a robbery, right? Robbery with a gun?"

"Just a robbery, a ten-thirty. I wrote it down."

"I see that," I said, almost kindly. "But what I'm asking is did it come over as a gun, too? You see what I'm asking here, right? Because if central said gun, you'd be thinking gun when you rolled up on the guy."

"I think it just came over central as a robbery." I nodded. Then she asked, "Should I write it down? Would it be better if I wrote it—?"

Jesus, she was scared. Now it was beginning to hit her, to really hit her. Soon she would be no good to anyone, but for the time being she was still with me and I wanted to keep her there until she told me everything there was to say, or at least everything she was able to say.

"Central radio's recorded, Officer," I said, "so writing down different isn't going to help, is it?"

"So, what do you want me to—"

"Just—then what?" I asked. "The job comes over. Then what? You and Holtz canvass around for the perps or what?"

"No, they were right there. We were parked right there, on the corner, and as soon as the job came over Donny was like, there they are. And he kind of laughed. Because it was weird. Because it was them. It was the big guy—the, um, the victim? And the littler guy was with him. And you could see they seen us the minute we seen them, and they like stopped. They stopped, said something, then kept coming right toward us."

"Where are you?"

"Broadway and Putnam, northeast corner. And they're coming south down Putnam. I get out. Donny stays in the car."

"Did you call for backup?" I ask.

"No, I—"

I sneezed from nowhere and it scared the hell out of her. She put a hand on her chest. She had a big ring and colorful nail wraps an inch long at least. "Holy Mother," I said. "Goddamn head cold." I blew my nose on a paper napkin I found on the concrete floor by my feet. I said, "Go on," and presently she collected herself and continued, now in a different voice. I figured I had ten more minutes tops until she fell apart.

"I was saying," she said. "We knew it was them, it was the really big one, the victim, he was really big. Like—obese."

"Yeah, he was."

"You know?" she asked, surprised.

We both waited for the other, until I asked, "You know he's dead. I mean, right?"

"Oh, my God—" She threw her head back.

"Officer, come on," I said. "Nine-millimeter hollowpoint to the pulmonary artery? You don't walk that shit off." I sneezed again and she tensed, facing me with an expression like horror. I didn't care. I wasn't here to make friends; I was here to shake her tree and see what fell out. "So, let's back it up. You get out of your RMP. Take me from there."

"I told you like three times."

"You got someplace else you gotta be?"

She hesitated, looking down at my hands. "You're not taking no notes."

"I have a good memory."

"Then why you want me to keep telling you?" she said.

"To make sure you got a good memory, too," I told her. "I write down what you tell me, then what I write down is what happened. But say you change your mind about what happened, then my what happened is different from your what happened. Get it?"

"No."

"Believe me, Officer, they will," I say. "So you better tell me what happened and it better be what happened."

"I am—I din't murder nobody."

"Look," I said. "I'm in a shitty mood, I'm sorry. I have a cold. I'm reading books again, which is always a bad sign, and my dog died last week. But, Officer, in about twenty-four hours every rock in the world is going to fall on your head and no one's gonna want to be standing anywhere near you when that happens. But I'm gonna be there. That's why you pay your union dues. And if I'm gonna be standing with you, I gotta know where you stand."

After a pause during which I could feel the turmoil in her, I thought for a moment that she was going to let the truth out. Instead, all she said was, "I'm sorry about your dog."

"It's okay," I said automatically. "She was old. It was her time. Do you understand what I'm telling you, Officer?"

"Yes," she said simply, not looking at me, but she didn't understand, not really. Maybe Georgina Reed had never watched television or read a newspaper. Or perhaps all she thought was that she was in trouble with quotes around it. "What kind of dog was she?" she asked, and I noticed she was now crying very softly, the tears filling her eyes without falling.

"Ah—a mix. A mutt, really. Not much of a dog, but one of the best people I've ever known."

Now the tears fell, gathered and fell. She made no sound.

"Okay, you want to have a nice cry," I said. "I can go out for a cigarette."

She closed her eyes and in a moment it was over. She drew a heavy breath inside her vest, bulletproof, then looked at me with a gaze cool with hatred or worse. She had a reserve of strength, I realized then, and for a moment that would never repeat itself in the course of our short acquaintance I was interested to know more about Georgina Reed, for strength is always fascinating.

"I din't murder nobody."

"No one's saying—" I started.

"Look at me. You think I could murder? I was afraid. I was afraid for my life."

"Officer—"

"I mean, you even know what it's like? When you're out there, by yourself, and somebody—somebody you don't know—hates you—and you only got a second—?" She stared right into me, daring me to answer.

"Yes, Officer," I told her, my turn to lie. "Yes, I do."

TWO

The basement door swung abruptly wide and there was Gordon Holtz. I recognized him at once. He'd been in a different platoon than mine, and we'd never ridden together, but for two years at least we'd worked in this same command, bringing law and order to the good people of Bushwick. He had thrust the door open so violently that it struck the wall with a sharp crack like a pistol shot that echoed in the basement, low-ceilinged, the walls painted a dirty ocher, lit by fluorescent tubes. Georgina started at the sound and turned to face her partner, who came right over. She stood and to my astonishment each wrapped the other in a bear hug, their bodies disproportionate and unlike and entwined.

"You okay, Gina?" I heard him ask into her ear, fully twelve inches beneath his, and she responded with a quick nod.

"How we doing?" Donny asked me, pulling a folding chair over for himself, his expression friendly, unperturbed, imperturbable, yet I supposed he actually wanted to know. He gave me his hand and took me in, his drowsy blue eyes flat as cops' eyes get. I knew the face, sure, but he saw me without recognition. I wasn't offended. Not a house mouse, I nevertheless had kept my head down when I worked patrol, trying to pretend being a cop was just a job.

Police Officer Gordon Holtz was a giant towheaded man, well over six feet tall with a barrel torso and callused hands and a knot of blond bristle above his necktie, all of it set off by a disconcertingly boyish face. With his wide-open demeanor he eased the tension in the room as efficiently as a golden retriever.

"Will Way," I told him. "I'm PBA."

"Okay." A dull expression.

"Your union guy."

"Okay."

"Patrolmen's Benevolent Association—?"

"Yeah, sure, I got it."

I wasn't sure he did. He seemed a little slow and too relaxed for the context. "That means you can talk to me," I said. "They can't."

"Who can't?"

"Brooklyn DA, bosses, Internal Affairs, whoever," I said. "They can't talk to you for forty-eight hours."

"Yeah, I know!"

"I'm on your side, so—"

"Great!"

"—maybe I can help you out."

"Great!" he repeated.

"What then?" Georgina Reed said, evidently the brains in the family. "What after the forty-eight hours?"

"Then you got no choice," I said. "You have to make your statement."

"Why?" she asked.

"Because those are the rules, Officer."

"What about the right to remain silent and all?"

"Constitution don't apply to cops, Gina," Holtz answered for me, patrolman wisdom, cop dogma, polished up on a barstool after hours in every sports bar in Nassau County. "Only the shitheads got rights, ha ha!"

"Is that true?" she asked me.

"More or less," I said. "You're a cop. Read the fine print. You have to give up a statement in two days."

"That seems—I don't know."

"You can always quit, you don't like it. Besides"—I sneezed violently into my left shoulder—"what you told me already doesn't make out an unauthorized discharge, much less a crime. Does it? So what's the worry?" Now I was looking at two blank faces. "Does it?" I said, opening my hands in fake dismay. "Come on, people. Where's the worry? He pulled out, right?"

Nothing.

"Oh, by the way, pistol or revolver?"

"Excuse me?" she asked.

"The kid's gun."

Reed consulted Holtz. Holtz consulted Reed. "I din't notice," she answered at length, looking somewhere. Holtz added, "You gotta ask the sarge."

"Who is—?"

"Sergeant Bear."

"Berrigan," I said with an inward sigh. "I'll be damned. He still on the job?"

"Yes," Reed said.

"He was there?"

"Yes," she said. "No."

"Yes, no—what is he, four-dimensional?"

"Not at first," she said. "Then he came. Him and his driver."

"Who is?"

Holtz shrugged and said, "New guy."

"Karpatkin," Reed said in vague tone, and I immediately forgot the name.

"They rolled up after," said Holtz. "After I called it in."

"Will you talk to them?" she said. "My sergeant vouchered the victim's weapon."

"Bear I can't talk to," I told her. "At least not on the record. He's a sergeant and not one of mine. The rookie guy—what's his name?—I'll try to get to him tonight."

"Will you?"

"Weather permitting."

"I don't understand."

"Shit storm is coming," I said to her. "And another thing, Officer, let's call Dewberry the perpetrator. Or the assailant. You call him the victim all the time, makes it sound like—like he's a victim."

After a pause she asked, "That his name?"

"Raquan Dewberry. Seventeen," I said, then I told her what else I knew, knowing it wouldn't help. "Long sheet for seventeen," I said, leafing through my disorganized and hastily scrawled notes. "Long sheet for fifty. Seven collars, starting age thirteen. Two prior YO adjudications. We're trying to get them unsealed, but they both look like assaults with a deadly. In and out of Spofford. Suspended FK Lane. Off to Tryon."

I watched Reed, whose eyes never moved from the floor.

"In other words, Officer, Raquan Dewberry wasn't getting out of the batter's box. He was never going to collect social security, so don't beat yourself—"

"You don't know that," she stopped me, angry. "That he was never—that he—" she began, searching in vain for words until she gave up. That was all I would get from her that night. I'd blown it with Georgina Reed, I knew. I'd not needed her to like me, but I'd needed her to tell me how it was. Instead, she ended up believing I was just another suit. I'd gone the wrong way with her, talking to her the Manichean way cops speak to one another when they want to pretend, forgetting Georgina Reed wasn't a cop.

I stood and so did they. For the first time I noticed her shiny new holster was empty. Holtz, too, was unarmed, the timeworn brown leather gaping at his side, the absence of his Glock 17 like a missing thumb or limb. Both their weapons were now in evidence bags somewhere, surrendered, proof of something, hers a single nine-millimeter round lighter than his.

My legs were stiff and I was suddenly very hungry. I'd missed dinner and blown three red lights to be here, running off the six miles from headquarters on Fulton Street in lower Manhattan to this Brooklyn backwater precinct less than thirty minutes after I hung up with Masterson. Mark Masterson was my hook at Internal Affairs. We'd been partnered up when I wore a uniform, but that was not why he fed me. He did so neither out of friendship nor corruption but because he believed so faithfully in the law that he felt constrained sometimes to break it. He knew that IAB in its zeal to clean house could scrub the walls down to the studs. Why he thought I shared his mission I didn't know. More likely he believed simply I'd take his information and not ask too many questions.

His telephone call had stopped me as I was heading for the door at Fulton Street, one arm already in my overcoat. Sheila Simmons, my police administrative assistant, had left, and my phone rang and rang. I picked up, supposing Kat had forgiven me. Instead it was Mark Masterson's familiar low, circumspect voice on the line, telling me we had a discharge in the 83 and if I hurried I might even beat him there. I blew him a kiss, slammed the receiver, and firewalled the accelerator all the way to Bushwick, not even bothering to find parking but leaving my sky-blue Ford with city plates on the walkway in front of the 83 house, a plasticized NYPD placard thrown on the dashboard by way of apology. Now, hours later, the adrenal hit was spent, and I'd begun to sense that strange dissipation I frequently felt at moments such as this, when the ship is sinking but I'm smugly ashore—moments when I remember we're each the author of our own fate, after all, so exactly what miracle do they expect from me anyway?

Nevertheless I asked Georgina Reed to wait for me upstairs in the juvenile room, to lock the door, and to speak to no one until I came for her. I was still working.

I didn't like the idea of leaving her in the stationhouse, which as early as then—11:47 on the night of—had begun to seethe with assistant district attorneys, assorted rat squad cocksuckers, women with plastic hair and microphones, random departmental hairbags wondering what the fuck, and a dozen chinless chiefs and inspectors and deputy commissioners from One Police Plaza hoping to keep their pensions when this thing blew up. And it would blow up, but for now I needed Reed quiet and Holtz all to myself. I needed to hear how he told his story, for two people never tell the same story when they're telling the truth. But after Georgina Reed had gone upstairs and I sat on a metal folding chair with Gordon Holtz for another half hour in the 83 basement I listened very carefully and probably shouldn't have been at all surprised that his story was the same as hers.

I sent him home.

Upstairs I tried the door to the juvie room, expecting it to be locked. Instead I pushed right in. The lights were on, but rather than Police Officer Georgina Reed waiting alone for me inside, her brown eyes wearily expectant, I found only three vacant chairs, mismatched, and a doughnut box yawning empty on the lacerated tabletop. I made my way back to the patrol desk, where on top of everything the tour was changing with the midnight platoon coming in. The desk sergeant and a lieutenant were hollering, directing traffic, and the feeling was violently alive yet static. Everyone was getting the word. I heard someone say, "The fuck's Georgina Reed anyway?"—a question I would hear more and more in the next few days. Reed had not made much of an impression on her peers, it seemed, and for my part I was looking for any woman in uniform. I could no longer picture her face. Yet Georgina Reed was nowhere in the press of blue, and after a while I felt like a dad who'd lost a kid at Macy's.

Back to the juvie room.

Then back downstairs.

Then up to the muster room, where I saw Sergeant Ralph Berrigan sitting with a civilian in the far corner. Berrigan was instantly recognizable: his squat muscular form, his Lord Kitchener mustache, his graying hair trimmed high and tight, all of him unchanged from my memory of him, from the time not so long ago when he used to give me orders. We saw each other at the same moment. He waved me over. I obeyed.

"Way! Will Way, come on over here, you old pussycat."

I ought to have anticipated the moment when I would see him again, having heard his name tonight for the first time in years, knowing Berrigan had a piece of this thing, but I was not prepared for the swell of the old familiar emotion I felt upon seeing him—an odd mix of respect, fear, disgust, and love combining to form nausea, as colors mixed form gray.

"Sarge, hey," I said, and he took my hand and pulled me in, the boar-bristle brush of his head scraping my chin, his body smelling of cigarettes and aftershave—the same smell, an outmoded smell, the smell of men when I was a boy. "How you been?"

"I'm a wreck," he lied, giving his chest a resonant gorilla pounding. He seemed not to have aged an hour. Berrigan was a righteous son of a bitch of the old school. He'd been on the job since they started making cops and had no patience for Kevlar and semiautomatics. He carried a revolver instead, a black and fiercely ugly Webley his grandfather used to shoot Protestants. I never impressed him much as a patrolman, yet he liked me a little because I knew how to read, a circumstance that simultaneously drew him to me and kept him always at a safe distance. I would read the ancients here in the muster room late at night whenever I could, whenever there was nothing much going on in Bushwick, or at least nothing I could do anything about. In this selfsame room, for instance, I read Hesiod in a library discard hardcover, underlining in pencil, *When you are building a house, do not leave it roughhewn, or a cawing crow may settle on it and croak at you.* "Look at me," Berrigan ordered. He had a thin smile, as thin and unwholesome as skim milk. "I'm falling apart."

He sat again. Meanwhile the man next to him hadn't risen or said a word, yet he examined me warily. Berrigan didn't bother to introduce him, nor did he introduce himself. I'd supposed he was a civilian boss, but now I wasn't so certain. Both were sitting near the open window, a half dozen cigarette butts pressed out on the sill marked with raindrops and pigeon shit. Outside, on Knickerbocker Avenue, I could make out the rear quarter panel of my Ford on the walkway. So far no one had towed it. A television truck had pulled up behind me, however, and another behind that. Things were getting going.

"Misplace somebody?" Berrigan said, laughing noiselessly, his torso going up and down, his white uniform shirt pulling away at the buttons, showing skin below, and hair. The old warhorse still refused a vest. With a jerk of his head Berrigan indicated the office behind him. The door was shut.

"Christ," I said, moving to the door.

The man beside Berrigan swore under his breath and started to rise but Berrigan took his arm. "Young Will is PBA," I heard Berrigan tell the man as I moved past them. "I'd let him go, Ronny. He's a dangerous man when his blood's up, ha ha!"

I pulled open the door on the back of Georgina Reed, seated. Across the table, on which there sat a cassette tape recorder and microphone, I saw a woman, blond, sternly beautiful in an unremarkable gray jacket. She examined me coolly while Reed turned with the face of a doe. "Hell is this?" I said to the woman in gray. There were other people in the room, but you could tell she was in charge.

"No, no, it's okay," Reed told me, hurriedly. "She's—"

"No, Officer, it's not okay," I answered sharply, then to the other, "Who are you? Cop? DA? What?"

"I'm not a cop," said the woman in gray, standing. More precisely she unfolded herself like a crane, for she was tall and all long bones. She was wholly unperturbed by me, and she may even have smiled ever so slightly, infuriating me unreasonably, when she asked, "Are you?"

"Hell you doing?" I said. Seeing her machine was still running, I stopped it. Then I hit it and pried out the cassette. "Fucking unbelievable."

"Hey, now," said the man with Berrigan. They were both watching from the doorway behind me. Berrigan's chest was going up and down, his blue eyes shining through slits. He was having a fine old time. "Hey, now," repeated the man. "Is that necessary, Officer?"

"Go get 'em, Way," Berrigan erupted. "Ha ha!"

"Hey, now. You—"

"Let him keep it," the tall woman said, folding herself back onto her chair. Her hair, which in the bleached fluorescent light of the room appeared blond at first, I saw now was a pale red. She had a complexion to match and green watercolor eyes that were intelligent and a little tired. "He may want it as a memento, but he probably won't need one."

"Whoever you people are," I told her, "you leave my men alone."

"He's PBA, Jackie," said the man with Berrigan.

"It's the forty-eight-hour rule," I said. "So fuck off."

The tall woman in gray considered me. "I'm gratified you follow rules, Officer," she gave out. "So refreshing. But Officer Reed here wanted to talk. Nothing says I can't talk to your man, if she wants to talk to me."

"She just changed her mind," I said and put a hand on Georgina Reed's shoulder, feeling her narrow collarbone beneath the strap of her bulletproof vest. "Let's go." Obediently she stood, and as we passed together through the doorway she exchanged a glance with Ralph Berrigan full of helpless apprehension on her end and almost jovial reassurance on his. I sneezed.

I was nearly at the door to the muster room when the tall woman called out, "God bless you," which made Berrigan erupt again into renewed peals of laughter that went through me like lead. Leaving Reed I walked back into the office and set the cassette on the table. With a finger I pushed it toward the tall woman. "I won't need this. You're absolutely right." She smiled wearily, almost kindly, not taking the bait. Our eyes met, and I saw that I'd need to get my house in order fast else she'd settle on it and croak at me.

THREE

In America killers disappoint. Never have I met a killer on our avenues or apartment houses nor inside a police station pen nor in the high-ceilinged court-rooms of Brooklyn Supreme who seemed quite up to the word. In the book of my experience a killer is just some skinny fatherless barely literate mope who points a gun at some other skinny fatherless barely literate mope who's done nothing so very terrible and yet—in the brutal, irrefutable logic of the street corner—deserved to die nonetheless. Georgina Reed was different, of course. She had killed, but she was no murderer. I knew that, not because she told me, repeatedly and unnecessarily, through a veil of inchoate tears, but because it made no sense to call Georgina Reed a murderer. Senseless crime usually makes sense.

But who knew. I'd been wrong before. The job is full of surprises.

Georgina Reed had given me her truth, but not the truth—not the whole truth and nothing but. What interested me more than her truth was her lie, for the most interesting truths in this business are always the ones hidden by lies. When you uncover the lie, well, then you have the truth. For the moment, however, her truth was enough to let me stand with her. I had to stand with her regardless, but it's always better when you can feel good about your man. Then you can stand a little closer.

Now on the corner where the thing happened, the rain on the windshield of my sky-blue Ford, I considered my next move. There was no reason for me to be here. I just came. I was a tourist, looking for souvenirs. I stepped out of the car and shut the door. I'd been here before, of course, to this very street corner countless times, but not once in the past four years. Was it four years already? Holy Mother, a lifetime ago when I worked a footpost, in Bushwick, in uniform. Once I rolled up here in time to watch a man bleed to death against this same rusty chain-link fence. He was very angry about dying and took a swing at me with a filet knife with a duct-taped handle and his curses flew out with blood and spit. We couldn't get near him. He died on his knees, genuflecting as if in prayer in the back of some dissolute church, beseeching whatever minor gods might have loitered here for—what? Forgiveness? Mercy? Vengeance, probably.

Bushwick was poor black then. Now it was poor black and pioneer white, a neighborhood of pit bulls and poodles, shotguns and strollers. The readjustment had taken less than five years. On this corner, for instance, I now saw the playful logo of an outpost of a SoHo seven-dollar coffee spot, a transplant from their Broadway to ours, the inside aglow with laptops even at this hour and white faces pressed to the glass, urban homesteaders priced out of Manhattan and Park Slope now questioning their decision to seek the real Brooklyn.

In the wan orange streetlight this stretch of road was less brutal than in daylight, but not much less. Broadway here cut a four-lane groove between hundred-year-old brick storefronts low enough to show a lot of sky above and even constellations and planets during rolling brownouts and the dark of the moon. An elevated train track put a roof on everything and made noise at twelve-minute intervals in both directions. There was nothing very special about any of it, in other words, except this was where everything started with Georgina Reed. Later—not tonight, but soon—this corner would become a makeshift shrine with flowers tied to the chain-link fence and handwritten condolence cards and prayer candles in tall glasses featuring the benevolent face of Our Lady of Guadalupe. Right now the corner teemed, but it was still all official: five command cars, a white go-to-hell station wagon with CRIME SCENE UNIT in blue block capitals along each side, MEDICAL EXAMINER written on something similar, and an ESU truck with a spotlight. Two cops were putting up a portable lamp stand, and there were uniforms everywhere and easily a dozen suits, either detectives or civilian bosses come down to stick their fingers in the dike.

Over the scene an irresolute spring rain came, cold and thin. My suit jacket spotted as I stood hesitantly by my Ford, still uncertain whether I should stay or go. Amid the general low sound of voices the generator on the lamp stand kicked noisily to life and everything changed at once from orange to white, like a theater set. Lit in the glare, the rain seemed more real than it felt. Now I could see yellow crime scene tape tied to the chain-link fence, then to a fire hydrant, then to an alternate side parking sign, then to a graffitied mailbox, and then back to the fence, segmenting a polygon of the sidewalk on the northeast corner of Putnam Avenue and Broadway the size of an eight-hundred-dollar apartment. I paced over, hands in pockets, harmless. Apart from the others a uniform stood alone securing the taped scene. He stood round-shouldered against the mailbox, paper coffee cup not steaming in his left hand, and he took me in with an expression of almost unbearable torpor.

"Hey, brother," I said, clipping my Li'l Sheriff Kit toy badge onto my lapel. He nodded in reply. Both of us stood there for a spell in the rain, facing in the same direction, downward looking, unspeaking, as if on the bank of a brown stream fishing or at adjoining urinals during intermission. There was nothing to say, nothing to see, except blood, and the rain was already washing that away. CSU had placed numbered evidence tents around the scene. By the fence, on the other side of the tape, I saw a rolled paper cone containing a dozen flowers, lying mournfully pink on the concrete getting wet.

I was done, ready to leave with the same nothing I came with. Before I walked away I turned to the solitary patrolman and said, "Least you'll score some good OT." His coffee came from the new place across the street, and the cheeky childish image in his hand in such a place seemed discordant, nearly blasphemous. He made a kind of laugh. He was young, impossibly young, and had a junior college look to him—a suburban kid whose first footsteps in Brooklyn were in uniform. Yet he already wore an expression I'd see a lot in the next few days, a look that seemed to suggest, *Ah, Jesus, here we go again—*

"Jesus, here we go again," I said aloud to myself, twisting the AM dial on the car radio to the news station as I drove west from Bushwick, waiting for word of Georgina Reed amid the neurotic cadence of weather, traffic, Monica Lewinsky, and advertisements for life insurance and automobiles with safety features and medicines with side effects that included dry mouth, bloody stool, nausea, and death. It had become a dangerous world. You couldn't be too careful.

On Atlantic Avenue there was little traffic, and the emptiness and stillness of everything at that early morning hour made my mind empty and still, and it felt good to think of nothing for a few blocks. After a few blocks, however, I thought of the tall woman with the pale green eyes and strawberry-blond hair. "Too pretty to be a DA," I said to myself. "Maybe a fed." So went my train of thought when I heard:

—shot dead tonight in Bushwick. Laquan Dewberry, seventeen of Brooklyn, robbed a grocery store and assaulted the cashier before making off with flowers and a candy bar before he was apprehended by police a few blocks away. Police say Dewberry then drew a gun and pointed it at a police officer who shot him once in the chest. Dewberry died at the scene. Another unnamed youth was arrested and charged with robbery. In sporting news—

"Raquan," I said peevishly into the void, twisting the volume down, then off. After a half mile I asked myself, "What kind of candy bar?" I was hungry, but this stretch of Atlantic was all gas stations and flat fixes at this hour and in daytime not much more. "Definitely a fed," I decided another half mile later, still talking to myself, supposing the tall woman in the gray jacket was too uptown for a downtown deal like the Brooklyn district attorney, but the idea that the feds were already sharpening knives for Georgina Reed gave me a chill. I counted assistant U.S. attorneys I knew and realized I knew damn few, and none well enough to send birthday cards to. I stayed away from the federal courthouse on Cadman Plaza whenever I could. It always felt like walking into the wrong homeroom. In federal court everyone wore ties. In federal court no one spoke Brooklyn. No one ever shouted in federal court and the hallways were never crowded nor reeking of weed with babies bawling in strollers and fistfights breaking out between factions and witnesses and girlfriends. Federal court was just different. Federal district court was clean.

My natural habitat, on the other hand, was state court, Kings County Supreme Court—down the block and around the corner, on the wrong side of the subway tracks. Brooklyn Supreme was not so clean, but at least it was real. Brooklyn Supreme didn't have candy-ass federal indictments for tax evasion and money laundering and white-collar bullshit whatever. Brooklyn Supreme had the crimes that made you mad—robbery, rape, riot. Murder could make you mad, often, so I couldn't imagine how the feds might look for a piece of Reed, but it had been a long day and I was already thinking of flowers.

I'd seen Raquan Dewberry laid out on the sidewalk, a midrange Polaroid and a close-up of his face, his tongue peeking out pink like a paradigm corpse, just waiting for Xs to be written on his eyelids, dead. Dewberry was a big kid with a hard face that death made harder. You could tell every day of his life he'd come up against a locked door, yet he'd made it to seventeen years old, which in some precincts was an accomplishment Mom could frame and hang on the wall. Boosting a candy bar made sense for Raquan Dewberry, nine candy bars even, but flowers—? It didn't fit. And in a murder story what doesn't fit is always useful.

"Flowers." I laughed out loud. "I love Brooklyn."

GARRITY

FOUR

Morning came on time, unfairly, and the bed was empty and cool where she had lain. Stumping sleepily barefoot down the long, long staircase, over the blue Persian runner, in my suit pants and egg-stained undershirt, I found Kat and Phillip waiting by the enormous front door, each looking at me with the same expression of tolerant amusement. I shook hands with Phillip with the exaggerated formality that had become our routine since I first refused his proffered fist on general principle.

"Good day to you, sir," said he, like an English butler.

"And a very good morning to you, sir," said I.

Meanwhile Kat was pulling his left arm through a raincoat with the fierce brutality only a mother can exert on her young. Like Kat he was slight, as weightless as a bird, with the same brown Paris eyes, the same blond Oslo hair. Here in the entrance to her Park Slope brownstone, all mahogany Victorian splendor, she had met me in the dark of the night wearing something negligible, her expression genuine, pleasurable surprise, telling me to come in, come in, that I was wet, that I didn't have sense to come in out of the rain, et cetera. She stripped me dry, fed me runny eggs, then took me to bed, where the tug of sleep pulled me under.

Now Phillip said to me happily, "I have a cultural studies quiz this morning!"

"Me too," I said.

"Paper's on the table," Kat told me with a prosecutorial glint in her eye.

"Front page—?"

"Metro. Below the fold."

"Garrity's colon will appreciate that," I said.

"What's a colon?" the boy said.

"A punctuation mark."

"No, it's not that! My grandpa has a colon!"

"Let me show you," I told him, pinching him above his left hip and igniting a riot of laughter. He slipped away and ran out the door and down the stoop, barely stable beneath a backpack, absurdly huge, looking like Buzz Aldrin on the surface of the moon. "Cheerio, my good man!" he called back.

I was seated in the parlor on a slippery yellow leather couch when Kat returned twenty minutes later. She leaned in and kissed me with intent, her cheek cold. For drop-off Kat had dressed with her wonted casual elegance: a pink cashmere sweater and buff-colored riding pants, the lingering damp from last night's rain giving a plausible excuse to have pulled on green wellies and a short waxed cotton jacket that smelled like a tent. "I haven't seen you in days and days and days!"

"Well, two," I said. "Read it?" The two-hundred-word article only referred to a *policewoman*, a *youth*, and an *uninjured male currently in police custody charged with robbery*.

"It's on the television, too."

"I suppose there was a lot of moral indignation at school."

"Actually no one mentioned it," she said, "but I was in a hurry to get back. I thought you were going to run away on me."

On a bright and cool October morning last year our two divergent orbits momentarily converged, as rare as an eclipse, in the park. I was walking Magdalene, who had already begun to move slower, to place her paws more warily as she walked, bearing with canine stoicism the tumors in her body I knew nothing about. Kat accompanied her neighbor who led a pair of corgis with identical simpering expressions and poufy haunches that seemed vaguely obscene, like Liberace's bouffant. Magdalene, an actual dog, disdained them with a noble hauteur as we passed on the path. Kat's neighbor, a superannuated hippie with a graying ponytail and chapped lips, asked if my doggie was friendly. "My doggies are very friendly," she said. "Aren't you? Yes, you are!"

"I, um—" I started, but then I caught sight of Kat and stayed. Behind blackout sunglasses Kat seemed to regard me with some small interest, the faintest smile playing on her wondrous pink mouth to suggest we each shared a common understanding of her neighbor, doggies, and the world.

"Does he want to play, your doggie?" said the neighbor.

"She," I said, as one of her corgis, a snowy white, barked at nothing while the other—jet black—made ropey turds on the grass. Magdalene began to urge me in the direction of anywhere else in the world while I stayed and stayed and took in Kat bit by bit. And that was how it started with Kat. We were as perfectly suited as only two mismatched people can be, and sometimes I saw in her face that she wondered what she'd been thinking when she fell for me. Once

I volunteered to take Phillip to drop-off and Kat politely demurred, offering a hurried excuse with an averted gaze. My sudden appearance in her morning sidewalk jurisdiction, which a certain set of Park Slope mothers patrolled with the same territorial vigilance as the popular girls' cafeteria table, would have raised too many questions. I understood. No one else would ever get us; it was enough that Kat and I did.

Kat overheard me last night, of course, as I gave Shawn Garrity the rundown in my sleep. Garrity ran the union, and I hoped I'd chosen words that fitted Kat's tender sensibilities. I knew we'd have to have a conversation about Georgina Reed at any rate, and I didn't look forward to it. I tended to piss her off when I spoke about cops, about the job. Kat had a sociolinguistics degree from Bennington, which she'd attended without the least sense of irony, and last Saturday we'd lost an entire morning, postcoital, on the subject of fascism, a political philosophy I had thought consigned to the dustbin of history. Evidently not. Kat insisted he was a fascist whereas I maintained he was simply a small man whom power had corrupted, he being the anonymous patrolman who'd hooked Kat's double-parked yellow Benz coupe to an NYPD tow truck and driven away with it, somewhere. There was a question of unpaid tickets, it developed, something on the order of seventeen.

"He wasn't a fascist, Kat."

"He was so a fascist," she said. I was on my back, counting shooting stars on her bedroom ceiling whereas she was sitting cross-legged and bare-chested, leaning forward and prepared to hit me again with her little ball of a fist. "He was fat, too. With a belly like this."

"A fascist, and fat. His name wasn't Goering, was it?"

"Oh, I don't know his name, Will," she said. "I didn't ask his name. I told him I would move it in like a minute. I just had to pick up my dry cleaning. And some yogurt. But he wouldn't even listen."

"For the record, none of that means he's a fascist."

"What was he, then?"

"Doing his job?"

"Such a cop," she said. "You always take their side. Oh, where's my yellow Benz? You have to find it, Will! Can't you call someone? Can't you fix my tickets?" I started laughing, which didn't help. "What—?" she said, and when I kept laughing she hit me. It hurt.

"Just stop getting tickets, babe."

"You can fix them," she said. "You're a cop."

"I'm hardly a cop. I dropped my gun in the ocean a long time ago."

She thought about that, suddenly serious, dropping the little girl act, which we both knew was an act—as much an act as mine. "Tell me again why you stopped being a police officer."

"I am a police officer."

"You know what I mean."

"I thought they were going to arrest me," I told her truthfully, but she didn't believe me.

Instead all she said was, "I have to tell you something, honey. I'm really not sure what your job is, what you do for the police."

"You know something?" I said, looking again at the ceiling. "I'm really not sure either."

At headquarters on Fulton Street everyone made sure to say hello. After I went by they began speaking again in low voices. Sheila was on me before I reached my office door. Sheila Simmons, my PAA, was six years younger, but nonetheless had been at this longer, so frequently she would point me in the right direction. Frequently she needed to.

"Mr. Garrity wants to see you," she said. "Soon as you come in, he said."

"How long's he been here?"

"Before me, Mr. W."

Already nine forty, I saw. Sheila was usually here promptly at eight thirty. I was usually here promptly at nine forty, but today I should've done better, even with only three hours' sleep. At least I'd shaved, using Kat's pink disposable and a bar of soap, but I should've shaved better, too. And in yesterday's suit, rainspotted and formless, I looked like surrender. In Sheila's hand was a wad of telephone message slips, which she passed me without comment as she left. I closed my door and thumbed through them, still standing. They were all from the press. *Please call. Urgent.* I bet. I recognized some names and separated those from the others, which I dropped in the trash. Then I dropped all of them in the trash.

Things were starting in Brooklyn. Driving in this morning I had—against my better judgment—listened to the news. Protesters were already assembling on Knickerbocker Avenue across from the 83rd Precinct stationhouse. As yet they were nothing like what they would become; rather they were drops from a sunny sky that precede an afternoon hurricane. They were just the familiar faces with one-size-fits-all placards ready to go on a moment's notice to provide a slow-motion rejoinder to the latest grievance or atrocity. Certainly Archbishop

Basil Bumpurs and his congregation would be there. They always were. They were polite enough. We would let them use the facilities and took them coffee when it was cold. And when they chanted *Two! Four! Six! Eight! We don't want no police state!* none of us took it personally.

Kat this morning mercifully had said nothing more on the topic of Georgina Reed. She had something to say, I'm certain. She usually did. She'd appointed herself my apologist, directing a public relations campaign at me on my own behalf, hoping to convince me I wasn't as bad as I seemed to myself. "We're not on different sides," she would defend me, "we just have different perspectives." That is, we both wanted the same thing, which was justice, but frequently her justice was different from my justice, just as our justice was different from their justice. Before the sun set that Wednesday, for instance, Archbishop Bumpurs would forgive Georgina Reed while demanding the Brooklyn DA indict her for murder. So, when Bumpurs and his flock solemnly intoned *No justice, no peace!* Kat and I wholeheartedly agreed, neither of us knowing exactly what that meant. And not for the last time would I wonder: If justice means one thing to you and another thing to me, is there a difference between justice and just trying to feel better about a shitty situation?

So that morning Kat knew better than to touch on Georgina Reed. Instead she kissed me a lot and before I walked out she said, "Oh, I wish we could go to the park instead and have a walk. This is lovely English weather. Look, I have my green wellies on."

"I noticed."

"You notice everything," she told me.

"Do I?"

"About me, you do. About everything else, not so much. I miss Magdalene," she said suddenly, the name making me stop on my way to the door. "We should get another dog, Will."

"We?" I asked. "Are you proposing?"

"What sort of dog was she again?"

"Part labrador retriever, part Presbyterian."

She smiled wistfully at a memory, her small face pretty and fresh. "Remember how she'd jump in the mud in the park on this sort of day and wallow like a pig? And we'd have to hose her off? I miss her!"

"She was old. It was her time."

"She was not!" Kat said, angry. "Why do you always say that, Will?"

"She was eleven."

"She didn't deserve to die because she was eleven."

"She had cancer, Kat," I said. "I gotta go. I'm late."

"I'm angry."

"It was eight thousand dollars, the operation. Eight big ones, Kat."

"It's just money," she said.

"How can you justify eight thousand dollars? For a dog?"

"She was worth eight thousand dollars," she said, so earnest that I was certain she'd begin to cry. "If you love her. And you did."

"I'm not going to say I love a damn dog. I love you."

"You loved her," she said. "You know you did."

"She was a good dog, but she was old. It was her time—"

"I know you loved her. I know it. After—after they took her away, and you were drunk, you asked me if dogs have souls. And you—"

"I really have to go, Kat," I said. "I'll see you tonight."

"Will you really?"

"Probably not," I said, leaning to kiss her, holding her, feeling her rise up on her toes, as she might have done when she was a twelve-year-old ballerina in Connecticut. "Probably not until 2002, come to think of it."

"I think they do have souls," she called after me. When Kat said it, I was already halfway down the stoop. Next door, her neighbor with the gray ponytail and chapped lips was on her knees planting bulbs in her miniature plot alongside her own identical stoop. Nearby, enclosed by a cast-iron fence, her corgis were busily consuming each other, head to tail, black on white, forming a perfect circle like an ouroboros, one of them yelping as if on fire.

"Maybe," I answered, pointing. "But not—"

FIVE

Down the long hallway, which grew longer and longer, like a horror movie hallway, I walked to see Shawn Garrity. Some of the other union men were gathered outside his door, which was conspicuously shut. Garrity always made a point of having an open door, and he always made a point of telling you that. The men turned to face me as I drew near and began shaking their heads in mock disbelief and exercising their wit—*Looking kinda tired, Way—Long night?—You know, you should go to Disneyland—What's that, your resignation letter?*—and one of them made the sign of the cross over my dead body—all which was meant kindly, of course, in the spirit of camaraderie, as at Stalingrad, but I was not in the mood. "Fuck you all very much," I said, and it came out like I meant it. They could take it. They were hard men, and we continued until we all felt foolish talking that way about it.

"No, really," one said, suddenly grave. "What's she saying? Your lady cop there?"

"What d'you hear?" I asked, genuinely interested.

"It's on the TV there. Your cop put one in his back. He gave her attitude so she put one in his back. Then she put one in his brain."

"And his hands were up."

"Walking to Mass."

"He was kneeling."

"With his little kid, they said."

"I heard he was fourteen."

"D'you talk to her or what, Way? Come on."

"I talked to her, sure," I said.

"Come on, Way," they all said. "Give."

"Said the kid pulled out," I said with a shrug. "So she dropped him. One shot to the body."

"To the brain?"

"No," I said, indicating my heart, "right here."

"Nice. Center mass."

"Why?"

"Told you," I said. "The kid was strapped."

"But his hands were up, right?"

"On his knees, right?"

"And the guy across the street who was upstairs looking said he was crying, the kid, begging for his life, but she put him down like a dog, he said."

"Believe her, Way?"

"Why not?" I said.

"'Cause it don't make no sense is why not."

"I say she shit her pants, your lady cop," another put in. I was just listening, in no mood for any of it, but Garrity's door was still shut tight as a submarine hatch and I had no place to hide. "What I heard is she shouldn't've been out there in the first place. I know the FIO in the Seven-five who ran a warrant with her in the Eight-trey last year and he says your Georgina Reed, she ain't no cop. Wouldn't even hit the door, he told me. Scared."

"Yeah, Way, I think I seen her once before. She ain't no cop."

"Yeah, someone said she ain't—"

"Hey," I said. "Hey, she's a cop."

"One of them diversity cops, you mean. Put her on a recruiting poster maybe."

"Put her on a desk."

"In Staten Island."

"Fuck're they thinking?"

"Just trying to send a message."

"Fuckin politics."

"It's all fuckin politics."

"You got that right, brother."

"So, Way, you believe this lady cop of yours or what're you telling us here?"

"Sure, I believe her," I said.

"Nah, fuck you, Way. You don't believe a word of it. I can tell from your face, ya fuck."

"Fuck's up with the flowers anyway?"

"What about flowers?" I asked.

"They're saying the perp he ain't had no gun anyway, just a bunch a fucking flowers, they're saying on the TV there."

"Who's saying?" I asked, at once interested.

"Fucking—the other perp's lawyer, the second piece—what's his name?"

"Ouellette."

"Dewberry."

"Nah, Dewberry is the DOA, ya fuck. I'm talking about the second piece."

"Ouellette, you mean."

"Ouellette's a lawyer," I told him.

"That's what I just said, ya fucking dumb fuck. It's the lawyer for the second piece, what the fuck's his name—Onan or whatnot—that was saying it was just a fucking flower and not no gun. On the TV news, he's saying it. I just saw."

"So what's the story, Way?"

"Kid have a gun or what?"

"Yeah, they get a piece off the dead kid?"

"Or all he had was a fucking flower?"

"Sure, it was a flower," I answered before I pushed in Garrity's door. "A thirty-two-caliber pink azalea."

Shawn Garrity, seated at his desk, was on the telephone, listening, nodding, saying uh-huh and other substitutes for words, unable to get in an actual word of his own, gesturing me over with a frantic movement of his big hand.

Garrity's office was less an office than the den of a large slow-moving mammal. He didn't work here so much as inhabit it. Garrity was the job and vice versa. Everything—somehow even the standing lamps and file cabinets—appeared creased and slept on. Beneath the worn leather armchair in the corner was dirty laundry, probably, or last week's lunch. And everything smelled faintly of Garrity.

I dropped into a wooden chair opposite. One leg was shorter than the rest. Garrity watched me with interest across a desk littered with mussed newspapers and takeout wrappers and letterhead ringed with faint sepia circles the diameter of the coffee mug in his hand, the one with the FBI seal. We trade trinkets like wampum in the law enforcement tribe. I waited, but whenever I stirred the chair shifted slightly but startlingly on its short leg, and each time I felt I might tip backward in a comic pratfall. Beneath it the world was unsteady. A good chair for an interrogation, I thought, thinking mine was about to begin. I was ready to confess.

Garrity lost interest in the telephone call now that I was here. He stood, probably without even knowing it. Behind him, through the windows that made the north and east walls of his corner office, you could see the East River and all the bridges to Brooklyn. A big man, Shawn Garrity had a jowly Black Irish face and gray eyes too small for it. His complexion was a mood ring. Barely forty years old, he had thick dark hair combed in the same part his mother had

made in his Marine Park bathroom. Being a cop was so bred into Garrity that
he never looked wholly right in a suit. He had only one, dove gray, and it fit his
obtuse form like someone threw it at him. The pants hung in the crotch and
his jacket was wrinkled like an old face. Garrity wore his suit whenever there
was a chance someone might point a camera in his direction, so he'd worn it
today. Three television crews lay in ambush for him in front, simultaneously
annoying pedestrians and attracting them. The press wanted Garrity because
they couldn't get at Reed, who'd been reassigned overnight to modified duty
in parts unknown. Our telephone number, on the other hand, was in the book.
Also, Garrity always said exactly what came into his head, which made fine copy.

That evening, New York City would be treated to the televised image of
Shawn Garrity hustling slope-shouldered into the cavernous entrance of 40
Fulton Street. When they cornered him barely ten feet before the safety of the
revolving door, the camera lights glinted on his broad pallid forehead. On the
eleven o'clock news, Garrity was glistening, glancing everywhere and at no
one. Kat would turn to me on the couch: "He looks like *he* shot Dewberry."
Garrity squinted his little eyes in the unflattering television light, and with the
microphones aimed accusingly at him he mumbled that *the union stands behind
its officers* before disappearing through the door. "*We stand behind our officers*,"
repeated the personality, arching a single well-plucked eyebrow as she stared
down the lens. "The words of Shawn Garrity, president of the Patrolmen's
Benevolent Association—"

"Stands behind them for the moment," I called from the kitchen, where
I was burning fish, "until such time as we revoke their membership cards and
all their parking privileges."

Kat switched off the television and from the dark and suddenly quiet parlor
her voice seemed very clear. "Why didn't they interview you, Will?"

"Because I would've told them the truth."

She didn't laugh on cue, nor indeed say anything for a while. As quick
as that, Georgina Reed became a wall between us. The truth was Garrity had
broken his own edict going on record, telling me to keep quiet until we lit upon
something plausible to give out. Meanwhile everyone else in the world was lining
up for the television: Reed's third-grade teacher, Holtz's aunt in Nassau County,
an anonymous man who'd seen something from the window of his third-floor
walk-up on Putnam. *I was in the bathroom washing my butt when I hears the shots.
Or just one shot. So I ain't seen nothing, but you ask me the police just shot that boy
for no reason. Ask anybody on the block. They all seen it. Lord have mercy.*

Garrity dropped the phone.

I asked, "Who was on the other end of that performance?"

"Tommy Janus. The lawyer."

"Among other things," I said. "Little early to start sniffing around for a settlement check, even for Tommy."

"It's not what Tommy wants, Will. It's what I want."

"Hell do you want from him, Shawn?" I asked, incredulous. "You know what Tommy is."

"I want Tommy. On this—" he began, and when I stood from my teetering chair to punctuate my reply he put up a cautionary hand, a gold claddagh ring glinting in the morning sunlight off the river. "I know you don't like him—"

"Kidding me?"

"—and mixed it up a little bit with the man there, but—"

"He fucking tried to—"

"Which is all ancient history, Will, am I right? Ancient history, now. I thought the two of youse shook hands already?"

"And washed mine after. With lye."

"Oh, come off it, Will. You know the rules of this game—Christ, as good as me. I'm not saying I'm gonna ask Tommy stand godfather to my kid, but he could be useful on this one. Agreed?"

"Useful how?"

"Look at the news. It's getting ugly out there, and Tommy's specialty is ugly, no? Look, we'll talk about the Tommy thing later, okay? You and me. For now just tell me again what she said, our man Georgina there, because I'm hearing all kinds of crazy crap and I don't know what to believe no more—I mean, Jesus and Mary, was the perp on his knees? Did she really hit the kid twice?"

"Who told you that?"

"It's what they're saying is all."

So I sat again and told him what I told him already. He listened, eyes at half mast, and it seemed to comfort him, like a familiar bedtime story. It took about two minutes to tell because there wasn't much to tell. When I was done, he kicked back in his chair and put a fingertip in his mouth and said nothing for a very long minute. He bit absently on his finger, then he examined it with a furious expression and asked, "They got a gun off the kid?"

"Yeah."

"And you believe her? I mean, believe her that the kid pulled out first?"

"I have a choice?" I asked. I shouldn't have said it, but I said it anyway because I wanted to know. I was supposed to know the rules, Garrity had just told me, and here I was breaking a rule by asking for a rule.

"Yes, you have a choice," he said, partly hurt, partly angry. "Yes, goddamn it. Yes. What the hell's that question supposed to mean, do you have a choice?"

"I'm just asking. Christ, Shawn," I said mildly. The wooden chair danced beneath me.

"Will," he asked again, "d'you believe her?"

"No," I said at length. "No, I don't, Shawn. Not all the way."

He sighed through his nose. "Brace her hard?"

"Hard enough. I just listened mostly. She gave me her version right off, but she seemed—I don't know—open."

"Open?" he said. "Open to what?"

"A better version."

He looked down and ran his palm roughly over his forehead. Behind his hand I saw him redden to his ears, but the color faded at once before my eyes like a magic trick. That morning everyone wanted my answer, but Shawn Garrity was the only one I had to tell. Yet he knew, I suppose, that we don't always have the luxury of knowing, so for the moment he let me off the hook. When he returned to his more usual temperature, Garrity swore and took it out on a ten-year-old twelve-inch television set next to an enormous ficus powdered gray with dust. He found the local news, no sound, featuring a man with a microphone backdropped by the stationhouse on Knickerbocker Avenue, where a dozen gray-haired citizens slowly circled with hand-painted signs bearing the quoted words of Martin Luther King, Malcolm X, and God.

"But I tell you what, though," he said, manipulating the remote control. "We're gonna back our man, Will. We're gonna back her because no one else— goddamn it." He was pointing the remote at the television and pressing buttons. Nothing happened. "So I want you out at the Eight-three at every change of tour—why can't I hear anything—?"

"Pass it here."

"I can figure this thing out," he said defensively, fingered the remote unsuccessfully for a moment, then he went on. "What I'm saying is, say someone's feeling talkative, I want you to make them not so talkative."

"Sure."

"Read me?" he said.

"Uh-huh."

"Biggest problem we have—" he was saying, now almost to himself, pressing buttons on the remote "—is someone wants to go on the record, unburden himself, you know?"

"Not our biggest problem, but—"

"Someone thinks he's helping, someone wants to talk to the press, rat squad," Garrity was saying, his voice falling as he lost more and more of himself in the remote. His voice became hardly audible, as if he was dialing down his own volume by mistake. He'd nearly forgotten I was there, it seemed, much less what he wanted to say. He was pushing buttons, pointing, hoping. Nothing was working for Shawn Garrity today. His entire world had shrunk into the small, General Tso's chicken–stained, rectangular shape of a remote control. He hadn't yet detonated with the realization that he was powerless to move events, even events as minor as the volume of a small television set, but you could tell it was only a matter of time. I could do nothing except watch, fascinated. In the meantime, from seventeen floors below, came the sound of sirens, ambulances, the city. Everything went on around us, untroubled by us. "Someone says something," Garrity kept saying to no one, peering hopefully at the television, which returned a sphinxlike silence, "and then he can't unsay it, you understand? And then we gotta—"

"Got it."

"—gotta have our man's back."

"Yes."

"She's all alone out there without us—what's her name again?" he asked me.

"Georgina. Officer Georgina Reed."

"Georgina Reed, Will. Georgina Reed. She's all alone, Will. All alone in the cold world."

"I know," I said.

"We're always alone, you know. A patrolman's always alone. But at least we have each other."

"Yes."

"IAB out there," he said. "The DA. The feds. *The New York Times*. All of them, circling like sharks. Like piranhas. Or hyenas. They don't care about her. They just want to use our man to sell their story, get a promotion, prove their point that we're all a bunch of—whatever they say we are."

"Fascists."

"And worse," he said to himself. "You know they smell blood."

"Of course," I said, wondering whose blood.

"Blood in the water."

"Yes."

"Pressure like that," he said. "Some young, idealistic patrolman might come forward. You understand? Think he's doing the right thing. Everyone wants to do the right thing. It's natural."

"Yes."

"I'm not saying a patrolman comes forward, he's a rat. No. I don't like that word," he said, now remembering I was here and giving me his earnest look to prove he meant it. The remote remained in his hand and he weighed it, like a man contemplating suicide might heft a revolver before placing the cold barrel against the roof of his mouth. "I'm not saying that. I don't call them rats. Some people do, you understand. I'm just saying you have to go out there, make sure before he goes outside the chain of command your patrolman knows the gravity of—of—"

"I understand."

He now began manipulating the remote control with greater urgency as Conrad Gilbert appeared on the screen. The commissioner walked to the newsroom podium at One Police Plaza, grim-faced, like the doctor who brings the bad news to the family in the waiting room. *We did everything we could—*

"Almighty Christ!" Garrity said at last, finally giving vent. He climbed heavily to his feet and underarmed the remote control to me. "Fix this damn thing."

Now Garrity was standing in front of the television, facing it, shaking off his suit jacket like the start of a bar fight. His shirt had pulled out in the back, and I could see the waistband of his white briefs. He seemed about to hit the set with one of his big hands. Meanwhile I was taking the batteries out of the remote, picking off the corrosion with a broken fingernail. "And not for nothing, Shawn," I asked him, "but why do you think there's some young, idealistic patrolman in the Eight-trey itching to turn rat?"

He turned and said wearily, sounding more like a human being than he had all morning, "Because there always is, Will."

"Why should he talk to me and not Internal Affairs?"

He looked astonished and opened his palms. "Because we're cops. You're a cop. And they—they're IAB!"

"IAB's cops, too."

"Just fix the damn thing. Will you fix the damn thing?"

"I can't fix everything for you," I said so low he didn't hear, and when I pressed the button the noise of cameras aimed at Commissioner Gilbert was like a nest of machine guns.

SIX

PAA Sheila Simmons stood waiting by my office door. I went inside, passing her without meeting her eyes, as if she was the teacher and I late again for class. We hadn't talked about Georgina Reed yet, but there it was like a stink in the dining room neither of us could politely acknowledge. Usually Sheila and I sat down on whatever interesting thing I had on my desk. And, whatever else it was, Georgina Reed was pretty damned interesting. I liked to get Sheila's take because she wasn't a cop, and her father wasn't a cop, nor were her brothers, nor her cousins, so she could give it to me straight the way the rest of the world saw it. With this one, though, I just wasn't sure.

There was a fresh stack of telephone message slips on my desk. I looked them over, still on my feet. "Betty Moon called. Again. That makes four times, Mr. W.," she said, still in the doorway, not leaving, not coming inside. I felt the weight of her gaze upon me. I nodded, said nothing, then I tossed the pink message slips on top of the others in the trash can.

"You want me to stop writing them down?" she asked at length.

"No, keep writing them down," I said. "I like throwing them out."

"What do you want me to tell Betty? She's angry."

"She's always angry," I said. "What'd she say?"

"She said she's angry."

"Anything else?" I asked.

"Only to tell you that you're—excuse me, Mr. W.—that you're a faggot if you don't call her right away."

"A what?"

"A faggot."

"I see."

"Betty has a way of putting things, doesn't she?"

"That she does," I said, sitting heavily in my chair. "Well. Don't believe a word, Sheila, though I once owned a David Bowie album—"

The telephone rang. I nodded for Sheila to pick it up, and she did. I took pleasure in hearing her telephone voice, which was adult and coolly efficient and made me want to be both. *Betty*, Sheila mouthed to me, her dark and sensibly manicured hand covering the receiver.

Betty Moon had the police beat for the *Brooklyn Daily News*, and Sheila put her above all the rest, thinking I liked her, thinking we were friends, because she knew we gossiped on the telephone on lazy afternoons like mean girls—who was on the outs at One PP, what lieutenant was boning which captain's wife, and so on. In person Betty Moon was five foot nothing with wide hips, and she always smelled like juniper berries and cigarettes, though I had never once seen her smoke. She had nimble fingers that were always in motion and never took her coal black eyes off you. I suppose she was Korean, but that was not a real ingredient of her personality. No husband on the scene, nor children—no room at the inn, I gathered. I liked Betty, true—how could you not? She was smart and relentless and whatever I told her on background stayed on background, although in truth every encounter with her gave me a frisson of nervous tension, wondering what she might spring on me or try to cajole out of me. I was her source, and she was mine. Our relationship was purely transactional, and I knew she'd deliver me if I deserved it.

I took the telephone.

"No, Betty," I said, my eyes on Sheila, who remained immobilized in the doorway, out of concern for me, I suppose. "I don't have your keys."

"Hilarious," Betty said. Her lost keys were a running joke. I forget why. "Georgina Reed. Start talking, Way. I'm on deadline."

"Hell, Betty, go easy on me. I haven't even had coffee."

"You're gonna have to say it eventually, Way, so you might as well say it to me," she said, and I believed she drew on a cigarette. "Open your mouth. Bend over. Time to take your medicine. The tape is rolling. Tell me to turn it off, you don't have any balls this morning."

"Betty, I—"

"Screw you, too, buddy," she said. "I know things about you, remember."

"Everyone's got secrets, Betty," I said. Sheila was looking at me with stern disapproval from the doorway. "But no one cares about my secrets."

"That might change," she said cryptically. "So how about it?"

"Sorry, Betty."

"What'd she say, Georgina Reed?" she said insistently. "I know you talked to her already. So when I say what'd she say what I mean is what did you tell her to say?"

"What—?"

"Just—just, okay," Betty Moon said, undaunted. "You won't give me what you got? I'll tell you what I know. Just grunt or something if I'm right so I don't lose my job. Just say la-de-dah." I exhaled loudly, and when I did not hang up she took it as permission. She told me what she knew, which as it turned out was all that I knew.

"La-de-dah," I told her.

Betty kept going in her hyperkinetic way, and I lost focus for a moment when she went off on a thousand-word-a-minute tangent about flowers, about the DOA's babymother, about Brooklyn, about women working the job, and when I tuned in again Betty was talking about Marlon Odom, now awaiting his turn at central booking in downtown Brooklyn. Odom was the second piece. I had missed Odom last night at the 83 since the squad had him nailed to a desk upstairs. They ended up putting Odom though the system, charging him with an acting-in-concert armed robbery with Dewberry as his unindicted co-conspirator—unindicted because Dewberry was dead, which in my view made the whole exercise a little precious. Some boss, however, thought that charging Odom would maintain the fiction that this was all just business as usual, just cops and robbers. Odom was up for arraignment today in Brooklyn Supreme, Betty told me. "See you there?"

"Why not," I told her. "Slow day."

"Funny. Odom hired Ouellette, you know."

"Charlie Ouellette? Tommy Janus's partner?"

"Was. Was Tommy's partner," she said. "They had a less than amicable split couple months ago. I think one of them ended up with Bea Katzenbach. Can't remember which one. Anyway, Ouellette's already raising hell."

"He's a lawyer. They're always making noise with the mouth."

"What's he saying about flowers, Way?"

"Flowers—?" I asked.

"Ouellette's out there saying the victim—"

"Perp."

"—says Dewberry didn't steal nothing. Said he was just bringing flowers to his babymom. Bouquet of pink azaleas."

"And a puppy."

"You know anything about it?" she asked.

"No."

"Not exactly a dangerous weapon," she said.

"Kid's so fucking huge, could kill you with a flower. Could kill you with a baked ziti."

"My point is are you sure about your cop?"

"The PBA stands behind our man," I intoned in Shawn's voice.

"Just how far behind is the question," she said. "Far enough you don't get anything on your jackboots, I hope. This is gonna get real brutal for you, my friend. Folks are already running for the exits. You see Whitey Fister's news conference just now? Said Georgina Reed's got the same rights as any other criminal defendant. And I quote."

"Holy Mother," I said, feeling the chill. "The Brooklyn DA said that?"

"Fister's up for reelection."

"Reed's not a collar. She's not under arrest."

"Yet," Betty returned. "Wanna synchronize watches?"

"How can he indict her? Doesn't make sense."

"Don't be stupid."

"I'm not stupid, I'm angry."

"Same thing," she said. "Fister's putting the case in the grand jury."

"On what evidence?" I nearly shouted. "There's nothing that makes out a murder charge here."

"So evidence matters, Way? Can I quote you, ha ha?"

"Seriously, Betty, fuck's Georgina supposed to do?" I said, now angry and not merely pretending for her benefit. "Cop says shut up and get on the floor, then shut the fuck up and get on the floor. An arrest isn't a debate, Betty. You think this perp Dewberry didn't know the drill by now? Fucker took his first pinch when I took my first communion."

"Will—"

"Fuckin politics, Betty," I said. "Anyone care if Dewberry drew down on a cop? Anyone? Shithead got what he was asking for, Betty—and you can quote me."

"You don't mean it, Will."

"What, too bellicose for that fish wrapper of yours?"

"Hey, it's your pension, buddy," she said. I could hear Moon's fingers banging away on her keyboard, and I could hear her breathe into the phone I imagined now caught between her ear and right shoulder. Also in the background I could hear the noise from her newsroom, the hum of voices under deadline, an occasional shout.

"By the way," I asked, "who's got this at the DA?"

"Kane. Jackie Kane. Just got off the line with her, matter of fact. Gave me even less than you. Why? Know her?"

"Maybe," I said. "Red hair, tall drink of water?"

"That's Jackie."

"Should I be afraid of her?"

"Depends what side you're on," she said. "And Will, you're gonna have to decide what side you're on. Sooner or later."

Before noon I walked from my building onto Fulton Street. One of this morning's television crews was still there, waiting dispiritedly. They didn't know me. That would change.

I crossed Pearl Street. The air was cold as March in the city is sometimes, when you think spring should be here already but isn't. There was no rain at least. Up Pearl, then down to the fish market, which didn't smell too bad because of the cold. I bought a couple salmon steaks to burn later then went up the block to Carmine's. The place had a pleasant walnut-and-nautical-whatnot atmosphere and was popular with both cops and low-rent suits from the office buildings farther down. Masterson wanted to meet here although the place was a twenty-minute walk from IAB headquarters on Hudson Street. Detective Mark Masterson never sweated meeting me in daylight, but he didn't think we should rub it in their faces either. We'd been partners before Masterson put in for IAB, so that would provide a decent explanation should a decent explanation become necessary. He hadn't gone to IAB for the gold shield but because he believed in it, and who was I to hold that against him? After all, there were easier ways to make detective and not become a pariah. When he went to Hudson Street we saw each other less and less, of course, but by that spring I could still count Mark Masterson on my short list of people in this world I could trust with my house keys.

He was already seated, already eating, when I came over. He kept eating. Linguini with white clam sauce, I saw, garlic and oil and pink-orange clams big as acorns.

"I got twenty minutes, Way."

We ate in silence and didn't talk about the thing we came to talk about. On the television above the bar was the situation—talking heads I didn't recognize plus a few faces I did: Georgina, Dewberry, not mine yet. The chyron I could scarcely read from my table apart from a few words such as TEENAGER, UNARMED, MURDER, and FLOWER. The isolated words were like clues in a children's game. *One of these things is not like the other.* At the bar itself a line of men sat not watching. Their coats and jackets were draped over their stools and their asses spread out. They were drinking their drinks and eating. All you heard were low masculine voices and the clean click of glass and ceramic and stainless steel.

After, we drew matchsticks. I lost, so I opened my wallet and threw some bills on the table and didn't wait around for change. Masterson stood, took his tie from inside his shirt, and I was following him toward the door when someone called me. I walked over and shook hands. He pushed paper downtown at One PP, another clean-fingernail cop like me. He introduced me to his crowd, cops in suits, but when I turned to Masterson he was already gone. Maybe he wasn't so happy about daylight after all.

I found him across South Street, next to a steel upright painted gray and graffitied. Overhead was the rush of cars on the FDR. Masterson, his red-orange hair flaming against the overcast, stood smoking a thin cigar and wearing a hard look. Saying nothing, we walked onto the pier over the river where the old tea clippers were docked as attractions. Kat and I had taken Phillip aboard on a winter afternoon, the first time in years I'd set foot on a wooden deck. I was a landlubber now. What would my father say? I'd grown up on the sea, and by Phillip's age the pitching ocean was more natural to me than the Q train clattering its endless way to Manhattan and back. On this dark water, in fact, this muddy East River that flowed wide and brown beneath the Brooklyn Bridge, I once made an illegal wake in the Sea Ray with a sixteen-year-old girl. The girl was Regine Pomeroy, we had been in love with each other, and the Sea Ray was a desert island we carried around with us for our convenience, remote from the populated world that was never more than three nautical miles away, but I was young at the time and didn't know, so that afternoon under the bridge became like all the other afternoons with Regine, and I forgot it until that moment when I stood with Masterson on the end of the pier.

"You gonna hook Georgina Reed?"

I asked my old partner the question when we stopped walking. You could see the big clock across the water on the Brooklyn side. It read alternately 12:37, 43 degrees, but it was colder than that with the wind blowing from the harbor, colder yet standing next to Masterson with his frigid demeanor. He nodded yes but answered, "Maybe," which came in a haze of cigar smoke instantly lost against the gray sky behind him.

"What's stopping you?" I asked. "I mean, I'm sure you got a great case. Except for no evidence."

"Working on it." His eyes flickered a moment. "The second piece. Odom. He has a story."

"Ouellette fed it to him."

"No," Masterson said. "Odom starting talking last night in the Eight-three squad before he lawyered up. Ouellette didn't figure into this thing until they got Odom downtown to booking this morning. Then Odom shut up and Ouellette started to talk."

I thought about that. "How'd Odom sign him, I wonder? Ouellette doesn't swim in shallow water."

"Basil Bumpurs tipped him, I'm sure," Masterson said. "Ouellette has a financial interest there. A regular contributor to the archbishop's collection plate, and not for the remediation of his sins."

"So, Odom—"

"Once the Brooklyn DA drops the robbery charge against Odom, he touches the city for a fat settlement check. Wrongful arrest or whatever. Ouellette will figure something to get his piece. Then Bumpurs will get his."

"'Drops the charge,' bullshit," I said. "They're arraigning Odom this afternoon in Brooklyn, for chrissake."

"Sure, the Brooklyn DA'll act all strong, maybe indict him, too," Masterson said, "but Fister's the French army. In two weeks he'll run up the white flag, give Odom a hearty handshake goodbye and don't let the jailhouse door hit your narrow ass on your way out." Masterson sighed or yawned, probably a yawn—he and I had been working different sides of the same street since yesterday evening, and he looked like I felt.

"You talk to Odom?" I asked Masterson after that sunk in.

"Yes."

"He fucks Reed, I suppose."

"Up the ass. A bad shoot, he says," he said with a shrug like an apology. "Yeah, I know, I know, that don't come off as exactly original, considering the source is a worthless sack of shit, but—Christ, Way, I just dunno. Fister and the politicians'll do what politicians do, and I got nothing to say about that, but between you and me there's something no good about this one. I dunno."

"Now you're talking like you're rat squad, Masterson."

"I am rat squad," he said, "but don't stand there saying you ain't thinking the exact same thing. You got your tail between your legs and don't say it ain't."

"Okay, partner, you're right. Georgina Reed's a stone-cold murderer," I said, annoyed that I was so easy for him to read. "She put him down like Dirty Harry."

"She tells it like it's a textbook line-of-duty discharge. By the numbers, one, two, three. She's got her whole story down neat and clean."

"Perfect's not good enough for IAB?"

"Perfect ain't real, Way. When the shit hits, people fuck up. They make mistakes. Then they lie about it. Hell, you know that as well as I do."

I began to argue, but the look he shot me as a punctuation mark to his last sentence changed my mind so I pretended to be angry instead. "How do you have Georgina's story anyway? She hasn't gone on the record with anyone."

"She did with the DA last night. Or tried to, before you threw a hissy."

"None of that counts," I said, wincing at the recollection of William Way, Jr., assaulting a tape recorder in the presence of witnesses. "DA can't use none of that."

"And why in hell would she wanna?" Masterson drew the last lung of smoke from his little cigar then shot what remained into the river twenty feet below. "Besides, Jackie Kane thinks the both of youse were just putting on a show for an audience of one. Thinks you and Georgina had a chat in the basement about—well, about how to be perfect. She's not amused, by the way."

"That's not how I work."

"Don't worry, Way, I convinced Kane you ain't that smart," he said. "But I suggest you get your man on the record. But soon. Odom's already talking, and in the public mind the first to speak's got a monopoly on the truth. Once Odom's version sees light of day, your man's story's gonna sound a lot like—like a story."

"What's Odom saying, out of curiosity?"

He considered telling me before telling me. After all, his expression said, that's why we're here. "He fesses up to the robbery like a Christian, Odom does, excepts he puts it all on the DOA. Says he got nothing to do with it himself."

"So he lied."

"Basically. Says Dewberry knocks the cashier over, gives him a black eye, then he and him are coming along the sidewalk after. That's when your cops roll on em and try to put em under. But your DOA he ain't having none of it, Odom says, and then things get complicated. As things do."

"So far I'm with you."

"Not for long, partner," he said, "but one point for you is Odom's stoned to the bejesus when this all goes down. Maybe Dewberry, too, I dunno. We'll have his tox today, tomorrow the latest. Anyway, the guy Odom says Dewberry catches a little attitude maybe when your man Georgina orders him down. Says he ain't doing it, says he's sick of this, sick of that, sick of getting tossed, sick of getting his shit run by Bushwick cops, and so on and so forth. The usual mouth, plus maybe the DOA mighta got himself a little anger management issue there. So that's two points for your team."

"I'm counting."

"There's some words, some more back-and-forth," Masterson said. "And Dewberry won't go under. Got some flowers in his hand, I dunno, for his girl, and—"

"Nothing says I love you like stolen property."

"Flowers," Masterson snorted and shook his head. "That's what's gonna make this one different from the others."

"It's no different, Mark. Go on."

"That's kinda it, partner," he said with a half shrug. "DOA won't show his hands, so sayonara."

"Double tap?"

"One shot."

"One shot? In the back?"

"In and out," he said. "So who knows. Waiting for the autopsy."

"What's Odom say about it? I mean, was Dewberry running away or not?"

"Little vague there. Seems our Mr. Odom wasn't looking. Maybe he was running himself. But he heard it."

"So that's three for me," I told Masterson. "Plus you left out the part where Odom told you his running buddy pulled a gun."

"Oh, didn't I tell you? No gun, Odom says."

"Patrol vouchered Dewberry's thirty-two at the scene, Mark," I said. I heard my own voice, sounding more urgent. I had used up forty of Masterson's twenty minutes, and I felt him pulling away. "What's Odom's answer to that?"

"It's a flake."

I considered this a moment. "No, Odom has to say that, but it doesn't work. Think," I said. "Sergeant's on the scene two minutes after—two minutes, Mark—so where's Georgina supposed to come up with a flake in two minutes? What's she riding around with a box of Saturday night specials in the trunk of her RMP?"

"Who says the sergeant's there?"

"Plus her partner backs—"

"Donny Holtz's a moron, Way. You know that."

"Doesn't make him a liar," I said. "But Bear recovered the thirty-two when he rolled the body, so—"

"Berrigan was there—?" Masterson said, swallowing the information like a hairball. He knew Sergeant Ralph Berrigan as well as I did. Almost to himself Masterson said, "You confirm that with him?"

"Not official, Mark, I got no jurisdiction to sit down with a sergeant," I said. "But Bear signed the voucher. Check property, you think I'm wrong. A junk thirty-two with a broke handle and defaced serial. And I got somebody else on the scene, too. Haven't talked to him yet."

"Yeah, who?"

"Berrigan's driver," I say, snapping a finger. "Rookie. Forgot his name. He should confirm it, and that'll make three cops besides Georgina who put a gun on the DOA—three cops, Mark—so even if evidence doesn't count anymore it should count for something with us."

"Look, Way," he said, not unaffected. "I don't like Odom no more than you, but he's not my call. This one's going over me all the way. Georgina Reed is Inspector Danilov's case as of ten o'clock last night. The bosses are running it now, and I'll tell you, under the circumstances Odom's story's gonna have some legs."

"The circumstances being?"

"Christ, maybe you are as dumb as I told Kane," he said, shaking his head. "Read the paper, Way, look around—people out there're tired of cops shooting people."

"Even people who ask for it?"

"Who else do we shoot?"

"And if Georgina Reed just happens to be telling the truth?" I asked. "What about her?"

"Partner," he said, allowing himself a smile for once, "they already forgot her name."

MARLON ODOM

SEVEN

The DA had Marlon Odom up for arraignment at two o'clock. I went. From my office in lower Manhattan to Brooklyn Supreme was nothing, maybe ten minutes, with traffic, over our ancient Gothic bridge, altogether less than a mile in a straight line. But a mile in New York City divides worlds; you can walk two blocks to another country, and for all the difference between the financial canyons of lower Manhattan and the easy decay of downtown Brooklyn, the East River might as well be one of the seven seas.

At the courthouse I used the back door on State Street. The main entrance on Schermerhorn was choked off, the narrow street impassable with yellowy orange church buses and double-parked television trucks and media vans, their cameras pointed at what they would call a "lively, chanting throng" on the evening news. The throng in question was neither lively nor indeed a throng, in my opinion. Instead it consisted of maybe thirty of Archbishop Basil Bumpurs's geriatric congregation moving in a slow solemn plod. I glimpsed Bumpurs himself among them, his bare and shaven head shining like a beacon of hope and righteousness or whatever. The soundtrack was "We Shall Overcome," sung lowly and sad, as ever.

Across State, a hard, grim street lined with cyclone fence and razor wire, the courthouse faced the rear of the jailhouse on Atlantic Avenue. The back door was where you'd take your guy when you hauled him downtown to central booking, where the DA would take over. Going to central booking was like turning in your homework. Sometimes the DA would listen to your story and read your booking sheet and tell you to get the fuck outa town. Most of the time, however, that was all there was to it. Then you were done. Then you could go to bed. For your guy, though, central booking was only the beginning, and sometimes there was no coming out again. Just looking at the back door on State Street, you wouldn't know it was anything but a door.

Here cops stood smoking and passing the time, and there were prisoner vans parked on the sidewalk, idling, wreathed in their own exhaust. One was full of hookers, singing. They were in a fine mood, although it was late in the day for them. Usually you get your hookers booked in the morning and out of everyone's way. Marlon Odom was gumming up the works. More than four years had passed since I brought my last collar through the back door on State Street to put him through the system. Since then I'd begun to think a little differently about myself, but now as I felt my hand close upon the cold metal knob it was as though nothing had changed.

Inside was a court officer reading a tabloid. The cover story was something else. Georgina was still that fresh, although it didn't feel that way. Not even a day old and it seemed I'd been working Georgina all my life. The officer on the door was supposed to ask me for identification, but he didn't. I said, "Who's doing Odom?"

"Odom?" he asked, making a face.

"Guy from the TV. Big case with all the people outside for it."

"Ah, the guy," he said. "Pomeroy, I think, who can say." The name was like a blow, yet I didn't flinch. I just watched the court officer go down his clipboard with a big fingernail. "Yeah, Pomeroy."

"Since when does Pomeroy sit arraignments?"

"Since he's the chief judge and does whatever he wants. Big case like this one, probably put himself on it, who can say."

"So, they doing it in AR1 or what?" I asked him, moving away.

"Nah, people keep coming in, just look at it, not enough room downstairs, so they're doing it up in the big ceremonial, maybe, who can say, which is where Pomeroy likes it anyway—hey, hey, you need a key for that, you got a key?" I was walking to the private elevator. I answered him but kept walking, pulling the clattering metal gate closed behind me. My key chain was a janitor's key chain, everything on it: key to the Avocado King's 1973 boattail Riviera, to the bungalow on Melba Court which was never locked anyway, to the rental I shared with MK before she left, to my current home that was not home. You could reconstruct my entire life from age sixteen with this key ring, which also contained a little worn key that I'd won or bought or stolen a lifetime ago that fit the panel on the private elevator.

Upstairs in the ceremonial courtroom, Pomeroy's courtroom, there were more than the usual dozen who bothered to turn out for kith and kin at arraignment, but fewer than I'd expected and seemingly fewer yet in the wide-open space with great arched windows four stories tall and a gallery that stretched away in deep rows like a basilica. I walked hearing the echo of my own footsteps up the long aisle and took a seat up front by myself. A low balustrade separated the gallery from the empty well before a wide and exalted bench like an altar of dark wood aged nearly purple, and a handwritten sign posted here warned NO TALKING! POLICE LAWYERS PRESS ONLY! Some newspaper reporters sat farther down, talking. Betty Moon was not among them.

I waited. Presently more civilians drifted in, mostly lost-looking women with thick eyeglasses, gripping their patent leather handbags for dear life with both hands. In the gallery, already seated, it was mostly women as well, looking like the same. The gallery of any Brooklyn criminal courtroom is always mostly women—mothers of defendants, sisters of, silently weeping mascara-smeared girlfriends of. But these were not those. These were women from Bumpurs's church, the Brooklyn African-Baptist-Episcopal Cathedral way out on the east side of the borough, all of them shuttled here on repurposed school buses. They shuffled to their seats as if in church and were hushful as if in church and they brought with them the smell of church, of old wool and naphthalene and sweet outmoded spray perfume. They were each of them more than sixty years old, more than seventy. Some of the few men in wide ties and wide lapels actually wore brimmed Frank Sinatra hats with little feathers or held them piously in their hands. They all sat not talking, each looking straight ahead with a dark visage of stern disapprobation.

Up front nothing was happening. Nearly three o'clock now and the bench was vacant, which gave the place the slightly anarchic feel of an empty classroom. Now an officious-looking young-old woman in a sweater outfit stood at the prosecution table, but I supposed she was just the DA's paralegal, arranging matters. I waved to her, and with a face of prim reluctance she came to the balustrade, which I leaned on familiarly. She told me the judge was still at lunch.

"Long calendar?" I asked.

"No," she said. "Just the one arraignment."

Then, from a door behind the bench that led to the pens where the prisoners were kept behind blue-painted bars, appeared the tall DA from last night. Jackie Kane. With her came a well-formed black man I recognized at once from television and newspapers as Charles Ouellette. Somehow I'd never seen Ouellette in the flesh, which in retrospect seems odd inasmuch as he and I were opposite numbers. His job was to undo what I did and vice versa. He was my antimatter, and I suppose if we ever shook hands the universe would end. In person Ouellette was nearly as tall as Jackie Kane, with the build of a bantamweight. He dressed like you'd hope your lawyer would dress if you killed someone. His bright blue suit was just this side of garish, almost-but-not-quite clashing with his pink shirt with the white collar and French cuffs. A carnation blossomed hugely on his lapel. His complexion was caramel, and beneath an aristocratic nose was a neat pencil mustache. You could hear his rich operatic tenor from where I sat without hearing the words; he sparkled in conversation with Kane, who in marked contrast was glum and haphazardly dressed. She hardly faced him at all as Ouellette carried on in a fine flow of talk. She needed sleep.

Betty Moon landed beside me, in fact shoving her overstuffed canvas tote bags against me with a brusque and breathless hullo, but before she could say another word the door behind the bench opened again and Pomeroy stepped into his courtroom.

Just like that.

Dropped incongruously in the middle of that March afternoon, after four years, was Pomeroy, the Honorable Henry K. Pomeroy, looking remarkably like himself, like the Pomeroy I remembered. Apart from his hair, which had turned a rather startling white, he could have been the same Pomeroy I'd first seen twenty years earlier in the Tamaqua Marina. "All rise," said the clerk, and I did so automatically. Behind me fifty Brooklyn A-B-E congregants rose, too, some crossing themselves and genuflecting. Meanwhile Pomeroy took the bench, his black robe parting slightly as he moved above us to reveal his usual blue double-breasted Brooks Brothers suit, his usual rep tie, his usual white shirt buttoned down at the collar. His razor part was still a fresh pink scar, and in profile I recalled his sharp nose meant for looking down at you, looking down at you with a pair of unforgiving blue eyes. I felt my body of its own accord collapse a little as if to make myself as inconspicuous as possible, if not actually invisible.

Before my mind could accustom itself to the idea of Regine's father sitting not thirty feet from me, the clerk began:

THE CLERK: Number 43 on the arraignment calendar, docket ending 7642, People of the State of New York against Marlon Odom. Appearances, please.

MS. KANE: For the People, Jacqueline Kane. Good afternoon, your honor.

THE COURT: Jackie, hello. Charlie, good to see you again. Did you appear?

MR. OUELLETTE: No, your honor.

THE COURT: I beg your pardon. Let's have it.

MR. OUELLETTE: For Mr. Odom, Charles Ouellette, that's O-U-E-L-L-E-T-T-E, for the law firm of Ouellette and Katzenbach, 225 Broadway, New York, New York.

THE COURT: Did you put in a notice, Charlie?

THE CLERK: We have a notice of appearance from Mr. Ouellette.

THE COURT: Fine. Legal Aid is relieved. Where is Mr. Hendrix? He was just here. Someone notify Mr. Hendrix he is relieved. Well--

THE DEFENDANT: Can I say something? I want to say something.

THE COURT: Speak to your lawyer, Mr. Odom. Mr. Ouellette, are you retained?

MR. OUELLETTE: I've been retained. That is, actually I'm representing Mr. Odom pro bono.

THE COURT: You put us all to shame, Mr. Ouellette. You are a credit to your--

THE DEFENDANT: Excuse me, your honor, your honor, I have something I need to say.

THE COURT: Mr. Odom, you have a very capable and dare I say it civic-minded attorney to speak on your behalf, so let me advise you to speak--

THE DEFENDANT: But what I want to say is, what I want to say is I have my constitutional rights.

THE COURT: Indeed you do, Mr. Odom. And I daresay you will need them. Mr. Ouellette, maybe you can help us out.

(Whereupon, the defendant conferred with counsel.)

MR. OUELLETTE: Thank you, your honor. We're ready to proceed. There was just a small misunderstanding.

THE COURT: Very well, perhaps we can move ahead. People, do you--

THE DEFENDANT: Your honor. Excuse me, judge, your honor. What happen here ain't right. It ain't. What happen here is fascism pure and simple. The boy got shot right in front of me, and they be arresting me and charging me with shit I ain't done. And the gun he had he ain't had. So it's a travesty, man.

MR. OUELLETTE: Judge, I--

THE DEFENDANT: And they took my watch at the precinct.

THE COURT: Excuse me?

THE DEFENDANT: Breitling watch. Them cops took it. And my benefit card, too.

MS. KANE: Your honor, I wonder if we could approach.

THE DEFENDANT: I'm going to have to sue somebody. You wait.

THE COURT: Step up.

(Whereupon, there was a pause in the proceedings.)

THE COURT: On the record. Mr. Ouellette, do you need a moment with your client?

MR. OUELLETTE: No, thank you, judge. We're ready.

THE COURT: I understand we have a disposition?

MR. OUELLETTE: Yes.

THE COURT: People, what's your offer?

MS. KANE: People are offering an A.C.D. and time served.

THE COURT: Mr. Ouellette, I'm going to hazard a guess Mr. Odom might find the People's plea offer acceptable?

MR. OUELLETTE: He does, your honor.

THE COURT: Mr. Odom, is that what you wish to do? You wish to dispose of this matter this afternoon?

THE DEFENDANT: Huh?

(Whereupon, the defendant conferred with counsel.)

MR. OUELLETTE: We're ready.

THE COURT: Mr. Odom, you understand that the People will be adjourning these felony charges against you in contemplation of dismissing them six months from now provided you live a law-abiding life. Is that what you want to do?

THE DEFENDANT: Yes, your honor.

THE COURT: Very well. A.C.D. But, Ms. Kane, before we proceed, I need you to place on the record the basis for this offer.

MS. KANE: Your honor?

THE COURT: These are serious charges against Mr.
Odom. He was charged with robbery and assault and you
come before me to say, well, maybe not. I think it
appropriate that you make a record why the Brooklyn
district attorney has seen fit to dismiss this case for
all intents and purposes.

MS. KANE: Interest of justice, judge.

THE COURT: A noble sentiment to be sure, but one
might suppose the interests of justice underlie all of
the district attorney's actions.

MS. KANE: Yes, your honor.

THE COURT: So, would you care to state any other
basis for your decision not to proceed against Mr. Odom
as charged?

MS. KANE: Your honor, I--we have insufficient
evidence to prove the case against Mr. Odom beyond a
reasonable doubt, so we are--

THE DEFENDANT: Excuse me again, your honor. I have my
constitutional rights. Due process and shit. I want my
due process. I want what I deserve.

THE COURT: Well, Mr. Odom, it appears you are not
getting what you deserve, and for that you should be
thankful. Please sit down.

Afterward, Archbishop Bumpurs's flock began to file politely to the exits, making no sound whatsoever apart from the shuffling of a hundred churchgoing shoes and one somewhat perfunctory hallelujah. A moment later a court officer unhooked Odom, who looked behind him, uncertain what came next, rubbing his wrists, running his eyes over the gallery beyond me, looking among all the unfamiliar faces for a familiar face, for Mom. There was no one. No one spoke to him. After all, they had come not for him but for the idea of him. But I had come for him.

He was, however, built to disappoint. Marlon Odom had a feral expression and a hollow set to his eyes from a lifetime of living at night on a diet of dollar slices and rock cocaine. Turning, he hiked up his worn-out pants, which sagged to reveal stained purple boxer shorts. His hair was a rat's nest and no one would ever kill him for his sneakers. I didn't make Odom as anybody you had to keep an eye on. I mean, you wouldn't leave your wallet on the table with the guy, but he was just standard-issue mutt, nothing major league about him. Yet despite all that, Marlon Odom knew something I didn't.

Beside me Betty Moon was scratching away on her notepad. "Well, that was entirely predictable," she said. "Should've stayed at my desk."

I didn't answer and wasn't looking at Odom anymore. My eyes on their own went to the bench, where Ouellette stood in conversation with Pomeroy, both of them laughing about something I couldn't hear. Pomeroy then strode off the bench, sweeping his robe behind him, but as he did his eyes passed over the courtroom gallery and alighted for the briefest imaginable instant upon me—so I thought or more accurately felt, for an electrical current seemed to flow through me in that moment, then once again he was gone.

EIGHT

I stood beneath the arched limestone entrance of the courthouse and watched as three battle-weary yellowy orange school buses, BROOKLYN A-B-E CATHEDRAL painted by a childish hand on their sides, vied with television trucks and prisoner vans, stopping traffic for three blocks along Schermerhorn. Polite, slow-motion congregants lined up to board, a gentleman in a pork-pie hat and matching houndstooth jacket helping up a sturdy woman twice his girth then himself taking the first step with elaborate caution on artificial knees. The process was fascinating but interminable, yet no one honked nor gestured through open windows as expected. No one was going to honk or gesture at these buses, not today. Their diesel engines meanwhile rattled and spewed an acrid, oily exhaust over the scene.

"Pray for me, Babes," I said sincerely to no one.

"Hope Odom gets his watch back," said Betty Moon, appearing at my side, startling me, flicking something surreptitiously into the street. The smell of cigarettes came with her as she drew up too close, as ever disrespectful of boundaries, personal boundaries least of all.

"It wasn't his watch, Betty," I told her. "It was the proceeds."

She laughed in her creaking way and set her tote bags on the ground and rummaged through one. "Be able to buy a few of his own soon enough. Soon as Ouellette files his lawsuit against the city."

"Dewberry'll get more. Too bad he's dead."

"Which raises a question, doesn't it?" she said, straightening up and looking right at me with her almond eyes. "Dewberry have family? I mean he's got a babymom. Which implies baby, *n'est-ce pas*?"

"Once Ouellette files suit," I said, "Dewberry's gonna have fourteen baby-mothers. Not to mention a couple absentee fathers and some third cousins he never met. Fucker's gonna have more family in death he ever had in life. More, period."

"More what?"

"Bumpurs'll canonize him, start selling souvenir T-shirts and snow globes with his face. Raquan Dewberry, patron saint of Snickers bars."

"Ouch, Will."

"Just tell me how come every time this shit happens they gotta turn the dead guy into a paragon?"

"Maybe because you can say things like *every time this shit happens*," she said. "Anyway. I tried to run down the babymom, who the flowers were for—"

"You don't know Dewberry had a kid, Betty," I answered testily, suddenly warm for a fight if only to defend myself. "You don't know he had a babymom, or who the fuck the flowers were for. Far as you know he was bringing her a candy bar."

"Aren't we caustic today?" she said, not paying particularly close attention to me but writing in her notebook instead. "Pour Drano on your Froot Loops?"

"You and the television, you just repeat what Ouellette says and then it becomes gospel, and everyone starts thinking Georgina shot the kid for target practice on his way to cure cancer. How the hell's Georgina supposed to defend herself against that?"

"I thought it was your job to defend her," she said. "You got any information on Dewberry's family or what?"

"Why?" I said, knowing exactly how I sounded but oddly incapable of doing anything about it. I just kept rolling downhill. "So you can get Grandma Dewberry on record saying he was a good kid and didn't deserve to die?"

"Did he?"

"Well. That's why we're in Brooklyn Supreme, isn't it?" I said. "Though given what we just saw up there, I'm not convinced the DA's in the truth-and-justice business anymore."

"Whitey Fister's in the Whitey Fister business. Same as ever," she said, writing in her book. "But if it's any consolation to you—and it sounds like you feel sorrier for yourself this afternoon than for anyone else—Jackie didn't look too happy to be doing the DA's dirty work, did she? For a minute I thought she was gonna puke on Ouellette's thousand-dollar-an-hour Italian loafers."

"Fister bought Odom's testimony," I said in a more neutral voice. "For the grand jury. That's all that was."

"Georgina makes strange bedfellows."

"Tell me. Brings together enemies and separates friends."

"Nevertheless," Betty said, "surprised as hell to see Jackie Kane making nice with Ouellette. She has a certain reputation."

"Does she? I once gave a girl a reputation."

"Assume you don't mean the former Mrs. Way."

"No, I didn't give her anything, except the opportunity to make lemons out of lemonade. What's the story with Kane? I know nothing about her."

"Straight shooter," Betty said, writing. "Straight arrow. Just not straight."

"As in—?" I said, making a gesture.

"Yeah, Way. It's been known to happen."

"That's crap."

"Because she's beautiful?" Betty said. "Because she doesn't wear flannel shirts and file her middle finger?"

"For a news reporter, you know a hell of a lot," I said, but she didn't laugh. "I really don't see the DA's play with Odom. Sure, Odom can get the DA his murder indictment, but then what? They go to trial, no jury's ever gonna go for Odom over Georgina, cop or no cop. No way. Even assuming Odom isn't dead in a year, even if he doesn't OD or wreck his new Lamborghini, no jury's gonna believe a damn word out of his mouth. I mean, worst Legal Aid attorney in Brooklyn could prove Fister dropped Odom's charges to buy his testimony. All Georgina will have to do is squirt a few with those big brown eyes and say—"

"Is that how she got to you, Will? You big softie—"

"She's no murderer, Betty," I said. "Maybe she's no cop either, but either way you don't indict her for it. And you don't take her to trial."

"Fister doesn't want a trial. All he needs is an indictment to keep Bumpurs and *The New York Times* off his ass until election day. After that everyone'll forget about Georgina Reed."

"Oh, no one's gonna forget—"

"We'll forget her, Will," she told me, speaking as seriously as she ever did. "This is New York City."

Betty Moon was right, of course. A couple years later we would watch downtown Manhattan dissolve into a brown cloud that spread the stink of electrical fire over Brooklyn for weeks—we've already forgotten that, so is it any surprise that no one remembers Georgina Reed? We forget well in this town. We don't have time to give a fuck about you, then we forget about you. Our collective memory dates back twenty minutes, so we always crash the same car. It gives us our scattershot vitality. It's why New York is different from every other great metropolis of the world. In London or Rome they live with their ancestors peering out from every ancient edifice. In New York we tear everything down, fuck it, build another.

"Besides. Election, hell, what's Fister worried about?" I said. "He's got better job security than a sub-Saharan dictator."

"Not if he screws the pooch on this."

"And who'd be quixotic enough to take a run at him?"

"Our friend upstairs, what I hear," she said.

"Ouellette?"

"Pomeroy," she said. "Oh, fuck me—there's Jackie."

Betty snatched her tote bags and darted after Jackie Kane, who was already walking purposefully off with long strides. Next to her was a massive office detective in an unbuttoned black leather three-quarter Gestapo coat, struggling to keep up on tree-stump legs. Betty threw herself bodily in front of the prosecutor, and it struck me again how tall Kane was. The pair stood disproportionately together and I watched from a safe distance as Betty made her frontal assault. I heard none of it, but after a moment Betty gestured in my direction. Kane turned to face me, appraisingly, unemotionally, unimpressed. I did nothing.

Then, distinctly, I overheard Betty say, "Will Way. He's PBA."

"I know who he is," the assistant district attorney said in a voice that matched her cold gaze.

I did not like being looked at that way, and I might have said something to make me unpopular with the detective, yet immediately Jackie Kane spun away and that was that. Betty was busily scratching something into her notebook, and I found myself alone on the gum-speckled sidewalk with the detective in the leather coat. He stood there as if to say my only way out was retreat. He had a huge, florid face and he smiled at me with it. Then he stuck a bent cigarette in it. We were fifteen feet apart, our bodies by chance having fallen into the same attitude. He made no move to light his cigarette, and I might have told him what I thought of him, and Kane, and Fister, and all who comforted themselves with the notion that they were the hand of the Lord on the world, that the worst evil is always perpetrated by those who believe they're doing good, that the belt buckles of concentration camp guards were embossed *Gott mit uns*—God with us—but oddly enough his self-satisfied smile left me completely calm. I was in a peculiar mood that afternoon, ready to kiss or kill, like James Bond, so I smiled back and said, truthfully, "Your fly's open." He made a single bark, which was his laugh, then he produced a lighter that had been in his fist all along. He used it and I left him there.

NINE

Fifty minutes later I was in Bushwick again. I wanted to be at the 83 before the tour change, to talk to the men doing a four-by-twelve. I was late. There'd been roadwork then a car accident then a warehouse fire, and Atlantic Avenue was solid red for two miles and the car horns still resonated in my ears. I'd considered hitting my lights and siren or working my way east along the side streets, but I ended up waiting with everyone else. Usually I play the hand I'm dealt.

Television trucks with upraised antennas made a phalanx across Knickerbocker Avenue from the stationhouse, brick with slits for windows and bastioned like a medieval fort. Waiting in the late afternoon sun, looking cold and bored, stood cameramen and crews and nearby a small coterie of sightseers, just curious, not yet aggrieved. Though the day was lowering gray I wore anonymous sunglasses. A man with a microphone trailed me from my double-parked Ford, asking rhetorical questions. I was not in the mood. Georgina Reed still seemed like something private, like a shameful family secret to be whispered about if mentioned at all. Already I was sick as hell of reporters. They were embarrassing.

"Hey—hey, buddy," the guy was saying, "gimme a break, huh? Just tell me what you're feeling today?" My mind boggled, but I managed to ignore him until I reached the stationhouse door where in desperation he grabbed at my arm—not taking hold exactly but making contact enough to break the plane between us. I turned on him, and I imagine my demeanor was disciplinary for he fell back a step. He had a high freckled forehead with basset jowls and basset eyes. Yet he gamely persevered, asking in a familiar radio voice, his microphone offered, "*Yet another police shooting, Officer. But this time the victim is an unarmed teenage boy, doing nothing more than walking home—*"

"Unarmed?" I said. "Bullshit unarmed."

The reporter moved in a step, wary yet encouraged, knowing he'd gotten his knife into my oyster shell. Speaking into his microphone but looking straight at me, he asked, "*Police maintain that the youth was armed, but a grieving New York City wants to know: where's the proof?*"

"Besides a loaded thirty-two in his hand?"

"*—shot in the back by a hardened ex-Marine with years patrolling the mean streets of—*"

"Fourteen months."

"*—refused to cooperate with prosecutors investigating the—*"

"As was her right."

"*—last night arrested the victim's childhood friend Marlon Odom in what his legal team have characterized as a desperate bid by cops to—*"

"To arrest an accomplice to robbery and felony assault."

"*—to silence the sole witness who came forward only to—*"

"Cash in."

"*—young honor student at Franklin K. Lane High School in Brooklyn who—*"

"Was expelled in ninth grade for shooting a classmate in the leg."

"*—neighbors say dreamed of one day being a veterinarian—*"

"Because he had a pit bull?"

"*—corner of Putnam and Broadway. Laquan was carrying only a bouquet of—*"

"Raquan," I said, and now I recognized the guy. He was on news radio all the time, speaking in an authoritative and streetwise voice that made you believe he knew the truth and was letting you in on it. You'd never put this face with that voice, however, and the jarring juxtaposition made this moment—what is this anyway? are we on air?—even more surreal, as if I'd entered a dream state. Nor did it help that I was strung out from stop-and-go traffic, too little sleep, and too much caffeine.

"Excuse me?" he said.

"Raquan. You people keep saying Laquan."

"You certain?" he asked in a conversational tone, lowering his microphone.

"Unless they misspelled it on his twelve-page rap sheet," I said. "Catch my drift? And Odom's not an eyewitness, he's a perp. And tomorrow he's gonna be a plaintiff, which is why he has a legal team, not Legal Aid."

He continued, "*District Attorney Weldon Fister caved to outrage from community groups, including Archbishop Basil Bumpurs of the Brooklyn African-Baptist-Episcopal Cathedral, whose activists today surrounded the downtown courthouse loudly demanding justice for young scholar Raquan Dewberry, lighting bonfires and blocking traffic for hours. Fister responded by announcing that he would—*"

"Paint Bumpurs's toenails if he asked."

"*—dismiss charges against Marlon Odom—*"

"Two weeks earlier than expected."

"—say Odom will give testimony in the grand jury, but will he be alone? Will this senseless and horrible murder be enough finally to bring even just one cop forward to testify against a fellow officer? Or will the famed blue wall of silence continue to protect cops who kill?" I had already turned to leave when he said, "Will you tell me—"

"No."

"Can I get your name, Officer?" he asked.

"No."

"Do you work at the Eighty-third precinct?"

I swung open the door. I meant to answer no, but what came out was, "I'm not a cop."

"Probably wish you weren't," I heard him say before the heavy metal door slammed closed behind me.

Inside I drew a breath. *Must be the haircut,* I decided. Never in my life have I been seen as who I am, as who I believed I was at that particular moment. Instead I was ever the previous iteration of William Way, Jr., the version I had shucked off to become whatever I had then become. As a cop I was never a cop—I was the professor, the one who read books in the muster room. In college, during my foreshortened sightseeing tour of Georgetown, an abortive classicist, I was the Brooklyn Boy, concrete in my veins, zip guns in my pockets. At Xaverian High School, on the *Saturday Night Fever* set of Bay Ridge, I was the one non-paisano, the blondish kid from all the way across the borough. With Regine Pomeroy, I was—to her mother at least—the urchin, the Gerritsen Beach urchin who waxed boats, shanty Irish on the make, sliding over to Manhattan Beach, where I didn't belong, trying to get my hairy paws on her daughter. And at home, eight years old, alone with my father on Melba Court, I was not his, he who raised me, but my mother's son, whose face I knew only from the photograph the Avocado King still kept in his dresser drawer, under rolls of socks along with the leatherette box containing a blue-and-white ribboned star and a folded certificate, creased as if never once read, attesting to his *conspicuous gallantry and intrepidity at the risk of his life above and beyond the call of duty, in dense jungle northwest of Cam Lo to extract seven men of a heavily besieged reconnaissance patrol,* et cetera.

Even now—even in my current apotheosis as PBA trustee for Brooklyn North—I'd been mistaken for something I never truly believed I was: a cop, a flatfoot, dragging my sorry ass into the house to start my night's tour. In each new chapter of my life, whenever I was mistaken for someone I once was, I wanted to say, Don't you see how I've changed? But you cannot shed yourself like a cicada. You layer from childhood until you can scarcely move. That's what it means to grow old, I suppose, to become immobilized by what you've been. So, I was a cop because I'd been a cop, and because I still cut my hair like one.

As for what I was at the core, that remained to be seen. *I know who he is*, Jackie Kane had said. I should've asked her to tell me. I'd have been interested to know.

I came onto the floor in front of the desk sergeant and saw faces turned to me, trying to ascertain with patrolman eyes whether I was friend or foe. You'd see that same appraising once-over on the street—cop radar—but now it was in the house. They were all on edge, and trying to pretend everything was cool only made it worse. Being a cop is all about arranging things in your head. You got to be expert at that after a while, but it took a toll. The men on duty tonight had all shoved Georgina Reed into a box, but arms and legs kept reaching out from under the lid. Already there were telephoned curses and bomb threats and tomorrow morning tires would be slashed along Bleecker Street, where everyone parked his off-duty ride.

A lot of men were silhouetted behind the glass half-wall of Captain McCosker's office. One of them was Sergeant Ralph Berrigan. He opened the door and ordered me over. Then some other men inside called out. "Get in here, Way," they said. "G'wan, get in here, ya fuck!" They were merry enough. I kept walking, giving them a lazy wave, saying I would catch them later, maybe. They were drunk or well on their way. I can't tolerate a drunk, particularly when the drunk is me.

Upstairs I waited for the lieutenant to gather his men in the muster room. I sat where I would sometimes sit in the dead of night when the world was quiet around me, reading my Greeks and Romans, trying to know myself, trying to practice moderation in all things, knowing I could never step twice in the same river, and so on. Here was the little office, just off the muster room, where Jackie Kane had sat with Georgina before I walked her out. *I know who he is*, the bitch.

As the men filed in they saw me. *Ah, hell*, their faces seemed to say. A few I recognized, including one kid I'd pulled from a wicked jam with the civilian complaint board. But for me he'd be bagging groceries in Massapequa right now. He gave me a nod, nothing more. The lieutenant brought the men to order, then he left the room because I told him to. He was a boss. When he was gone I shut the door and told them to stand easy. They didn't move. They all wore that same forbearing expression of a dog beaten for no reason it knows but believing it deserved to get beaten nonetheless. So I made it quick. I told them

I was their union trustee and if they had any questions I was their man. I told them the forty-eight-hour rule was in effect, and one raised a hand to ask what that meant. Everyone turned to her, the dumb kid in class.

"It means shut the fuck up, soldier," I said in a grave tone, as a joke, but no one laughed. The joke made everything worse. "It means they can't talk to you for forty-eight hours."

"They—?"

"IAB or the DA or the bosses. Nobody."

Nothing.

"Nobody but me. So if any of you saw anything, know anything about this situation we got going here, you just sit tight. You want to talk to someone, come to me."

Still nothing. I gave them a once-over. I wanted to see who was scared, who was not. All were young. All were trying to let it roll off their backs. All were suited up and ready to go into a world that hated them more tonight than usual, but none of them let on and I loved them for it. So help me God, I love cops. I wish I could've been one.

"You need a lawyer," I said, "I'll get you a lawyer. You need to talk, throw up, shit your pants, anything, call me. I'm here. Clear?"

Nothing.

"We clear?"

"Yes, sir."

They stood looking at no one until I let them go. Then there was the sound of boots on linoleum, and I followed downstairs to the complaint desk, where I asked the sergeant for the telephone. With the tour change finished the floor was clear and quiet except for the men still inside the captain's office. Every now and then a terrific explosion of masculine cheer burst forth. I dialed Garrity. He was not in, so I called Kat. The sound of her voice was like medicine. I asked her if she wanted to go to Norway.

"Sure," she said. "Why Norway?"

"No one honks in Norway, I read somewhere. Or shoots anyone."

"Sounds quiet."

"Tonight," I told her, meaning it.

"Okay," she answered, meaning it.

"Fill the bathtub with raisin bran so Phillip won't starve to death while we're gone." Neither of us spoke for a moment. We just felt each other along the telephone line, then a sort of hurrah came from the captain's office.

"Where are you?" she asked with a laughing lilt.

"Eight-three."

"Sounds like a hockey game," she said. "Are you coming tonight?"

"I don't know. I bought a fish."

"*Bought a fish*? Is that like cop talk, like you're in trouble or something?"

"It means I bought a fish," I said. "A salmon. I have to be back here at midnight, so maybe I can't come. Everything's going to hell. Everything is—you're probably sick of having me there anyway."

"I'm not very."

"You certain?" I asked.

"You're very useful. You can reach all the burned-out light bulbs I can't."

"Goodbye, Kat."

"Will—" she said, at the moment I was about to hang up the line.

"Yes?"

"Come. I have a sudden inexplicable urge for salmon."

TEN

As I passed the captain's office Berrigan fell out with his powerful arm comradely around another man I didn't know, and my eyes went automatically to his shirt collar. The 108—Queens, for chrissake. They'd come from all over town to send off McCosker. Police Commissioner Conrad Gilbert was cleaning house at the 83, beginning with the CO, Captain McCosker. I said "Sarge," but kept walking to the door. Berrigan pretended to be dismayed. "Way! Wha the fuck?" he said, moving down the hallway at a slight angle. "Come along like a good boy and have a snort with your old cap." I obeyed, as ever.

A mostly empty bottle of Bushmills was the only thing remaining on his office desk, and McCosker alone sat behind it. Everyone else was standing. Everything else had been cleared out or boxed up or was just gone. The office was a casket. Captain Michael McCosker had been precinct commander the last three years I worked patrol, and I hadn't been his favorite. The only reason I was standing here now was because I was with Garrity, we both knew, but it didn't matter. When the world shifts, you take what you find. McCosker's eyes were hollow and lonely, yet a phony smile hung on his face, on everyone's face. I was probably smiling, too, like a phony.

Berrigan poured me a slug of whiskey in a paper cone that began to dissolve at once. I tossed it back, and the liquor tasted like paper but felt good and made me want another, from a glass, from a heavy glass someplace dark where I wouldn't have to talk to anyone, or smile. There fell a sudden and obvious pall, and to keep things moving McCosker said to me, "Busy day for the PBA." He raised his cup, which was not a paper cone but a coffee-stained ceramic mug, BEST DAD EVER! Mickey McCosker was maybe fifty years old and there'd be nothing for him after Georgina. He was out, reassigned to the archives bureau in Staten Island. He was the first to fall, and he hadn't even been in Bushwick last night. He was home in Syosset with his beagle.

"Doing my best, Cap," I said.

"Well. You do that, William. She's a good man," he said wistfully, his life in the rearview mirror. "They're all good men."

Berrigan said, "Garrity must be crapping his pants," and everyone let go at
the idea of Shawn Garrity crapping his size 44 pants. I followed on this theme,
something about Garrity in an enormous diaper. Someone smacked me on
the back. Whiskey sloshed onto the floor, and I knew I had to get the hell out
of there. I lingered another five minutes, then I pushed through to McCosker.
He shook hands without meeting my eyes. Everyone said so long and I walked
out. It was the saddest party I'd ever seen.

More than anything I needed to get into the clean evening air again, even
if it was bristling with microphones and antennas, but Ralph Berrigan called
out behind. "Let's walk," he said, and taking my upper arm he directed me
away from the front door and instead along the long hallway to the fire exit. A
sign said an alarm would sound, but if it did I heard nothing. We came onto
Bleecker Street, empty, well away from the television trucks and everyone. Even
so Berrigan waited half a block before asking, "How we looking?"

"They ACD'd Odom. He's going to testify against Georgina in the
grand jury."

"So what?" he said after several paces, like a man trying to convince himself.
"Fister wants to sign that shithead up? Go ahead. He can have him."

"What's Odom gonna say?"

"Gives a fuck? I don't," Berrigan said. "DA's got nothing without he gets
someone someone's gonna believe, and no one's gonna believe this hump. He
can talk all day long. Everyone'll know he cut a deal with the DA. Forget him.
He's no worry. I'm not worried."

We walked along and two things occurred to me. The first was that Berrigan
was not drunk, nor at least as drunk as he'd made out before. The second was
that Berrigan was worried, or at least somewhat on edge. The idea braced me.
I'd never seen Berrigan worried. Hell, I'd never seen him on edge. I had, on the
contrary, seen him stand in the middle of Central Avenue and quietly examine
the state of load of his Webley after one round from an upper floor of Hope
Gardens penetrated the left quarter panel of our RMP and a second landed on
the asphalt at his feet.

"There's no worry," he went on. "All these people out there with the signs?
Racist cops, don't shoot me, or whatever the fuck they say. I mean, look at that—"
He gestured to the cars parked on the sidewalk all along Bleecker. Each had a
flower tucked under the windshield wiper, a single pink azalea. "It's a protest,
I get it. You protest, you got to protest something, right? So what're they
protesting? What do they think? They think Georgina threw a shot at the guy

there 'cause—what?—'cause she hates the kid she don't even know?—'cause he's black?—'cause she's a racist?—'cause she's a racist and don't even know it?"

"I don't know," I told him the truth.

"I mean—look at her—what is she—?" he went on, leaving the obvious fact of her flesh unsaid. "What is she, a racist against herself? Maybe she should go shoot herself, I guess they're saying. Maybe she's such a racist she should shoot herself in the head, she hates herself so much, I dunno."

"Or maybe they're just fed up."

"Of what?" he said, nearly laughing.

"Of living here. Being poor. Getting stopped. Getting frisked. Getting arrested. Getting shot. Getting killed. By us," I said, and he threw me a side-eye glance full of disdain and bewilderment, and for a moment I felt the same uncomfortable timidity I'd often felt with him when our nighttime conversations in the muster room turned philosophical. Berrigan seemed always to seek me out whenever I was sitting alone upstairs, digesting events with cold pizza at four in the morning, reading the *Meditations* or worse. Berrigan never knew what to do with me. He would look at my books, sometimes ask about them, never scornfully yet always with an unformed smile on his weather-worn face, the slightest lift of his absurd Lord Kitchener mustache, whenever he would ask, "Hell you get out of that paperback book anyway, Way?" Berrigan might have been a caricature, and therefore easier to ignore, except I realized he actually wanted to know. While I could never answer such a question without sounding ridiculous, one night I read him a single phrase I'd just underlined:

What discontents you? That men are wicked and do wicked things? Then take heart for we are all thinking creatures, made for one another, and understanding is a necessary part of justice for no man does wrong except out of ignorance.

"Bullcrap," he said lightly then, looking at the cover. "Guess Marcus Aurelius ain't from Brooklyn. Men here don't do wrong outa ignorance, Way. They do wrong 'cause they want a pair of Air Jordans."

"Yeah, fed up," Berrigan said to me now as we walked along the darkening street. "Be a lot more fed up we didn't take their calls, we stayed in the car and let them eat each other, breakfast, dinner, and dessert. Why do they call us?" he said, and I answered him by rote—*To make things better*—like a schoolboy, one of Berrigan's aphorisms, a declaration he demanded of us at every roll call, an easy distillation of all the complex reasons why we take the calls, why we get out of the car, why we do what we do for a living instead of driving a cab or fixing faucets or selling avocados, for example. "And if we don't make things better, they get worse," he said, continuing his catechism. I nodded amen. "We're not the problem, Way. You don't like how we police your world, see how you like it if we don't."

"I don't think they're saying we—"

"Leading cause of death of black men is black men," he said. "Not cops."

"I don't—"

"Fuck that," Berrigan said. "Don't hold up a sign telling me some brother's life matters after you just put him in the ground."

I decided to let him talk. As he went on I became aware of the shift in our relationship. Before, in uniform, I'd been just another rookie for him to keep an eye on, and not the class valedictorian by any means. The tables had not turned exactly, but now at least we had our eyes on the same men. That made me if not a peer in his view—for the world hadn't altered radically enough to allow that— then at least now I was someone more substantial. Not so very long ago there were few in the world whose good opinion mattered to me more than his, so to have Berrigan speak to me now as something near an equal felt unreasonably flattering.

"Look, between you and me," he said, "so maybe Georgina wet her knickers a little bit. Maybe she went too quick to the gun. You gonna blame her? You put her in a situation where she's gotta shoot or wait around and find out the guy means business? Say she waits. Say she keeps it holstered. Now she's dead. Lesson learned. Won't make that mistake again, ha ha, will she?"

"No."

"Put yourself in Gina's shoes," he told me. "I mean, yeah, she's a woman. Okay. On the small side, maybe. Not threatening. You think some scummer like Dewberry's gonna let her put him under without a fight? No way. You're small, not aggressive, with the perfume and the long fingernails there—you know—"

"I know."

"—what're you supposed to do, the guy won't go down?" he said, opening his hands. "Ask nice?"

"And that's what happened here?"

My question started as harmlessly rhetorical, but by the time it reached the punctuation mark it had become a real question. And I wanted the answer, suddenly aware Berrigan so far had said nothing about the better reason Georgina Reed drew down on Raquan Dewberry: that Raquan Dewberry had drawn first. Last night I hadn't spoken to Berrigan about Georgina—officially I wasn't speaking to him now—so all I knew about the situation I'd gotten from Georgina and Donny Holtz. Berrigan I knew came on the scene too late to have seen anything, arriving with his rookie driver after Holtz radioed for backup. By then Raquan Dewberry was already on the sidewalk, already dead, and Berrigan had done little more than roll the body and voucher the gun he recovered beneath. Berrigan, of course, believed the same about me: that I'd gotten the whole story and knew all there was to know. As a result we were two eleven-year-olds with a waterlogged *Penthouse*, hopefully speculating and drawing faulty conclusions based on flawed information and a fundamental lack of understanding of the nature of things.

"Fuck yeah, that's what happened," he answered affirmatively. "You're her, Gina, what choice you got? Listen, Way, I'm no dinosaur. I'm no fucking brontosaurus here. I seen some women do this job good. But, Jesus, some people. Take my driver—what's his name?—Karpatkin—take this probie Kevin Karpatkin fuck they give me as my driver. There's one useless little pussycat I ever saw one. Couldn't punch his way out of a paper bag. I was Dewberry, and Karpatkin tried to hook me? Forget about it. I'd shove Karpatkin up his own asshole and shoot three-pointers with the guy. Almighty Christ, you could partner up the both of them, Karpatkin plus Gina, and still Dewberry woulda run up on her. That's why she got no choice."

"No choice?"

"Except the gun. Old days," he said, laughing at the recollection of the old days, "old days, fuck, you didn't go to the gun. You settle business with these." He held up his two big meat hooks to demonstrate, knuckles scarred to make his point. "Now it's official in the department—no fists, just the gun. Read the patrol guide. You got kids coming into the job now, out of the academy, they never mixed it up, not once, not never. Everyone's too quick on the gun, ask me."

"Sure."

"You take a cop like Donny," he said. Gordon Holtz was Berrigan's kind of cop, the kind that cracked skulls and didn't read Seneca in the muster room. "Dewberry woulda took one look at Donny and give up. I surrender. But even if he put up a fight, Donny wouldna needed no gun. Only Gina she—"

"Donny was there, Sarge."

"Say again?"

"Donny was there," I told Berrigan, repeating what I knew. "At the arrest. He was backing Georgina when the kid pulled out—I mean, right?"

"Donny said he was backing Gina, then Donny was backing Gina. I wasn't there, Way, was I?"

"No."

"The story is Donny was on the second piece, Odom. Odom was Donny's collar. Only I'm saying in general, Gina, she ain't got no choice when a guy won't go under. That's why you don't put a man like Gina on patrol, like I told McCosker fifty times. Only he don't listen."

"Right."

"So everyone's back there in the office tonight saying, *Mickey, you got corn-holed, you ain't do nothing,*" he said. "Meantime I'm thinking, *Exactly, Mickey, you ain't do nothing.* Only what can he do? He don't let Gina patrol, then the ACLU and Bumpurs come in and say it's discrimination they don't let her work. So he lets her patrol and now what're they saying?—it's discrimination she killed the guy. Can't win." His laugh dripped acid.

"Sure."

"And not for nothing, but what discrimination?" he said, still lightly caustic. "Everyone crying discrimination when they can't do the job. People ain't the same, Way, what can I say? Everyone wants equal rights, I get it. But people ain't equal, so how you gonna have equal rights?"

"I think you're talking about something different now."

"What different?" he said, scowling, slowing his pace.

"Equal rights doesn't mean we're all the same, Sarge," I said. "Just that we should all get our shot."

"Gina got her shot. One round. Center mass at five yards," he said, laughing, genuinely amused this time, and I couldn't help but laugh with complicity alongside him. "Not too damn bad for a virgin, am I right?"

"But, I meant—forget it."

"What?" he asked.

"I'm just saying I don't see the race angle here."

"Check your calendar, Way," he answered. "Everything's got a race angle now."

"No, I just mean—how can they say she's a racist, she's—?"

"She's a cop," he answered. "Doesn't matter what color's under the Kevlar, once you're blue you're blue. That's all they see."

"All we see, too."

There followed the briefest imaginable pause, during which Berrigan decided to take this as something like a joke. "Way, you old pussycat, you're still soft," he said and put a big heavy arm around me, pulling me right in as we walked. I knew he didn't mean pussycat exactly and I knew he didn't mean soft either. Up close I smelled his antique smell. "Gimme a ten eighty-five here. God help us, we got a bleeding heart in the house—"

He stopped at once. Rounding the corner I saw three yellowy orange BABE school buses now double-parked in front of the 83 stationhouse. Berrigan dropped his arm from me and his eyes went flat. A uniformed cop held back traffic to allow the congregants—gingerly, arthritically—to alight on Knickerbocker Avenue and then to gather into an orderly cartel on the sidewalk behind wooden parade fencing painted blue. Most of their signs and placards were the familiar usual, but tonight every third person carried a bouquet of azaleas, pink and rolled into a paper cone. A small folding table was set with coffee and boxes and patterned tins and when we passed a delicate old woman in a hat offered us homemade cupcakes on a tray. Berrigan took one and asked the woman if she needed anything.

"No, honey," she said. "We're all just getting settled in here."

"Well, Miss Janice," he said, "you know where the ladies' room is, don't you?"

"Yes, darling, I remember."

"And tell Latrice I keep hearing good things about him," Berrigan said. "So good that I'm wondering if they're talking about the same Latrice, ha ha!"

"Whoa now, honey, ain't I got my eye on him and you both?"

As we continued for the stationhouse door they began to sing "We Shall Overcome," and a man with a bouquet began delicately to place azaleas under windshield wipers. Berrigan ate his cupcake in two bites and watched them with a complicated expression, vanilla frosting on the corner of his mustache. "They're just ignorant is all," he said without meanness. "You see, Way, that's why they do us wrong, call us murderers, racists. All wrongdoing comes from ignorance, so you have to try to understand. Understanding is part of justice."

"What'd you say, Sarge?"

"You never heard that, Way? You like to read, I remember," he said, and I understood that Sergeant Ralph Berrigan had no memory of that conversation in the muster room so long ago, but that he had afterward made the words his own and was now handing them back to me as a present. "It's Roman, you know."

ELEVEN

"Medicine," I told Kat the moment she swung open her front door, an enormous carved affair with thick beveled glass refracting the light of a brass chandelier overhead. I'd driven from Bushwick, so lost in dark thoughts that it wasn't until I parked my Ford too close to a fire hydrant near Kat's brooding brownstone in Park Slope and threw a plasticized NYPD placard on the dashboard that I even noticed the pink azalea under my windshield wiper. I threw it in the gutter.

"Poor baby," she said, the look of happy surprise on her face changing to fake-real concern. "Oh, what hurts?"

"My conscience."

"I'm putting Phillip down," she said, and I watched as she flew light-footed up the long mahogany staircase in black yoga pants, making no sound.

"I feel better already," I called to her, and I watched and watched.

"Come up when you're sedated," came her voice. "He has a question."

In her stainless-steel kitchen I poured something into a juice glass and drank it off, a quick hit, efficient as a paid assassin. "Hell, yeah," I said to the empty air and waited for the burn to fade. Then I followed upstairs, plodding heavily as if into a halftime locker room, the score 28–3. "You live in New York City and have two flights of stairs," I told her as I came upon the third-floor landing. "That's really all anyone needs to know about you, socioeconomically speaking."

"Perhaps," she called from Phillip's room. "But I still don't have my yellow Benz back."

"Working on it, doll."

She appeared in an overlarge knit sweater that she had pulled over her forearms, smooth and small. She kissed my cheek then skipped away down the stairs, saying, "And don't tell him anything scary. Last time you gave him nightmares."

"Did I—?"

"Something about owls. And the old gray wooly, whatever that is."

Phillip was in pajamas, in bed, his huge eyes shimmering in the orange streetlight that leaked through the old shutters in the tall and narrow windows that faced the front. When I opened the door, he pushed himself up against the headboard and said to me, "Good evening to you, my good man."

"*Bonsoir, mon ami*," I said. "How was your quiz? Get an A?"

"They don't give grades in my school."

"Good. Life is a pass-fail course."

"I got a sticker, though," he said. "Magdalene was a girl dog."

"Yes, she was," I said, and it seemed perfectly fine to hear her name when he said it. I sat next to him. He smelled like shampoo and toothpaste.

"Did she have puppies?"

"No."

"Girls have puppies," he informed me.

"I had her fixed."

"Was she broken?"

"Fixed so she wouldn't have puppies."

He considered that, and although I could scarcely discern his small face in the thin light I knew the expression on it showed dissatisfaction. "Didn't she want any?"

"What do you think?"

"I think so. It's natural," he said. "You should get a dog."

"Why?"

"So you'll be happy again."

"I am happy. My apartment's too small anyway," I said. "I only like great big dogs, not ankle-biters."

"What's an ankle-biter, ha ha?"

"You know the lady next door with the little dogs with no legs? Ankle-biters." He began to giggle, guiltily, knowing I had said something naughty but delighted to share in being naughty.

"They do so have legs, ha ha," he laughed.

"You turn them over, they have a million little legs like centipedes," I said, demonstrating with my fingers then tickling him.

"No, they don't!" he tried to say, half-believing, his tubular little body twisting, kicking.

"Shush, now, or your mom will hear!"

"I can't, ha ha, because you're tickling me!" he managed to gasp out.

"Oh, sorry," I said, stopping. He heaved a great sigh, and I stood. "Now, go to sleep."

"Centipedes only have a hundred legs. That's why they're called centipedes."

"They're called centipedes because they cost a penny," I said. "Now go to sleep."

"You lie a lot."

"Do I?" I asked defensively. "No, I don't."

"What toys d'you have when you were a kid?"

"Let me see," I answered. "I had a water moccasin. Some gasoline."

"Seriously," he said in a voice very much like his mother's. "What was your favorite?"

And in his dark bedroom I tried to think back twenty-five years, to the time I was his age, but while my childhood was atraumatic neither was it filled with toys. The Avocado King's idea of fun was to give me an iron rake to clear the little driveway in front of the Melba Court bungalow. When I got underfoot he'd tell me to run around the block as quick as I could, then do it again in the other direction. Nevertheless one birthday my father gave me an orange helicopter that would circle a point on a stiff wire tether. You could make it hover and land and fly backwards, but it never left the circle. I told Phillip about the helicopter and how I used to lie on the floor in my bedroom and pretend I was rescuing injured men, plastic green toy soldiers with bent bazookas, flying them to safety from dense jungles in faraway places with strange names.

"You had a house when you were a kid?" he asked.

"Sort of."

"Whoa, you're lucky."

"You have a house, Phillip."

"This is a building."

"I got news for you. This is a house," I said. "I live in a building. There are a thousand people in it. Here it's only you and your mom."

"Wow, you know a thousand people?"

"No. I don't know any of them."

"That's weird."

"This is New York City," I said. "It would only be weird if I knew my neighbors. Now, good night."

"Will—" he said at the last possible moment, my foot already in the hall. "Tell me again about the old gray wooly."

Downstairs Kat was cross-legged on the couch in the parlor, eating an avocado. It looked familiar. On the enormous television was Shawn Garrity, looking shifty and damp, captured this morning outside headquarters. "He looks like *he* shot Dewberry," Kat said as I continued to the kitchen where I dropped the salmon into a skillet and lit the gas. "Will you turn that off, please?" I called. She complied, and in the welcome quiet there was just the sound of Kat singing lightly to herself. Then the singing stopped. Then I heard a newspaper thrown. When I came over her knees were pulled up and she wouldn't look at me. "I just read the paper." She gestured savagely at a tabloid on the floor, the *Brooklyn Daily News*, which lay open and scattered. "Have you?"

"No," I answered carefully, getting ready for whatever was coming in my direction. "Strangely busy today."

"Oh, you really should read it, Will," she said in a mordant tone, which made me deeply uneasy, as she was never that way with me. Our arguments had never been arguments. They always had a fence around them. "Page three."

I went to hands and knees on the carpet, searching through the deranged folds of newspaper until I found the headline:

COP UNION BIG: FLOWER VIC A "S*HEAD"

I stopped, dropped, and rolled, as if on fire. "Goddamn you, Betty Moon," I said aloud, knowing I had only myself to blame. On my back now, on the thick woolen carpet, I lay looking at the parlor ceiling fourteen feet above—ornate cornice molding, rococo plasterwork, roses, fruit, friezes, eggs, darts. I had really never noticed it before, and now it peered back at me with stern Victorian righteousness. "Oh—fuck me."

"Darling," Kat said in the same voice. "I'm so proud of you. I never realized you were a union big."

"Kat—"

"You sure it's not a typo? You think maybe they misspelled—"

"It's not what—" I tried to say, pulling myself up, kneeling before her on the carpet in supplication.

"Holy Mother, Will," she said, all sarcasm gone, leaving pure anger or if not wholly pure then anger alloyed with disgust. Her face was one I'd never seen, as anger was a stranger to her. She hadn't even the profanity for it, so for the occasion she had to borrow mine, using my own vocabulary to tell me what she thought of me. "How could you say something so cold and awful?"

"Kat—"

"Oh, don't—"

"Listen," I said, imploringly. "Listen, Kat. Okay, so everyone can call Georgina Reed a racist and a murderer, but God forbid I go on record and call a spade a spade and—" The sudden open shock on her face stunned me into silence before I realized she simply hadn't understood: a misunderstanding, yes, but under the circumstances a misunderstanding of the most vicious sort because it fit. Worse was the realization that she was no longer willing to give me the benefit of the doubt, which she'd always done before whenever I crossed a line. "No—no, Jesus, I don't mean—"

"I got it, Will," she said, but her frosty stare told me the damage was done.

Now the stink of burning fish wafted in from the kitchen, and in fact a gray miasma had begun to form in the parlor, unnoticed by either of us. "Son of a—" I said, hurrying in, but the smoke detector tripped and the alarm echoed throughout the townhouse. A light flashed brightly someplace. I dashed the skillet off the stove and stood on a chair, swinging with a kitchen broom awkwardly at the alarm fixed to the lofty and ornate ceiling. At length I managed only to knock it off along with a section of plasterwork, which fell. Amid the cacophony Phillip appeared in his pajamas. "Are we on fire?" I heard him say sleepily before he walked to a keypad on the wall and pressed some buttons. Silence fell. No one spoke. Kat coughed.

"I'm sorry," I said after she'd sent her son bleary-eyed back upstairs.

"You should go," Kat said.

"I should," I said, as if it were my idea. In my hand I held a thirteen-inch piece of ceiling, unsure what to do with it, wanting to fix it, knowing I couldn't. "I have to go out to Bushwick. The midnight crew is coming on and—"

"No."

"No what?" I said.

"I don't mean you should go because you're busy. I mean you should go."

"Oh, Kat. Really?" I asked. "Are you really gonna make a fight out of this damn newspaper?"

"Whatever he was, that boy. Whatever he did. Whatever you—you policemen think he was, he was still a boy, and now he's dead. He was alive yesterday and today he's not. And you can't talk about him like—" For a moment she couldn't speak. No, she wasn't tongue-tied, I realized. She knew exactly what she wanted to say. She just couldn't say it.

"Good night, Kat," I said, placing the section of ceiling carefully on the carpet, the world turned upside down.

"Last week I told you I didn't know what your job was," she said. "Well. Now I know."

TWELVE

For a while I just walked around Park Slope. After seven blocks I realized I was cold and remembered I'd left my overcoat in Phillip's bedroom. Then I remembered my keys were in the pocket of my overcoat, but I continued toward my building, a twenty-minute traipse, and somewhere along the way I started thinking of Regine.

Of all the things in my head at that moment, of all the things I needed to sort through, I needed Regine Pomeroy least of all. Yet there she was, her memory sparked by the sight of her father this afternoon in his courtroom, by his eyes passing over me as he walked off the bench. She was always there, I suppose, waiting like a virus in remission to overcome me when my resistance was low. Still, I had no specific thought of her, much less the hollowness that frequently accompanied the recollection. There was only the renewed weight of knowing that sooner or later there'd be a reckoning, and my heart told me it would be sooner. After all, I'd waited almost fifteen years.

I walked chilled to the bone through the entrance of my apartment building, and the doorman said, "Welcome home, Mr. Way," without sarcasm. He was a compact, handsome man of middle years with a nobility of deportment that overcame the necessary servility of his polyester uniform. Indeed the striped pants and gold buttons gave him an almost military bearing, and he spoke with a majestic accent of someplace in Mitteleuropa that never failed to make me conscious of my own south Brooklyn mother tongue.

"Frederick," I said in a voice fit for the confessional. "I'm locked out."

"No problem, sir. Don't you worry about a thing, Mr. Way. You come with Frederick now, and Frederick'll fix you up right away." He always spoke to me as if I were a boy, or slow-witted, and with a hand on my arm he moved me paternally toward the elevator bank. In the lobby there was enough room to be congenial, but in the elevator car it was too close so we rode in silence, both of us looking politely at the ceiling, our wristwatches, Frederick humming Jerome Kern for seventeen floors. I smelled burned salmon on my clothes.

Upstairs the elevator door slid open to reveal a hallway of doorknobs. One of them was mine, I gathered. You could never be sure. Once I stepped off on the wrong floor and—drunk, cursing the lock—awakened a frowsy neighbor at two in the morning and for an instant thought it was me. Now I followed Frederick, matching his brisk pace. He began going through his enormous ring of keys, saying, "Just a moment, just a moment now, just wait for Frederick." And I waited, and while I waited nature called, loudly, and still I waited, and while I waited my neighbor—shirtless, dreadlocked, tattooed, smiling broadly—appeared in the doorway opposite. The skunk stink of a joint followed him out into the hallway along with a thumping backbeat and a small dog, yellow, with the face of a jackal.

"Kaseem, hey," I said wearily, neighborly, but Frederick gave him a steely stare over his shoulder. He disapproved of Kaseem, one of the building's subsidized tenants, no visible means of support, and more than once told me that sort of fellow shouldn't be living here among reputable people, which made me wonder what Frederick thought about me.

"Yo, Mr. Will," Kaseem said, as another dog joined the first, identical. "Thought y'all was the pizza man, yo! Freddie, yo! Freddie—? Freddie—?"

"Young man," Frederick boomed. "My name isn't Freddie. Where is your shirt? And we've talked many times about that other thing. The other thing, I'm telling you. That smell."

"I locked myself out," I said to no one. Christ, I had to pee.

"Dang!" Kaseem said. "Come in! We can catch *Wheel*. I got it taped. I just phoned for pizza. Four large. Extra cheese. And a mess of garlic knots, yo." The dogs had their noses on me, insistently taking inventory of where I'd been. I let them. There was nothing I could do. I stood immobilized by events and waited as Frederick continued looking for the correct key, talking lowly to himself. Now the first dog began to bark, a sharp piercing bark. "Quiet, Shiny," Kaseem said. Half an octave higher it would have passed beyond human hearing, but as it was each bark went through me like a nail. I was afraid I might leak. Now the second started in. A door opened down the hall. Someone stood there in disapproving silhouette, hands on hips. "Shiny! Shooshka, quiet!" Kaseem was saying without meaning it, like a new parent who secretly thinks it's cute when her toddler crayons your couch. "We got neighbors, yo."

"Four pizzas?" I said, trying hard. Frederick was still working.
Woof!

"Oh, hell and death!" the doorman said to himself, stamping.

"Yo," Kaseem laughed, a big genuine laugh. "I eat three pizzas by—"
Woof!

"There you are, Mr. Way," Frederick said at last, pushing open the door to my darkened apartment. I hastily left him hectoring Kaseem in the hall and took care of business, the relief like climax. Then I walked around the place in the dark like a cat burglar. I'd not cleaned for days, and it stank like takeout. I opened a window. The night breeze blew in irresolutely and I stood there with the lights out, all south Brooklyn before me, and above it came airplanes in long procession, their landing lights blazing brighter than Venus, which yet hung above the rim of the horizon. Loosening my stained tie I walked into the kitchen, where a long chef's knife, a wedding present, remained unwashed on the cutting board. I hefted it thoughtfully then placed it against my carotid artery, for fun, for size, for practice, pressing the blade so firmly to my skin that I could feel my own heartbeat transmitted along the handle, steadily, hastening by not so much as a beat, for there was no cause for alarm—even I didn't take myself seriously.

Once I thought I was someone, then one day I realized I was someone else—how the hell did that happen? "So you may never be the man you always wanted to be," I said aloud, taking my spare keys, my spare overcoat, and walking out the door, "but at least you can be a force of evil in the world."

Twenty minutes before twelve I walked up to the 83 desk. Outside, the yellowy orange BABE school buses had gone for the night and the stationhouse lay mostly peaceful and unprotested. Inside it was the turnout for the midnight tour, so men were coming on and men were going off, walking outside to find azaleas under their windshield wipers and their tires slashed. Even so, a slow night at the 83. Word had gone out at every roll call that no one was to take a job, no one was to get out of his car. For the next week you couldn't get arrested in Bushwick unless you did it in broad daylight in front of three observers from the United Nations. Commissioner Gilbert wanted no one in Brooklyn to have an excuse to do what they were going to do anyway.

The desk sergeant nodded hello to me. I was a feature here again, known. Down the hall I saw two plainclothesmen in the captain's empty office. McCosker was long gone. The office was so brightly fluorescent that the men seemed like cutouts, blankly menacing. I asked the sergeant about them and he shrugged. "Rat squad?" I said. Another shrug. He didn't want any part of it, even a part as small as saying yes. That was the atmosphere. No one wanted to be next out the door.

I made a perfunctory knock. "Hello, gentlemen," I said to them, two white men, plainclothes. Both wore the same impassive expression, as if they knew I was going to raise hell and didn't care. The older one had gone a little soft but he wasn't a bus driver yet. He sat at McCosker's desk like he owned it, which pissed me off. Nevertheless I said without teeth, "Get you some coffee?"

"No, thanks," said the younger one. Despite the cool night he wore a thin knit sport shirt and his nipples stared like headlights. His arms were very strong and tattooed with the eagle, globe, and anchor. He was a big-necked man—no neck really, just a line on the back of his head where the barber stopped cutting.

I said, "Guess that means you've had our joe before, ha ha."

Nothing.

"Once is enough, huh?" I said, still trying. Neither man tipped his hand, however; they just took me in with blank eyes in flat faces. I gave up. I exhaled dispiritedly and said, "Yeah, thought so."

"Thought so what?" the younger one said in due course.

"Let me ask you," I said to him. "How many Internal Affairs men it take to screw in a light bulb?"

He shot a glance at the man at the desk, seeking approval to hit me. The older man had folded his hands together in front of him and sat clenching them rhythmically so they seemed like a heart slowly beating on the desktop where there were still circles from McCosker's bottle of whiskey and Father's Day coffee mug. That was all he did. Otherwise he remained motionless. The younger one asked me, "You somebody up in the squad here or something?"

"The answer is 'That's not funny,'" I said to the man at the desk. "I can always tell an IAB man. No sense of humor at all." I was looking at him because he was the one in charge. The jarhead I didn't even notice anymore, but he told me to piss up a rope. "There, you see?" I said. I advanced toward the desk. "You want to tell me what you're doing here?"

"Hell are you?" said the younger man, putting his body near me.

"It's the forty-eight-hour rule," I said. "You talk to my men, I'll make trouble for you."

"And you'd be right if you did," said the man at McCosker's desk. He unclasped his hands and made a gesture toward the younger man, who reluctantly stepped back. "Wouldn't you, Officer Way?" Hearing my own name spoken by a stranger made me falter to a degree, like losing the anonymous quality of dark sunglasses or the safety of flipping someone the finger behind the wheel of your car. Perhaps sensing this, his gaze softened yet he remained empty of any human motivation I could fathom. "But you got it all wrong," he told me. "We have other business here tonight." He produced his card from an inner pocket and slid it across the desktop. I read it but left it there. In the trash basket behind the desk was this afternoon's *Brooklyn Daily News*, neatly folded open to page three.

"You mind if I ask what business that is, Inspector?"

"Had a dog shot last week. Neighbor saw a patrolman throw the shot," he told me straight-faced, using each word carefully. "So. We're looking into that."

A moment went by during which we regarded each other.

At last, smiling a little more than I had all day, I moved toward the door. "Hilarious," I said. "I take back what I said before—"

"Hold up, Officer Way," the IAB inspector said. I was already in the hall, but I turned to face him again. He hadn't moved an inch. "Something I have to ask you, you like jokes so much. How many cops it take to throw a handcuffed prisoner down a flight of stairs?"

"Excuse me?"

"I asked you," he said, very serious now, "how many cops it take to throw a handcuffed prisoner down a flight of stairs?"

I shook my head.

"None. He fell."

DONNY HOLTZ

THIRTEEN

Thursday at nine Police Officer Gordon Holtz duly appeared, as ordered, at 315 Hudson Street in the city. Hudson Street was Internal Affairs. Holtz didn't bother to tell me until he was already there. He called from a payphone, speaking with a buttered roll in his mouth evidently. I was still in my underwear, still unshaven, still watching the morning news in my kitchen when he called. I ought to have gone back to the 83 for the tour change at eight, but when my alarm rang after three fitful hours of sleep I reasoned it away. Even half-awake I knew I was done with events, even if events weren't yet done with me.

On television they were still talking about Dewberry's memorial service at BABE Cathedral yesterday evening. A fistfight had broken out in the nave. There were factions and divisions among the mourners, the reasons unstated. Cousin went after cousin, nephew after aunt. Someone's grandmother was carried out on a litter in a dead faint or cardiac arrest. Archbishop Bumpurs momentarily reimposed order from the pulpit through the force of his enormous personality, but things soon devolved onto Malcolm X Boulevard, where they really got ugly. As many ambulances were on scene as television trucks, but under the circumstances patrolmen from the 81 precinct hung back and watched on the perimeter with tasers and truncheons and military-grade cans of mace. Instead unarmed community affairs police in more benign light blue uniforms and baseball caps waded into the fray urging calm and distributing pamphlets. One was beaten nearly to death along with seventeen civilians hospitalized at last count. There were no arrests, but four cars were overturned and an appliance store down the block set ablaze after being stripped of car radios and microwave ovens as *residents mourned the murder of one of their own by Brooklyn police officers widely seen as out of control*, the anchor reported dolefully before moving on to national news. I yawned, then my phone rang.

"Goddamn it, Donny," I said when he told me. "Fuck are you thinking?"

"I just thought it was just the usual. I dunno."

"The usual? This shit happen to you all the time?"

"I dunno. Sit you down," he said into the receiver. "Ask you questions and stuff."

"Jesus, Donny. Just stay there. Stay there, okay?"

"Okay."

"Don't go inside," I said.

"Okay, boss."

"I'll be there in ten minutes," I told him, already pulling on yesterday's pants, which were the pants from the day before.

"Okay, boss. They said—"

"Said what?"

"Said I could bring a lawyer, I wanted."

"Holy Mother—just stay there, Donny. Don't go inside."

Forty-five minutes later I found him, inside, in uniform, huge, freshly shaved and redolent of Irish Spring soap and Desenex foot powder. He was sitting spread-kneed on a wooden bench in IAB reception, which had the sour tang of steam radiators and bureaucracy. I sat with him on the bench and he talked nonstop for an hour, I swear. I hardly listened at first. I couldn't focus. My mind was slow and fast. And there was something between his teeth. He was talking about his shield number and he was talking about how it had been his father's number, then he was talking about fishing, for God's sake, then about anything that came into his golden retriever head, so it took me a while to realize he was scared. The realization that Gordon Holtz had enough sense to be scared made me revise my opinion of him, and I began to listen.

"Oh, hey—" he said so suddenly that I started. "Was a truck outside, outside on the street there, double-parked, double-parked in the no-parking. Big white box truck there, with a lime on it or something. And it had your name. I wanted to tell you."

"Avocado," I told him, knowing he'd seen one of my father's delivery trucks.

"Huh?

"It was an avocado on the truck you saw. You said lime."

"Yeah, yeah, avocado. With a face," he said. "And like a crown or whatever? And your name—William Way—that's your name, right?"

"Ain't me, brother."

"William Way, it said. And son, it said."

"I've seen those trucks around," I told Holtz, noncommittal, as much as I'd ever admit. "Shoulda wrote a ticket, Donny. For the double-parking. Tow that son of a bitch out to College Point."

He laughed only because I smiled. Then, both of us still smiling, he said, "They modified Gina, you know. Out to College Point."

"I heard."

"They put Gina in the impound lot. You know what that means, doncha?"

"Yeah."

"Ain't never gonna see her no more, are we?"

"Nope."

We weren't friends, Gordon Holtz and I, but in this place he knew I was as good as it would get. He relaxed a little, and his talk remained desultory but steady. Like a bad hangover, everything was okay so long as he kept moving. Or maybe he just wanted to get the talk out of his system before they brought him inside and put him in a wooden chair at a long wooden table in a room with a two-way mirror. Now he was telling me how his service gun, his piece of shit semiautomatic Glock, once jammed up on the range and took a good five seconds to clear.

"That's life and death right there, my friend—five seconds," he said. "All over by then. That's all she wrote." He had never fired his weapon in anger, he told me when I asked, and I understood that the idea of getting killed in the line of duty haunted him less than getting killed because his gun jammed. He then fell quiet for the first time in an hour, pausing, breathing audibly, before saying, "That's what all them with the signs and flowers out there don't get."

"Tell me."

"They don't get that out there, on the street, it's just seconds. It's a split second," he said. "They say we murder some guy 'cause we hate him. 'Cause we're racist or whatever and hate them. But how can you decide to hate somebody in a split second? You can't."

"No."

"So, yeah. You fuck up, sure. Everyone fucks up. But I'd rather fuck up and come home, you know? I don't want to fuck up and be dead."

"No, you don't."

"But how's it murder, I fuck up?" he said. "I mean—say I'm right, and I take the shot, then I'm a hero. They give me a medal. But I fuck up, then I'm a murderer? I'm a racist? I don't get it. In half a second, I'm a murderer or I'm a hero. You're one or the other, I mean, it should be something more than luck, you know?"

Hudson Street always depressed the hell out of me. The brown walls closed in. I caught a whiff of urinal cakes in the heavy air. Men came and went. Two walked by and regarded us, saying nothing. Each had the dull glazed expression that seemed to follow from a career of distrusting the people you were supposed to trust. Every time someone passed I looked into his face and he into mine. At IAB you had no idea who was a friend. I hadn't told Mark Masterson I was coming down. There'd been no time. Were he to come by it might be uncomfortable. A PAA sat behind the reception desk. So far she'd said hello to everyone who passed, attaching name and rank to her incongruously light and pleasant good morning. I was paying attention. I wanted to know if an unfamiliar face came in, someone the PAA had never seen before.

At one point I felt hostile eyes on me and saw an IAB detective glowering from the corner with crossed arms. He had a brief, whispered conversation with the PAA, who seemed embarrassed and suddenly disorganized. She shot me a horrified look as the man walked over to ask my name in an overtly correct, officious voice. I told him and asked his. "Detective Ed Margulies. Are you a lawyer?" "Now, is that nice?" I said, then he told me to leave. I said I was staying. He insisted. I told him to go fuck himself, whereupon the conversation became pointless and I lost interest. I felt him hovering over me, radiating heat. He was a weedy man who probably enjoyed his work. When he stumped off on size nine and a half shoes Holtz grew dark and quiet.

"His name isn't Ed," I told Holtz. "It's E.D."

"Huh?"

"Takes five Viagra just to play solitaire, you know?" I told him with a gesture for emphasis.

"Ha ha, funny," Holtz said weakly, not listening.

"With Polaroids of his mother."

"Ha ha," he said, and I stopped trying to cheer him up. The detective reminded him why he was here, I suppose, and he no longer felt so talkative, even if the talk was only to keep at bay an emotion he'd never felt before.

Presently a uniformed patrolman came into reception from the hallway. The PAA didn't say hello.

I didn't know him either, but he was escorted by an IAB inspector named Sheldon Danilov, who gave me a nod of uncomfortable recognition. On a winter evening a month earlier, when the narrow streets and lampposts of lower Manhattan were black with ice, I attended a sedate little celebration at Hudson Street for Mark Masterson. He had taken his promotion to second grade, and there was a Carvel cake and several stiff figures standing around eating it in a conference room that was probably wired. After, a few of us made our careful way over the slick sidewalks to a nameless saloon on Spring Street that was very snug and dark inside and had a warm wooly church smell. There the party improved a little. Masterson introduced me to Danilov, who ran his unit at IAB. Danilov had been cheerful enough that night, all lit up on a string of martinis and greatly amused at the idea of letting a PBA man in on the fun. He pulled me into a corner and told me amusing anecdotes to show he wasn't bad through and through. Then around two in the morning a vodka sadness overcame him and I was afraid he was going to tell me his life story. I didn't want to hear it and knew Danilov would regret it in the morning. Besides, there's never anything anyone ever needs to explain to me.

Today, Danilov was different. He said my name and took my hand, but the motion was purely mechanical; I doubt he was even aware of it. He asked what I was doing here in a voice that struck the precise midpoint between a casual question and a bald accusation. The patrolman with him meanwhile loitered at a cautious distance, safe behind Danilov's protective gut. I noticed Gordon Holtz give him a nod but nothing more. The patrolman gave the impression of a minor film-noir villain, the greasy type who gets what he deserves in the first reel, shot or shoved screaming off a skyscraper. He even had a thin mustache. I was trying to make out the name written on his tag or at least the gold numerals pinned to his uniform collar because I knew he was important. Danilov followed my eyes and got the idea. Now he told me to leave and meant it. "All right, let's go," Danilov said, and as they moved toward the door I read the patrolman's collar pin: 83.

"Who's that cop?" I braced Holtz after they'd gone.

"Carpet, maybe?"

"Carpet—?"

"Kevin—or Kyle," he said. "I dunno. One of the rookies. Works steady four-by-twelves on our platoon. Bear's driver."

"Berrigan's driver?" I said, astonished, the pieces falling into place. "That was Kevin Karpatkin?"

"Yeah, that's it," Holtz said. "So?"

"Fuck's he here?"

"I dunno. Ain't see nothing."

"What do you mean, ain't see nothing?" I said, angry.

"I mean he wasn't there, with Gina and me, when she—you know—when it happened or whatever. Came after, with Bear."

"So if he wasn't there, why's he here?" I asked again, still angry, as if it were Holtz's fault.

"Maybe orders?" he offered. "Like me?"

I didn't buy it. I was thinking a white shirt like Danilov had better things to do than walk a rookie patrolman around like he owned a piece of his ass if all the rookie patrolman had to offer was nothing. I was also aware that Karpatkin had never told me what he saw because I never asked him. I should have sat him down, I knew. That was a mistake. Before I could consider that, however, the detective from earlier came over and again told me to leave. He'd been lingering by the reception desk while I talked to Danilov, and now he seemed emboldened. He put his fists on his narrow hips and waited. I'd lost all fight by that point, so I obediently said okay and buttoned up. I shook Holtz's hand and left him there. The detective said nothing more to me but seemed almost disappointed—for fifteen minutes he'd been getting himself all worked up to come back and shoot me if necessary.

FOURTEEN

Uptown, Tommy Janus happily reported a grand jury had voted an indictment against Georgina Reed. Janus had a hook inside Brooklyn Supreme maybe or the DA's office because the news wasn't in the open yet. I'd caught a yellow taxi up from IAB headquarters on Hudson to the East Forties, and all the way the driver was listening to the radio report on the big march in Bushwick that was getting going. Thousands were expected. There was nothing about Georgina herself, however. As early as then, Georgina Reed had become almost irrelevant to the enormous thing she'd set in motion, essential yet unimportant, like whoever it was that shot Archduke Ferdinand. I asked the driver to turn the radio off as soon as I got in, but he only turned it down. I nearly said something about that, then I saw he was black. Of course he wasn't going to turn off his radio, not that day, not for a white man with hair cut like a cop, and when I stepped out on Park Avenue I gave him a twenty-dollar bill to cover an eleven-dollar fare. Immediately I felt ridiculous. What the hell did I have to prove?

Janus's address was high rent. On the sidewalk I looked around, a little disconcerted, always a little out of place in midtown Manhattan. I get light-headed north of Houston Street, and sometimes my nose starts to bleed from the altitude. Upstairs Shawn Garrity was with Janus waiting. "Way, you magnificent dumbfuck, d'you really call Dewberry a shithead?" Janus said to me at once, smiling broadly, laughing with professional admiration and striding across his carpeted office to shake my hand. He thought my comment had been a shameless defense of the indefensible, and he thoroughly approved. I said nothing. Neither did Garrity, who I'd missed this morning at headquarters.

Garrity had hired Tommy Janus as private counsel for Georgina Reed. Garrity knew how I felt about it but hired him anyway. Georgina needed someone good, and Janus was good, I admit. I just didn't like him. While Janus had been partnered up with Charles Ouellette they'd grown fat on cop cases: misconduct, misbehavior, false arrest, malicious prosecution, civil rights violations, section 1983 cases, *Bivens* claims, and the occasional eye socket fractured with the blunt end of a police radio in the back seat of an RMP while resisting arrest, supposedly. So fine, most of Janus's courtroom histrionics had a point. I didn't like that he did his job well. Or that he enjoyed it. Or that he got rich doing it. "God, but you're a man of tact and consideration, Way," he said, still laughing, still holding my hand. "Even I wouldn't say that about a dead perp—not a dead schwartze perp especially, and sure as hell not on the record, ha ha."

"Okay, Tommy, thanks."

"Even if it's true," he went on. "Particularly if it's true, ha ha. Don't you know the deal? Don't you read the newspapers, Way? Fucking guy gets shot by cops there, you put a motherfucking halo on his motherfucking head. You put fucking wings on the guy. Right? He never done nothing wrong not never. Understand?"

"Okay."

"You build a monument to the guy," Janus went on. Garrity listened. "That's what you do, Way. You don't tell the truth, what are you, stupid? No one wants to hear the truth about this guy. No one wants the truth, period. Truth only upsets people, Way, what's wrong with you? People already made up their mind what happened out there and you go upsetting people by telling the truth? Fuck are you thinking? You think this's about Dewberry got shot 'cause he's a shithead? Because he deserved it? No. He didn't deserve it, even if he deserved it he didn't deserve it. So he's a perp, so what? So he's a shithead, who cares? Doesn't matter Dewberry put the gun in his own fucking mouth and pulled the trigger—you gotta say he died 'cause cops are fascists and you're really sorry about it. That's what you say."

"All right, Tommy," I said in the spirit of cooperation. After all, we were now teammates.

"You say it's a teaching moment. You say the department will learn from the blah, blah, blah. You get it? Shawn here was a little—you know—" he said, with a glance at Garrity. "But I settled him down for you, told him you were just backing your man there."

"Tommy, how're you gonna help Georgina out, saying you're sorry all the time?"

"Murder trial is different, Way," he said. "I'll say it different to a jury, sure, but right now no one cares about a murder trial. Guilty, not guilty, that's not important. I'm talking about now. I'm talking about looking like police get it. D'you get it, Way?"

"Get what?"

"Get it's bend-over time for cops, Way," Janus said. "Either get it or get out of the way, 'cause that train is coming through! Toot toot!"

"Sure, Tommy," I said, as he blew his whistle. I was not in the mood and grew taciturn, and the conversation continued without me. Garrity and Janus seemed to be getting on like fraternity brothers, and watching the pair of them agree with each other made me feel like the odd man out, like the kid at the grown-up table.

"The indictment came down in Brooklyn," Janus said to me almost as an aside. Garrity already knew.

"Holy Mother—" I said. "What's the top count?"

"Murder two," he said, opening his palms to me. "What'd you think, Way? Public urination? Dis con?" Janus was still walking around his office, talking. I was seated on a chair that seemed to swallow me like a grouper. As Janus went on and on I sank deeper and deeper inside. I asked if Georgina knew. Janus didn't answer. He held up two fingers, like the pope in benediction, to indicate that he was not through talking. He was one of those lawyers who has to stand when he talks. I don't even know why he had a chair behind his desk. In fact his chair was spun around to face the window, and above the expensive view I saw a concrete sky threatening rain. Tommy Janus had thrown his jacket over his chair and wore shirtsleeves and suspenders. He had a nice tan for March and bright teeth and a flat stomach and all his hair but was rumored to wear lifts in his pointy shoes. Garrity let him talk. We were paying him.

"Does Georgina know?" I asked a second time.

He stopped and faced me. I saw no lingering animosity there, although a year ago we'd gone at it in a hallway in Supreme. I'd nearly thrown him against a wall. Court officers had been summoned. Janus hadn't taken it personally, however. Lawyers in my experience take as much interest in insult and discord as doctors in the naked human form. "No," he answered plainly, unapologetic.

"I'll tell her," I said.

"I'll arrange a surrender with Crimmins," Janus said. "We'll do it friendly."

"When?"

"I'm on it, I said."

"Who's Crimmins?" Garrity asked.

"Montgomery Crimmins," Janus answered him. "He running this one for DA Fister."

"What about Kane?" I asked Janus.

"Who?" Garrity asked.

"Jackie Kane," I said. "Her case."

"I just don't understand," Garrity interjected, suddenly angry. "Indicted? I mean indicted with what? I mean, all they got is this, this—what's his name?"

"Odom," I said.

"They got this guy Odom," Garrity said. "What is he? He's nothing no one's gonna believe for—"

"They got somebody else," Janus interrupted. "Someone seen something. Seen something that fucks Georgina but good."

I asked, "You know or you guess?"

"It's my opinion," Janus said somewhat haughtily.

"So you guess."

"My opinion costs three hundred dollars an hour, Way, so you tell me if it's a guess," Janus said. "They got a witness. A real person. Not Odom. And dollars to doughnuts Officer Holtz is your rat."

"It's not Holtz," I said flatly.

"A cop!" Garrity said.

"Why else he's at Internal Affairs right now?" Janus said. "Shining shoes?"

"It's not Holtz," I repeated. "I don't read him that way."

"You don't read him that way," he repeated, winking at Garrity. "What are you, a mentalist? You gonna bend some spoons with your mental powers or something?"

"Fuck you, Tommy," I said without much heat.

"No offense, I'm just saying you don't know," Janus said. "I mean, I know you hope Holtz didn't rat his partner there, particularly since it's your job to make sure he don't rat. And I don't want to say this in front of Shawn and all, but the fuck's this guy doing at IAB in the first place? You couldn't get him out of there? Send him to Vegas? Throw him in the trunk of your car? I mean, hello, Way—what kinda moron are you?"

"I don't know, Tommy, how many kinds are there?"

"Knock it off, you two," Garrity said. "It doesn't help. We have to circle the wagons here, not fight with . . ." His voice trailed off, disconsolate.

"There was another guy at Hudson Street this morning," I admitted weakly after a moment. They both waited for more in silence, but I was just staring ahead, knowing Janus had a point about Holtz. He would have even more to say about Karpatkin.

"Cop?" Garrity said at last, speaking his fear aloud, blue on blue, hoping I'd say no, knowing I'd say yes.

"Yeah. Eight-three patrol," I told them. "Probie named Karpatkin, first name Kevin—"

"Probie?" said Janus.

"Probationary," I said. "A rookie. Berrigan's driver. All I know is an IAB inspector was walking him out of Hudson Street when I came in, which I don't take as a good omen."

"And Berrigan is?" Janus asked.

"Patrol sergeant," I said. "He was on scene."

"During—?"

"After," I said. "Didn't see the shot. All he did was roll the body and recover the weapon."

"You talked to him, the sergeant?"

"Under the rose," I said. "I can't take a statement from a sergeant, not officially, but we have a history."

"So this Karpatkin—"

"Didn't see Georgina throw the shot either. He was with Berrigan."

"So why're we worried," Garrity put in, meaning he was worried. "If your rookie wasn't there, what can he say to hurt us?"

"He can say whatever the DA and Internal Affairs want him to say," Janus said ominously. "They need a witness. Maybe they went witness shopping. You tell us, Way. What kind of man is this—again?" He held up his hand for the name.

"Karpatkin."

"Spell it."

"R-A-T," I said. "Maybe."

"This Karpatkin character strike you as somebody looking for a gold shield the easy way?"

"I'm not sure turning rat is easy, Tommy, even if you get your step," I say. "Next twenty years you eat lunch by yourself and hope someone doesn't drop you down an air shaft. I'm sure you know the feeling."

"So what'd he say?" Janus asked.

"I didn't talk to him," I confessed.

"What do you mean you didn't—?" Garrity said to me.

"Just that."

"Will, Jesus Christ—" Garrity said, his big face coloring. He was already looking for someone to blame; as early as that, before the ship even sank, Shawn Garrity was pointing at icebergs.

"Shawn, please, please," Tommy Janus intervened unexpectedly, the unlike-liest cavalry of all. "If this character wants to say he seen something he ain't seen, how's Way here supposed to get in front of that?"

Behind him on his wall, along with diplomas and bar certificates and framed awards, were several large courtroom sketches of Tommy Janus in pastel chalk: Tommy Janus at the plaintiff's table, Tommy Janus cross-examining cops, Tommy Janus making a rhetorical point to the jury with a finger upraised. In one of them, I believed I saw myself seated in the front row, an expression on my face fit to hang a dog, but unlike Tommy I was roughly sketched. I wasn't important.

FIFTEEN

I drove to Queens, where Police Officer Georgina Reed was serving her modified duty at the NYPD auto impound lot in College Point. All the way I didn't listen to the news. I'd gotten enough news for one day, and now it was time to give some away. Instead I tuned to the seventies station for a few exits on the Long Island Expressway, but Karen Carpenter singing "Rainy Days and Mondays" reminded me of my father, the Avocado King, of driving on summer mornings in his boattail Riviera, and that reminded me of Regine Pomeroy, and I didn't want to be reminded of her, so I shut the radio off and thought about Kat instead. I wasn't sure what to do about her. I didn't know how to convince Kat she was wrong about me when I knew she was right.

I arrived at College Point supposing I was too late to do any good, that I'd find Georgina Reed already gone, already in custody, yet when I pulled off the highway I didn't see a single official car, neither blue-and-white nor more ominous unmarked black. Instead I found only the expected acre upon forlorn acre of confiscated automobiles arranged in ragged rows that stretched out in parallel toward Flushing Bay. College Point was detention hall for cops, for those One PP didn't want around but couldn't fire. They dropped Georgina here until they could figure what to do with her. She still had her white shield—they hadn't suspended her nor even put her on leave, supposing someone might get the right idea if they had—but her gun was already in the evidence room, Exhibit A, a murder weapon, maybe. So, while the department awaited events, they put Georgina Reed in a small room behind a smeared Plexiglas window reinforced with vertical steel bars. *Get used to it*, I couldn't help but think.

The impound office was nothing more than two conjoined job-site trailers raised on concrete blocks temporarily thirty or forty years ago. A few other cops were here, a few other reprobates, none in uniform since it was College Point so fuck it, all of them working at dirty beige computer monitors or standing at sea-green metal filing cabinets peeling paint. Like all cop places—like all complaint rooms, or 124 rooms, or locker rooms, or muster rooms in every stationhouse in New York City—the College Point impound office was half church-basement rummage sale, half postapocalyptic future.

On the other side of the window was a Puerto Rican kid yelling. With him was a girl, maybe sixteen. She was holding a fat-faced baby and wore a tired expression, too much makeup, and a red push-up bra. A Betty Boop tattoo was mostly visible on her left breast. As I waited our eyes touched briefly, and I had the sobering sensation that her life's story had already been written. I listened to the kid, and Georgina's weary brown eyes passed right over me. Then she saw me.

Meantime the kid wouldn't shut up. The gist was cops *had towed his fucking truck and told him it was in fucking Queens but now that he'd taken three fucking buses and a fucking cab to get to this fucking shithole he wanted his fucking truck so where the fuck is it motherfucker and it better not be fucking scratched yo.* He was yelling effortlessly in English and Spanish, and Georgina was telling him to calm down but really she didn't care. She kept looking at me, wondering why I was here, knowing it was no good.

I sat and waited, a memento mori in her foreground. I knew IAB could kick down the flimsy door any minute and this could be my last run at Georgina in the free world, but to be honest it was cathartic to listen to the kid rant. He was very good at it. When I get angry I just shut up. It all goes to my spleen. Not this kid; with him it all poured out. Georgina was just waiting for him to draw breath so she could tell him his truck was in the Bronx. I was sitting in a row of fiberglass seats, pale green and orange. Kat had the same chairs around her marble breakfast table, I realized, scored in a SoHo atelier and priced accordingly. Here they were just crap like everything else. I smiled, imagining telling Kat. Then I remembered I couldn't. Before my smile disappeared the kid asked, *what's so fucking funny why you smiling at me yo*, then he decided to cut his losses and push open the door and walk out trailing exclamation points and ampersands and asterisks for all concerned. "Fuck you fucking fascist cops. Always be killing people, stealing people's motherfucking rides." The girl followed, casting me a vulnerable, apologetic look before she left. "And fuck fucking Queens."

Georgina and I walked onto the lot. In the overcast she looked gray, and there were lines at the corner of her eyes and alongside her mouth. She would never see twenty-three again. She had gone straight to thirty-seven. We stood on the half-frozen mud and there was still a little snow from a week ago, before the world changed. My second-best overcoat was in the car, and I was cold.

"You've been indicted for murder," I told her straight out.

"Okay," was all she said.

I waited, watching her, open to changing my opinion of her. It was why I came, after all. "You can expect to be arrested. Your lawyer is trying to arrange a surrender, but circumstances being what they are—"

"Okay."

"Today, probably."

She drew a breath that rattled in her chest, then she asked, "What do you mean by circumstances?"

"Because of everything. They might want a public arrest. Perp-walk you and the whole nine yards."

"Will you be there?"

"We have a lawyer for you," I told her. "His name is Thomas Janus. He's— very good."

She inhaled deeply, then she let it out. Behind her a stand of pale dried weeds undulated to and fro in the indifferent breeze, as if underwater. We were between two rows of impounded cars. The rear of one nearby caught my attention, a familiar yellow Mercedes S500 coupe, a Wharton sticker above a Bennington sticker above six or seven Westhampton Beach parking stickers. "How do I do that," Georgina said, bringing me back to the present, "how do I get arrested?"

"Listen," I said. "Right now I need you to tell me something. You got a guy Karpatkin on your roster? A rookie, drives Berrigan?"

"Kevin Karpatkin," she said, and the name seemed to do nothing but sow confusion. "Yes."

"He was there. He was at the scene, yes?"

"Yes. I already told you that. You din't write it down."

"What's he know?" I asked.

"How do you mean?"

"It's a simple question, Officer."

"I don't know," she continued, still confused. "He came later. Everyone came later. It was a big mobilization, the whole command almost. But he wasn't there when—when the victim died. Is that what you're asking me? Why're you asking me about Kevin Karpatkin? Because you forgot?"

"Because you got indicted," I said, feeling time slipping away. "Which means the DA has evidence on you. I want to know if it came from Karpatkin."

"No," she said, not a denial but a statement. "No, it's the other. Odom. Him and his lawyer. But they're lying. They're on television, saying I shot the victim in the back—but that's not true. They can prove that's not true, can't they? I mean, he wasn't even there so how can he say?"

"What do you mean?" I said.

"I mean the medical examiner can prove I din't shoot him in the—"

"No," I said. "What do you mean Odom wasn't there?"

"He's telling everyone. He's on TV saying it, but he's a liar. How can they convict me if he's a liar? He must of told the DA."

"Sure he did, but Odom's not enough," I said. "He's a dirtball and the DA's trying to clean him up—they dropped the case on him yesterday—but he still stinks too bad and the DA knows it. They need someone to back Odom in court, and I know they got a cop. I just want to know is it Karpatkin or—?"

"No."

"—or Gordon Holtz?"

"Donny?" she said, facing me with huge hurt eyes. "No, no, Donny would never—"

"He may not have a choice. The shit clock is ticking."

"Not Donny, no."

"Think, Officer," I said. "Karpatkin wasn't there. Donny was. Donny can back up Odom's story, so just—just, could it have been Donny?"

"No, no," she said, starting to unravel. "No one was there. You're not listening. I just told you. That's why I din't have no choice. I din't have no backup. Why won't you believe me? The victim. I ordered him down. I unholstered my weapon. He had something. I reacted. My training. My training—"

"Either the DA got a lie from Karpatkin or the truth from Donny. Which?"

"I don't know."

"Tell me."

"I don't know!" she said.

"Then tell me what happened, you can do that."

"I did already," she said, "only you din't write it down so you forgot."

"I didn't write it down because you lied. Now tell me the truth, Officer. Tell me or to hell with you," I said and nearly meant it, for the desire to walk away was overwhelming and it would be convenient for my conscience to let her end it for me.

"I din't murder nobody."

"I don't care."

"I din't—" she said.

"This isn't about the truth, it's—" I started to say before realizing I sounded like Janus. "Okay, it is about the truth. Only you have to tell me, else I can't do a thing for you." I couldn't do a thing for her regardless, I knew.

Nor did I have much faith that I'd get everything from her now. With Georgina I was just squeezing the middle of the tube. Yet I wanted to know, and I knew I'd never again be able to ask. After tonight she'd be beyond my reach. Overhead seagulls joined the traffic and horns on the expressway and airliners on final into LaGuardia. I looked upward, squinting into the surprisingly bright overcast. The gray birds wheeled against the gray backdrop of cloud, turning in tight semicircles, one or two breaking formation to swoop low and examine us with their cruel petulant faces, faces like old women, or dinosaurs.

"He din't have no gun," Georgina said at last, her voice very far away. She was telling me the truth at last, but it was someone else telling it to someone else. Georgina Reed had left.

"Who didn't?" I asked very carefully.

"The victim. Dewberry."

"Go on."

"Odom had the gun," she said.

"Wait. Odom pulled it?"

"No."

"I don't understand."

"Odom ran," she said. "When Donny and me got out to make the stop, there was some words with the victim. Then Odom ran off. Fast. Donny went after him in the RMP."

"And you stayed on Dewberry."

"Yes."

"Dewberry didn't run?" I asked.

"No, I—I think he was too—too obese to run. He stayed. He was yelling at me."

"So, Donny—fuck—Donny wasn't there when you—during the shooting?"

"No," she said.

"Odom neither."

"I was all alone, don't you see?" she said. "By myself. No backup. I din't have nobody. And the victim, he wouldn't show me his hands. He wouldn't go down. I told him to. I kept telling him. He yelled at me. Said he wasn't and I'd have to kill him only I wouldn't because I was just a bitch in a uniform or whatever. He was holding something, flowers, and he wouldn't drop them on the floor. And he moved toward me, and I couldn't see his hands, like he was hiding something else, and I thought—"

She realized I was no longer meeting her eyes but looking behind her. She turned on instinct and there along the gravel drive into the impound lot were three unmarked cars. No sirens, no lights. There was no need. They moved with the slow inevitability of fate foretold.

"You thought?"

"I thought he was going to kill me with what he had. Only he didn't have nothing. Are those men coming for me?"

"The thirty-two Bear got off Dewberry," I said, my mind in motion, trying to put everything together before the cars stopped. "Donny got that from Odom?"

"Yes."

"And you flaked it on the guy."

"We had to." She nodded. "Don't you see? No one would believe it—if all the victim had was—was flowers. Why didn't he just drop them on the floor? They were just flowers."

"So it's Donny," I said, more to myself than to Georgina Reed. "Only Donny had something to sell. Only Donny had something to lose."

A car door behind her, then another and another. Neither of us turned.

"It wasn't Donny," she said to me with touching innocence, wanting to believe. "He went to IAB this morning, you know. He backed me a hundred percent. He told them Dewberry pulled a gun on me, so I shot him. In self-defense. That's what he told them. So you're wrong about him. He wouldn't do that to me."

Inspector Sheldon Danilov came up with two men, one with a pair of silver handcuffs ready in his right hand. "Hullo, Way," Danilov said, neither unfriendly nor triumphant.

"Do we need those, Inspector?" I asked.

"Procedure."

"She's still on the job."

Danilov considered that then nodded at his man, who pocketed the bracelets and led Georgina Reed away, a hand on her upper arm. He was the younger man from last night in McCosker's office, I realized, the one with the Marine Corps neck. After he put Georgina in the car he said to me, "Get some rack time, funny man, you're looking dog-ass tired." I saw Mark Masterson standing to the side. He met my eyes but that was all. After they drove away the impound lot seemed like a forsaken waste. The sun hung low over the rows of cars. There were only seagulls and airplanes now. The pale weeds went back and forth on the breeze, and I was very cold.

SIXTEEN

I started for Brooklyn with the purest of intentions but changed my mind the instant a green-and-orange neon sign, O'Somebody's Bar & Lounge, hove into view in the disorderly tangle of *streets* and *avenues* and *roads* also known as the borough of Queens. I pulled to the side and killed the ignition. I needed liquor and besides, I was already lost. I couldn't even find the expressway, for chrissake—*fuck fucking Queens is right, little brother.* Inside, the guy set me up with no conversation. It was that kind of place. Then I asked him for the telephone and he dropped an ancient dial affair on the bar next to my empty shot glasses. The first had been brutal, but number three I hardly tasted. After the whiskey went to work I dialed IAB looking at my watch—late now, nearly six, but Georgina had ended nine-to-five for everybody. "Remember me from this morning?" I asked the PAA. "I was with the big blond uniform, the one that wouldn't shut his mouth?"

"Yes, sir."

"He still there?" I asked her.

"Just a moment, please." Her hand covered the receiver and the barroom was so quiet I could hear the PAA speaking to someone without the words coming through. "I'm sorry, sir, Inspector Danilov is in the field."

"I didn't ask for Danilov. I asked for the cop."

"I—I'm sorry," she said. "Inspector Danilov is assigned to Officer Holtz."

"Of course he is," I said with a bitter smile, deciding immediately to go for the extra point. "Then can I speak to Kevin Karpatkin instead?"

"What's the name again, please?"

"Karpatkin," I said.

"There's no Karpatkin working for Internal Affairs."

"Maybe not yet," I told her, "but I bet you see him at the office Christmas party."

"I'm sorry?" she said, and I imagined the PAA at her neatly organized reception desk. I had scarcely noticed her this morning except to see that she was set heavy and well put together. Working the desk at Hudson Street was the wrong job for her, you could tell. When she said she was sorry she meant it. There was something she wanted to tell me, I knew, because it was impolite to keep it from me and she was not raised that way. All the way home on the train she'd be sorry to have been between them and me.

I replaced the receiver in the heavy Bakelite cradle silently and looked around. Inside it was dark and unpopular. There was the not unpleasant smell of burnt coffee. Three barflies sat alone and unmoving, forearms upon the bar like the gnarled roots of trees on a sidewalk. They had different problems. A dim evening light fell in from the street through two rectangular windows of frosted glass. After several minutes I heard the muffled suck of a toilet in the middle distance, and then the bartender reappeared. I hadn't realized he was gone. He eyed me, but I wanted to stand pat for now. I needed to think.

I took the phone again and dialed the 83 desk.

"This is Will Way. Who's this?"

"Sergeant O'Somebody."

"What a coincidence. Berrigan working?"

"Berrigan's doing midnights," he said.

"You got a Karpatkin on the four-by-twelve roster? First name Kevin?"

"Hold on—who's this again?" the sergeant asked me with a voice like a crew cut.

"Will Way. I'm PBA."

"How do I know that?"

"Yeah, can't be too careful these days, Sarge, can you?" I answered. "How about I tell you McCosker's got a beagle named Fred?"

"Hang on," he answered, and I heard him set the receiver down. The truth was I had no clue what McCosker called his beagle, only that it was old and leaked. From the receiver, while I waited, came the sounds of a police stationhouse, which despite everything always gave me a nostalgic stab. Now it sounded like men bailing a sinking lifeboat. "Karpatkin," the sergeant said, his voice oddly loud in my ear. "Supposed to be on, only he ain't. Struck off the roster, and if you ask me why the answer is I dunno. We set?" Next I called Garrity. It rang and rang, and when the machine picked up I put the receiver down. I sat there stupid, eyes focusing and refocusing. After I don't know how long I looked up and saw myself in the mirror, a dull listless expression on my face framed on the top shelf among bottom-shelf liquor. *Hello, young man! Did you know an exciting career awaits you in law enforcement?*

"Hey, buddy," I said to the bartender, who was doing the crossword in yesterday's *Brooklyn Daily News*, the one with my epitaph in it. I gestured to the television. He responded by clapping the remote on the bar. With very particular dexterity, I turned it on. *Wheel of Fortune*. Pat Sajak and Vanna and vowels. Kaseem would be watching, the enviable motherfucker, moving through life unsullied by events, every day a treat, stoned, devouring leftover pizza shirtless and famished, Shiny and Shooshka biting each other's face on the floor—

Then there was Mayor Weyman Desmond in the Blue Room at City Hall. No sound, and when at last I figured that out, I heard

—whose testimony made it possible today to have an indictment handed up against those officers responsible for this horrendous crime, this monstrous betrayal of their public trust. This young officer, this one hero cop—I'm not afraid to call him a hero, no, because a hero is what he is. He came forward to shatter the blue wall of—

I gestured to the bartender. Same again. Let's go let's go let's go. Meanwhile I was trying to shut the television off but my fingers were anesthetized inside insulated gloves and I only made the volume uncomfortably loud. The men sitting nearby were moved from their torpor to throw me malevolent glances and unspoken curses, then I dropped the remote on the floor, where it disappeared among the stool legs in the murk.

—and makes me very, I should say enormously proud to be mayor of a city where we have a police officer willing to do the right thing, to do the right thing in the face of pressures of which I'm sure you're all aware. No, I've been asked by DA Fister to refrain from identifying this, ah, hero by name. And I'm sure you understand why that is.

The mayor paused and arms shot up all around him like bayonets. I stopped listening. So that was the news, I thought. Nothing new. They turned somebody to get somebody. They got a hero to get a murderer. To them cops are only heroes and murderers, virgins and whores, yin and yang, white and black, anything more complex would never fit into a headline. Newspaper ink doesn't come in gray. Whoever had testified against Georgina Reed was no hero, not through and through. No one is ever anything through and through. I knew about their heroes. I'd seen their heroes before. Their heroes were heroes only because they came in from the cold twenty minutes before the other guy. Their heroes were heroes because the DA sat them down in a windowless conference room and told them what was going to happen if they didn't put their name on the cooperation agreement, for nothing makes you feel more heroic than the scare of upstate prison—nothing, that is, except the realization you don't necessarily have to go.

That's why—as much as I wanted to believe it was Kevin Karpatkin, with his rat name and rat mustache—I still believed it was Gordon Holtz.

I dialed Garrity again. This time he answered on the second ring, breathless. "Mayor's on television with Gilbert," he said. "Right now."

"I know."

"He's not saying who, but it's a patrolman, Will. It's a—one of my men."

"I know."

"One of my men's a fucking rat. I don't—what are you doing? Where are you?"

"Drinking rotgut whiskey in a dive," I admitted, for contrary to Phillip's bedtime indictment I didn't lie a lot.

He sighed, his breath sounding heavy and moist. "I thought—"

"I was."

"Fine time, Will."

"None better," I said, raising an empty shot glass. *Here's to heroes, may they all get what they deserve.* Then I told him what Georgina said. I gave it all to him with no punctuation.

"So, wait, wait, wait. I don't understand," Garrity said. "The gun Dewberry had wasn't his gun?"

"No. And he didn't have it."

"And he—wait, what?—didn't have it?—didn't have what?"

"The gun."

"The gun he had—" Garrity started.

"The gun he had he didn't have."

"What is this, who's on first?" he said, hopelessly lost. "Whose gun didn't he have? I mean—whose gun did he not have—?"

"Odom," I said. "It was a flake, Shawn. They flaked it on the guy after he hit the sidewalk, to make it pretty for IAB."

"Huh?"

"They planted the gun, Shawn."

"I know what a fucking flake is, Will," Garrity said, defensive, pretending to be angry. "I used to work the street, you know. I used to. Back in the day. So I know. Okay. Let me think. Shit. Shit. Who—planted the gun? D'you know?"

"Georgina and Holtz."

"Wait—"

"Holtz and Georgina," I said.

"She told you?"

"It wasn't leprechauns did it."

"And you think it was Holtz went over to IAB?"

"Yes," I told him.

"And you think Holtz told IAB it was a—"

"Yes."

"—flake, but," he said, "you don't know. I mean, not for sure you know it was Holtz went over?"

"No, Shawn, not for sure. It's just my opinion, and I know my opinion's only worth twenty-one dollars an hour, unlike our new friend there, but think about it—there's no one but Holtz. The rookie, Karpatkin, he wasn't there, so what's he gonna say?"

"He coulda lied, like Tommy said," Garrity said. "Get a promotion. Get off the street."

"Sure, but the fucking guy Karpatkin's been on the job what? Three months? Little soon to get jaded and pissed off and want out, wouldn't you say? Karpatkin doesn't make sense, unless he really is a fucking hero. And omniscient. But Donny Holtz on the other hand, fuck—he doesn't sign his name on a co-op agreement, he's cooked. Goodbye pension, hello Attica. So Donny makes the most sense as our hero cop." Garrity said nothing, so I went on. "Even if he's not a hero, Holtz still fucks us."

"How?" Garrity asked.

"Because if Holtz told IAB he saw Dewberry draw down on Georgina, that's the version we're stuck with."

"What's wrong with it?" he asked.

"Apart from being bullshit, I assume you mean?"

"Yeah, I—"

"I happen to prefer the truth here anyway," I say. "I mean, if it's just Georgina on the corner, it's her word against Dewberry. And Dewberry ain't talking, so Georgina wins. She takes the stand, tells the jury what she told me, squirts a few, and worst case maybe she goes down for misdemeanor evidence tampering. Sure, she's upstate a few months, but then she can write a memoir, go on Oprah—"

"I don't think it's funny."

"Am I laughing?" I said, and I wasn't. "But if Holtz isn't the hero—"

"You mean if he lied?"

"Right," I said, still not laughing. "If he told IAB he saw everything because he's there backing Georgina, he can't very well be chasing Odom around the block, can he?"

"So?"

"If Holtz's on the corner with Georgina, then Odom's on the corner with Georgina," I said. "And if Odom's on the corner with Georgina, then he's an eyewitness, too. Just like he says."

"Except he's lying."

"So is Holtz," I said. "And Georgina'll have to lie, too, unless she wants to go against her partner. Get it? Everyone's a liar, and trial will be about whose lie is best."

"When isn't it?" he said, and hung up.

Mayor Desmond was still on the television, wagging an obscenely priapic index finger at me. I had another drink.

—and let me just say, in answer to your follow-up question, that some police officials have stated publicly that Laquan Dewberry—this dead child, this scholar, this aspiring veterinarian—may have acted inappropriately, like a—well, I'm not going to repeat the vulgarism—like an s-word, it has been said, but let me just say that this name-calling, this blaming of the victim is—

Desmond always spoke like the editorial page of *The New York Times*. His words came out perfectly, like orderly little tin soldiers off to an imaginary war. I hit the remote and the television—a Zenith set with faux wood side panels, like a Ford Country Squire—went gray along with everything else, and the barman set me up again. I had one more for the road, then another, then I stopped counting because I couldn't count.

Next thing I remember is being astonished Kat was still awake.

"Oh. You 'wake?"

"It's eight thirty, Will."

"Still dark!"

"Where are you?"

"Queens. 'M lost."

"What're you doing in Queens?" she asked.

"Sorry wake you."

"I'm awake," she said.

"Time's it? Told you. 'M lost. Took a turn and. Got lost. Just like that."

"Can't you ask—"

"Fuck fucking Queens, ha ha!"

"Will."

"Fascist towed my truck, ha ha!"

"Oh. You're really drunk."

"I am. Kat. Reminds me. Saw your car!"

"My car—"

"Yellow Benz. Saw it. It's. Over there."

"Will—" she said.

"Something else. Sorry. Wanted to say. Sorry. Kat."

"You're sorry?" she said. "About what?"

"Disappoint you. Ashamed me."

"I'm not. Not really," she said. "I thought about it all day. I think you were just trying to defend Georgina. It's just you can't say things like—"

"Didn't mean shithead. Kat. Just meant shithead. Understand?"

"Oh, Will."

"You don' understand."

"I'm trying," she said.

"Tommy says. Tommy says not tell anyone truth. Sorry. Told the truth."

"Who's Tommy?"

"New friend."

"Will, can't you just ask someone to—"

"You don' understand. Kat. I don' understand."

"Will. I'm sorry," she said.

"Sorry—?"

"I saw the television. I know they arrested Georgina, and I know you wanted to help her."

"I couldn't anything."

"But who's the other one?" she asked.

"Other what?"

"The mayor said there were two."

"Two?"

Next I remember I was in a taxi.

Next my face was in the toilet.

Next I don't remember.

KARPATKIN

SEVENTEEN

I looked for Holtz downstairs in the pens. The pens inside Brooklyn Supreme stank like jail: like shit and bleach, like school lunch, like the projects, like the cinder-block stairwells in public housing projects where I spent my probationary year after the academy. I did midnight tours for eleven months, walking vertical patrols with Mark Masterson in Hope Gardens, where there was little hope and no garden. "Guess they hope someday they get a garden," Masterson once cracked with a straight face, as close as he ever got to humor. When I got home in the early morning MK would make me strip and shower and would seal my uniform in a black plastic garbage bag. I owned four uniforms because we didn't have a washing machine. On my regular days off we would walk to the self-serve on Gerritsen Avenue and read magazines between the machines and old ladies would beam at us because we were beautiful and did not belong here and our future was bright. After MK left without fanfare one afternoon I moved by myself into an apartment with a washing machine, but of course by then my clothes didn't stink.

Gordon Holtz was not in the pens. I found him sitting at a desk in the little room the court officers used down the hallway from central booking. He was on the telephone. He didn't look like a prisoner. He didn't even look upset. He smiled a distracted hello but remained on the telephone. There were about five court officers sitting around in their white sleeveless shirts, none of them talking. They didn't know who I was exactly. I wasn't supposed to be here. Holtz wasn't supposed to be here, either—in this room, on the telephone—but court officers think they run the show, and I suppose they figured Holtz was on the job so no way was he going in the pens with all the other criminals.

I leaned against a file cabinet and waited. Now we were all listening to Holtz and pretending not to. He was talking to his wife. You could tell she wasn't doing well. He was telling her not to worry and to remember what they talked about and that it would all work out okay. Very awkward to hear a man speak that way, so after a couple minutes I stepped out, walking to the open courthouse lobby, where a row of metal detectors stood like guillotines. Already the place was filling up with women in Sunday hats. Outside, through the revolving doors, you could see a yellowy orange BABE school bus double-parked, then another pulled in behind and let more of Archbishop Bumpurs's congregants out into the day, a Friday that had broken absurdly sunny and soft.

Daylight hurt. I felt like shit. I'd barely made it to Fulton Street alive. I told the driver to pull over twice. I persevered, but like all my victories this one passed unrecorded. It felt oddly quaint to be hung over, a nostalgic visit from the good old bad old days, which were themselves an improvement on the bad old bad old days when I was never hung over because I was never not drunk. Sheila Simmons had some idea how it was, accustomed as she was to my ways and knowing the rest from rumor and hallway innuendo. She went easy on me. She brought me black coffee, hot and hot, until she felt it safe to hand me my messages. Garrity was not in, she told me when I asked, and she shut my door silently. Alone with my coffee cup on a barren desk I sat wondering about Kat and what had happened last night. Since we started last October I hadn't gone out on a real bender, so she had no idea how it could be. After being a better person with Kat, I'd started to be who I was.

I opened *The New York Times* past the front page, past the Metro section, my eyes shut tight, to the safety of the crossword puzzle. Ordinarily I might have done it in bed with Kat, her small body, firm as a trout, pressed to mine, our legs twined. Together we could've banged it out in twenty minutes flat. Today, however, I'd gotten only 3-down, ABSCESS, before my coffee went cold. The word made me queasy and I looked for my trash can, full of message slips, just in case. I was not smart enough for a Friday puzzle anyway and found myself by accident on the op-ed page—

> *which brings me to this question: Where exactly was the police union through-*
> *out all this? Even if we accept at face value the word of its president, Shawn*
> *Garrity, that his union did not actively interfere in the department's internal*
> *investigation, the P.B.A. certainly did nothing to help investigators either.*
> *Instead the P.B.A. stood mute, or when it did speak it was only to say that*
> *the union "stood behind" the officer who gunned down a teenager on a*
> *Brooklyn street, his back turned, his hands in the air. His crime? The theft*
> *of a candy bar—*

I noted unemotionally that the gentleman held a distinguished chair in law at Georgetown, where I had lingered a semester, and he had letters after his name. But he had never been shot at, I was certain, nor had he ever done a vertical patrol in a housing project, nor once arrived home to have his wife ball his tweed jacket with the leather elbow patches into a plastic bag because it reeked of human misery. Then again, I had done these things, and I wondered now if it mattered. I always believed rolling in the dogshit of the world had made me wiser in compensation, but possibly all it did was make me stink.

Also in the newspaper that day was a cartoon. Here was Shawn Garrity, his huge face and neatly parted hair instantly recognizable on three pot-bellied chimpanzees holding gloved hands over eyes, ears, mouth. Garrity's frequently televised expression of benign bewilderment was strikingly well realized, and I felt an involuntary smile twitch on my cheek, humor and nausea commingling for a giddy-sickly moment. Then in the background I saw a young monkey, cavorting, pointing to the grown-ups and holding a sign: "YOU S*HEAD!" That was me, the little monkey with the sign. It was not drawn to look like me or anybody. It was just a monkey.

I pushed today's message slips around the desktop with my fingertip. None were from Kat. She rarely left messages anyway, I told myself. She'd just call and call until I picked up. Here were some others. Mark Masterson. Betty Moon, twice. And here was one from Pomeroy. I picked it up, wondering what the hell. Before the realization that Justice Henry K. Pomeroy had telephoned could fully register, however, Sheila gently opened my door to inform me Gordon Holtz had been arrested overnight. She'd just heard it on the radio.

Now, waiting for Holtz in the lobby of Brooklyn Supreme, I found myself by a directory listing all the judges in white capitals, slightly off-kilter, as if typed by an old machine. Here was Pomeroy's name, above all the rest. Glimpsing my face two days ago reminded him he had a daughter named Regine, that's all. I could reconstruct Wednesday night's dinner conversation at Dover Street, Pomeroy still in jacket and tie, sitting across from Saint Ann, just the two of them in the big empty old house by the sea eating pork chops and apple sauce, and during a lull—

THE COURT: Ann. You'll never guess whom I saw today.

SAINT ANN: No, Henry. Whom?

THE COURT: That boy.

SAINT ANN: Which boy, Henry?

THE COURT: Billy Way's son. From Gerritsen Beach.
Her friend.

(Whereupon, there was a pause in the proceedings.)
SAINT ANN: Will?

When dinner was over and they were in bed, perhaps even after the lights were out, his wife would suggest, in a casual tone, "Henry, why don't you give him a call?" The idea that these events took place on Wednesday night in Manhattan Beach in one form or another gave me a set of complex contradictory feelings, all of them rather mild, however, because by then I'd grown accustomed to the idea of Regine Pomeroy having gone over the hills and far away.

Gordon Holtz was off the telephone when I returned. With an imperfect mind, for an hour, I'd been trying to fathom the DA's move on Holtz. I was unpersuaded by his arrest. For me it didn't change my thinking that Holtz was the rat and if anything proved I was right. If Holtz had signed a co-op agreement with the DA, I believed, they'd want to hold him with something stronger than his childish signature on a dotted line. A felony indictment was stronger, and the DA could keep that above his head until Holtz gave them what they needed. And what the DA needed was his testimony against Georgina at trial. It wasn't a cooperation agreement, in other words. It was a bill of sale.

When I came in Holtz was very breezy with me, like the guy in the emergency room who jokes with the doctors and nurses to prove he's fine really and not going to die. "Hullo, Donny," I said, my voice frosty. The thought that he was the *as yet unidentified police officer* made me see him differently, no longer a golden retriever. Nor did his grinning and mugging seem to charm the court officers very much. They stood with their hands in their pockets and slit smiles attached precariously to their faces. They were telling him it was all bullshit. They were telling him everything would come out in the wash, that it was all fuckin politics, et cetera, but what they were really thinking was that this was the man whose partner unloaded on a kid, shot him in the back maybe while his hands were up. None of them could hold that against Holtz, not really. But still.

I asked the sergeant if I could have a few minutes. They all left. One of them remained outside the door for the sake of form. You could see the back of his head in the window, and occasionally he looked inside. I sat across from Holtz and waited for a wave of blue-green nausea to pass over me like the angel of death. Holtz just waited. He was not in uniform. He was instead dressed for Sunday dinner with the in-laws in Mineola. He wore pleated khaki pants and a polo shirt. His forearms were like hams and covered with stiff blond hair, and he'd put on cologne for the occasion. Even so, even out of uniform, he could only be a cop; you'd never mistake him for anything else—in a towel, naked, in drag wearing a boa, Gordon Holtz would still be a cop, and if it came to it the jury wouldn't need evidence to convict him.

"Donny, listen up," I said to him. "Gotta ask you something."

"G'head," he answered with a full mouth. Going to jail had given Gordon Holtz an appetite. The court officers had let him order lunch, and he was at work on a sixteen-inch Italian hero, a family-size bag of potato chips, and a half-sour pickle, washing it down with noisy gulps from a liter bottle of Manhattan Special.

"How well d'you know Georgina Reed?"

"Gina and me been partnered up, what?" he asked me. "Like seven months almost."

"Good cop?"

"Yeah. I mean, you know," he said with a shrug, meaning no.

"Get along?"

"Sure, we get along. She's real nice, Gina."

I said, "She ever snitch you out, you think?"

"Snitch me," he said, eating. "I ain't done nothing to snitch, my friend."

"Just would she—if it came down to it," I said. "If it came down to her or you. Would she go over on you?"

He swallowed and looked at me with his drowsy blue eyes. "Put it that way—I mean, who wouldn't?"

Carefully I asked him, "That work both ways, Donny?"

"How you mean?"

I looked right at him and waited. Holtz began to smile when he caught the upshot. "Oh, no, no," he said. "Not me. Really? I ain't no rat. Come on, boss, look where I am!" He had a yellowish dogtooth. I waited. "It's the guy. Carpet. Bear's driver. He's your snitch. Gotta be. He was at IAB yesterday."

"So were you," I said.

"Orders, I mean, why'd I call you to come down, I was a rat?"

I leaned back and pretended to relax. "He's our snitch, you think? Karpatkin?"

"Wasn't me, I tell you that," he said. "Yeah, must of been him. Right?"

"So how's Karpatkin our snitch? What's he got to sell the DA?"

"I dunno. He was there with Bear," he said. "He didn't see nothing."

"That's what I'm saying. He didn't see the shot, right?"

"No," he said, taking a bite of sandwich, more relaxed today than this time yesterday, when he was sweating through his uniform on a bench at 315 Hudson Street. "Because he couldn't of."

"Because he wasn't there."

"Right."

"And you didn't see it either, the shot," I said.

"Sure, I did."

"That's what you told IAB," I told him. "You told IAB yesterday you saw Georgina take the shot?"

"Absolutely," he said. "Guy ran up on her. Pulled out. What choice she got? Him or her. So, boom."

"And the guy—the fat one—he pulled out."

"Of course," he said.

"And you saw that, too."

"Of course."

"Only you didn't," I said, looking right at him. "You didn't see none of it. I mean, come on, Donny. It's me here. I'm not your mom. You and me, let's cut the fucking fairy tale, okay? You were down the block on the second piece when Georgina popped her guy."

"Yeah, who says I was?"

"Georgina says. I talked to her yesterday. So come on," I told him. "Fuck you think I'm saying here, Donny?"

"What are you saying?"

"I'm saying I know the deal, Donny. Georgina told me," I tell him. "You roll up and Odom legs it. You go after Odom in the car, and by the time you get him under, Dewberry's dead. Georgina tells you she thought he was armed. Only he wasn't, was he? Was he, Donny? So you fix that. Right? Lucky you, Odom's got a piece-of-crap thirty-two in his shorts, so you flake it on the fat guy—"

"I didn't—" he started.

"The DA just indicted you for it," I said. "For evidence tampering, Donny. Where d'you think the DA got that idea? Karpatkin? Karpatkin wasn't there. Fuck's Karpatkin know about it? Nothing."

"I dunno. Bear, maybe."

"Berrigan's not there either. No one else is on the corner except you and Georgina," I said.

"Maybe Odom said."

"Yeah, Odom already said what he's saying, and he ain't saying that. He's on probation, so he goes back to jail if he admits to the gun," I told him. "That's why I know the DA got the story from you."

"Me—? The fuck—?" he said, genuinely astonished.

"You told IAB. You testified in the grand jury, didn't you?"

"Why—why would I fuck myself?" he said. "Fuck would I wanna tell the rat squad I planted a fucking gun for?"

"So you can tell it at trial."

"Yeah, that don't even make no sense," he said. "I—I don't even follow you, boss. You're just talking stupid now. Why do I wanna say that?"

"Stay out of prison."

"Stay out of prison? Look where I am!" he said. "I just caught a case!"

"Yeah, what kind of case, Donny? Evidence tampering, jaywalking, and misdemeanor nose picking. Big fucking deal. So, what'd Kane promise you anyway?"

"Fuck is Kane?"

"The DA," I said. "What'd she promise you on the sentence, Donny, if you testified for her? Something really painful, I bet. Like maybe she'll make you clean erasers behind school for a week? Maybe come over and wash her Suburu? You made a deal with her, didn't you, you rat motherfucker, so you better tell me or—"

"Tell you what?" he said, sounding defeated.

"What's the deal?"

"What deal?"

"It's what I'm asking you. You give up Georgina, and the DA doesn't indict you as an accessory. They consent to ROR at arraignment, and you sleep in your own bed tonight, never set foot on Rikers. Sound familiar? Just nod yes."

The sergeant came inside with some men. Holtz said nothing, and I slammed my hand against a file cabinet. Two court officers stood him up. He seemed unaware of them, and he allowed his arms to be pulled gently behind him and handcuffed. "Showtime," one of the COs said, and as they took him to the hallway I saw they had strung together two sets of handcuffs as courtesy. Yet before they left, Holtz stopped and turned to me from the doorway, not meeting my eyes.

"Must of been the rookie. Carpet."

After he was gone his lunch was still there, half of it. I was looking at the remains on the paper plate when the sergeant came back in. "Gonna do the arraignment in the ceremonial upstairs on account of all the people onlooking. Pomeroy wants to do it up there, so that's where we got your friend." I said, "Brother, he's not my friend," and immediately I wanted to take it back, not because it was untrue but because anyone might've said the same thing and I wanted to believe I was different. But you can take nothing back in this world. *Take that back!* Something kids say. We pass into adulthood, where there are no magic words anymore and sorry is all we have left, about as pointless a word as I can imagine.

EIGHTEEN

I skipped Gordon Holtz's arraignment. I couldn't face Pomeroy, not even from the safety of the front row of the gallery in his courtroom. Instead I cabbed out to Queens again for my car, finding it with three orange parking tickets under the windshield wiper but no pink azaleas. Back at Fulton Street I didn't reach my desk before Sheila Simmons directed me down the hall. I went, obediently. There Tommy Janus was on his feet inside Garrity's office with some other men from the organization, all of them seated around Garrity's desk as if he were a campfire.

"There he is," Janus said to me, smiling broadly when I came in. "Another hero cop, ha ha!" They all laughed and eyed me in a way that made me think I'd been a topic before I walked through the door. I suppose I was. Georgina was my case, after all. And I had fucked it up, or that was the general idea. Everyone watched me sit down. The only chair left was the one with the uneven leg. As I sat, Earl Dillard held up this afternoon's *Brooklyn Daily News* with a three-word headline in huge capitals:

ONE HERO COP

Beneath the headline was the rookie's face. Betty Moon had the name. She was not supposed to have it, but she did. "Fuck this guy Karpatkin come from, Way?" Dillard said. I didn't answer. I just looked.

"He doesn't know," someone said at last.

"Nice," another voice said privately.

"Our own fucking guy don't know who it is turned rat."

"Guess you were wrong about Holtz," Garrity told me, not unkindly.

That was the day New York City caught its first glimpse of Kevin Karpatkin. While I had already seen him in person, hustled out of Hudson Street by Inspector Danilov yesterday, that moment never seemed to count. My second impression is what stayed: a grainy black-and-white studio photograph enlarged too much. The headline seemed almost sarcastic since the photograph in question was reproduced from Karpatkin's Far Rockaway High School year-book circa 1996 and showed a dopey eighteen-year-old boy with a bowl cut, unfortunate ears, and the faintest suggestion of the villainous mustache he would wear only slightly more emphatically as a probationary police officer in Bushwick. In the photograph Kevin Karpatkin was the kid you'd beat up or just ignore, the one who played third clarinet in stage band, the one who ate in the cafeteria by himself.

Also, I realized with a jolt, Karpatkin had been at the 83 on Wednesday night when I had given the four-by-twelve platoon my sales pitch, all of them standing at attention after I told them to stand at ease. I hadn't noticed him then, nor had he paid much attention to me. Kevin Karpatkin had heard every word of mine yet somehow remained unpersuaded that I was his best friend in the whole wide world. I might've taken him aside then. I ought to have taken him aside then, sat him down, listened to his story, told him to keep his mouth shut. That was my job, after all. Instead, a few hours later—as I lay staring at the dark ceiling in my bedroom, still redolent of Kaseem's weed habit, aware of every passing ambulance and fire engine on the street below—Kevin Karpatkin would tap timidly on the captain's office door and tell the IAB man seated there that he was no longer so certain Raquan Dewberry had a gun under his dead body. In fact, Karpatkin would tell him, Dewberry never had a gun. Until he did.

Jug-eared, pencil-necked, appropriately rat-whiskered, Kevin Karpatkin hadn't been a cop very long. He had worked 83 patrol for just three short months out of the academy. Three months would be the extent of his tour in Bushwick, however, and nearly the end of his time in uniform. A year later Kevin Karpatkin would be an IAB detective with a gold shield, promoted out of patrol, never again to leave his sinecure in 315 Hudson Street without someone to hold his hand. That, however, still lay in Karpatkin's future. Wednesday night he was yet a patrolman, eating his midnight lunch in the 83 muster room, perhaps in my old spot, when at last he put down his cheese sandwich. He might not have fully understood the man at the desk in McCosker's office who told him to empty his locker. Karpatkin, his muddy brown eyes unblinking, probably just stood there, uncomprehending. Then the IAB man would have had to explain, "You don't work here no more."

Now everyone in Garrity's office was talking at once.

"Look at this guy."

"Karpatskin."

"Kin."

"Huh?"

"Kin not skin. Can't you read?"

"Fucking looks a rat, the fuck."

"Like the rat fuck he is."

"Fuck is this guy?" Dillard asked me again. Earl Dillard was pushing sixty with a hurricane-beaten face and the slim form of a Dodge City gunslinger. He'd been with the union forever and was hard in all the places Garrity was soft. I'd encountered him maybe half a dozen times in my four years at the PBA, each one a picnic that made me close my office door afterward and walk in circles for an hour. Gray and dangerous, Earl Dillard still kept a revolver on his person. We union men were on the books as cops, but for us weapons were purely ornamental, like cuff links or St. Christopher medals. My own pistol I'd dropped in the Atlantic Ocean long ago and never wanted another. I suppose in Dillard's case the little ugly snub-nosed Colt .38 Detective Special strapped to his bony right ankle was superfluous. If Earl Dillard didn't have a gun handy he'd just find something else to kill you with.

"Lives with his mother," someone was saying.

"Packs lunch for him, probably."

"Packs him a ratty little lunch."

"Cheese for the cheese-eater."

"When did we know?" Dillard continued, to me. My job was to answer his question. My job was to know things before anyone else, before they appeared in the newspaper. My job was to make sure they didn't appear in the newspaper. I felt the heat of Dillard's gaze on me, but I didn't meet his eyes.

"Way red-flagged him yesterday," Garrity said to the room in general, and I loved him for it.

"Sheldon Danilov walked him out of IAB," I said, "when I was up there with Holtz."

"Fat Danilov, that child molester."

"And you didn't do nothing, Way?" Dillard said.

"No," I answered.

"Beautiful."

"What's he say anyway, the rat?"

"Says Georgina dropped the guy and made it look he pulled first."

"Paper says that?"

"Didn't do nothing," Dillard said, shifting uncomfortably in his seat.

"Fat Danilov probably offered him a lollipop."

"Paper don't say that."

"What'd you want me to do, Earl?" I said, suddenly not in the mood. "Hit him with the car door?"

"Just step inside my office, little probie."

"Take it easy, Earl," Tommy Janus said. "Someone wants to lie, he's gonna lie."

"How d'you know?" Dillard asked Janus.

"That's a snitch face."

"Rat-face rat."

"Know what?" Janus asked.

"Know the guy Karpatkin's selling a lie to IAB?" Dillard said.

"Karpatskin was—now you got me saying it, dick."

"Has to be a lie," Garrity said. "Karpatkin wasn't there when our man took the shot. He came up with the sarge after, so what could he say that's true that hurts our man?"

"What sergeant?" Dillard asked.

"He sees the plant, paper says. Don't it?"

"Says he saw it, he says."

"You wanna Hertz doughnut?"

"Something like that. They don't say for sure."

"Ow! Ya fuck!"

"Just read it."

"Hurts, don't it?"

"Catamite."

"Will you fucking schoolchildren put a sock in it," Dillard said to everyone, and for a moment they did. "Who's the sergeant, I'm sitting here asking."

"Ralph Berrigan," I told Dillard, "but—"

"Then that's that," Dillard said, his face making the rictus that passed for his smile. "Bear's old school cop—"

"Berrigan's Eight-trey?"

"Fuck's a catamite?"

"Bear Berrigan's a fucking dinosaur throwback to another epoch."

"That doesn't even—"

"He's Jurassic."

"Berrigan's so cop, why don't he kick some sense into this guy?"

"No shit. Some half a fag in my platoon jumped the chain of command I'd—"

"Way already got the story from Berrigan," Janus said.

"That right, Way?"

"Not on record," I said. "But yeah, he backs Georgina. So does Holtz, at least to me."

"So they lied."

"Good for them."

"I'll call Buddy Garner at the SBA," Garrity said. "Maybe someone on his end can reach out, see if Berrigan'll say something official before the department shuts him up. I don't want this turning into a jurisdictional stink—"

"Karpatkin might be on the level," I said. "At least—"

"I just don't think you should be going around calling people fags is all."

"Say again?" said Janus to me.

"You got some special reason why you don't?"

"I mean, okay, Karpatkin's saying the gun's a flake," I said. "Well, no shit, it is. Question is how's he know it's a flake if he didn't see Georgina plant it? I mean, he may be lying but telling the truth."

"What are you, a philosopher now?" Dillard said. "Either the rat's on the scene or he ain't. Either he's lying or he ain't."

"Rats is rats."

Janus said, "If he's lying it don't matter if he's telling the truth."

"What I mean is we don't know what he told IAB, do we?" I said. "Maybe he sees something after he rolls up on the scene. Maybe he hears Georgina say something, do something. All I'm saying is we don't know. Or maybe—oh, fuck it."

"Rats leaving a sinking ship."

"No, no. Way's got a point. The guy may be a hero cop," said Tommy Janus, "but he's not clairvoyant on top of it."

"Fuck's a lying fuck."

"Yeah."

"Your ship's sunk, you catamite."

"All I'm saying is," I said, but I didn't think anyone was listening to me anymore, "all I'm saying is how does IAB know Georgina flaked the gun if Karpatkin wasn't there to see it?"

"Way, get off of Holtz already," Garrity told me. "I know where you're going."

"I'm just saying," I said. "Holtz was there. Karpatkin wasn't. So what if?"

"I ain't sinking."

"You're a catamite."

"The trick," Janus said, still on his feet, "the trick is catching Karpatkin in a lie. I don't care if he's telling the truth, if he's lying he's done. That's how we win in court."

"Yeah, so she sees some big mook coming up on her and she freaks."

"She don't know he's a kid in the dark."

"Plus it's a brother. Fuck's she scared of?"

"Seriously?"

"She dropped him 'cause she's scared."

"That's all that matters."

"Mutt was asking for it."

"I'd just like to know what the fuck happened is all."

"Self-defense. Pure and simple."

"What happened? Dumb fuck, when was this ever about what happened?"

"No," Janus said with such force than everyone went quiet. "None of you meatballs get it. Same goes for Georgina goes for Karpatkin. The DA proves she lied? Won't make no difference she tells the truth. Truth don't matter in Brooklyn Supreme, not in the end. All that matters is the lie they catch you on."

NINETEEN

Half past six at night, still at my desk. No call from Kat, of course. She subscribes to *The New York Times*, I was thinking. Goddamn newspaper lands on her stoop every morning with a thud in a blue plastic bag that is the perfect size for scooping dog crap from the sidewalk. Funny the things you miss. Of course Kat always turns first to the op-ed page, even before the crossword. Now when she thought of me she'd think of a monkey.

I was looking at the message slip Sheila had left with Pomeroy's name on it. Filled with sudden resolve, nearly angry, I put on my second-best overcoat and left. I drove to Brooklyn Supreme supposing I'd find Pomeroy gone. My plan was to thumbtack a message to his locked door, hoping he'd come to his senses over the weekend and we'd go back to the same relationship as before, which was to say no relationship at all. Yet there he was. Even before I went inside the building, even as I stood outside gazing at the Jovian heights of his courthouse, I saw a single window bright against the deepening nightfall and knew it was Justice Henry K. Pomeroy. "Thinks being a judge's a real job," I said aloud, and for fifteen minutes I loitered in front of the courthouse, cold, waiting to feel ready. After fifteen minutes I didn't feel ready, only ready to get it over.

Inside, the lobby so full of people only this morning was now empty and dark. A lonely court officer sat upon a high stool by the metal detectors, reading in a pool of wan light, his feet not touching the terrazzo floor. "Pomeroy," I said. He made an ugly face and put two fingers to his hairy ear. "Pomeroy?" I repeated, adding a polite question mark and displaying my Li'l Sheriff Kit toy badge to let him know I wasn't asking directions.

"What—you got a warrant, Officer? To sign?" He inserted a thumb in his paperback as a bookmark. "Because you got a warrant, you gotta see Judge Ciavatta there."

"I don't have a warrant."

"Not Pomeroy, you know. He's chief judge. He don't do warrants after hours. You wanna see Ciavatta, then?"

"No."

"You ain't got no warrant? 'Rest warrant? Search warrant?"

"No."

"I'll call upstairs for youse."

He asked my name and wrote it into a ledger with a ballpoint pen attached to a bead chain, and I walked to the elevator. I felt his eyes on me. He still thought I had a warrant. When I pressed the button my hand shook a little. Just cold, I told myself. Upstairs on the top floor no one was around and it was dark. I walked one way, then the other. In a moment a door opened, making a bright rectangle with the silhouette of a man. He said my name as a question. For a moment I thought it was Pomeroy, but even when I realized it wasn't I was still rattled. I followed. We walked along a narrow corridor behind many courtrooms. You could see inside. One after another they yawned black and deep. In daytime lives changed inside. Now they were just rooms.

We came to Pomeroy's chambers, his name lettered on the door in gilt. He was on the telephone, the man told me, so would I please wait, please have a seat. I waited with the man in a small rectangular space. On his desk the man had dinner set out for himself, takeout, and the room stank like an uptown 3 train. I sat on a narrow uncomfortable chair between two beige filing cabinets. Through a half-open communicating door marked private I could hear Pomeroy's voice very clearly. There were no magazines to read. At the same instant I realized Pomeroy had stopped speaking the door swung fully open.

"There's the ancient mariner now," Pomeroy said to me, immediately giving me the old worry he'd forgotten my name. He showed a genuine smile, and I sprang up like a puppy and gave him my paw. He was giving it one hell of a shake and his cool blue eyes looked me over appraisingly. "Come in, come in," he then said, ushering me. He wore an unloosened tie but a navy cardigan in lieu of his suit jacket. His desk was a dark walnut affair in the shape of a bank building adorned with carven pillars and capitals. I recollected the desk at the Dover Street house, in his private room upstairs where we were forbidden but sometimes went in minor acts of teenage nihilism, tiptoeing around as if in a tomb before dashing out again. Even more evocative of that unforgotten time was the smell in this place, which was the smell of Pomeroy, the smell of whiskey and leather, or who knew what—medicine cabinets, or Doublemint gum, or witch hazel rubbed on a freshly shaved chin, or the starchy smell of changing rooms in Madison Avenue men's stores. I really had no idea, but it was his smell.

We sat together in two deep club chairs, for ten minutes talking about nothing—or rather he talked about nothing while I nodded and gave short answers, eloquent as ever in the presence of Regine Pomeroy's father. But it was just a sniff under the tail, polite conversation in which we each avoided certain topics, Regine most of all. I supposed we'd get around to her sooner or later, for that surely was the point. We had run out of talk nearly when his telephone mercifully rang. When his law secretary cracked the door, Pomeroy frowned but stood and walked behind his desk to place the receiver on his ear. "Conrad—" he began, and I rose thinking I should leave but Pomeroy gestured that I stay. I stood nearby, my hands clenched so tightly into fists that they tingled a little when I opened them, and the blood returning felt like spiders. Meanwhile I ran my eyes cautiously around his office. I'd been here once, four years earlier, but then I hadn't even made it past his secretary. There were no diplomas on his wall much less any certificates or other framed accomplishments. Pomeroy was not that way, although one might say there was something prideful in how he undersold himself. Upon a narrow wall by the window, however, I saw several photographs. These were what I wanted to see.

I moved casually to the window, hands behind my back, as though I feared he might suspect me of shoplifting. After a moment of pretending to take in the view of Schermerhorn Street—where fifteen minutes earlier I stood looking up, where this morning Archbishop Bumpurs and his flock vowed they shall overcome—I sidled casually to the photographs, and at that moment Pomeroy hung up. "Sorry, sorry," he said, giving me a start, and in three strides of his long legs he was upon me. "Ah!" he said with a gesture to the largest photograph. "There's the whole crew, hmm?"

Yes, here was the whole Pomeroy crew all right—Pomeroy and his three women in another age of the world. Here was Pomeroy himself, his hair, which had since gone white, seeming nearly black, although I knew it'd been the same red-brown as Regine's, just as her eyes were the same blue and turned down in the corners in the same way. This Pomeroy was the Pomeroy I knew first, more immediately familiar than the man now before me. In the muted Kodachrome print he stands behind his wife and daughters on the sand of a pink beach. Regine is a coltish twelve, smiling with braces on her teeth. Next to her a teenaged Pamela scowls, her shapeless legs the image of her mother's who stands in a primly skirted one-piece, hand raised against the Bermuda sun. Others on the wall caught my eye. Here was Saint Ann—as Regine canonized her devout mother so frequently I could think of her by no other name—in a studio portrait, lambswool sweater and gold crucifix, gazing at some distant, faintly pleasing point—heaven, probably. Here, too, was Pamela with a curdled expression at her graduation but wearing contact lenses and a little makeup for a change, her mother next to her in a flowery hat. Pamela with a blond baby boy. Pamela and a toddler harassing a dachshund with a stick. Pomeroy in a blue blazer and brick-red pants standing with the same boy against a backdrop I knew at once to be the view of the ocean behind the house on Dover Street. Among all these was a photograph of Regine Pomeroy, age seventeen, in a plain frame. She stands on skinny legs on the prow of her father's boat, and the sea is behind her. She wears a T-shirt pulled over a yellow bikini and is barefoot. She laughs at the camera. Or rather she laughs at me, for I took that picture.

I became aware of Pomeroy next to me, his breath soft but vital and regular. He seemed to become aware of me at the same moment, and he moved away. "So—" he said, bending somewhat gingerly as he retrieved a bottle from a number of bottles inside a credenza piled high with legal documents, with blue-backed briefs, motion papers, exhibit books. He shoved a crystal tumbler into my hand and said with a wink, "Interesting times." I didn't know if it was a toast or a commentary on current events, but to be safe I raised my glass. We drank and were both quiet a moment. I hadn't eaten a thing all day, and I wasn't altogether happy about four fingers of scotch neat. This morning I'd had the original idea of never doing that again, and of telling Kat that vow by way of penance. But after a drunk like that you always decide either to clean up or just have another drink. I'd done both. "The Chinese curse, hmm?" Pomeroy said. "*May you live in interesting times*, ha ha!" I laughed on cue, and his blue eyes shone. "That was your commissioner on the telephone. I'm afraid the poor fellow finds the times too interesting by half."

"Yes."

"But you have a piece of this lamentable affair," he told me.

"Georgina and Holtz are mine, yeah."

"So I gathered from your rather spirited defense, shall we say, of Officer Reed in the *News* yesterday, ha ha."

"Yeah, that—"

"In future, it would serve you well to let the press intuit your thoughts, Will, rather than hear them aloud, unexpurgated, and for attribution, ha ha."

"Lesson learned."

"Betty Moon isn't a bad egg, you know," he said. "I've known her years and years. She'll cadge you all day for a story, of course, but she won't put you on record unless you give her the okay. But at the end of the day she's in this to sell newspapers, and *l'affaire Georgine* has become something of a cottage industry to her. And to a number of others, naturally."

"Yes."

"Sure, it's an ugly business," he said, examining his drink with a dissatisfied eye. "With their signs and their flowers. All afternoon they were outside that window, these pitiful old women of Basil's, shivering in the cold, believing in their cause so completely. Your heart just breaks."

"Sure."

"Not what this city needs, either. Another bloody mess."

"No."

His eyes fell hard upon me and he waited. He seemed content to say nothing, whereas I heard the silence echo though the entire building. It quickly became unbearable, so to keep the conversation moving I said, with more vehemence than I really felt, "It's all such—nonsense, you know, Judge."

"How do you mean, Will?"

"The flowers and marching and all," I said, "and everyone acting like Dewberry was such a sweetheart. Everyone saying Georgina shot him for no reason, like she's a racist. He wasn't, and she's not."

"But surely, Will, you don't disagree there're grounds for an indictment. After all, Mr. Odom swore under oath in the grand jury that Officer Reed shot his young veterinarian friend in the back—"

"No, my God, she shot him here—!" I said immediately, hand on my heart as if pledging allegiance. Dewberry's autopsy report wasn't public, but Masterson had given me an abridged version over the phone. I was primed to tell Pomeroy something he didn't know, but when he laughed I shut up.

"I'm afraid I'm making a rather small joke at Whitey Fister's expense," Pomeroy said, smiling, and when I realized it I felt foolish and young. Most of Pomeroy's rather small jokes, like most of his seemingly innocuous questions, were meant to measure you. Again I'd come up short. "But I'm afraid our current district attorney has no sense of humor whatsoever. We ought to remedy that, ha ha. But I take it you've read the medical examiner's report?"

"Yes."

"So the DA's star witness is somewhat off. About one hundred eighty degrees off, in point of fact, ha ha."

"Not sure it matters anyway," I answered, still glum.

"Perhaps not, now that the DA has a more credible witness—a police officer, no less—to corroborate Mr. Odom's account."

"Karpatkin can't back Odom, Judge. I don't know what Karpatkin can say that Fister can use against Georgina. He wasn't there," I said, then almost as an afterthought, "Hell, Odom wasn't there either."

"How do you mean?"

"I mean Karpatkin didn't see anything, and Odom's flat-out lying. That's the DA's case against Georgina Reed. That's why it's all so infuriating, when the truth is she—"

He raised a hand and I shut my mouth obediently. "Just to play devil's advocate with you, Will. Mr. Odom is a witness to this incident, and the DA's entitled to his testimony regardless of whether he's of a disreputable character or his recollection of the incident differs from—"

"But that's just it, Judge," I said in a rush, realizing I knew more than he did for once and feeling a sense of exhilaration at the idea. I pushed forward in my chair. "Odom's a liar."

"Of course that's your—"

"No, the DA put Odom in the grand jury to say he saw Georgina shoot Dewberry in the back, but—"

"He was mistaken, Will," Pomeroy said. "It's a mild embarrassment for the DA to be sure, but really that sort of thing happens with alarming regularity at trial. You can't imagine how many times I've heard two or three eyewitnesses give accounts that differ wildly. People under stress particularly are—"

"He's not just mistaken, Judge. He's lying," I said. "Odom didn't see the shot. He couldn't have. He wasn't there."

"Of course he was there, Will, and the difference between his recollection and—"

"No, Judge, I mean Odom wasn't there. As in he wasn't there." I said it, feeling oddly triumphant, like a cat with a cockroach, pleased to show Pomeroy what I knew and what he didn't. "Odom dipped—I mean, he ran off when Georgina moved on Dewberry. Her partner followed Odom and they were a long block away and around the corner when Georgina dropped her guy."

Pomeroy fell silent, and so did I.

The idea that I should've said none of this occurred to me, of course, in an abstract and theoretical way, like one of the Ten Commandments, but at the moment I wanted only to show him something. So later, when it became important, I couldn't console myself believing it had all been just a lapse in the heat of conversation. My only defense is that at the time I told Pomeroy I'd asked for nothing in exchange—nothing, that is, except his unspoken acknowledgment that I was no longer his boat boy.

He turned my words over in his mind for a moment as I took a long pull of whiskey and watched for some indication of how the balance of this conversation would go. Part of me expected he'd change the subject to something safer, and another part hoped that he would. He didn't. "Then Officer Holtz wouldn't have seen the shooting either," he told me.

"No."

"I wonder why the district attorney was so insistent on having his testimony in the grand jury, then?"

"Holtz never testified."

"I daresay he did, Will. At any rate I signed a material witness order for Mr. Crimmins. Which implies that the DA at least believed Holtz was a witness, hmm?" he said, then seeing my expression change he asked, "You didn't know?"

"No," I stated the obvious.

"This is somewhat embarrassing. I might've imagined your man would've told you."

"That son of a bitch."

"As I say, interesting times," he said. "But I shouldn't feel very unloved, Will. On a case such as this one, Whitey Fister's obscure doings in the grand jury are of little consequence one way or another. People will believe what they want to believe about your Officer Reed, regardless of what the eyewitnesses say and no matter what the evidence shows."

"How can the truth not matter?"

"Oh, the truth matters very much, more than anything," he said, "but your truth is different from mine just as it's different from everyone else's. The facts are not necessarily dispositive of the matter, and often they only just get in the way."

"I don't understand."

"Facts are raw material, Will, a base element. We use facts to build truths— as many truths as there are builders—as bricks can make either a penthouse or an outhouse, as carbon becomes a diamond for your finger or a lump of coal for your stocking, ha ha. I needn't tell you that in certain neighborhoods of this city at this very moment they're crying *Murder!* whereas you would certainly say, *Let's await a full and fair investigation.*"

"I don't need an investigation," I said. "I know Georgina Reed's not a murderer."

"Well, then, you've rather just proven my point, haven't you?" he said with the slightest smile imaginable. "You believe you know what happened, as do they. You believe you know the truth, as do they. You each have your own distinct truth, built from the same facts. You each have the truth that's true for you."

"Truth isn't subjective."

"What could be more subjective than truth?" he said. "How can something be true to you if it doesn't inhabit your heart?"

"The truth is the truth. What happened is what happened."

"And, like wives and sweethearts, may they never meet, ha ha," he said, raising a glass. "It's almost as if the act of perception alters the thing, isn't it? As in physics, quantum mechanics and all that."

"Physics, judge?"

"You know those laboratory experiments proving a particle or some such thing is here when I look at it, and there when you look at it, and someplace else entirely when neither of us is looking. If nature's a matter of perspective, why not human nature?"

"A trial isn't a laboratory experiment."

"Oh, I daresay it is, Will," he said. "A criminal courtroom is a laboratory built for understanding not quarks or jellies under a microscope, but instead the most complex thing known to us, the human soul. Most of the time, of course, a criminal trial is about nothing more profound than whether that sad-looking fellow over there snatched your pocketbook, ha ha. But with Georgina Reed, well—now, that would be an experiment worth watching, wouldn't it?"

"You think Georgina's soul is that interesting, Judge?"

"Oh, it's not her soul but ours that a trial would put on vivid display," he said. "But there'll be no trial, alas. I imagine Whitey Fister's just doing his imitation of one of those great leaping jungle apes that shake their pink bottoms at their enemies and throw turds to impress them. You've spoken to Officer Reed, I take it? You think she would comport herself well on the stand?"

"I do. People will believe her."

"Most likely the same people who believe her now," he said ruefully, "though she's not uttered a public word. Which you'll agree with me is a curious thing, hmm?"

"She'll tell the truth."

"Which is?"

"That she was scared," I said. "She didn't murder anyone."

"But then there's this troublesome gun that Officer Karpatkin speaks of—"

"So what she planted a gun?" I said. "She was scared, not a murderer."

"Tell me, if the defense can lie to prove their truth, why can't Mr. Odom lie to prove his?"

"What's Odom's truth?"

"Surely you know better than I," he told me. "You worked among Mr. Odom and men like him for—the better part of ten years, did you not? Would you say he and his friends in Bushwick and Brownsville and the housing projects of East New York think of the police in the same way as they think of the police in Park Slope and Brooklyn Heights? And is Mr. Odom wrong for believing what he thinks?"

"Belief isn't truth."

"Belief is the truest truth, Will," he said firmly.

"You can't convict Georgina with belief. Not in court. That's what they do on the street, with their signs and banners—"

"And you've acquitted her on the same basis," Pomeroy said.

"Georgina Reed didn't murder anyone," I told him in a defeated voice. "I don't care how many signs and banners Bumpurs puts up—"

He smiled a little. "Basil Bumpurs is a friend—a contributor at least, ha ha, and I certainly want him by my side in the fall primary. He's as fine a man as you could wish, yet never could you shake him from his conviction that Officer Reed is a murderer."

"Why?"

"Because it's true," he said. "To Basil, it's true that Officer Reed shot Mr. Dewberry for no damn reason."

"Why?" I said again.

"Because it accords with his belief."

"Which is?"

"That police officers shoot black boys for no damn reason."

He stood and by tacit agreement we moved on. He seemed tired of Dewberry, and I was just tired. He moved to the cabinet and freshened our drinks without comment. Mine was still pretty fresh. He sat wearily, like an old man, placing his hands upon his knees. I was still unused to his hair, which was the purest white although he was no older than my father, not even sixty. Our eyes met, and it was uncomfortable because in that moment we were each unguarded. We drank, and it seemed he was casting about for a way to turn the conversation to the reason he wanted to see me in the first place. While I waited, unmemorable things were said, and he tried to make the longer, silent interludes seem intentional by assuming a distant clever smile, as if to suggest he wanted nothing in the world more than to drink whiskey in the company of his boat boy.

What shit, I starting thinking about then. *Let's go, already. Ask me. Just ask me.*

And I was ready with my answer. *No, Judge, I didn't see her once, not after that whole thing in Massachusetts. Um-hmm. I know. Well, I was married but it didn't take. No. No, no kids. I had a dog, though. No, she died, couple weeks ago. Yeah, I know. I miss her. She was old. It was her time. No, I haven't been to Gerritsen Beach since I don't know when. I'm in Park Slope now. But Regine—Jesus, Judge, no—Yeah, I tried to talk to her after, but she never—I just don't know what else I could have done, so—No, I don't know why she did it—Anyway—*

I waited. Nothing. It showed an unexpected, uncharacteristic weakness on his part, that he had to work his way around to it. I nearly said that single word—*Regine!*—so we could get it over with and I could then do us both a favor and disappear. Yet there we sat, drinking, nodding politely at each other. I began to feel his whiskey.

At once he seemed to brighten. "Ah, well, I suppose we'll see," he said, and I believed he smiled his old smile at me, and his blue eyes flickered darkly, and all at once I was seventeen again, sitting in the dining room in the redbrick green-roofed house by the sea. Regine is next to me, her foot pressing mine under the dining table. There are potatoes wrapped in aluminum foil and roast beef and cucumber salad and everyone is drinking milk from tall orange glasses patterned with circles and diamonds. Pomeroy is speaking to me from across the expanse of tablecloth, asking me questions over placemats sewn by Pamela in ninth grade. He is wielding a carving knife and everyone seems to await my answer. Pamela is there and Saint Ann, too, all of them looking at me, waiting, but later, when I bicycle home to Gerritsen Beach, on dimly lit and desolate Knapp Street, I think, *What was his question?*

MASTERSON

TWENTY

There was Regine again. We'd not said a word about her, Pomeroy nor I, yet her absence from our politely pointless talk had made her more tangible than if she'd walked through the door. She stared openly from our conversation as she did from the collection of photographs on his wall—here was the whole crew, all right, before the shipwreck—and her name punctuated every sentence spoken between her father and me. She was a hundred periods in a hundred sentences, a hundred quiet commas, the silent consonant in every tenth word. She inhabited that conversation as she inhabited me still, unseen and unheard, somewhere deep, always there.

Saturday, 9:37 in the morning. I was home at the home that was not home. The weedy stink of Kaseem's morning bake had mostly dissipated, and his dogs had quieted to a manageable regularity. The sun was well up over Brooklyn and reflected off the silver rooftops of Park Slope in a perfect blaze of light. Feeling meek beneath the power of heaven, I started to clean my place, vacuuming in my shorts, spraying the bathtub on my knees as though in an act of contrition. In the kitchen closet I came upon a forgotten bag of dog food and everything stopped for a while. I sat down on the floor and felt my eyes burn then felt ridiculous because she was just a dog. I walked down the hall to the garbage chute and let it go. By the time I returned—thirty seconds later, at least—Kat still hadn't called, so I organized my liquor cabinet, which was just a Christmas-present Chivas and a half-empty bottle of Wild Turkey under the sink.

When the bottle was mostly empty I drove to Fulton Street. There I sat. Some wiseass had clipped yesterday's cartoon and left it on my desk, the monkey circled in blue ballpoint: "Way YOU are my hero cop!!!" I dropped it into the trash, atop yesterday's message slips, and looked at the crossword for something to do. I was on a roll. I'd written SOUVENIR and ALOOF when the telephone rang.

Detective Mark Masterson said, "Working on a Saturday?"

"On my résumé."

"Well," he said, "don't let me interrupt."

"Not much on it, partner. So far all I got was I was a cop. Then I was an unemployed cop, twenty minutes from now."

"Say you resigned," he said, "so you could spend more time with your family."

"Except I don't have one."

"You got the old man. Hell, I'd resign to go fishing with him," Masterson said. Though he'd met my father only twice, that was enough. The Avocado King was universally loved. "Give him my regards."

"I sold avocados for six months," I said, pretending not to have heard. "I could put that. What's that qualify me to do, besides sell more avocados?"

"Sell guavas, maybe. I dunno."

"There should be more on my résumé, don't you think? This is not where I was supposed to be, Mark."

"You drunk, Way?"

"Enough to know to pretend I'm not."

"All steady there, partner?" he asked.

"Never better."

"Okay, well—" he said.

"Which is a pretty sorry fucking thing to say, come to think of it."

"What is?" he asked.

"I've never been better than this. That where I am is the apex of my—ah, fuck it."

"Will—"

"I have been better, you know. Just not for a long time."

The line went silent for a while and in the silence I realized I wasn't at all drunk, not even a little. Then he asked, "Out of curiosity, where were you supposed to be?"

"What do you mean?"

"You said you're not where you're supposed to be. So I'm just asking you where you're supposed to be?"

"Ah, hell. I don't know," I said. "Accomplish something. Be something. Do something. Write the great American limerick, I dunno. Forget it. What's on your mind, partner?"

"Meet me," he said. "Something you should see."

"I gotta run to Bed-Stuy. Ouellette's press conference."

"Odom's lawyer?"

"At BABE Cathedral," I said. "Wanna go? Should be enough disinformation there to make Goebbels blush."

"No thanks," he said. "But call me after, you don't get lynched."

I hung up and promptly went back to what I had been doing, which was nothing.

Then I was thinking about Regine.

Then I left the office for the press conference in Bed-Stuy but instead found myself taking the split off the bridge and driving south toward Dover Street and the sea. I didn't drive down her old block, but I idled for ten minutes nearby. Because this was Manhattan Beach there were no pedestrians and few cars. Here was our famous park to the right, where the ocean fell gently upon a crescent beach and the elm trees looked down. Now off-season, the cyclone fence was in place but I might have clambered over and found the very spot where I'd said the words "I," "love," and "you" in that precise order for the first time in my life, but I didn't even get out of the car. It was enough to stay nearby and to remember her, which meant remembering the ravening urgency of her kisses when there is still surprise in them, when she is sixteen and smells sweet and does not let go. I recalled one time in particular: we kiss on the grass inland from the beach then walk home along Oriental Boulevard to Dover Street. I do not go inside, unwilling to submit to the patient tolerance Saint Ann throws my way. Her prayer, of course, is that I am something temporary, a momentary fascination that will lose its sparkle when Regine comes to her senses or turns seventeen. Ten minutes after, I say good night to Regine and leave her by the side door. I am on my bicycle, on Knapp Street, pedaling toward Gerritsen Beach. I can hear them even as I turn toward my father's house on Melba Court. He is there, sitting on the porch lit with the light of a yellow bulb. June bugs beat against the screens. I smell them as I pass, as I step around and over them: the men and the stink of flat beer and spent cigarettes and aftershave. They sit on colorfully webbed beach chairs. The aluminum grieves beneath them as they shift to shake my hand. My father sits above them, enthroned on a white rattan armchair, on a thin cushion stuffed with redwood shavings, the king upon his throne. WM. WAY & SON NY'S LARGEST AVOCADO DIST'R read his trucks—his trucks too small for his trademark, his trademark too ambitious for his trucks. On them he spells out my unwanted patrimony above the image of an anthropoid avocado wearing a jeweled crown. Men at Terminal Market ask my father, "Who's Sonny anyway, ha ha." Sonny takes on an unseen presence within the realm. He is a personality, a regular card. Dock men blame Sonny when a crate falls from a pallet, or a shipment goes to Bayside by mistake. Sonny actually appears in the flesh one winter's day. I think, why the hell not? I am the

Ampersand Son, and I cannot live forever in the same bedroom on Melba Court with the orange shag carpeting and Rush and Van Halen arranged alphabetically in purple milk crates. I try business. I buy a leather-bound organizer. I receive a complimentary subscription to *Forbes*. I wear a jacket and khakis and a new shirt from the men's department at Macy's in Kings Plaza.

So yes, Masterson, I sold avocados. I lasted six months. Then I became a cop.

I suppose liquor—the liberal and amiable consumption of it—was the only thing Pomeroy had in common with my father. By age ten the Avocado King had me measuring out highballs in the kitchen for his Gerritsen Beach hangers-on. I could have tended bar at fourteen. That had been my youth—a little dodgy in some respects, but no great trauma. I have no excuse for what I became. My mother didn't leave me on anyone's doorstep except my own.

Summer afternoons on Melba Court, and there was always the astringent smell of bourbon in the kitchen and ice cubes from spent glasses in the sink, smoothly melted like little bars of soap. There was always my father's voice on the porch, radio baseball, the shivering clap of the screen door closing. Intermittently there was the hoarse laughter of men who had seen more of the world by twenty than I ever would, even with my time in uniform. As much as cops liked to pretend, we knew Brooklyn was not the shit. As warm as it ever got for us, it was never as warm as the jungle.

My father appeared unannounced in the 83 stationhouse in Bushwick one midnight when I was a patrolman. Unwillingly, knowing what would happen, I introduced him around to the men lolling in the muster room between tours. He charmed the hell out of everyone as feared, and ten minutes later they were wound around him in a circle of hilarity while I fell into my traditional role of satellite. Within his gravitational field I become his little moon, cold and distant, with an orbit so wide that I can scarcely be seen to move at all.

Leaving the stationhouse that night, after he had made more friends in my platoon than I'd made in two years, he became downcast and mum. As I walked him from the stationhouse we passed the flagpole where a POW flag flew loose in the night breeze. My father rarely spoke of his war, so when he dutifully rewound the halyard onto the cleat and squinted in the floodlight I prepared myself, but all he said was, "NVA lost more they can count." When the topic of war arose there always seemed more important business for my father elsewhere. In consequence I never knew what he or the loitering gray souls of my old neighborhood had seen over there, yet the pale outlines of war were written on their faces and showed in the deliberate movement of their bodies, in their readiness to burst forth into heavy laughter, and in their sullen quiet when left alone. You could tell that a hundred years before they found themselves drawn to my father's front porch they had lain in a sandbag bunker or hunkered down in a paddy as magnesium shells burst like dandelions overhead. They had all decided if they ever made it to ask no more than to sit and listen to baseball under the setting sun in the sea air of home. That would be enough, and that was enough.

My father could still be seen in photographs sent across oceans to a woman who was by then already plotting her escape. He is there in square images, white-bordered, color-fading, edge-curling photographs of men in a jungle clearing, a snake hanging dead from a vine, a dirt-road ville, a squat hootch with a roof of corrugated tin, men atop an artillery emplacement, one flashing a peace sign, another displaying what could be a human skull. On the backs of these photographs my father had written captions in his unlearned scrawl. *Back from patrol—Long way from Brooklyn!—Me and Roger C. in base Khe Sanh.* In one my father looks right at you. Impossibly young, shirtless in a bucket helmet, dog tags dangle from his neck, fragmentation grenades from his belt, tools of the trade, one hand resting casually on his hip. His smile is an inscrutable sentence punctuated by a cigarette. Next to him is a skinny kid in Buddy Holly frames holding the biggest gun I have ever seen.

Pomeroy sat out that war, but never would I have known if the Avocado King hadn't told me, seemingly apropos of nothing, one bright morning when I'd overslept. He related only the fact of it, but from his lips it seemed much like a measurement of the man. I never got my father, so different were we, yet I did live under the same leaky roof with him on Melba Court and could not help but accumulate a certain amount of basic information about him, much as Mowgli would have come by a working knowledge of gray wolves, having been raised by one. I knew, for instance, that my father would have thought nothing of Pomeroy missing the war, nor have given a damn for whatever explanation Pomeroy gave for his deferment. "A medical," my father had told me that bright morning, with a near smile to indicate that neither he nor anyone else in south Brooklyn believed it. "Bum ticker, he told us."

At the same time, of course, the Avocado King hadn't bothered to wait for the draft. Instead he was already in advanced infantry training in Reedsville, Georgia, when I was born, leaving the formal status of my entry into the world somewhat informal. Until that bright morning I believed only that, to my father,

Pomeroy was simply a fellow seagoing hearty, the occupant of the adjoining slip at the Tamaqua Marina, a tall affable man in faded Nantucket reds whose Hatteras Sportfish—a fifty-three-footer that might have shipped our little Sea Ray as a runabout—his son bilged from April until October. They drank beer and gin together on deck chairs in the marina and laughed as only adult laughter can sound to a kid, but of course Pomeroy never came once to our front porch on Melba Court.

My father reserved opinion on how men made their way in the world— judging neither Pomeroy nor certainly those men who draped themselves over our porch on summer afternoons so languidly complacent that I had to step over them, walking on tiptoe as if passing through an opium den. So on that bright morning when he told me about Pomeroy's heart, my father's words had a false quality, and I paid attention. This was after Regine Pomeroy and I had begun to walk with a hand in the other's back pocket, after I had begun to eat my dinners at Dover Street, to be more vocally disdainful of the Avocado King and his idiosyncrasies, to dress less like my old haphazard self and more like the tall man in the adjoining slip.

One summer morning I awoke late to my father performing his usual number of push-ups on my bedroom floor, and to make conversation I asked about a particularly ugly scar beneath his right shoulder bone. "Self-inflicted," he said. "Fell out of a Bangkok whorehouse." "Fell or pushed?" I answered. By then of course I had seen the leatherette box in his sock drawer with the blue-and-white-ribboned star inside, so I asked him for the first time about Cam Lo and his conspicuous gallantry and intrepidity. He shrugged, answering with his wonted obscurity, "I suppose I was gallant and intrepid. Mostly stupid and lucky, but you can't put that on a citation. More lucky than stupid, else I wouldn't be here. Then where the hell would you be, boy?"

"Here," I answered.

"Oh, you think?" he said, smiling.

"Maybe."

"Maybe get Lemons to adopt you, you like it so much in Manhattan Beach."

"Lemons?"

"What we called Regine's dad, back in the day."

"Why Lemons?"

"He was—kind of—a sourpuss—" my father began, but he checked himself, adding only that Pomeroy had no war, that some sympathetic family doctor had written a note to explain to the board that Pomeroy's heart was not an ordinary human heart. In that instant my father's voice was unlike his, as if someone else were speaking, someone absolutely human. "Big deal, Dad." My witty answer. He told me "Yes it was" in the same tone. He then lifted himself off the carpet and before leaving told me I might understand someday.

Now, I suppose, is that future someday, now that I am whatever I have become in the interval between that bright morning long ago and today. I still do not know what my father hoped I'd understand, not for certain, yet I believe I'm entitled to one guess. While it would have meant absolutely nothing to him that Pomeroy sat out the war on a contrived deferment, what I have at last come to suspect is how it wounded him to know it meant nothing to me either.

But who can say? Who can say what thoughts fill another man's head, much less put a price on them? If MK left me, believing I had become a man other than the one she wed, a man without a moral compass, my own feeling was that I simply lacked the phenomenal arrogance needed to pass judgment on another. I had no better idea why Pomeroy stayed home than why my father went. Or why he remained overseas until my mother threw up her hands with me in them. All of these decisions were made in my prehistory, and my only contact with that age derives from sitcom reruns and a 1964 Pontiac Tempest we drove until 1987, when finally it collapsed under the weight of its past, as do we all. The Tempest gave me no greater understanding of a time when *I Dream of Jeannie* was in black and white and I had a mother. Under these exotic conditions, never again to be repeated in the history of the world, my father went to war.

All the same, I suspect the reason he went was the reason he stayed. He stayed three tours, he stayed until my mother gave up on him altogether and decamped to parts unknown. My father would have gone for the boys he knew, for the south Brooklyn boys whose fathers had fought another war in another place. And he stayed for the same boys, because they would have been the same sort of boys who as men would sit on our front porch. He stayed until the world had changed, until the Swinging Sixties had choked on its own vomit and died. He came home at last—spat on at JFK Airport and called a baby killer in his 1st Cavalry uniform—to find his son in a wicker basket on the doorstep, care and feeding instructions blown away on the breeze. Our first conversation must have consisted of me asking, "And who, sir, might you be?" followed by thirty-odd years during which he tried to answer that question in his own way.

They were going, so he went. They were dying, so he stayed. He told me as much once. I know nothing about war nor can I guess, but I know something about the Avocado King and a little about men. Men together make fearsome achievements. Men together build cathedrals, great ships, dams, highways, rockets. Men die in jungles for no better reason than the men they're with. Yet men together burn crosses and ovens to put other men in. That is what I know of men, but knowing is not the same as understanding, so I will not say I understand my father or the choices he made. Nor will I say Pomeroy made the wrong one, nor express an opinion either way on the subject of my mother. Nor can I say I would have done differently than any of them. I have never built a cathedral, and my insignificance to the universe is only a thin comfort, for the one thing more oppressive than a longing to be something is the slow realization you never will—

Big deal, I'd said to my father. He likely went to Terminal Market that morning believing that was as much headway as he would make with me on the subject of Pomeroy. Yet the idea like a little virus had entered my blood, and afterward it festered and infected my thoughts about Pomeroy when I ate dinner on Dover Street, when I piloted his Hatteras into the slip, when I climbed with him into the attic over rolls of pink insulation the time the wasps were getting in. And it was on my mind when I sat in a cheerfully dreadful hospital waiting room in Worcester, Massachusetts, where Regine lay somewhere behind a door. What my father had said that bright morning was still with me even as late as that Friday evening when I sat in Pomeroy's chambers in Brooklyn Supreme drinking whiskey and not talking about Regine. My father's words had meant something to me no matter how frequently I tried to convince myself I was a thing of the world formed wholly independent of him, not simply illegitimate but parthenogenetic, a fatherless son of Juno cast at birth upon obscure Gerritsen Beach. I was wrong.

TWENTY-ONE

Forty minutes later I was in Bed-Stuy, taking Ocean Parkway through the beating heart of Brooklyn, through Midwood then the Flatlands then East Flatbush, neighborhoods I scarcely knew, places I never went, not as a cop nor as an unarmed man. I might have been in Elmira. I was a stranger in my own hometown, like Elvis.

Everyone had a microphone that week. Marlon Odom took his late that Saturday morning in a low-ceilinged hall adjoining the Brooklyn African-Baptist-Episcopal Cathedral. The cathedral—formerly the church of the now-deconsecrated Roman Catholic parish of San Vito—loomed over a lively block of Malcolm X Boulevard in a distant corner of Bedford-Stuyvesant. The cathedral had recently been repainted a bright and cheerful mustard yellow and featured a Times Square–style ticker tape displaying passages from the more belligerent prophets in red letters eighteen inches high: PURSUE THINE ENEMIES! THY MEN SHALL FALL BY THE SWORD! THEY SHALL BE CONSUMED BY WRATH AND FLAMES! et cetera.

The cathedral itself was in need of repair. Bricks had fallen from its towers, a congregant brained just last Thursday. A brief service was read. A full recovery was expected, but a little money had changed hands nevertheless. Today scaffolding had been erected on the eastern wall and a long section of sidewalk cordoned off with tape. Workmen mixed concrete in a trough, speaking Urdu and looking cold. This was all to be expected, of course. Catholic churches were always falling to pieces. I never once attended Mass on Gerritsen Avenue without hearing a monotone plea for the building fund or the roofing drive or a second collection to repair the Blessed Mother's shrine, which had tipped over. When they shook the wicker offertory basket on the six-foot pole in front of my father he would grudgingly toss in a few bits with a roll of his eyes.

My business here required me to take notes and make skeptical expressions from my seat in the back. An ass-watcher by trade, I am content in my vocation, pleased to see the world from behind, fighting rearguard actions in battles noticed by none. I sat alone, arriving early with nothing better to do. I supposed I was done with Georgina Reed, that I had played my hand, shot my bolt. Still, I came, the inertia of events buoying me along, like a mostly empty bottle of Wild Turkey on an ebb tide.

The hall began to fill. Television crews were testing their lights, brightening a makeshift stage at one end of the hall from time to time. I looked at my watch. Ten twenty-seven, and I became aware of a faint familiar smell. Here in this room yet lay the cafeteria stink of decades of shepherd's pie, peas and carrots, and stewed tomatoes eaten by generations of good Catholic children in ill-fitting woolen uniforms. And in the hallway outside, even before I sat, I caught at once the ancient mingled odor of mimeographed assignment sheets and liquid soap and holy water and linoleum hallways with construction-paper scenes and hard fiberglass chairs in the principal's office and the pink granules the janitor would sprinkle from a Chock full o' Nuts coffee can on pooled vomit then sweep it all away as we stared in disgust and fascination from our desks—the smell of Resurrection School in the Beach and of Xaverian, my high school in Bay Ridge, and of Fontbonne, hers—the smell of childhood— the smell of Catholicism—the same comforting stink of slow strangulation.

Marlon Odom was now front and center. Charles Ouellette beamed at his trophy. Since his arraignment three days ago Odom had shifted out of his crotch-sagging baggies into a snappy suit, beige, four-button, with a maroon shirt and tie to match. Ouellette had also taken him to a barber, and his hair was now smartly trimmed into a neat fade. There were two karats in each earlobe and a titanium Breitling Chronomat on his wrist. Odom was smiling broadly, chatting away affably with all and sundry, pleased with himself, pleased to be at the center of the universe. All of it was new to him and wonderful. The violent death of his homeboy on a Bushwick street corner was the apex of Marlon Odom's life. From here it all would be downhill.

Archbishop Bumpurs's congregants began to assemble, shuffling stiffly into the former cafeteria of the former school of the former church with little conversation and set expressions upon their dark and unreadable faces. They came in, his Babes, bringing their now-familiar scent of old lady perfume and mothballs and evangelical piety. I watched with a fascination that might have been love or ridicule, unsure myself. How alien they were, sitting there on folding chairs stenciled s. VITO R.C. CHURCH, their hands on their laps holding tracts and pamphlets and dog-eared missalettes, as placid and noble as Indian chiefs. I could not imagine them in their daily lives. I could not see them doing anything but praying and protesting. I could not see them washing dishes, for example, or doing the crossword. They seemed not only from another place but another time, such as a movie from the Ford administration on videotape; their polyester clothing seemed pointed, their hair slept-on, their complexions bad. Their colors were slightly off. They needed adjustment. And they all looked so purposely and unfalteringly holy, as if God mattered to them more than anything—God, and funny hats. They really believed, you could tell, the lucky dopes. What a gift it would be to believe like that, I felt myself thinking enviously. What a relief it would be to think that something, anything came after all this noise and movement here on planet Earth. I had long since abandoned the notion of heaven and hell, quaint absurdities peddled by women in hoods and men in colorful gowns, yet I still wanted something at the end of everything—a signpost in the void to inform me I was right, that the end is the end and that God is not dead because he never existed, for knowing there's nothing beyond nothingness is more unbearable than nothingness itself.

I once had the conviction of a Babe, the faith of a child, which is to say I was told what to believe and believed it. I said my prayers and believed there was a great and complicated world out there, a world of television news anchors who had answers, of banks and corporations and governments running everything according to plan. I believed in nuns and postmen and senators and men with ties and the world at large seemed so imposing and I understood none of it, but that was okay. Then, slowly, as if a curtain were drawn away, the workings of the world were laid bare. Walter Cronkite was selling ad time. Father Mike fondled altar boys in the sacristy. The postman no longer wore a uniform and smoked weed in his truck. The earth was changing, the planet warming. You could no longer trust the sky. Danger was rife, but it all made perfect sense: the world was not a mystery but a creation of the people in it. There was no larger plan. That was it, I suppose; I'd lost the sense of mystery, the belief that an unseen hand moved creation. When everything became clear in its shoddy human mundanity, when I understood everything, that was when God went away. When you know everything, there is no need for faith. Ten years on patrol in Bushwick proved I knew all there was to know, yet even before that was a hospital waiting room in Worcester, Massachusetts, where Regine lay somewhere behind a door.

Now it was almost noon. Everyone seemed to wait for someone who never arrived, but no one became impatient. Betty Moon dropped into a folding chair next to me without saying hello, rummaging through one of her overstuffed canvas tote bags with her head down. "Where are my fucking car keys?" I didn't answer. I remembered I was theoretically pissed at her, but at the same moment decided I didn't care—that the headline was my own fault, and what happened in newspapers wasn't real anyway. We sat without talking. She was writing in her notebook. I looked at my watch.

"What's Crimmins's first name?" she asked abruptly. "Selma or something?"

"Crimmins?"

"DA on Georgina. Hello! McFly! Oh, you're useless," she said. "Plus you smell like vodka, you alcoholic."

"And you smell like cigarettes, you—smoker." She wasn't listening. "By the way, what was the brawl about?"

"Brawl? And it's Montgomery," she said, still writing. "Selma—duh."

"Here. Dewberry's memorial Wednesday night. On the TV, I saw it."

"Money," she said. "Cousin that's handling the donation fund bought a microwave oven with it. And a houseboat."

"A boat. Wonder what he's gonna name it."

"And Dewberry's babymother went after his girlfriend with a diaper bag."

"No, really?"

"Said she was just a side piece and scratched her eyes out. You know a lawyer named, ah—" she looked at her notebook "—Herman Wrublewicz? I can't read my own writing. I'm a fucking pig."

"Should I?"

"Ex-Legal Aid, now on his own out in Hicksville. Stood up for Dewberry at arraignment on his robbery case last year." She was writing again, distracted. "Just filed a notice of claim for a third of any future settlement between the city and Dewberry's estate."

"He retained by the estate?"

"No."

"Working with Ouellette?" I asked.

"No."

"Do anything whatsoever to earn a cut?"

"No."

She was writing, not listening anymore. "Hey, Betty."

"What—?"

"I think I thought of a name for that boat."

Nearby a television cameraman was at work. A woman stood there, a familiar face from CNN, dark bob, pretty, bored. She dropped down closer than necessary to me on a folding chair, talking into a flip phone and making sharp gestures with pointed fingers. Her face said twenty, but her hands said thirty-five. When she stopped talking she frankly met my gaze. An invitation. Women sometimes mistake me for someone they want to meet. "You look like you're having fun," she said to me, throwing me a softball. A thousand witty replies flew on instinct to my head, but I just shrugged. She made a smile and didn't leave, on purpose doing nothing I couldn't interrupt if I felt like it. She gave me just enough of her Zelda Fitzgerald profile to tell me that, but instead I stood and retired to the far wall. Now she and Betty were talking, and a moment later they both looked in my direction. Betty laughed mercilessly. This hall was still a school cafeteria.

I told myself I missed Kat, that I wanted only Kat, but I wondered if I simply lacked the spirit to start again. I already saw the next two weeks with Zelda—two weeks of winsome conversation at dimly lit Manhattan restaurants and opening doors for her and kissing in yellow taxis and moonlight walks on the beach or whatever. And I knew I could sustain it for two weeks, like a man treading water, but after two weeks would come the questions, the disclosures, the revelations, the explanations, the arrangements, the sullen silent moments at the dinner table, the dental floss on the bathroom floor, the strange marks on the bedsheets, and at once it was all so dreary. We were tired of each other before we even met.

I had dialed four of Kat's ten digits when Bea Katzenbach spotted me and made her plodding way over. There was nowhere for me to hide, but part of me welcomed the obligation to pocket my phone. Beatrix B. Katzenbach was Ouellette's new partner, a self-styled friend of radical causes, a criminal lawyer of some local reputation, a gigantic putty-colored pudding of a woman with red lipstick drawn defiantly across her lips. She had no use for makeup, so she wore it in a minor act of rebellion against herself. She was dressed in an amorphous green garment. She rooted herself before me on the black-and-white checkerboard linoleum.

"Will Way. How's the Benevolent Association these days?"

She said it with a weary perfunctory sarcasm, which was exactly what I expected under the circumstances. I'd known her a few years, during which we'd crossed swords a few times. Usually she won, but I'm not a sore loser so we became friendly without being friends. Bea came with the job. Before William Way, Jr., came along she had no doubt entertained herself similarly with my predecessor. She pretended to be the Bleeding Heart. Which obliged me to be the Fascist. I played along, if for no other reason than to show her what I was by pretending to be what I wasn't. I was tired of the pretense by now. So was she, yet we went through the motions nonetheless, as elaborate in their rules and routines as a Japanese tea ceremony.

"Fine. Fine," I said, giving her the obligatory half-smirk. "How 'bout you, counselor? How goes the revolution?"

"Hanging by its fingernails as ever."

"Dirty fingernails, I bet."

Ouellette & Katzenbach, LLP, was filing civil suit for damages against the city on behalf of Dewberry and Odom, the point of this press conference. No one was surprised. After all, this whole thing happened in the United States of America. The only wrinkle was Katzenbach. She was no ambulance chaser, that much I knew. She wasn't one of those remoras, those suckerfish that fix themselves to the underbelly of every heartache and joyride them to the bottom. She actually believed in her signs and banners, and there had been one or two moments, in courthouses or in sad crowded places such as this, when I understood from the set of her eyes that she recognized that I knew it—and that I respected her for it. As for what she thought of me, I couldn't say, yet she often sought me out in those same places when she might have talked to someone more useful. She might then prolong the conversation unnecessarily, telling me she didn't believe I meant what I'd just said, giving me the benefit of the doubt in an act of secular faith I frequently didn't deserve.

"How'd you end up on this one, Bea?" I asked her now. "The huddled masses don't pay?"

"Oh, they pay all right. But they don't pay money, and they don't pay me."

"This one'll pay," I said, cocking my head at Odom in his new suit. He was cavorting onstage, posing with admirers, giving out both high fives and low. "One hundred fifty-five mill—isn't that what you're looking for?"

She shrugged, maybe a little uncomfortable with the idea. Money may not have been her thing, but it was the blood of her enemy and Bea Katzenbach was a zealot in the service of her own nature. She leaned in. I smelled powder or hand cream, which seemed unlikely—the smell of a grandmother's bathroom, upstairs. "I'll take an even ten, but you didn't hear that from me."

"Ten million buys a lot of Molotov cocktails, Bea."

"That it does, that it does."

"Odom get any of it?"

She gave a pained smile, the creases bunching up around her mouth, ruining her line of lipstick. "Laugh it up, Will Way. You won't think it's so funny when I come after you. Well, Garrity won't anyway. But then he wouldn't, would he?"

"He's a true believer."

"In the wrong things," she said. "You on the other hand might think it's funny. Maybe that's why I like you a little."

"Why's that?"

"Because you don't give a damn."

"What don't I give a damn about, counselor?"

"Anything."

"That's not true, Bea."

"About none of this you don't," she said, making a gesture that took in the whole cafeteria and everyone in it. "What you do give a damn about is anybody's guess. Maybe you don't even know yourself, Will. Or maybe you just forgot."

I must have made a face that showed I wasn't very amused, because she looked at me with eyes gone hard beneath her gray-blond hair cut into a bowl. She said, "But that's right. I named the PBA as a defendant, too—you didn't hear that yet?"

"No."

"I'd like to say it's just business, Will, but it's not."

"Oh, this is personal?" I asked.

"Yes. Yes, it is," she said. "And a couple years from now Shawn Garrity's gonna write me a check to prove it. And Mayor Desmond's gonna write me a bigger check. And that's going to be a good day, Will Way."

I thought it over, realizing that for the first time Bea Katzenbach and I might actually be having a conversation and no longer playing our joyless little game. "It's just money, Bea," I said as coldly as I could manage. "Just dollars and cents. Won't change a damn thing, and what's more you know it won't."

She considered what I told her, then—more seriously than I'd ever heard her speak to me—she said, "I don't make the rules, Will. I can't burn their houses down or put them up against the wall, even though the bastards deserve it." She shifted heavily on her feet. "But I can take their money. The rules say I can take their money when they lose. And they lost, and by God I'm gonna take their money. And yours, too, don't forget that."

"It's not my money, Bea," I said, looking away. "Or theirs. You just have your hand out, like everyone else. You can take their money and call it justice, but do me a favor and don't pretend to me of all people."

I wasn't telling her anything she didn't already know, and if it broke her heart she didn't let on. "So what's justice, then?" she asked as if she didn't care about my answer.

"I only know what it isn't, and this isn't," I said. "What should I tell Garrity when he stops sobbing?"

"Tell him to pay me."

"Why the hell should he?"

"Because, Will Way, my dear old friend, you tried to throw a blanket over this. And if I thought it would mean anything to you, I'd tell you to go to hell for that. And I'm not talking about Garrity or the union now. I'm talking about you."

"Me, huh?"

"Yes. Because of all of them down on Fulton Street you were the only one that knew better. This was the one when you should've stood up, Will. And you didn't. You sat down."

She left. I watched her go.

TWENTY-TWO

Betty Moon was already on the attack by the time I returned to headquarters. Garrity was doing his best, but she was giving no quarter. Holding the telephone an inch from his ear, as if it was a steam iron, the expected pieties were flowing out of him but I saw it was only a matter of time. Already his broad forehead was dewy and pale and soon the whole marble façade would crumble away to reveal the rough brick and mortar beneath, which was Shawn Garrity. He was not cut out for Georgina Reed. Garrity could only be the cop when the cop was the good guy, which meant he'd missed his moment by three or four generations.

He should tend bar, I once told him. Irishmen are only useful pouring drinks, pounding a beat, or saying Mass. We have a way with drunks, criminals, and God. Garrity had been an okay patrolman by all accounts, but he would have made a lousy priest; he took sin far too seriously. That left tending bar. I'd offered him this career advice gratis late one evening when he was sitting with his size fourteens on the desktop. Neither of us with anywhere to go, he was musing on some shindy with one city agency or another, nothing involving us. *They should do this*, he was saying, *and they should do that*. Shawn Garrity had a saloonkeeper's ability to find the safe middle ground, to make senseless people see sense and with a few words have them shaking hands and singing "I'll Tell Me Ma." "When this union gig plays out, Shawn," I said to him then, "maybe you got a cousin can set you up behind the stick?" He waved the thought away and kept talking, but I'd already stopped listening. Unlike Garrity, I couldn't work up any genuine interest in anything not affecting me directly, which in those days was hardly anything.

Garrity was a politician, after all. He was one of them, or he wanted to be. He was going places. He had a secret idea of himself, I knew. To his credit Garrity did the work, but to him it was always more important that he be seen doing it. And he was good at it, bless him. Part of his particular genius as a politician was pretending he wasn't. Wearing his one suit he'd dismiss the mayor and the commissioner and the DA as the suits. At precinct meet-and-greets he would wade right in, pressing his fleshy palm onto blue backs like he was still one of the men, telling them how he'd make the suits dance, laughing his big laugh, swapping lies about knocking heads back in the day. They loved him for it. And he loved them back. No matter what else he was, no matter what else he would do, Shawn Garrity was unquestioningly loyal to his men. Whether you were trying to take away their cost-of-living adjustments or put them in jail, there he would be, immovable as a donkey, braying no. You might dismiss it as a benign form of stupidity, this mindless loyalty to the idea of the job, but there were times when it was strangely comforting just to get behind the tribe and say to hell with all the rest. Yet sometimes I thought Garrity's devotion to his men was too conjectural a thing, as if his men were idealized and faceless to him, clearer in the abstract than in the particular. With Garrity there was always that—the miles between the men and the man.

Standing now in his doorway, I felt his eyes come out to me imploringly. Georgina Reed was killing him, you could tell, eating him from the inside out. His eyes were ringed and he slumped visibly, even seated. The words came automatically now. Drop in a quarter and you got *Stand by our men* and *The grand jury has spoken* and *Inappropriate for me to speculate* et cetera. I'd heard it all before, and so had Moon and she wasn't having it. Her teeth were on his ankle and she wasn't letting go. At last I took the telephone from his hand. He didn't protest. It was slippery.

"Find your keys?" I said. "Oh, that's her name—No, I didn't—Tell her I don't watch CNN—Tell her I don't even have a television." Garrity was staring at me. "Listen, you got your statement from Shawn, so off you go, there's a good chap. And run the nice picture of him for a change, not the one where he looks like they're removing his appendix." I set the phone into the cradle and sat on the chair with the uneven leg. Betty was still talking when I hung up. You could hear her voice in the receiver, distant and censorious, until there was nothing. At first Garrity took it out on me, because I was handy. I let him, figuring it was a nice purgative for him. I was a dose of ipecac. He got it all out.

Then he began feeling sorry for himself. "What the hell do they want anyway?" he asked weakly, plaintively. He slumped further into his chair.

"Not money." Bea Katzenbach didn't need the PBA's money. She had New York City on the hook, and New York City was good for it. The city was enough, but it wasn't enough for Katzenbach, I knew. Katzenbach didn't need our money, but she needed us to pay. I waited for Garrity to make some sign that he understood that—he was the politician, after all—but all he did was look lost and sad. He couldn't see the endgame. He was staring at the board and wondering what the hell to do with his pawns.

"They're suing us!" he cried, in laughing disbelief.

"I heard."

"You heard," he said, scoffing. "Now you wanna tell me maybe what I'm supposed to do about it?"

"Pay up."

"Funny," he said. "It's not a joke, Will. You think this is a joke?"

"No."

"Pay up," he said and shot air through his nose. "What'd we do to get sued? Nothing, that's what."

"That's why they're suing us."

"How can they sue us? Tell me that."

"Come on, Shawn," I said. "You think baseball is the national pastime? Fuck that. You should have told Moon something like that, instead of—what did I hear you say? *It's sad that Mr. Odom has chosen to politicize this tragedy—*"

"What the hell's wrong with that?"

"First place, Shawn. This wasn't a tragedy. A tragedy is you end up fucking your mother because you're—"

"Oh—" He winced. "Don't say things like that, Will."

"Sophocles, Shawn—? Anyway, Odom didn't politicize this thing. We did. All the bad guys did, including us. Mostly Fister and Desmond and Gilbert did, but we did, too. Odom's just joining the party a few days late."

Shawn Garrity gave a grunt. "We're not the bad guys, Will. They don't need to tap us—"

"You're not listening, Shawn. It's not about the money."

"Then what's it about?" he asked.

"Say your puppy craps on the living room carpet. You rub her nose in it—"

"That's not how you housebreak a—"

"No," I said. "But it makes you feel better, doesn't it? Katzenbach caught us crapping on the carpet is all. And she's rubbing our noses in it."

His phone jangled noisily, startling him. He looked at it and paled. Four days of Georgina Reed and the man was afraid of his own telephone. He picked up, delicately. "Hello—?" Tommy Janus. Garrity relaxed a little and put him on speaker. Tommy had heard the news. He thought Odom's lawsuit was brilliant, but it pissed him off. He was calling from his Bentley, driving through nameless smokestack New Jersey. His voice kept cutting out. It was annoying. He was laughing and the expletives dropped like meteorites. Katzenbach was a cunt, he said. She was a fat castrating hippie cunt, and Ouellette was a schwartze whoremaster. Ouellette banged paralegals and cocktail waitresses; they were always laying bastards on his doorstep, the satyr. The altar boy in Garrity winced, but Tommy Janus made him feel better than I did. Not once did Tommy Janus suggest we pay up.

Janus was talking about a motion he wanted to make. He wanted to ask Pomeroy to dismiss the indictment against Georgina Reed. "That's ridiculous," Garrity said. He was looking at me like it was my idea. "Pomeroy's no dope, Tommy. You try to get cute and—"

"Maybe he'll go for it, who can say?" Tommy said. "This thing's gotten all political all of a sudden and maybe Pomeroy's looking to throw some piss water on Whitey Fister for the primary, who knows? Pomeroy's gonna make a run for DA this fall, you know."

"That's just talk," Garrity said. "Pomeroy don't wanna be DA."

"How d'you know he don't? You got a hook in there?" Tommy Janus asked. "I mean, I know you know the man, but d'you know him like you know him?" Garrity's eyes flashed over me. "There's been some moaning about that, you know," Janus went on. "About Pomeroy on the Georgina case, I mean. With him having been at One PP and all, and now wanting Fister's job on top of it." In fact, there had been a single article in this morning's *Post*, the only city paper that leaned unapologetically to Whitey Fister. The article now lay open before Garrity on his desk, and from my teetering chair I saw Pomeroy's face staring back at me from an oblique angle, an older photograph, a Pomeroy without white hair. He had been a deputy police commissioner before he took the bench as a justice in Brooklyn Supreme, but that had been years ago when I wasn't paying attention. Along the way up Pomeroy had acquired a few friends, but that's no sin. In New York it helps to have friends. I had a few myself, and one of them was Justice Henry K. Pomeroy.

"I know him, sure," Garrity said, "but I got no sway there—other way around, if anything." Again, Garrity's cool gaze passed over me, this time with an expression on his face I didn't like. For the first time since this thing began Garrity seemed to recollect my connection to Pomeroy. How much he remembered I couldn't say, but certainly Shawn Garrity still recalled it had been Pomeroy on the other end of the telephone four years earlier recommending a certain bright young patrolman for a job. Certainly Garrity then wondered why the chief justice of the Kings County Supreme Court would take an interest in an obscure patrolman, no matter how bright and young he may have been. Garrity would've known better than to ask a lot of questions, however, understanding a recommendation from Pomeroy was not just a recommendation.

Later, however, I told Garrity myself. And I told him about a domestic call I'd taken at a certain two-story brick semidetached on Eldert Street when I worked patrol in Bushwick. I told him about a white woman with red lipstick and a man named Pie whose face I broke. I'd gone to Pomeroy, I told Garrity, because I had nowhere else to go, believing the next knock on my door would be IAB. And when Garrity asked in a mock-casual tone of voice how I knew Pomeroy to begin with I told him that, too. I didn't tell him everything, of course, but I told him enough. Garrity filed it all away.

"I'm not afraid of Pomeroy," Tommy Janus was saying, meaning he was. "Arrogant prick, everyone's afraid of him. Thinks he's God on the throne, but I'll do it. I'll shove a motion up his ass, make him decide it one way or the other, on the record. I'll make him say the fucking indictment's legit or it ain't."

"What motion?" I said.

"Motion to dismiss the indictment," Janus said. "Ain't you listening, Way? Say the evidence in the grand jury's insufficient. Say this rat bastard Karpatkin couldna seen shit, and the other douchebag—fuck's his name?—Odom lies like a rug."

"Come on, Tommy. No way the court's gonna dismiss," I said, unable to say Pomeroy's name aloud, and Garrity seemed to register that as he looked at me a third time. Now I recognized his expression, an expression I rarely saw on his open face and one never before aimed at me—suspicion or distrust, the look of someone looking at a stranger in the body of a friend. "DA can indict a ham sandwich, Tommy," I continued, "you know that. Anything Kane gave the grand jury's gonna be good enough for the court, particularly a case like this. No way they're gonna toss Kane's indictment. Bumpurs would run riot."

"Crimmins," Janus said. "It's Crimmins's case now. Jackie Kane's out. I got it official."

"What do you mean Kane's out?"

"Gone. Off the Georgina case," he said. "And not for nothing good riddance. She's about as good as they got in the DA."

"Why's she out?" I said.

"My guess? Melanin deficiency."

"Excuse me?"

Janus laughed at me over the phone. "Come on, Way, I thought you were the brains in that outfit. I mean, you didn't never notice? Jackie Kane's white as rice. But Monty Crimmins? Well, what can I say? The brother's even got dreadlocks."

Garrity immediately said, "Get outa town, Tommy."

"Get out nothing, this is Brooklyn we're talking about, Shawn," said Tommy Janus, laughing at us both now through the speaker. "You got your archbishop there, Bumpurs, he don't like Jackie on it, and if Bumpurs don't like it then Fister don't like it, not in an election year he don't. But Pomeroy's a closet racist, they say, so it all evens out. That's Brooklyn for you right there. You don't like me, I don't like you, but since we're both in agreement we get along just fine."

After Garrity left, I stayed. The Saturday afternoon atmosphere at 40 Fulton Street was heavy yet desolate, the deserted fortress of a defeated army. A few people were around, and they all knew about the lawsuit. On someone's television set I saw myself in the background of the press conference in Bed-Stuy. There I was standing against the cafeteria wall. All I needed was a blindfold and cigarette. *Vive la France!* We had already lost, or that's how it felt. In the empty hallways were some angry noises of disbelief, but close to the surface was a tacit understanding that Georgina Reed was our man so we collectively shared her guilt. We were guilty. I was guilty. There was Bea Katzenbach, of course, but I'd told myself the same thing even before she cast the verdict into words. All she'd done was save me the effort.

I had other business, of course, other work to keep me busy. Men in uniform were still punching people on their noses, getting drunk, urinating on geraniums. In other words cops kept doing things everyone else did, except everyone else wasn't a cop. And everyone else didn't have Will Way, Jr., standing by with a bucket and mop. So for a deluded moment that Saturday I played house, pretending to do the sort of nonsense I used to do before Georgina Reed. Sheila Simmons had piled three days of it neatly on the corner of my desk, complete with notes and recommendations taped to each file in her neat handwriting. I blessed her silently and had a look at some of it. But it was just work. I did it, knowing all the while I was not yet done with Georgina Reed.

The telephone rang and punctured the solitary quiet of my office. By then it was after five, and I was sitting with the overhead lights off. Through my window twilight blushed the city pink for our sins. "PBA," I answered anonymously.

"Way, Christ," said the efficient, no-frills voice of Detective Mark Masterson. "I've been sitting here waiting for you all day already."

"Sorry, partner. Some shit went down."

"Yeah, I saw you on the TV," he said. "Didn't look too happy in the cathedral there."

"Brick fell on my head."

He told me to meet him at headquarters and hung up without saying goodbye. I sat for a while longer in the soft light of evening wondering what the hell. We always did our thing at Carmine's, never at Hudson Street, so now I started concocting wild scenarios featuring me in handcuffs. In the end I went anyway, accepting it was a thing I had to do. I always went when he called and always took what he gave, often not even picking up the check, knowing Masterson wasn't doing me any favors. Masterson was a cop. Masterson had always been a cop and came from a cop family, a genuine blue blood. I never asked why he left patrol, or why he tipped me, but I suppose even Internal Affairs wasn't cop enough for Mark Masterson. He wanted to be a supercop, not satisfied merely to police the police. He wanted to watch the watchers.

I walked to IAB headquarters, across lower Manhattan and up Hudson Street, more than a mile in the cool evening air. I didn't mind, and by the time I arrived I'd shaken the feeling of foreboding. Resuming my hard wooden seat in reception where I'd sat Thursday morning with Holtz I began to feel oddly ambivalent about everything. I'd accustomed myself to having lost, I suppose, and the idea didn't hurt—it was rock bottom, but rock bottom was the only place you could relax around here, so I relaxed. I nearly resented Masterson trying to slap me out of it, pulling me to my feet, pouring black coffee down my throat, pushing me fully clothed into an ice-cold shower.

The polite PAA was not here, and I kept waiting for Detective Ed to kick me out again. I would have gone meekly. Those few who passed barely gave me a glance. On his way out the door one said, "Oh, hullo, Way," in a polite if not actually cheerful tone of voice. To him I was not a monkey but a robin, prefiguring a springtime return to business as usual after a brief, violent winter. *Why, here's good old Will Way*, his face suggested, *come to plead for some flatfoot caught peeing on the geraniums, ha ha.* While I waited for Masterson I thought of things cops used to do to get in trouble, purely nostalgic thoughts of bygone days, like the fear of nuclear war.

Masterson at last reckoned I'd waited long enough for our business to seem like business and sent a PAA to fetch me, a black kid about twenty-five years old who wore thick eyeglasses and an unkempt asymmetrical afro. He looked like the smart kid in class, like the treasurer of the chess club. He led me to Masterson, who neither stood nor shut his door. When he spoke his voice was all business, and I nearly laughed when he put a large envelope in my hand.

TWENTY-THREE

Afterward I walked magnetically in the direction of the nameless saloon on Spring Street where we had toasted Masterson in February after he took his step. The city was dark as the city ever is, office lights of windows sixty stories overhead the only stars available to wish upon. By now my mood was even harder to diagnose. Elation and dread, I decided, supposing that Masterson's envelope contained the answer to everything, and I wanted to know as much as I didn't. Either way I knew it would hurt. Inside I took a stool but didn't drink, instead thinking of a time not so very long ago when we'd sat in a marked patrol car, just Masterson and me, the world black around us, our faces lit only by the dashboard and the orange vapor lights we slowly passed beneath, one after the other, through Bushwick. I knew I'd still follow him through a door or into an unlit stairwell when we heard the smash of gunfire and he said let's go.

I tore open the envelope.

> INSP. DANILOV: Okay. The time is now 10:31 in the P.M. My name is Inspector Sheldon Danilov of the Internal Affairs Bureau, N.Y.P.D. We are present in the Eight-three precinct stationhouse. With me are Detective Mario Grimaldi of Brooklyn North Homicide, and Assistant District Attorney Jacqueline Kane of the Kings County District Attorney's Office. Also present is Police Officer--state your name please.
>
> P.O. KARPATKIN: Kevin Karpatkin.
>
> INSP. DANILOV: Spell it.
>
> P.O. KARPATKIN: K-A-R-P-A-T-K-I-N.
>
> INSP. DANILOV: State your shield and command, Officer.
>
> P.O. KARPATKIN: Eight-three patrol. Shield 8-4-6-2-7.

INSP. DANILOV: We are investigating a line-of-duty
shooting incident that occurred earlier this evening
within the confines of the Eight-three precinct Bushwick.

MS. KANE: Will you swear him, please?

INSP. DANILOV: Oh, yes. Officer Kilpatrick, do you
swear to--

P.O. KARPATKIN: Karpatkin. I'm sorry.

INSP. DANILOV: Don't be sorry. I beg your
pardon. Officer Karpatkin. I'm sorry. Do you swear
or affirm to tell the whole truth and nothing but
the truth?

P.O. KARPATKIN: I swear.

INSP. DANILOV: We were talking earlier, Officer, and
I think at some point you took a call from central radio.

P.O. KARPATKIN: Yes.

INSP. DANILOV: Who took that call, you or--

P.O. KARPATKIN: Sergeant Berrigan took it, um. I was
the driver. Like I said.

INSP. DANILOV: For the record you're talking about
Sergeant Ralph Berrigan of your command?

P.O. KARPATKIN: Yes.

INSP. DANILOV: Go on. You were his regular driver?

P.O. KARPATKIN: I was his regular driver.

INSP. DANILOV: For how long?

P.O. KARPATKIN: Excuse me?

INSP. DANILOV: How long had you been assigned to
Sergeant Berrigan as his regular driver?

P.O. KARPATKIN: Maybe like a month.

INSP. DANILOV: So that was right out of the academy?

P.O. KARPATKIN: No. I had, um. There was a problem I
had with the, other, ah--and Sergeant Berrigan thought I
should drive with him for a while and see how it goes.

INSP. DANILOV: What problem?

P.O. KARPATKIN: No, nothing. Just a personal thing.

INSP. DANILOV: Okay.

P.O. KARPATKIN: So Sergeant Berrigan thought it was a
good idea.

INSP. DANILOV: Okay. We were talking before about what happened earlier tonight. You got a call. Start there.

P.O. KARPATKIN: We got two calls real quick. The first was a robbery. A 10-30 robbery on, ah, Gates.

INSP. DANILOV: Gates and what?

P.O. KARPATKIN: Let me check. Gates and Broadway.

INSP. DANILOV: You're looking at your memo book?

P.O. KARPATKIN: Yes, sir.

INSP. DANILOV: I'm going to need a copy of that.

P.O. KARPATKIN: Yes, sir.

INSP. DANILOV: What was the second call?

P.O. KARPATKIN: Like right away. Maybe three, four minutes after.

INSP. DANILOV: I asked you what, not when.

P.O. KARPATKIN: I'm sorry. The second was a 10-85, officer needs assistance.

INSP. DANILOV: Was that over central or--

P.O. KARPATKIN: Yes. No. It was point to point. I recognized her voice. It was Officer Reed. She's in my platoon. We do four-by-twelves.

INSP. DANILOV: That's Police Officer Georgina Reed?

P.O. KARPATKIN: Yes.

INSP. DANILOV: Go on.

P.O. KARPATKIN: She gave a location. She and her regular partner were patrolling sector Boy. She gave a location. Which was where the, ah, the incident was, and Bear, Sergeant Berrigan instructed me to drive there and I did.

INSP. DANILOV: That was where?

P.O. KARPATKIN: Putnam. Corner of Putnam and Broadway.

INSP. DANILOV: How long did it take to get there?

P.O. KARPATKIN: Like, nothing. It was right there. Like a minute maybe.

INSP. DANILOV: What did you see when you arrived?

P.O. KARPATKIN: There was two officers. It was Officer Reed and her regular partner. Holtz, I think.

Yes. And there was two perps. One was down but I didn't
see him until I got closer. The other Officer Holtz
already had under. He was by the fence.

INSP. DANILOV: You saw Officer Reed?

P.O. KARPATKIN: Yes. I saw her.

INSP. DANILOV: Tell me what you saw.

P.O. KARPATKIN: She was there. What do you mean?

INSP. DANILOV: What was she doing?

P.O. KARPATKIN: Nothing, really. She was there.

INSP. DANILOV: What happened when you arrived?

P.O. KARPATKIN: We got out the RMP.

INSP. DANILOV: And then what?

P.O. KARPATKIN: We went over and Officer Holtz
informed Sergeant Berrigan what had occurred.

INSP. DANILOV: What did he say?

P.O. KARPATKIN: Basically she was in the process of
subduing the perp and he reached for a weapon. And she
shot him. Once.

INSP. DANILOV: You heard Officer Reed say that?

P.O. KARPATKIN: The sergeant told me after.

INSP. DANILOV: What did Officer Reed say? What did
you hear her say yourself?

P.O. KARPATKIN: She wasn't really talking to me or
nobody. Not at that time. She was kind of out of it.

INSP. DANILOV: What do you mean out of it?

P.O. KARPATKIN: Upset. She was real upset.

INSP. DANILOV: Then what happened?

P.O. KARPATKIN: Sergeant Berrigan went to her. He
took her service weapon out of her hand. Because she was
still holding it.

INSP. DANILOV: She was still holding her pistol?

P.O. KARPATKIN: Yes. And Sergeant Berrigan took
it and told her to sit. So she sat on the curb for a
minute.

INSP. DANILOV: Did she say anything at that time?

P.O. KARPATKIN: Not that I could hear. She was
talking to my sergeant. I would say she was very upset.

Like crying. He was trying to get her to like calm down,
I guess. He had an arm around her. Like a hug kind of.

INSP. DANILOV: Don't guess. Go on.

P.O. KARPATKIN: Sergeant Berrigan put Officer Reed in
the car and instructed me to notify central that there
was a line-of-duty shooting.

INSP. DANILOV: There was a victim on the ground?
Let's talk about him.

P.O. KARPATKIN: Yes. I saw him when I came over. He
was dead.

INSP. DANILOV: Did you call an ambulance?

P.O. KARPATKIN: He was dead.

INSP. DANILOV: I'm asking did you radio for a bus?

P.O. KARPATKIN: I didn't. Someone must of, though,
because there was an ambulance that came.

INSP. DANILOV: When?

P.O. KARPATKIN: I can't say. They said he was dead,
too. Anyway everyone started coming right then. It was a
busy scene. Everyone mobilized.

INSP. DANILOV: Did you make any observations of the
victim on the ground?

P.O. KARPATKIN: I'm sorry?

INSP. DANILOV: Did you go over to the man who
was down?

P.O. KARPATKIN: Oh, yes.

INSP. DANILOV: What did you do?

P.O. KARPATKIN: Sergeant Berrigan ordered me to
handcuff him.

INSP. DANILOV: Handcuff him?

P.O. KARPATKIN: Yes, sir.

INSP. DANILOV: He was dead, you said.

P.O. KARPATKIN: Procedure, sir.

INSP. DANILOV: And did you?

P.O. KARPATKIN: No, sir. He was too heavy. I told
Sergeant Berrigan he was too heavy to move and I needed
help. And that I believed he was dead anyway.

INSP. DANILOV: Did your sergeant do or say anything?

P.O. KARPATKIN: I can't remember.

INSP. DANILOV: I wanted to ask you. Did you notice anything else about the victim on the ground?

P.O. KARPATKIN: Such as?

INSP. DANILOV: We were talking before and you mentioned a gun.

P.O. KARPATKIN: Yes. He had a gun.

INSP. DANILOV: The man on the ground had a gun?

P.O. KARPATKIN: Yes.

INSP. DANILOV: In his hand or what?

P.O. KARPATKIN: No, it was under him.

INSP. DANILOV: You saw this?

P.O. KARPATKIN: I saw the gun.

INSP. DANILOV: You said it was his gun but it wasn't in his hand.

P.O. KARPATKIN: No.

INSP. DANILOV: So why do you say it was his gun?

P.O. KARPATKIN: I--I think you asked me did I see the gun and I said I saw it.

INSP. DANILOV: I asked you. Wait. Now I'm asking you how you know it was his gun?

P.O. KARPATKIN: Because he told me.

INSP. DANILOV: Who told you?

P.O. KARPATKIN: My sergeant.

INSP. DANILOV: He told you the gun was under the man on the floor?

P.O. KARPATKIN: That's correct, sir.

INSP. DANILOV: What's correct, that you saw it or that he told you?

P.O. KARPATKIN: My sergeant showed me. I saw it.

INSP. DANILOV: You said it was under him, but you said the man on the floor was too heavy to move so I'm asking you when did you see it?

P.O. KARPATKIN: It was after Sergeant Berrigan rolled him.

INSP. DANILOV: Sergeant Berrigan rolled him over?

P.O. KARPATKIN: Yes, sir.

INSP. DANILOV: And that's when you saw the gun?

P.O. KARPATKIN: That's where Sergeant Berrigan recovered the gun. Under the gentleman on the floor.

INSP. DANILOV: Again, did you actually--did you observe Sergeant Berrigan roll the victim?

P.O. KARPATKIN: I--I was present at the scene.

INSP. DANILOV: And you saw the gun?

P.O. KARPATKIN: I saw the gun. Sergeant Berrigan showed me.

INSP. DANILOV: Can you describe it for me?

P.O. KARPATKIN: Handgun.

INSP. DANILOV: Was it a revolver or a pistol?

P.O. KARPATKIN: That I--I think it was a black revolver. Small caliber. Sergeant Berrigan vouchered it. I didn't.

INSP. DANILOV: Is that all you remember?

P.O. KARPATKIN: Yes, sir. For now.

INSP. DANILOV: I don't understand. Are you planning to remember more later?

P.O. KARPATKIN: Sir?

INSP. DANILOV: Do you have anything more to add at this time?

P.O. KARPATKIN: Only I'm sure the victim on the ground was not breathing when I saw him. If that's what you're asking me.

INSP. DANILOV: Okay, that will be all. Thank you, Officer Kirkpatrick.

P.O. KARPATKIN: Karpatkin. I'm sorry.

INSP. DANILOV: Karpatkin, okay, my apologies. I'm going to ask you not to discuss your statement with anyone. That includes police, press, or anyone representing the police union, okay? Thank you. The time is now 10:44. This concludes this interview of Police Officer Kevin Karpatkin.

Masterson had given me IAB's first run at Police Officer Kevin Karpatkin on the night of. It was like opening a Christmas present and getting socks.

"So he lied," I said aloud in the saloon. "Big fucking deal."

Karpatkin had lied, of course. Tuesday night when I was downstairs in the Eight-three basement with Georgina Reed, Kevin Karpatkin was upstairs in the muster room with Danilov and Kane, telling them a story to back a brother cop. Twenty-four hours later he would put down his cheese sandwich and become a hero. Twenty-four hours later he would say he hadn't seen a gun until he did. I supposed that Masterson wanted me to read Karpatkin's interview because he thought I should know, probably because it would be important to lawyers that Karpatkin had backed Georgina off the bat. And while I had sense enough to realize that, of course, I wasn't reading Karpatkin's interview transcript as a lawyer but as a different form of life. The way I read it, Tuesday night Karpatkin did the right thing and lied, but Wednesday night he did the right thing and told the truth.

I showed the transcript to Shawn Garrity on Monday morning. I sat on it all day Sunday. I might've driven it to Staten Island and caught him on the way to Mass, of course, or just left it on his doorstep with the papers, but I didn't. I was still thinking about the expression on his face when we were talking about Pomeroy. That was the beginning of the long goodbye, I knew, the slow-motion dissolution of something into nothing. I had seen it before in my wife and recognized it now in Garrity.

Monday I set it on his desk. He didn't ask where I got it. He knew better. For a minute at least after he read it he seemed lost in contemplation of a ferry progressing up the gray-brown East River far below, like a beetle on the sidewalk, and I thought we were done. When I was already at his door, however, he said, still looking out the window, "This information will come out, you think?"

"You mean if we don't bring it out?"

"Or the DA doesn't," he said, turning in his chair to face me.

"And we don't want it out, Shawn?"

"Either way you read this, we don't look too good, do we?" he said. "I mean, we got a patrolman tells a lie to back Georgina. Next day he rats her. Doesn't look good, I think."

I remained in the doorway. "What hurts Karpatkin helps Georgina."

"I'm not talking about him," he said. "I'm thinking of the—of the overall picture, Will. My duty is the overall picture, not a single patrolman."

"I thought we were supposed to back our man."

"They're both our men."

"Not for long," I said.

"I'm asking what happens if the DA doesn't disclose this?"

"They have to."

"But what if they don't?" he asked, insistent.

"If the DA hides it, well—" I said "—well, they're fucked."

"Why?"

"Because they have to turn it over, one hundred percent," I say. "Karpatkin's a prosecution witness, Shawn, no matter what else he is, and the law says the DA has to disclose witness statements to the defense. Also, you ask me it's *Brady* material—"

"Which is?"

"Evidence Tommy can use to cross Karpatkin at trial. Impeach his credibility with the jury."

"How does he do that with this?" Garrity asked.

"You know, *Were you lying then, Officer, or are you lying now?*"

"But he's telling the truth now, Will," Garrity said. "Isn't that the point?"

"Doesn't matter, isn't that what Tommy said? Trials aren't about the truth. They're about what the DA can prove."

"What's this prove?"

"Karpatkin's a liar," I said. "It proves he went along with the flake and kept his mouth shut until he could get something out of saying different. Tommy could take the shine off his halo. It's all good, clean fun, of course, but come to think of it maybe it's better for Georgina if the DA sits on it."

"Explain."

"The DA follows the law and discloses it to Tommy, which they have to, like today? Fine, the DA takes a few lumps, but I think they can explain it away. Sure, both Georgina and Karpatkin come off bad, but Georgina's the one on trial," I told him, thinking aloud. I shut his door and moved to a chair, the one with the short leg. "But the DA pretends this thing doesn't exist, throw it down a memory hole? And then Georgina blows trial? This thing's a get-out-of-jail-free card. No question. Appellate court will reverse her conviction on a *Brady* violation before Georgina even gets on the bus to Attica."

"So what do we do with this?" he said after a moment. Everything seemed very quiet.

"You're asking my advice, Shawn?"

"Yes."

"Wait for the DA," I said. "Under the United States Supreme Court's landmark decision in *Brady v. Maryland* the Brooklyn district attorney has a clear and unequivocal legal obligation to disclose this transcript immediately to the defense. Therefore they won't."

He thought about it. "I want to run this by Tommy."

"No."

"Hell not?"

"I don't trust Tommy Janus to wait. I don't trust Tommy Janus period."

"Tommy's Georgina's lawyer."

"Shawn, listen," I said. "We don't lose anything by waiting, and besides, I didn't find this thing in a box of Cracker Jack, okay? This comes out in the open before I know everything's copacetic with my people, some of them could get burned."

He nodded, and certainly he understood. Yet if he didn't pass Karpatkin's interview transcript to Tommy Janus that same Monday, he certainly did by Tuesday. And by Wednesday I was off the case.

JACKIE KANE

TWENTY-FOUR

The frosted glass door read HOMICIDE BUREAU. Jackie Kane's office was on the fourth floor of the district attorney's office on Joralemon Street in downtown Brooklyn. She wasn't in, the detective on the desk told me. "Over in Supreme. Courtroom, ah—seven-one-eight," he said after painstakingly running a cracked yellow fingernail down a clipboard, following the finger's slow progress through reading glasses set low on a broken nose. I could wait, he offered. So I waited. It was just the two of us. In the quiet he paged deliberately through a *Better Homes & Gardens*, not reading it, just looking at pictures of homes and gardens. He was one of that sad-eyed, used-up variety of civil servant, government surplus. Either I could start a conversation or leave. I left.

I had no reason to be here, or no official reason anyway since Garrity had pulled me off the case a month earlier. Under torture Garrity might confess he didn't blame me for the shitshow Georgina had become, but he blamed me nonetheless. He framed it in a way to preserve my dignity, saying simply that he didn't want "the union messing around in this Georgina business no more, so why don't we just let Tommy run with it, you know, it's in the courts now anyway," et cetera, but we both knew what it was. I didn't complain.

On Joralemon again, in front of the Municipal Building, a gypsy cab let out a bride and groom. She was fat and comely, like an operatic soprano. He was a stick. His beard looked like someone had drawn it onto his sunken cheeks with a marker. Strangers clapped and cheered, then the couple went inside, the same romantic setting where MK and I had signed our papers. A few years later we signed different papers, and that was the end of that.

I crossed Joralemon Street in a sudden dark spirit of mind, making traffic stop, to a concrete square in front of Brooklyn Supreme where a growing but still largely diffident number of Free Georgina! adherents had organized a torpid little counterprotest a hundred feet or so from the familiar congregants from Archbishop Bumpurs's cathedral. With the exception of their lapel ribbons— yellow for Free Georgina! and black for the Babes—the two factions were indistinguishable. They dressed the same, looked the same, and both carried the same placards demanding the same things: TRUTH! and JUSTICE! and NO MORE LIES!

Inside the lobby of Supreme a hundred people were lined up before the metal detectors, making a trail of humanity that stood and moved and talked and smelled and dressed as only they might in Brooklyn, New York. My turn, and the court officer gestured me forward. His face said that he'd had just about enough emptying pockets into plastic trays and running his wand over groins and crucifix arms, tired of feeling strangers' asses through polyester pants. I walked through the rectangular frame with the same faint sensation of foreboding I always had playing Operation in Sally Joyce's basement, angling the forceps toward the broken heart or charley horse, knowing the buzzer would buzz but believing I was safe the very moment before it did. *Buzz.* The court officer raised his chin at me, *You know the drill, buddy,* and I guessed it was the cheap alloy of my Li'l Sheriff Kit toy badge. I showed him, and he gave me all due respect.

Assistant District Attorney Jacqueline Kane was sitting in an uncrowded courtroom gallery upstairs. I slid into the row behind her. In the well, two lawyers were busy pissing each other wet. I guessed the judge was doing her civil calendar because there was no one sitting handcuffed at the defense table, no one in a beige DOC jumpsuit looking lost. Instead there was only a guy in a yarmulke taking notes. That went on for another ten very long minutes and at one point Kane faced around to the clock on the rear wall, but she didn't notice me. The expression on her face showed weary indifference, but it was a good face—clean and honest, a soap commercial, like an idea of America I once had. When the judge could take no more she sent the lawyers out, but afterward you could hear them going at it in the hallway, bawling like fishwives. Some personal injury thing. The plaintiff had tripped on her landlord's stoop, Wrublewicz said, and now she had irreparable injuries. She was scarred for life. She was traumatized and could never work again, but she would settle for low five figures nonetheless.

In my row sat an old woman of forty-three, holding a worn testament with the BABE crest gilded on the leatherette cover, patiently waiting for her son Rufus the double-murderer. Jacqueline Kane was waiting for the same guy, but not to blow him a kiss. I touched Kane lightly on the shoulder. She turned and looked first at the woman. I spoke her name and her eyebrows lifted in mild surprise, like birds I drew in kindergarten on construction paper. Jackie Kane had strawberry-blond hair and green watercolor eyes and up close I saw she was smaller and more delicate than I had realized. She recognized me, of course. *I know who he is,* she told Betty Moon.

"Talk?" I whispered, and Kane gestured with her head toward the bench without removing her suddenly interested eyes from me. The gesture meant she had to wait, but it was not the fuck-off I expected. She faced forward again. The clerk called another case and two new lawyers came forward and for twenty minutes it was a rerun of the same bad movie we'd just seen. Meanwhile Kane seemed unable to forget I was behind her, for her posture remained uncomfortably perfect, or so I thought. At 12:50 the judge told everyone to return at 2:15 and walked off the bench. Jackie Kane said "Jesus H. Christ" audibly and left without a backward glance, yet there she stood in the hallway when I followed.

"No," Kane was saying to the woman. "Your son's lawyer didn't show up. So they're going to call his case at two fifteen."

"Two fifteen—?" said the woman in an island accent, her expression lost and mournful, a black ribbon pinned to the lapel of her purple churchgoing pantsuit. "Will anything happen?"

"He is going to be sentenced today, ma'am. That's the plan."

"Sentenced?"

"To prison, yes," Kane said.

"Rufus in prison already. Three years, almost."

"He's in jail, ma'am," Kane said, her eyes registering that I stood not ten feet away. "He was convicted last month. On both murders. Today the judge is going to sentence him to upstate prison."

"But he don't do nothing. He promise me he don't."

"You should talk to his lawyer, ma'am," Kane said.

"When will they be letting him out to come home?"

"I don't know, ma'am."

"God bless you, lady," the woman said wearily, turning away. Nearly at the elevator bank she said, to no one in particular, "Rufus lawyer not very good, I think."

"Neither was Rufus," I said to Kane when we were alone. She was tall and didn't apologize for it, wearing shoes that nearly let her look me in the eye.

"What do you want?" she said to me, her voice cool, her expression a few degrees warmer. She was older than me, but so is everyone. Her hair was unremarkable except for the color, which was really very beautiful. Her skin was pale and lightly freckled and she had very long unmade-up eyelashes. Instinctively I wanted to see whether she had a ring. Her left hand, however, was obscured behind a big accordion file resting on her hip, which had only a slight outward curve to it as Jackie Kane was pretty much straight up and down.

I put out a hand. "Will Way," I told her unnecessarily.

"I know." *I know who he is.*

"I'm the PBA trustee for Brooklyn North."

"We met."

"Sort of, I guess." My hand was still hovering out there, defying gravity like a cartoon coyote that doesn't realize it's run off a cliff. She let it linger there a second more, then she took it with long, slim fingers as air-conditioned as her voice. "ADA Kane," she said, "but I suppose you know that already. Don't you, Officer Way?"

"Will." I nodded and smiled involuntarily. She was talking to someone other than me, to someone she thought I was and probably was to some extent. I said, "Should I call you ADA Kane or will just ADA do?"

She relaxed a little and said, "Jacqueline."

Jacqueline, I thought and gave a single nod. A start. I figured she didn't like me because she wasn't supposed to like me, but if that was the only reason I could live with it. "In that case, Jacqueline, I take back what I said before. You can call me William." I knew that I was smiling a little and I didn't know how that would translate with my new friend Jacqueline—probably not well, I decided, but it was really beyond my control. I wasn't playing with her.

"So, William Way of the PBA," she said with something like a sigh. "What can I do for you?"

"You know I was wondering that myself just now."

"I don't get it."

"Yeah. Funny, right?" I said. "I mean, wouldn't it be crazy if we managed to help each other out? You and me, I mean."

She was astonished and didn't try to hide it. "Why in hell would I want to help you?"

"Because—I don't know, Jacqueline—" I started. "Because—because I thought you might give an actual fuck, you know?"

Georgina was no longer hers either, I knew. The popular idea that Brooklyn DA Whitey Fister had swapped Kane for Crimmins, white for black, seemed plausible enough, predictable even, yet I didn't buy it. Something told me there was more there. I believed she'd quit the case, and I wanted to know why. Like me she'd been there from the start. She'd sat with Georgina Reed in the muster room before I stopped her, and of course she'd shaken hands with Kevin Karpatkin before he became a hero. But mostly I recalled the empty expression on her face the following day in Pomeroy's courtroom when she dropped the case against Marlon Odom. *We have insufficient evidence to prove the case against Mr. Odom beyond a reasonable doubt,* she'd said then, which loosely translated from the original bullshit meant someone told her to drop it. I didn't care who or why, since the answer was perfectly irrelevant. All I wanted to know was why Kane didn't like it—and I believed she'd tell me now that we were both sidelined. Irrationally I trusted her. That I knew hardly a thing about Jackie Kane didn't matter. What mattered was she knew all about me. *I know who he is.*

"Give a fuck about what?" she asked.

"About what happened—what really happened out there, and proving it, letting people know the truth. Am I wrong?"

"I know what happened out there, big guy."

"Do you really?" I asked her, certain I was no longer smiling. The question or the sound of my voice seemed to affect her. "Do you really, counselor? Because everyone's out there saying they know, but no one knows. I mean, I don't—not everything, and nothing I can prove anyway—and I bet I have as much on this caper as you."

"Oh, you think?"

"That's right. I'm not as dumb as I sound," I said. I have a south Brooklyn accent you could carve your initials on. She loosened.

"All right—just," she said, sounding exasperated more than angry, "just tell me what you're saying, because I—"

"Just talk, Jacqueline. That's all. Nothing on the record. Just a friendly conversation. I won't hold you to anything." When she seemed unconvinced, I said, "Come on, Jacqueline. Georgina didn't murder no one. What's more, you know it."

"Do I?"

"I think you do," I said. "And I don't think you like how your boss is trying to prove she did. That's what I think you think."

Clairvoyance made her angry, so Jackie Kane fired back, "And I suppose I think Raquan Dewberry was just another shithead who deserved to die."

I winced at the cheap shot but answered, "Don't believe everything you read, counselor. You'll start telling me witches live in gingerbread houses."

I kept waiting for her to walk away. She didn't, but she made a face that shamed me a little because of what was behind it. While the hallway was by now mostly empty, I felt exposed under her gaze. I didn't want to talk about my fifteen minutes of infamy here or anywhere, yet I wanted her to know I'd already acquitted myself of all wrongdoing. "Look," I said. "I never said Dewberry deserved what he got, but—"

"How twentieth century of you."

"—but I'm not gonna let Bumpurs build a shrine to the guy either. Dewberry was—"

"So wait. Let me understand," she said, catching an attitude. "Dewberry didn't deserve what he asked for? Or he asked for something he didn't deserve? I'm confused here."

"Funny," I said, "but why not? I'm always asking for things I don't deserve, Jacqueline. Why else do you think I'm here? Come on. Guy's a fucking mutt. Five minutes before Georgina rolled up he was robbing a bodega with Odom."

"He boosted a bunch of pink azaleas, Way."

"And a Snickers, don't forget," I said. "Not fun-size neither."

"Still not really a capital offense, I thought."

"Yeah, stealing while black, okay, I get it," I said. "I guess in Bushwick they call that grocery shopping."

"You just trying to piss me off?"

"Yes," I answered truthfully. "And not for nothing Dewberry dropped the cashier on his ass. Remember him? Francisco Espinel, right? No one ever talks about Francisco Espinel. Dewberry put him in the hospital unconscious, for chrissake."

"He didn't go to the hospital."

"Not what I heard," I lied.

"Espinel RMA'd at the stationhouse," she said, "so if you—"

"If Espinel went down to the Eight-three, counselor," I said slowly, "the fuck didn't you run a lineup with him? At least get Espinel to ID Odom as a perp?"

"I did, but you're—" she started angrily. Then she stopped and very nearly smiled. "Okay, Way, maybe you're not as dumb as you sound. Okay, sure. Espinel ID'd Odom. A solid lineup hit. So just say it, just say what you wanted to say. No, fuck it. I'll say it for you. Yes, I had a felony case on Odom. And no, I didn't want to drop the charges. Is that why you wanted me angry? That what you wanted me to tell you?"

"No."

"So what the hell do you want me to tell you?"

"Why you didn't," I said.

"Didn't what?"

"Like it."

"Oh, who cares now?" she said, exhaling. "Doesn't change a thing anyway, how I felt about it."

"You sure?"

"It doesn't, okay?" she said. "Maybe then but not now."

"Why not now? They deport Espinel back to Trini or something?"

"No," she told me in a weary voice. "No, he stopped cooperating when he saw what this was. Now he's got a lawsuit against Odom, I heard."

"No shit. Bea Katzenbach?"

"Herman Wrublewicz—?"

"Why sue Odom?" I asked no one.

"Odom's who punched his eye. Gave him a million-dollar mouse."

"Look, counselor," I said. "Georgina's not a murderer, that's all I'm saying here. She shot him because—"

"She shot him because—"

"—because she was scared, Jacqueline," I said. "First she was scared of Dewberry. Then she was scared of you."

"And what's so scary about Dewberry?"

"Seriously?"

"Yes, in fact. Have you ever asked yourself that?" she said. "I mean, if this all went down in Park Slope and Dewberry was just a seventeen-year-old Jewish kid, in any arrangement of the universe would Georgina Reed have shot him dead on a street corner?"

"Of course not, counselor, but nice Jewish boys don't rob bodegas on the way home from violin class," I said. "Nice Jewish boys don't have seven prior arrests or a running buddy with a loaded revolver in his pocket. And when you order nice Jewish boys down they don't give you mouth, so let's not pretend Dewberry's dead because he's black like that's the whole story. I'm talking about a Bushwick street corner here, not the sociology department faculty lounge." She was silent for a while, and I made the mistake of thinking I'd scored a point for the home team. "I mean seriously, Jacqueline, I worked that street corner, and out there your airy-fairy feel-good bullshit doesn't—"

She interrupted, "Why'd you say Odom had a gun in his pocket?"

For a moment I hesitated, unsure how bad it was; at the same time I was aware she'd just beaten me with my own stick. Trying to make it seem intentional, and maybe it was, I told her, "The gun Berrigan vouchered off Dewberry—it was Odom's thirty-two, wasn't it?"

"Who told you that?"

"Answer my question," I said, "then I'll answer yours."

"They're the same question, Way."

"Odom admitted it was his. Didn't he?"

"Eventually, but I'm fairly confident he didn't confess it to you, too, so I'm asking again how do you know?" she said. Meeting her gaze was like looking at the sun. "Georgina or Holtz? Had to be one or the other, Way, so which? Tell me now, or I'll turn my back."

"Georgina," I said at last, and the information seemed to make no dent on her. She was looking elsewhere now, all fight gone from her. In the light from the big window there were lines in the corners of her eyes you'd never notice when she was looking right at you. "They're all lying, each for their own reasons," I said. "Georgina and Odom. Holtz and Karpatkin. Everyone's a fucking liar. Even people who don't know they're lying."

"It's too late for the truth," she said with half a heart. "This thing's a scavenger hunt now. Everyone's just looking for random crap to help their side win."

"Maybe," I said, "but you indicted this case, Jackie. It's your burden of proof, not Georgina's, and if you indict her with lies and bullshit she should go home."

"What lies do you think I've ever told anyone, out of curiosity?"

"You put Odom in the grand jury," I said. "You put Karpatkin in the grand jury. You knew Karpatkin changed his story—Christ, you were in the room— but you put them in the jury anyway because—"

"Actually, I didn't."

"This was never a prosecution, Jacqueline. This was about taking down a cop as—as a Band-Aid on cancer," I said. "This was about pretending the problem is cops instead of something no one wants to talk about. Because no one knows how to fix it. Your boss wants to throw a bone to Bumpurs to get his votes in the fall. And Bumpurs wants Georgina's head on a spike so he can pretend we're making progress. But we're not. We're going backwards. We're just throwing virgins in volcanos, hoping to make it rain. You say Dewberry didn't deserve it? You're right, but Georgina doesn't deserve it either. And if I have to stand up for any one of the lying motherfuckers in this story I'm gonna stand up for her because she's the only one that deserves it."

"I just told you I didn't indict her," she said, evidently unmoved by my rant. "Then who?"

"Crimmins," she said without expression. "Montgomery Crimmins. It's not my case anymore."

"Quit or fired?"

"None of your business," she said. "But you're correct. I was in the room with Karpatkin when he backed your man, though he seemed a lot less sure about it in person than he does on paper. Where did Janus get the transcript, out of curiosity?"

"Janus—?" I asked with a terrible presentiment.

"This morning Tommy Janus filed a motion to dismiss the indictment," she said. "He's alleging prosecutorial misconduct and a *Brady* violation. He says Karpatkin went on record with IAB backing Georgina, but when Donny Holtz went under he changed his story and ran home to mamma. I assume you're aware of all this, officer, since you just told me more or less the same thing."

"I didn't know," I said, almost to myself.

"Kind of bonkers Tommy would have an IAB transcript, huh?" she said in a false light tone that went right though me. "I mean IAB's pretty selfish with their toys. They don't like to share."

"I didn't know Tommy—"

"I mean, far as I know the only person in the world with Danilov's transcript was Danilov." She shifted the big file on her hip, and I assumed she was done with me. Yet she went on, saying, "And I'm willing to bet he didn't pass it along to Tommy Janus. They're not particularly close."

"I don't know for a fact where Tommy got it."

"You don't seem to know very much all of a sudden, Way," she said. "Funny, you seemed to know everything just a minute ago."

"I—Tommy didn't get it from me," I said, another technical truth. "That's all I know."

Her eyes became bottomless green pools and she rose to her full height in front of me. After what seemed a very long time she lifted her chin, as if I'd just confirmed a fact about me she already suspected. "You're right about one thing, Officer," she told me before she walked off on long legs. "Everyone's a fucking liar."

I kicked around in the hallway after she'd gone and knew she was entitled to her opinion. A moment later, filled with a sudden urgent resolve, I hurried after her, supposing I'd catch her downstairs or walking back to Joralemon Street. Perhaps I could say something to change her mind about me, because all at once it became important that she did. I woodpeckered the elevator button until the door slid slowly, agonizingly slowly, and I saw an imperfect reflection of myself scarred on the scratched metal, obscured by marker graffiti. The door opened one floor down and I swore a private oath. Two twenty-year-olds got on and continued an angry conversation, wholly indifferent to my presence. They stank like weed and everything was nigga this and muthafucka that. One of them kicked the elevator wall, hard, and just like that I was a cop again.

"Muthafucka wanna put me in jail. Fuck, bro. What I do?"

"Yo fo real, nigga ain't even—"

"Shorty come up and say shit on me yo. Call the cops yo."

"Ten years is some motherfuckin shit for—"

"Who say ten, bro?"

"Bitch Legal Aid lawyer say ten—"

"Yo nigga, fo real I ain't got time for that—"

"Ten years smackin no bitch yo—"

"Yo messed up, bro. Attempt murder yo ain't even hurt that bitch nah sayin?"

"Bitch always be askin for it too yo."

"Shit I was some white dude—"

"Yo muthafucka, you some white nigga you ain't—"

"Yo fo real I some white nigga I ain't get—"

"Word."

"Fuck the system, bro."

"System fucked nigga nah mean?"

"Cops bust into my crib yo throw me down front of my moms. Like I'm a criminal yo."

"Racist cops ain't never give you no justice, bro."

"Fuck justice."

I was watching them in the reflection, and now the bigger one noticed. "Yo you lookin at somethin, nigga?" he said to me. I suppose he didn't like the expression on my face.

"Yo bro—" said the one with arms like weeds in a cautionary voice to the other.

"Yo what you starin at, nigga?"

"Bro don't he a cop yo."

The elevator doors opened and that was that. Followed by the other, the bigger one swaggered into the lobby and through the revolving doors into the daylight in front of Brooklyn Supreme where EQUAL JUSTICE UNDER LAW was written on marble high above factions circling with placards and posters, signs and ribbons, black and yellow, protest and counterprotest. I stood for a while and my heart felt light in my chest. I knew how little it would've taken for this moment to have gone another way, simultaneously relieved and disappointed. I could've dropped him in one hit, I knew, and Jesus Christ I wanted to. So help me I wanted to. He would go right down. I knew the type. There was no fight to him, except with his girl. I would've tinned the court officer at the desk with my Li'l Sheriff Kit toy badge and he would've asked no questions, except maybe whether I wanted to put the guy under. When I had come down from thinking that, I went through the revolving doors and drew a long breath of springtime air and wondered how the second guy—the skinny amigo with the docile cast to his eye—knew I was a cop. *Must be the haircut,* I said to myself.

TWENTY-FIVE

In Garrity's defense Tommy Janus could have gotten Karpatkin's interview transcript on his own. I wasn't the only sneak in New York City, and Janus had money and actual influence, so when I walked down the hall to Garrity's office that afternoon I had no intention to pick a fight. But I wanted to know nonetheless. He was not in, which was probably a good thing. Garrity didn't return that day and by the following morning I decided I didn't need to hear him deny it. By then the *Brooklyn Daily News* had the story. The headline used up a lot of oxygen. Tommy Janus's motion to dismiss alleged that the People of the State of New York had elicited perjured testimony to secure a murder indictment in a high-profile, politically important prosecution during an election year, an allegation we either believed or ignored according to the color of our ribbon.

I watched from afar, pretending to have no interest, but when Janus's motion came on before Justice Henry K. Pomeroy two weeks later I made my way to Brooklyn Supreme for old times' sake, taking a break from another day of doing what I used to do before Georgina hit. I pushed my way through the plaza in front of the courthouse and the well-mannered and mostly homogenous Free Georgina! and Babe factions and made my way up the courthouse steps. Both contingents gave me the same heedful eye as I passed, their faces peering at me beneath the heavy burden of their shared history. The black ribbons knew me, of course, and were formal if not polite, some nodding in recognition, believing I was not saved but savable. The yellow ribbons were somewhat warmer, knowing I was on their side for the time being but for my own purposes and that I would betray them eventually, for that is how it's been since time immemorial with well-meaning white folks everywhere, as it was in the beginning, is now and ever shall be, world without end, amen.

For twenty minutes before Pomeroy took the bench I stared at the backsides of grown-ups from my seat in the last row of the courtroom, reading the graffiti scratched with keys and bottlecaps on the wooden benches.

DAQWAN FUCK DENISE
83 COPS IS ALL FASHIS

JUSTICE=TRUTH
DONT SHOOT
STACK MONEY BOYS
JUSTICE IS JUST US

Betty Moon came in. I didn't wave hello, nor did she notice me skulking in the rear like the remedial in class. Jackie Kane never showed. I'd hoped to cross her path, believing our business unfinished. Instead the prosecutor waiting in the well was Montgomery Crimmins, a dark-complected black man of medium height with shoulders like a linebacker, a handsome ordinary face, and a head of neat baby dreads. Tommy Janus stood at the defense table, opening his arms in welcome as two court officers escorted Georgina Reed from the rear door. She sat, handcuffed, not speaking at all to Donny Holtz at the far end of the table. Holtz had been released on his own recognizance and was now dressed like a suburban dad in cargo pants and an off-brand polo shirt as if he planned to go to Action Park in Jersey with his twelve sons after this court thing was over. Georgina had been remanded to jail, of course, yet she wore not the expected beige overlarge Rose M. Singer jumpsuit but civilian clothes, a little makeup, and sensible hair. Someone had brought court clothes to Rikers for her—a boyfriend, maybe, or a mother. I had no idea. I knew nothing about her, I realized, not even the basics. Like everyone else, I was guilty of making Georgina into an idea and no longer a person. Seeing her now, leaning forward in her chair because of the bracelets, she seemed so small, an impossibly small target for all of this, for how could anyone taking aim at her even get close? She looked like a dental hygienist.

Charles Ouellette watched from the front row and from time to time exchanged daggers with Janus, like cheerleaders who'd kissed the same quarterback. I noticed Janus was nearly identical to Ouellette in dress, form, and figure—white and black bookends who together made a stunning contrast to Irving Meltzer, one of the union's more regular lawyers who Garrity brought in to stand up for Holtz. Meltzer was our go-to guy for desk-appearance tickets and parking tickets and jaywalking tickets, but not murder. All pointed knees and elbows, in a jacket not a suit, Meltzer had the comb-over of the year and a pigeon chest that nevertheless produced long, discursive, unpunctuated sentences in a deep rolling tenor. He peered at life through droopy aviator eyeglasses, green tinted, behind which you could see his milky magnified eyes blink very slowly at you.

Pomeroy took the bench without ceremony and for ten minutes there was the expected obscure legal tennis on the record by the lawyers, but as things wound down Pomeroy mentioned—as if the idea had just dawned on him—that he'd ruled on Tommy Janus's pending motion to dismiss. I'd nearly forgotten it until then. So had everyone else. All expected the motion to be resolved with a one-line decision—*motion denied*—but instead Pomeroy had written a seventeen-page ruling that he asked his law secretary to hand down. I remembered him from my late-night reconnoiter of chambers weeks earlier when he sat eating takeout while Pomeroy and I didn't talk about Regine for an hour. He came into the well and ever so slowly—licking his forefinger as he did—passed the stapled pages to the lawyers and then as a courtesy to the five or six reporters seated in the front row of the gallery. At once the reporters in a body turned to the last page of the decision where instead of the expected "is hereby denied" they found "is hereby granted."

At once the reporters began to murmur among themselves, and Ouellette read the decision over Betty Moon's shoulder. Pomeroy silenced them and said, "Counsel, you'll observe the court has granted the defense motion to dismiss the indictment," which was how the rest of us found out what just happened. None of the lawyers knew quite what to say, and for his part Pomeroy seemed annoyed and ready to leave. In fact he stood and unzipped his black robe. Crimmins at last spoke, or rather he began to make a helpless strangulated sound that Pomeroy terminated with an upraised hand before it could form into something more intelligible:

```
    THE COURT: People, the Court in fact was very
generous in allowing the district attorney to re-present
charges to the grand jury and--
    MR. CRIMMINS: Judge, I--
    THE COURT: Just a moment, People. And counsel for
defendant Holtz, what's your name, sir?
    MR. MELTZER: Me?
    THE COURT: Yes, you, sir. Did you make an appearance?
    MR. MELTZER: Nobody asked.
    THE COURT: I'm asking. Make your appearance, sir.
    MR. MELTZER: For Mr. Holtz, Irving Meltzer. That's
Meltzer with a Z not an S, 301-1/2 Old Country Road,
Hicksville, New York.
    THE COURT: Pleasure to meet you, sir. I think your
phone is ringing. Thank you. Why don't you turn it
off now?
```

MR. MELTZER: It's my wife. It's Shirley. Mrs. Meltzer.

THE COURT: It's a pleasure to meet her, too. Mr. Meltzer. Mr. Meltzer, you can either turn off the phone or surrender it to my sergeant.

MR. MELTZER: I'm sorry. I think there's a button or something.

THE COURT: Very good. Mr. Meltzer, do you wish to join in Mr. Janus's motion?

MR. MELTZER: His motion?

THE COURT: Off the record.

(Whereupon, there was a pause in the proceedings.)

THE COURT: Mr. Meltzer?

MR. MELTZER: Thank you, your honor, Mr. Holtz joins the motion that you were just talking about just now.

THE COURT: Very well. Motion granted. The indictment is dismissed against defendant Holtz without prejudice.

And I will say at this juncture, as I state at length in my written decision, that I have grave concerns about the district attorney's practice before the grand jury in this matter.

MR. CRIMMINS: Your honor, I--

THE COURT: And, Bob, maybe you can help Mr. Meltzer with his phone? Thank you very much. No, Bob, put it in the bottom drawer.

In any event my decision on the motion is meant to reflect those concerns. The People's flagrant violation of Brady v. Maryland, namely their failure to make a timely disclosure of impeachment material to the defense regarding their witness Karpatkin's previous denial of knowledge of matters at the heart of his testimony to the grand jury, cries out for a penalty. And I have adjudged dismissal of the indictment as an appropriate sanction.

MR. CRIMMINS: Your honor--

THE COURT: As further sanction you will see I'm also precluding the testimony of the witness Karpatkin from all further proceedings in connection with this prosecution.

MR. CRIMMINS: Including trial?

THE COURT: You spoke, Mr. Crimmins?

MR. CRIMMINS: Your honor, does the Court's ruling preclude the testimony of Officer Karpatkin at trial?

THE COURT: I believe I said all further proceedings, Mr. Crimmins. Trial would be a further proceeding, would it not? Assuming, naturally, that there is a trial.

MR. CRIMMINS: Judge, I--

THE COURT: You will observe the dismissal is without prejudice, People. So you are not precluded from re-presenting charges to the grand jury if you can manage to do so without further infringing the constitutional rights of the defendants.

MR. CRIMMINS: Judge, I--

THE COURT: I hope that is all sufficiently transparent, People, because whenever I have to sort out this variety of nonsense it only serves to make me very tired. Let's set a date. I'll give you two weeks.

THE CLERK: May 11, judge?

THE COURT: May 11 good for everybody? Very well. May 11 for the People to re-present charges to the grand jury, if they so choose. You do intend to re-present, Mr. Crimmins?

MR. CRIMMINS: Your honor?

THE COURT: The district attorney does intend to re-present charges against both defendants?

MR. CRIMMINS: Yes, I--

THE COURT: I will look forward to seeing you all then.

MR. JANUS: Judge, judge. Please. In light of the court's ruling, I wonder if your honor might set bail on my client?

THE COURT: No, Mr. Janus, I don't think so. Not at this time. Mr. Crimmins has indicated he plans to re-present, and we can take him as a man of his word. If he is unable to secure an indictment by May 11, I will entertain your application. Perhaps in the interim the Brooklyn district attorney will be able to secure some

```
reliable evidence to renew our faith in his apprehension
of the most basic elements of his public trust. Remand
continued. Good day to you all.
     THE CLERK: Remand continued.
```

Pomeroy then swept from the bench with his black robe following like a separate thing of great billowing folds, and for a long moment the courtroom remained absolutely still. The newspaper reporters in the front row were the first to snap out of it. Betty Moon darted to the balustrade on her short legs and began assailing Crimmins, who did his best. Irving Meltzer meanwhile stood, yawning audibly, and asked the sergeant to return his phone. Janus and Georgina were still seated, wrapped in close conversation. Donny Holtz lumbered out and a woman flew to him, hugging him, kissing him, embarrassing him.

Also in the gallery were the usual uniformed cops who came to every appearance to sit in silent witness to the proceedings. Garrity didn't send them; they simply came. There were also several civilian men and women who sat mute. All were black, but whether they were Babes or Free Georgina! was anyone's guess, and their silence baffled me. I then realized they likely had no clear idea what had just happened. Neither had I. I sat silent and alone in the back row watching as Montgomery Crimmins, at last able to be openly angry and not merely politely dismayed, shoehorned a thick accordion case file into a leather litigation bag and strode toward the courtroom door. "Of course I'm going back to the fucking grand jury," he said to Betty Moon, his voice no longer so mellifluous, his handsome face now like the wrath of God on earth.

Tommy Janus wanted to let Garrity pat him on the head, so we shared a cab back to the city, meaning I paid the fare. By then Garrity had gotten the news along with the rest of New York City, and he stood waiting at headquarters with the other trustees and staff. Everyone let up a ragged sort of cheer as we stepped off the elevator. Janus absorbed all the handshakes and back slaps and congratulations, mumbling self-effacing comments to no one and shoe-gazing. He was in a disgustingly chaste mood all of a sudden, which made him unnatural, like a tame honey badger. Just three months ago we would've peeled his skin if he'd dared to darken the threshold of 40 Fulton Street. Now everyone wanted to touch the hem of his garment.

I slipped away unnoticed to my office. Sheila followed. She didn't like Janus either. There was a pink message slip in her hand. "Mr. W.—"

"No, Sheila, I don't think we should get Tommy a Carvel cake," I interrupted.

"Mr. W., I—"

"Hell you wearing, Sheila?"

Everyone at the organization was a die-hard Free Georgina! zealot, of course, and had donned yellow ribbons weeks before it became a sociopolitical fashion statement—de rigueur in certain tonier zip codes of New York City, where support for Georgina Reed had little actually to do with Georgina Reed, much as Christmas does just fine without Christ—but on Sheila's lapel I now saw two ribbons, one yellow and the other black, entwined.

"Looks like a bumblebee landed on you," I said. "Lucky I didn't swat it with a newspaper."

"I'm showing my support, Mr. W."

"Garrity sees that black one he'll have a conniption."

"I wear it just the same," she said.

"Don't you like cops anymore, Sheila?"

"Some I do," she answered me seriously, as if I'd asked her seriously, but when her expression remained grave and thoughtful I realized we were going to have the conversation we'd been avoiding since March. "Some I don't."

"So you don't think cops are fascists?"

"Not the ones I know," she said. "Just the ones I don't."

"Why just the ones you don't know?"

"I don't like to say, Mr. W."

"Tell me," I said. "I want to know what you think."

She considered that before saying in her precise, reticent way, "I guess you have to say I have a trust issue."

"Me, too," I said.

"With police—?"

"With everyone," I said. "But you better pick one side or the other, don't you think? You can't be on both sides."

"Everyone wants to be on a side, but there's only one side," she said, lifting her chin defiantly. "Georgina's not a side, Mr. W. She's just a black woman the system's trying to keep down."

"What system?" I said. "Jesus, Sheila, if we're not the system, then I don't know who is. And we're the ones trying to back her out of this mess with her head still attached to her body."

"Well. Another system's trying to put her in jail."

"I've been behind Georgina longer than anyone," I said, dropping into my chair, enervated. "What, am I supposed to wear a yellow ribbon to prove it?"

"Maybe you don't want to take a stand."

"I'm not the one wearing two ribbons, Sheila."

"I can be for both."

"There are sides, Sheila," I said, "like it or not. People with black ribbons want Georgina in jail. They say she's a murderer, a racist."

"This black ribbon isn't for Georgina," she said in a flat tone. "It's—"

"No shit, it's not."

"—it's for the young man that died and—"

"The young man Georgina killed, you mean."

"—and for racial justice."

"Racial justice?" I said. "What's racial justice?"

"Justice for people of color, Mr. W."

"How's that different than justice for white people?"

"It just is," she said.

"So justice comes in colors? Can I collect all six?"

"I don't think we can talk about this, Mr. W.," she said.

"Come on, Sheila, give me a break. There's one justice. And justice is blind."

"Not color-blind," she said. "I mean, maybe it says that on the building, equal justice or whatever, but what it says outside's not always what they do inside."

"What building?"

"The court building. Brooklyn Supreme."

I knew nothing of Sheila Simmons. Every day for four years I'd seen her, talked to her, brought her birthday presents, flowers on Secretary's Day. I liked her. She liked me. If I ate the gun tonight, she'd be one of the five people at my closed-casket funeral, looking a little ashamed and not crying very hard. Even so, we were strangers, I realized. We would always be strangers. Our skin was between us. We'd never spoken so openly about race before, following the tacit compact of intentional myopia that allows black and white to come together in this town, but now here it was—race straight up with a twist of gender. "Just you look at Officer Holtz now," she said. "He's a white man. He's not in jail, now is he?"

"He—" I started to state the obvious, at least what was obvious to me, but immediately I gave up. Sheila was right, of course; we couldn't talk about race. She believed her truth that was true for her. I could tell her she was wrong, but she could tell me the same thing. "I don't know what you're saying, Sheila. Are you for Georgina because she's a black woman or against her because she killed Raquan Dewberry?"

"I can be both."

"Georgina's a racist?"

"Maybe," she said. "Maybe she's just not aware. Some people are racist and not aware. Because of the system they're in."

"Like me?"

"I know you're no racist, Mr. W. I know you," she said. "But I don't know Georgina like that. Or that judge."

"What judge?"

"The one on the case," she said.

"You saying Pomeroy's a racist, too?" I said, astonished.

"Well. It's common knowledge," she said, crossing her arms over her chest.

"Pomeroy just dismissed the indictment against Georgina, for chrissake."

"Exactly. Georgina killed an unarmed black boy for no reason, and Judge Pomeroy just lets her go free," Sheila said. "If that isn't racist, Mr. W., then I don't know what is."

"He didn't let her go—"

"Besides. He's only trying to embarrass the DA. Because of politics."

"Whitey Fister is white. As his name suggests."

"Anyway—" she said, handing me the message slip and opening the door. "He called again."

"Pomeroy?"

"And Kat, too."

"Really—?" I said. "What'd she say?"

"She told me not to tell you."

"So why're telling me?"

"Because, Mr. W., it's been a while since she called, and I just guessed you'd want to know."

"Thank you, Sheila. And Sheila—?" I said, and she faced me before walking out. "If you were to wear a ribbon for me, what color would it be?"

"For you, Mr. W.—? I can't even say."

When she left I took a cool regard of the pink message slip with *Henry Pomeroy* written on it, a familiar name but an unfamiliar number, not Pomeroy's courthouse line. Nor was it the Dover Street number, Regine's number, which I still knew by heart fifteen years after I last dialed it. I dropped the slip in the trash and said to myself, "Gray."

TWENTY-SIX

The first time I heard the word "subpoena" I must have been about seven years old—Nixon, Watergate, men on the television set, men seated at a table, a close-up on their faces, thick dark plastic eyeglass frames, questions from a disembodied someone, a gigantic steel microphone planted right there. I understood none of it, of course, but whenever I hear the word even now I think of Archibald Cox. Who he was I have no clear idea. All I remember is the Avocado King flicking cards at the television set whenever Archibald Cox appeared. He had Annie Oakley aim with a playing card, my father. Curiously enough I also remember that when Nixon resigned I bawled my eyes out. I ran to the cellar at Melba Court, ashamed in front of my father, though tears rolled down his own cheeks every time he listened to *Greatest Hits of Italian Opera*, a four-record set purchased at a Gravesend stoop sale for three dollars with a nonoperational Dust Buster thrown in. I don't know why Nixon made me cry, but I was sure Archibald Cox was to blame.

A knock on my door during dinner.

I was sitting on the floor in front of the television in my home that was not home. On the menu was leftover Vietnamese and a bottle of Chivas. My dinner guest was Bugs Bunny. Very funny, in fact I was laughing my ass off when I heard the door. Getting up was the problem, and I was encouraging myself, hands on knees. "Arise, Sir Loin of Beef! Arise, Earl of Cloves!"

One of the two detectives at the door I recognized at once, yet I couldn't place him. He smiled because I was smiling in a T-shirt and boxer shorts, and I took what he handed me, supposing he was friendly for no reason other than I knew him from somewhere, someplace. "Have a nice day, Officer," he said with a twinkle in his gimlet eye before I shut the door. The instant before I tore open the envelope I recalled he'd been with Jackie Kane, smoking a bent cigarette outside Brooklyn Supreme the day she dumped the case against Marlon Odom. *I know who he is.* I swung the door open, but the hallway was now empty but for an overtone of weed and the thump of bass. The door across from mine cracked opened and Kaseem's head appeared, more weed, more bass, and seeing me his expression turned docile. "Yo, Mr. Will, y'all see them big dudes?" he said, stepping shirtless into the hall. "Five-oh. Damn."

"Police?"

"Thought they was for me yo."

"What'd you do, Kaseem?"

"Nothin," he said. Shiny and Shooshka walked out and belligerently smelled my bare toes. "Nothin big-time anyway. Know how it is."

"So why you worried?" I said.

"Yo, Mr. Will, them fascist cops need a reason to fuck wichoo?" he said. "They always be fucking with me yo. Telling me I fit the description."

"What's so funny?" I said as a smile broke over his scowl.

"You," he said, laughing infectiously, even if it was the result of an alpine high. "Yo, man, y'all in your draws."

"My what?"

"Draws, bro. Y'all be in your draws."

"Oh," I said, realizing it.

One of the dogs barked. The other walked down the hall smelling the crevices and corners.

"Y'all wanna come in?" he said. "Come in, bro. I got some people here, but they all good people, nah mean? We just be chillin and whatever. Have ourselves a little celebration."

"What's it, your birthday, Kaseem?"

"Nah, man. Just celebrating life. Put some pants on. Come in, yo."

"Thanks, but—" I started, and he caught me reading his arms. The words in ornate script were difficult to make out against the dark canvas of his skin, but he held them out obligingly. On the left, FEAR NO MAN. On the right, TRUST NO BITCH.

"Yeah, stupid, right?" he said in a subdued tone, almost apologetic. "I have that done when I was young and all cavalier and shit, trying to figure my game out, ya know? I was rolling with my boys in Brownsville then and I ain't give a fuck about nothing, nah mean?"

"But now you do?"

"Now do I what?" he asked.

"Give a fuck?"

"Course. Ain't you?" he said. "Now that I'm living the life, you know? Got me a free crib, benefit card. Big settlement check from the lawyer."

"You have a lawyer, Kaseem?"

"Herman Wrublewicz, man. Yo, he hook me *up*. After them dudes shoot me. Check it, bro. Breitling watch. Now I own all this shit I *gotta* give a fuck, nah mean? Be responsible and whatever. You gotta believe in something, else what are you? Nothing, man. Yo, y'all wanna see something, Mr. Will? Check this out." He turned around and showed me his naked back where BELIEVE IN JUST US was written in six-inch Gothic script. "That's what I'm about now."

"Got that for your girl," I said. "How cute."

"Nah, man," he said. "She split with the baby."

"Then it's a good thing it doesn't say *Believe in Kaseem and Sally*. Might make things uncomfortable, you get another girl. Unless her name is Sally. Nah saying?"

He looked confused. "No, no, no, bro, y'all ain't read it right. Look," he said, turning around again. "It say *justice*."

"Then I got some bad news for you, Kaseem. Who inked that for you?"

"Just some shorty I know on my old block," he said.

"Don't trust that bitch anyway. To spell."

"Yo, man, y'all still ain't get it. Suppose to be that way," he said. "Read it fast."

"I'm just fucking with you, Kaseem," I said. "*Justice is just us*. I get it. It's what Bumpurs always says."

"Who?"

"Archbishop Bumpurs."

"Oh, yeah, yeah, yeah—that angry old bald dude on the TV," he said with a gesture, "always getting folks all hesticated, like my moms, making noise, agitating, only I don't pay him no mine. Dude needs to have him a smoke, ask me. And relax, yo. Sorry if I offend you, Mr. Will, if y'all into religion or protesting or whatever he do. I ain't know you believe in God."

"I believe in dogs," I said. "Not your dogs, though."

"For real. They kind of stupid, but they mines. Y'all gotta love something when they yours. Why ain't y'all come in? We just doing nothing, kicking it."

"No, I—" I began, but he was laughing again. "What—?"

"They just black, man. They ain't gonna rob y'all or nothing."

"Jesus, no. It's just, I—" I said.

"Yo, Mr. Will," he said. "Y'all ain't know no black folks to chill with, do you?"

"You kidding me? I'm Brooklyn born and raised."

"For real?" he said.

"Gerritsen Beach."

"That in Brooklyn?"

"It's over there," I said, gesturing somewhere in the direction of south by southeast.

"Where—?"

"You know where Manhattan Beach is?"

"In Manhattan."

"Manhattan Beach's in Brooklyn," I said. "You know Marine Park?"

"No."

"Sheepshead Bay?" I asked.

"No."

"Gravesend?"

"Oh, yeah, yeah, yeah. I know where you talking about now. Y'all talking about *south* Brooklyn, man. Y'all talking about *white* Brooklyn."

"Where do you think you're living, Kaseem? Injun country?"

"Park Slope is just white, Mr. Will," he said. Shooshka was peeing on a fire extinguisher. "Where y'all be talking about is *poor* white. Poor white is whiter than white, yo."

"I don't get it."

"It's like this," he said. "Like here, like Park Slope they all pretend they be like Attica Fitch or whatever talking about equality and justice and shit with their ribbons and whatever and whatever but when they see a brother on the block they dial nine-one-one and hide under the bed, nah saying? Poor white they don't even bother."

"Bother to what?" I asked.

"To pretend."

"That's not true. In high school my—"

"Oh, man!" he said, opening into hard laugher. "Y'all ain't gonna tell me some of your best friends is black, was you? Oh, ha ha."

"He was."

"So y'all have a black friend in high school down there in Manhattan Bay or wherever. That's cool, that's cool," he said, coughing. "But I bet that dude come to school in a armor car. Ain't making fun of y'all, Mr. Will. I'm just saying it as it is."

"Well."

"Where this boy now?"

"I'm not really sure," I said. "I heard he went to law school. I haven't seen him in—in a long time."

"So, what, the brother ain't fit in your world no more, 'cause he a lawyer? Or 'cause he a black lawyer, ha ha?"

"I'm going to put some pants on, Kaseem," I said. "I'm getting cold."

"Nah, man, I think y'all getting warm, nah saying?"

In my apartment, Bugs Bunny still paused on the screen, I opened the envelope the detective had served on me. Then I sat on the floor and hit play. *Don't you worry, never fear, Robin Hood will soon be here—*

Inside the envelope was Archibald Cox.

Shawn Garrity handed the subpoena back to me, unimpressed, when I arrived for work the following afternoon. My head was in a vice. I'd forgotten to shave. Garrity was on the telephone, laughing it up with Tommy Janus when I went in. He stopped smiling and pressed the receiver into his shoulder. "What?" he said as if I'd extracted the word with forceps. He handed the subpoena back and in the same voice told me to show Irving Meltzer.

"Irving's Donny's lawyer," I said in weak protest. I didn't like Meltzer as Gordon Holtz's lawyer, and I sure as hell didn't like him as mine. Meltzer with the comb-over and radio voice belonged in Long Island misdemeanorland, but the organization had spent all our rainy-day fund on Tommy Janus once it started to rain.

"So?" Garrity said, annoyed.

"So maybe there's a conflict of interest or something. I don't know."

"So?"

"Plus Meltzer's a fucking lightweight, Shawn. Come on."

"Someone dropped a subpoena on Way here," Garrity said into the phone. Then to me: "Who sent it, Tommy wants to know."

"Crimmins," I said.

"Crimmins. Yeah, the DA guy," Garrity told Tommy, and then, "Tommy says Monty's just fucking with you."

"What am I supposed to do?"

"What's he supposed to do?" Garrity said into the phone, then: "Tommy says blow it off."

"It's a subpoena, Shawn. You want me to blow it off?"

He wasn't listening. He was on the phone. I could hear Tommy's voice. "Tommy says Monty's just fucking with you 'cause he's pissed his case got shit-canned and he thinks you had something to do with it."

"Fuck I have to do with it?" I asked.

"It's just what Tommy's saying is all, what can I tell you? Show it to Meltzer. What—?" Garrity said. "Ha ha, Tommy says you don't like Irving go hire Bea Katzenbach. And shut the door behind you, I'm working here."

In my office I moved some papers around for ten minutes, trying not to look at the *Brooklyn Daily News* Sheila Simmons had brought in with a coffee. She had thoughtfully opened it to the page featuring a photograph of Pomeroy standing next to his car beneath the headline:

ACCUSATIONS OF RACISM LEVELED
AGAINST GEORGINA JUDGE

Sheila had said nothing, nor had her demeanor suggested the article proved anything, but I had taken her point directly. I shut my door.

Assistant District Attorney Montgomery Crimmins answered his own telephone. I asked him what the hell. "Oh, that," he laughed. "I just wanted to get your attention, Officer. Forget it's a subpoena. Say it's an invitation for a friendly chat."

"Why not just send an invitation?"

He laughed again. "Rip it up, then. Rip it up if you don't believe me. Go ahead." I set the phone on my desk and ripped the subpoena down the middle. He said, "You feel better now, Officer?"

"No."

"How about let's meet up?" he said.

"No."

"Tomorrow work?" he asked me.

"You're a persistent son of a bitch, aren't you, counselor?" I said. "Why meet?"

"You might learn something. I hear you're a guy who likes to gather all sorts of information. Fair to say?"

"No."

"Friday?"

"No."

"All right," he said and exhaled. "I suppose it's too late to tape that subpoena back together."

"I'll be there in an hour," I said.

"I gotta be in Supreme—"

"Take it or leave it, counselor."

"Guess I'll see you in an hour," he said, and there was a pause. "By the way, you're not bringing a lawyer, are you?"

"Does Irving Meltzer count?"

He laughed again and hung up and I was left holding the receiver, thinking about curiosity and its unhealthy connection to cats. I set the telephone back into the cradle only when a faraway female voice told me to. On my desk was the afternoon newspaper, and throughout my ninety-second conversation with the prosecutor I'd been staring fixedly at the black-and-white image of Pomeroy, which had a kind of soporific effect on me. The article told me nothing I didn't already know, but now a few hundred thousand strangers also knew. The photograph was the sort taken with a long lens from a hiding place in a grassy knoll or a stakeout car, a halftone image that would make the pope look shifty. Here was Pomeroy in a seersucker suit and Panama hat, his early summer look, unlocking his Lincoln, casting a backward glance right at you. Christ, he looked old. And guilty. Whatever Betty Moon wrote he did, you just knew he'd done it. I already knew the story, of course, so I knew that Betty had shot wide of her mark. Even so, she'd gotten close enough that I believed every other word.

The Brooklyn judge who threw out murder charges last week against a police officer who gunned down an unarmed black teen last March has a history of racial hatred and intolerance that have led some to question his fitness to preside over the case, some say.

Justice Henry K. Pomeroy reportedly fell out with his youngest daughter over her affair with a black man, an anonymous source has told this paper. Regina Pomeroy was just eighteen years old when she became romantically involved with a classmate against her family's wishes. Pomeroy sent his daughter out of state to discourage the affair and later directed her to an abortion clinic in Massachusetts, sources say.

Approached yesterday at the downtown courthouse, Justice Pomeroy refused comment. However, one acquaintance in Pomeroy's prestigious, predominantly white Manhattan Beach community recalled that the affair was "never discussed" in the neighborhood and that such a relationship could well have made Pomeroy "uncomfortable."

This unconfirmed report adds heat to an already simmering pot. Pomeroy drew fire last week when he dismissed the indictment against NYPD officers Georgina Reed and Gordon Holtz, the defendants in the racially motivated murder of Raquan Dewberry, 17. Critics have complained that Pomeroy's ruling was based upon a legal technicality, but Thomas Janus, who repre-sented Reed on her motion to dismiss, disagreed, saying, "Technicality? Sure, it's a little-known legal loophole known as the Due Process Clause of the Fourteenth Amendment to the United States Constitution."

Reached for comment, Brooklyn DA Weldon Fister urged Pomeroy to step aside in light of these revelations but denied that his unusually vocal opposition to a sitting judge bears any connection to widespread rumors that Pomeroy's name has been circulating among Brooklyn Democratic Party officials as a possible challenger to the widely unpopular Fister in the upcoming primary.

Yesterday's alarming development brought the Brooklyn DA into rare alignment with a longtime tormentor, Archbishop Basil Bumpurs of the Brooklyn African-Baptist-Episcopal Cathedral. "Do I think [Pomeroy]'s a racist?" Bumpurs said. "I'm not going to get drawn into name-calling, but what I will tell you is my community needs more justice, not more excuses. Remember justice is just us."

The article didn't hurt to read as much as it might have, and I wondered if that was because Betty had misspelled Regine's name. It was like reading about someone else.

TWENTY-SEVEN

On the fourth floor of the Brooklyn District Attorney's Office, in the Homicide Bureau where I'd waited for Jackie Kane a few weeks earlier, the detective on the desk didn't remember me. I tinned him with my Li'l Sheriff Kit toy badge and asked for Crimmins. "Wrong floor, boss," he said, looking up from his *National Geographic*. "You want the Civil Rights Bureau. That's on seven. ADA Crimmins, he's the one got that Georgina case now."

"Civil Rights?" I said. "I thought someone got killed here."

"Guess they must of violated his civil rights on top of it."

Upstairs, Assistant District Attorney Montgomery Crimmins looked worn and the fluorescent lights of the hallway treated him ungently. I suppose he'd had a really shitty week since Pomeroy pinned a Free Georgina! ribbon to his pinstripe lapel, but he gave me a smile full of teeth along with his hand, which was smooth and strong. With him was an office detective, a bantam Puerto Rican woman who looked like Maria from *Sesame Street* though her shoulder-holstered Smith & Wesson semiautomatic nine-millimeter SW99 absolutely ruined the look of her short cranberry red jacket. Together we walked like ducks in a row to Crimmins's office, the detective behind me making clear this was not such a friendly chat after all.

The view from Crimmins's office window featured the verdigrised cupola of Borough Hall across Joralemon Street and the jagged line of midtown Manhattan beyond. Montgomery Crimmins kept certificates and diplomas on the wall behind his desk and framed photographs of black men on another—not Malcolm X nor even MLK, but Duke Ellington and Ralph Ellison, I think, and a third I had no clue, autographed with a fat silver pen. The detective offered a seat, or more accurately directed me to sit. Crimmins himself sat at his wide and well-organized desk and fingered a pair of long, sharp scissors that looked like a graduation present or an assassin's stiletto. His office was very neat. Since court last week he'd shaved off his baby dreads. Now you could see the flat depressions of his skull.

Quickly the talk became serious. "Officer," he said, "I want you to testify for me. In the grand jury. At trial." When I said nothing he pretended to be embarrassed. "My ass is in sort of a bind, you know. Pomeroy—in his infinite judicial wisdom, the pompous fascist prick—dismissed my indictment and—I guess as a sort of fuck-you to my boss—barred Karpatkin's testimony from trial. So I find myself one witness short, ha ha, and I'd like you to help me make out an indictment against Georgina Reed. I'd like you to testify in the grand jury and then at trial I'd like you to give—"

"What are you, fucking nuts?" I said, unable to help but explode in dismay.

"No," he said calmly to prove he was not. "No, I'm not, Officer. What I mean is this. You're uniquely situated to give evidence in this case. You met with the perp—when was that?" He was asking the detective, not me.

"The night of," she said.

"The night of the murder in Bushwick—" Crimmins went on.

"The night of the line-of-duty shooting, you mean," I said.

"—on the night of the deadly shooting," he said, splitting the baby, "you sat down with the perp—"

"I met with Officer Reed—"

"—you met with the alleged—"

"—as duty required."

"—you met defendant Reed," he said, and before I could interrupt again he held up a palm, so close I could read his future. It was bright. "Just hear me out, Officer Way. Hear me out, then you can tell me to go fuck myself, okay? We're aware you personally met defendant Reed in the basement of the Eight-three precinct stationhouse that night. She confessed to you her actions in the attack. Am I correct?" I kept quiet. He asked again.

"You're absolutely correct, counselor," I said at last. "It was night."

"Please," he said, "I'm aware nothing legally prohibited you from speaking to the defendant—"

"Good to know, since it's my job."

"—and hearing her confession."

"Confession?" I said. "What am I, a priest now?"

"She told you what happened."

"We talked, okay?" I said. "At night."

"Gordon Holtz was there, yes?" he said, and then in fifty words or less laid out his entire case. "And the two defendants informed you that Reed shot an unarmed victim under circumstances legally insufficient to make out a justifiable LOD shooting, so to fabricate a false claim of such justification she planted a weapon on the victim's dead body."

"Now can I tell you to go fuck yourself?"

"Not yet," he said.

"And you can prove all that how, counselor?"

"With you, of course," he said simply, either a threat or a statement of fact.

"What happened to Holtz?" I asked, not bothering to be shy about it. All along I'd believed Gordon Holtz had cut a deal with the DA and that his indictment was purely for show. Now I was no longer sure. "You don't need me, you have Donny Holtz."

"I wanted him," he said. "I sorely did. He sat right there and I told him— well, I told him pretty much what I'm telling you now. I offered him an easy way out, but in the end I had to indict him as a felon. He's a good man, and I don't like breaking good men." *So*, I thought, *a threat.*

"You put Holtz in the grand jury."

"He took the Fifth," Crimmins said with a shrug of one shoulder. "Which tends to support my sneaking suspicion that Officer Reed may have committed a crime here. In my experience, people don't ordinarily take five when they're comfortable telling the truth."

"Holtz backed his partner, counsel," I returned, feeling a sudden warmth for the man, as I do for anyone who does the wrong thing for the right reasons.

"Which of course is very admirable, but—"

"It's more than that," I said. "When cops don't back cops, cops die."

"Some call it the blue wall of silence."

"Others call it loyalty."

"Let's say we cut the horseshit," he said, suddenly angry, wearing the face he wore when he stormed from court after Pomeroy dismissed his indictment. *Of course I'm going back to the fucking grand jury*, he had told Betty Moon, and here I was throwing a wrench into his well-ordered plans. "Okay? I mean, I get it, Officer. I get loyalty. I get backing your partner, but this isn't Holtz standing with Reed in the line of fire. This is Holtz refusing to raise his hand to tell—"

"And you think there's a difference?"

"Hell, yeah," he answered quickly.

"Counsel, it may surprise you to hear that cops—cops who are actually cops—would rather get shot on the job than bent over a desk by a bunch of lawyers and politicians and pencil-necked motherfuckers who have no idea what that job is."

"And what do you think the job is, Officer?"

"Getting it done."

"Okay—" he said, making a tolerant, infuriating smile. "So the job is getting the job done?"

"Fuck you, counsel. I'm sure everything's safe and clean for you here in your tidy retentive office, not to mention over there in court, but on the street corner the right thing is not always so obvious. Particularly when you have a half second to decide what the right thing is. You make the wrong choice? You get bagpipes, or best case someone like you waiting with a pair of handcuffs. You make the right choice all you get is you go home and sleep in your own bed one more night."

When the echo died down he said, "Believe me, Officer, things are not always so obvious in Brooklyn Supreme, ha ha. Matter of fact—can I tell you something about myself?"

"No."

"Okay."

"Look, counsel," I said, "if this is the part where you tell me your story, how you decided to fight for truth and justice or whatever you think your job is, I couldn't care less. So okay it's tough growing up black in Brooklyn. It's no picnic growing up shanty Irish either, I can tell you that."

"Hold on—"

"I mean, I'm sure you got tossed by cops a hundred times," I said, "but how's that cops' fault? You're tired of getting frisked because you fit the description, stop fitting the description."

Calmly he said, "Officer, you sound like a man arguing with himself." When I said nothing, he went on in the same easy tone. "For the record I don't have a story. I'm from Ohio and I've never owned a pit bull. Cops have never stopped me except once in New Haven for a—that reminds me, I think we can play the name game. Stephan says hello."

"Who—?"

"Stephan Morton?" he said. "We were in law school together. Up at Yale. Said he knew you from Xaverian—"

"No idea," I lied for no better reason than instinct told me to lie, as if admitting a high school friendship with a black kid I hadn't seen since would have given Crimmins an advantage over me. It made no sense. I was simply on edge.

"Must be mistaken, then," Crimmins said, knowing I had lied but not pressing the point, giving himself an advantage over me nonetheless. "I wish you'd help me."

"Why should I?"

He considered that. "What you just said, about loyalty, cops backing cops. I mean, I know you walked patrol for a while. In fact, just yesterday I spoke to your partner, Mark Masterson. I think you two remained in touch, haven't you? I mean, after he went to Internal Affairs." He said it as a matter of fact, as if to imply nothing at all. Then, as if to disperse the stink of it, he went on. "Someone once told me that policing is a game of inches. Well, I don't play for inches, Officer, and for some reason I believe neither do you."

"I'd take an inch," I said. "I'm just trying not to go backward."

"Ha ha, I understand the feeling," he said, supposing he had gained a little with me. I knew he was doing his best to establish a rapport, and not simply because he needed me. He wanted me to like him. Perhaps he had some misbegotten notion of the pair of us partnering up, fighting crime, and the realization that he may have cherished such an absurd, romantic idea made me soften a little. "One thing you can answer for me, Officer," he said. "Did Shawn Garrity pull you from this investigation, or did you quit?"

"Garrity pulled me," I said.

"Why?"

"Karpatkin."

"Of course," he said. "I'm sure Officer Karpatkin's rather dramatic appearance on the scene made things troublesome for you, ha ha. I suppose it would've been too much to hope that you'd quit in a froth of moral indignation. No? But I imagine Garrity's frustration. After all, it was your job to make sure police officers—what did you say?—backed other police officers? So they could get the job done? That all sounds very noble, of course." I didn't take the bait, and he continued. "But you do understand I want the opposite from you?"

"What exactly do you want, counselor?"

"The truth," he said.

"The truth. That's cute."

"I want you to tell the jury that Officer Reed admitted shooting Mr. Dewberry and flaking a gun on his dead body."

"Sake of argument," I said, "say she broke down in tears and confessed all that to me, did she also say why she shot the guy? I mean, isn't that kind of important to you?"

He reclined a little in his chair. "I'm just a prosecutor, Officer. Why people commit crimes is above my pay grade. Besides, motive is not an element of my burden of proof at trial."

"Crap. You want truth from me, counsel, then tell me the truth."

"I don't know why she shot him," he said. "I don't. And you can say, well, Monty, she was inexperienced, she was scared, or maybe she felt the young man disrespected her a little bit. Who knows, ha ha, maybe Mr. Dewberry in fact was acting like a shithead. But it doesn't matter, Officer. The short answer is I don't know and I don't care."

"What's the long answer?" I said.

His eye went momentarily to the detective beside me before he turned again to me and said, very seriously, "Cops shoot black men, Officer. I'm tired of it."

"Georgina Reed isn't cops," I said.

"She's a murderer. And frankly I'm sick of hearing cops explain themselves. I'm sick of the excuses, which by now all sound like—excuses. I told you I'm not in this game for inches. I'm in this game to change the game. At the end of the day Georgina Reed is neither here nor there. I'm not interested in putting Georgina Reed in jail. I'm interested in putting her uniform in jail, and everything it stands for, because that's the only way anything is ever going to—" Crimmins stopped himself and appeared to regret opening this window into his soul. He became sternly businesslike again, sitting up straight in his chair and fingering the scissors on his desktop. "She murdered Mr. Dewberry, Officer. That's why she tried to make it look like it was something else. Hell, I don't need you to tell me her confession. Georgina Reed confessed to murder the moment she planted that gun."

"You kidding?"

"Actually, no, I'm not."

"If she planted the gun—and good luck proving that to a jury, counsel— she had the best reason I can think of."

"Which is what?" he asked.

"You."

"What's so terrifying about me, Officer?" he asked with his jury smile.

"Everything you just said."

His smile remained but the life drained from it, and he said nothing for a while. I didn't either. At last he stood and buttoned his suit jacket. Then he walked to his window and with his back to me said, "She's innocent? Georgina lied to tell the truth? Is that what you're saying?"

"She doesn't have to prove she's innocent. She doesn't have to prove a damn thing," I said. "That's your job, counselor. She's a criminal defendant, and you put liars in the grand jury to make her a criminal defendant."

"If police can lie to prove they're not murderers," he said, "why can't Mr. Odom lie to prove they are?"

"Good luck proving anything with Odom. Jury won't even believe his name's Odom after Janus has five minutes with him."

"And I suppose you believe Karpatkin's a liar, too," he said, and I made a gesture. "By which I assume you mean he told a story to IAB on the night of the incident that exonerated defendant Reed."   ·

"Yeah."

"He backed a fellow cop," Crimmins said, his affect flat but his eyes bright, "like cops are supposed to do. Out of loyalty. So cops don't die. To get the job done."

"Go fuck yourself."

"In any event I take it your objection to Officer Karpatkin is not that he lied to IAB, but that he told the truth to the grand jury? Not that he's a liar but a snitch?"

"I—" I began, but immediately thought better of saying more. He was being a lawyer with me, a damn good one, building a trap for me with my own words. I wanted to back away, but my foot was already caught in the iron teeth of his logic.

"Yes, I understand," he said. "You think Officer Karpatkin is a snitch or a rat or whatever pejorative term the police like to employ in such situations. But a snitch tells the truth. I mean, ha ha, that's why you find them objectionable, isn't it? But if you object to Officer Karpatkin telling IAB the truth, it's because you must know the truth yourself. And you know the truth because Officer Reed confessed to you."

I had no answer. Or rather I had many answers but none that I could say out loud. Like a teenager sulking in my room I insisted to myself that I was right even though I knew I was wrong. He waited for me to get over it. I didn't.

Then what he said was this: "Or perhaps she didn't. Perhaps she didn't confess as much to you in so many words. You see, it's not particularly important how you frame your testimony to the jury because you know the truth just as well as I do. And I suspect you're as bothered by it as I am."

Still I said nothing, and he went on. "I need you to do something for me, Officer Way. I need you to be a cop again."

"Sorry—?"

"A cop will do whatever it takes to get the job done, isn't that what you just told me?"

"No."

"The job I'm offering you is the best job in the world," he said. "It's the job you signed up for. It's the job that maybe somewhere along the way you forgot about because out there sometimes it's hard to see. It's justice, Officer. That's the job I need you to do for me."

"Just us, huh?" I said. "Like Bumpurs says? Just you and me, counselor? Well, forget about it. There is no us."

He sat and became serious again. "I told you I know your problem, Officer. You've been looking for the right way out, only they won't let you. That's why Garrity took you off. Am I right?"

"No."

"Hell with Shawn Garrity. I can back you out of this and make you a hero," he said, and I smelled sulfur. "You do this thing for me—and you know it's the right thing, Officer, even if you have to hold your nose while you're doing it— you can write your ticket. Gold shield. Get out of that shitty office downtown and back into real police work. No one'll take your pension. I'll put that in writing."

"No thanks."

He stiffened. "I'll tell you something about Shawn Garrity, you really want to know. Garrity puts himself over like your daddy, but he's not your daddy. He doesn't give a fuck about you. All the time he's thinking about the job. You get between Shawn Garrity and the job, watch what happens. He'll forget your name. He'll leave you by the side of the road."

"But you are asking me to come between him and the job, aren't you?"

"Garrity's idea of the job," he said. "Not the job."

"Counsel, you're getting all metaphysical. Pretty soon I'm going to wonder if I'm really here."

"You need to decide if you're still a cop."

"I'm not a cop, counsel, you just said," I answered. "I just move papers around."

"Then I guess I'm talking to the wrong man. I thought maybe you could help me get some justice here."

"My hat's off to you if you know what that is."

"Sometimes it's as simple as sleeping better at night," he said. "Maybe all you need is a simple act of contrition." As he spoke he drew a stapled packet of paper from a file and laid it carefully on the desk in front of me. The transcript from Karpatkin's IAB interview. "Interesting reading?"

"Pomeroy thought so."

"Surprised a few people that Tommy Janus had it."

"He's a resourceful guy, our Tommy."

"Oh, I know all about Tommy," he said. "Any idea where he might've picked this up?"

"I didn't give it to him. I know that."

"You sure?"

"Should I call Irving Meltzer now?"

"I told you this was just a friendly chat, didn't I?"

"So you lied," I said, standing.

"I can't nail you for having this," he told me abruptly as I moved to the door. "But I can sure as hell nail Detective Masterson for giving it to you. Maybe that would mean something to you, but from what I see here today my guess is it wouldn't."

"Don't ever pretend you know a damn thing about me."

"I'm suggesting you get on the right side of this thing, Officer. While you can still choose sides."

Next to me the detective stood, ready to perform. Nor did I dismiss the possibility that she might. She was small, and small is dangerous. Yet all that happened that afternoon was I said, "Must be a comfort to have God Almighty kiss your ass every morning, counsel. Me, I never know whose side He's on."

Alone in the elevator I thought of a hundred really clever things I might have said to Montgomery Crimmins, but goddamn it, that's always the way it is.

HENRY

TWENTY-EIGHT

Irving Meltzer, Esq., served his motion to quash my subpoena and I duly appeared in a dark suit and unmemorable tie in Justice Henry K. Pomeroy's courtroom inside Brooklyn Supreme promptly at 9:30 as ordered. At twenty minutes before ten o'clock Montgomery Crimmins came through the big doors in back with a woman I'd never seen before. They walked to the prosecution table and he dropped a big file on it—*thunk*—all the goods they had on me, I supposed. Meltzer and I remained in the gallery and watched them calmly as Christians watching lions. The woman with Crimmins was very beautiful. "Probably fucking her nightly," Meltzer attempted to whisper in my ear with breath like a camel, but his voice seemed to have only one setting. Crimmins turned at that moment and stepped over to us. "Counselor," he said to Meltzer and took his hand. "And a good morning to you, Officer." He was smiling as if Meltzer was right.

Betty Moon entered soon after that. She spoke violently to Crimmins then dropped next to me and said nothing for a spell, a jittery caffeinated presence in my periphery, then she began pulling paraphernalia out of two or three over-stuffed canvas tote bags, arranging it all haphazardly on the wooden bench seat, then jamming it all back again to no apparent purpose. Then, standing in front of Meltzer and me, she put her ink-stained fists on her bony hips and asked if I'd been a bad boy. We talked of nothing important for long enough for each of us to realize the realignment of our previous relationship. I was no longer her source. I was her story.

At ten o'clock Pomeroy took the bench. The sergeant told us to rise. We did, obediently, and Meltzer and I stepped into the well and stood at the same faux walnut table where Georgina Reed had sat. The table was bolted to the linoleum floor, I noticed, and not because they were worried someone might steal it; I'd seen defense tables upended in Brooklyn Supreme when the guy blew trial, sometimes chairs thrown too. That's what sometimes happens on this side of the room, I was thinking, the defense side.

Pomeroy sat. He did not meet my eyes, nor did he once say my name. When he referred to me at all I was *the movant*, which was an improvement on *boat boy*.

THE COURT: On the record. Let's call it in.

THE CLERK: Number seven on the miscellaneous calendar, People of the State of New York against Georgina Reed and Gordon Holtz. Defendants not present in the courtroom. Counsel, your appearances, please.

MR. CRIMMINS: For the People of the State of New York, Montgomery Crimmins. Good morning, your honor. Good morning, counsel.

MR. MELTZER: Good morning, Mr. Crimmins. Good morning, young lady over there.

MS. BURNETTE: Assistant District Attorney Sarah Burnette for the People.

THE COURT: Counsel, now would be your turn.

MR. MELTZER: Yes, Judge, not a problem, not a problem at all. Irving Meltzer for Mr. Way, or should I say Officer Way, and that's Meltzer with a Z not an S and my offices are at 301-1/2 Old Country Road. In Hicksville. In New York.

THE COURT: Counsel. Ms. Burnette, nice to see you. Now that we're all friends, I have an application before me on a grand jury subpoena. You have the motion, People?

MR. CRIMMINS: I have it, but--

THE COURT: Counsel, step up.

(Whereupon, there was a pause in the proceedings.)

THE COURT: On the record. Counselor, I have received your motion to quash.

MR. MELTZER: Thank you very, very much, Judge.

THE COURT: Mr. Meltzer, I think you forgot to include the second page of your moving papers in your courtesy copy.

MR. MELTZER: Did I? I--

THE COURT: Mr. Crimmins, you have been served with the movant's papers, I take it?

MR. CRIMMINS: Yes, Judge.

THE COURT: Did you get Mr. Meltzer's page two?

MR. CRIMMINS: It's upside down, but I have it, Judge. I figured it out.

MR. MELTZER: Sorry, everybody. Sorry. I'm technically or technologically challenged, you might say. My wife, she--

THE COURT: I think I get the thrust of the motion, Mr. Meltzer. People, you do not wish to withdraw the subpoena, is that correct?

MR. CRIMMINS: Absolutely not, your honor. Officer Way is a witness to a homicide--

MR. MELTZER: Your Honor, how can he be a witness if he ain't even--

THE COURT: Counsel, I have your argument. Or four-fifths of it. If I understand your papers, you're contending the movant's conversation with defendant Reed was privileged in some manner?

MR. MELTZER: I'm saying he can't testify what she told him--

THE COURT: I'm trying to read between the lines in your brief. You're contending the movant cannot be compelled to testify in the grand jury, isn't that the gist of your application, Mr. Meltzer?

MR. MELTZER: I'm sorry, the what?

THE COURT: The gist of your motion?

MR. MELTZER: Yes, yes, it is, Judge. The gist. More or less.

THE COURT: More or less, counsel?

MR. MELTZER: I believe our contention, Judge, our argument, is in the first place Mr. Way refuses to give testimony against, ah, against his fellow policewoman Miss Reed there, and additionally any communication between them was privileged like you said so how can he be a witness? Please, it's ridiculous. Am I right?

THE COURT: And, People, you contend otherwise?

MR. CRIMMINS: We do, your honor. We believe
Officer Way has evidence relating to a homicide under
investigation by the Civil Rights Bureau of my office and
should be compelled to give that evidence to a grand jury.

THE COURT: What evidence?

MR. CRIMMINS: Defendant Reed made incriminating
statements to Officer Way concerning the homicide
incident.

THE COURT: And your belief is based upon what,
Mr. Crimmins?

MR. CRIMMINS: Yes, Judge.

THE COURT: It wasn't a yes or no question, People.
I'm trying to get at whether you have a good-faith basis
to issue a subpoena or whether you're just rubbing your
lucky rabbit's foot and hoping for the best?

MR. CRIMMINS: No, your honor.

THE COURT: Why don't you tell me why you believe
defendant Reed made admissions of wrongdoing to
the movant?

MR. CRIMMINS: The subpoena is based upon fact, or
upon information and belief. In utmost good faith.

THE COURT: Mr. Crimmins, I'm not even going to
attempt to parse your answer--

MR. MELTZER: Your Honor, with all due respect or you
know, the D.A. there, the gentleman over there with the
young lady--

THE COURT: I believe you're referring to Mr.
Crimmins, counsel?

MR. MELTZER: Yes. The D.A. over there who's doing the
talking, he wants to go on a fishing trip for evidence
and put Mr. Way in the grand jury and make him swear to
tell the truth but what's he supposed to say anyway?
How's he even know? How's he a witness? I don't get it.

MR. CRIMMINS: Judge, you have our opposition papers.
Our argument is that--

THE COURT: Hold that thought, People. I feel
certain you're about to embark upon an argument of such

```
monumental eloquence that it would carry all before it,
but I'm afraid your words would be wasted on me.
    MR. CRIMMINS: Judge?
    THE COURT: I'm going to recuse myself from
consideration of the pending motion to quash. As it
happens, and for the record, I have a relationship
with the movant, a relationship of a personal nature,
so under the circumstances it would be the prudent
thing for another judge of this court to consider the
instant application.
```

And with that, all heads turned comically to me. Meltzer was whispering "The fuck—?" privately in my ear for all the world to hear, and Pomeroy had already adjourned the case and left the bench before Crimmins came to his senses and asked to "inquire if I may, Judge, about the nature of this personal relationship with Officer Way?" Pomeroy didn't bother to disguise his annoyance at the question, but annoyance was all it was. When he left I couldn't help but feel disappointed. I had wanted to hear Pomeroy's answer. I had always thought our relationship strictly impersonal.

I had a few hours to kill before my name appeared in the afternoon newspaper, so I walked from Brooklyn Supreme to Park Slope, down Atlantic then Flatbush then south on Eighth Avenue. Garrity wouldn't miss me. In fact, he'd be relieved. Around me now Garrity was twenty years older. Already he'd begun to treat me courteously, actually excusing himself by me in the hallway at headquarters as if I was a stranger, probably on Tommy Janus's three-hundred-dollar-an-hour advice. Like Crimmins he certainly had a file on me. Crimmins had been right about one thing at least—Garrity was not my daddy. Of all the looks the Avocado King had thrown me over the course of my life, he'd never once looked at me as Garrity now did.

Even so, Garrity, Georgina, Tommy Janus—all of them and everything seemed thankfully a world away as I walked along the quiet Victorian streets of that brownstone neighborhood where the trees had broken into spring green and the air felt like Easter. Each step forward took me backward a little, for this was the time of year, when the air was this way, that the boats went into the water in Gerritsen Beach. For years I'd missed it, but it came back to me now with sudden clarity, our annual rite of spring with my father and the other men at the Tamaqua Marina reveling in the turn of the season, drinking morning cans of beer and flicking spent cigarette butts into Plumb Beach Channel, the King already in shorts, his legs brown. And each spring as a boy I washed the winter off Pomeroy's big cruiser, which filled the slip next to ours, dwarfing my father's Sea Ray. Pomeroy thanked me. He paid me in cash. Later I fell in love with his daughter, and then she was gone. That was our relationship of a personal nature.

Kat was at the door of her townhouse, a small suitcase in her left hand. "Oh. Can you fix this thing?" she said when I hove into view, as if I'd only just run to the corner store for a carton of milk in my pajamas.

I walked up the stoop. "What thing?"

"The—I don't know what you call it. The deadbolt thing. It's stuck or something."

"Okay," I said, locking the door, which gave a respectably heavy, reassuring click.

"I'm leaving," she told me when I handed back her housekeys, our fingers touching.

"I thought you left."

"I mean I'm going to Shelter Island for the weekend," she told me. "I'd invite you, but I hate you."

"Your mother hates me too."

"She doesn't hate you like I do, though," she said. "She's just scared of tall policemen. She voted for George McGovern, you know. Oh—goddamn it, Will, I'm furious with you. Why haven't you called? I left you like four messages. You know how humiliating that is?"

"Kat—Christ."

"Stop it," she said. "You can't just disappear for days and weeks. Say you're sorry."

"I'm sorry."

"But you're not, though," she said. "You're never sorry for anything really. You're never sorry because you think the world is oh so unfair to poor sad Will Way so you always have an excuse to do or say whatever you—"

"Kat, I—"

"—which is just fucking ridiculous. I mean, really, Will. You don't have any excuses. You don't."

"No."

"You're exactly where you put yourself, every time," she said, and I was looking at her, recalling with immediate regret how she was, how we were when we were. I moved to kiss her but she didn't let me. "I have to go. My car's here."

I followed her gesture to the street where a black Crown Vic idled, and behind the rear glass Phillip waved. I waved back. "Your yellow Benz still in College Point, I guess—?"

"I got it back. No thanks to you."

"I'm sorry."

"Nine hundred dollars," she said. "Sorry for my car, or—?"

Her driver honked. Or maybe a car behind his honked because the black car was blocking traffic on her narrow street. Three cars were now lined up, waiting. "What's that?" I asked her, indicating.

"It's a Free Georgina! ribbon, silly," she said unnecessarily. "I'm treasurer of the mothers' chapter at school. Hold this." She handed me her suitcase then she unclasped the yellow ribbon and fixed it to the lapel of my suit jacket. She was standing a step above me on her townhouse stoop, so we were eye to eye.

"Ah, hell, Kat, I don't wanna wear—"

"You have to," she said. "After all, you can do more for her than all of us. We're having a fundraiser Tuesday night, by the way. Maybe you can say something? Can you come? Everyone knows you're for Georgina."

"You're having a bake sale for Georgina—?"

"Not exactly, but it was Karen's idea," said. "The fourth grade's doing scenes from *Pirates of Penzance* with costumes and then there's a benefit auction for Georgina's legal defense fund. Every family in the lower school has to donate something. Catherine's putting up their lodge in Telluride for a week, can you believe it? With lift tickets and a housekeeper. Bidding starts at ten thousand."

"Dollars or lira?"

Another honk, more impatient than the first, and we started down the stoop.

"We could take Phillip," she said, "if I stop hating you by ski season."

Honk.

"On second thought," she said, "maybe you oughtn't come Tuesday."

"Why not?"

Honk.

She stopped walking and touched my arm. "Because of that—that thing you said, in the newspaper—you know—that *shithead* thing. Some people— the ones who don't know you—think you're a racist."

Honk.

"I don't get it. Do people think I'm a hero or a racist?"

"Maybe it's possible to be both?" she said with a frown.

"Shot by both sides. Story of my life."

"I think everyone's a little confused right now." Brightening, she said, "I love you again, though!"

Honk. Honk.

"I'm glad," I said, meaning it. "But, Kat, you know you and your friends—you know you can't do anything for Georgina, don't you?"

"What do you mean, Will?"

"Bake sales don't help once you lawyer up."

"You can help if you want to," Kat told me, kissing me at last, tentatively, almost carelessly, but the taste and remembered feel of her, unfelt for so long, weakened me with love or limerence. "You can try."

"Maybe I don't want to," I said, fingering the ribbon on my lapel.

"Well. It's really not about Georgina anymore anyway, is it?" she said. "You leave that ribbon on, Will Way. I'll be back Sunday. Goodbye!"

She stepped to the car door, but I stopped her. She looked at me, her face bright and happy. "Kat," I said. "I'm going to be in the newspaper again. This afternoon."

"Oh—" she said, the sun of her smile fading behind a cloud.

"Nothing horrible, just—"

She considered this a moment then asked, "Is that why you came to see me?"

"No."

"Why did you come?"

"I miss the hell out of you," I said.

"Do you—?" she asked. Time stopped, and I nodded yes. Tears filled her eyes but did not fall, and she said, "Well—let's just—let's just see when I get back," and she stepped into the waiting Crown Vic. "Oh—!" she said, rolling down the window as the car began to move off. "Don't go near the co-op with that yellow ribbon! Or the yoga place. Or the tea place. Or anyplace with a black sign in the window."

"Why not?"

"Everyone's picking sides and getting angry all of a sudden," she called through her window somewhat embarrassedly before the car drove away and she was gone again.

TWENTY-NINE

Before seven o'clock that evening my father came for me in the emergency room. I was sitting on the slippery paper on the hard upholstery of the examination table since my room had no chair. It was uncomfortable. The room stank of disinfectant, which made everything worse. They wouldn't let me leave unattended, so I went down the long list in my head until I at last came to my father. When he arrived I was no longer very drunk and somewhat chastened by the afternoon's events, so when he asked me the obvious question I told him as little as possible.

"I got punched," I answered.

"Never give the old man more than he asks for," my father said. "That's your motto."

"In the eye. Okay?"

I opened my good eye to find the Avocado King in all his glory examining me critically over a cheap pair of drugstore half-frame reading glasses. "Ooh-wee. Gonna have one beaut of a shiner, boy. Who socked you? Girl?"

"Just—someone I pissed off," I said. "What else's new? Let's get out of here."

"Ask for it?"

"Sure. Probably. Fuck knows."

"Probably," he repeated. "You know, kiddo, *you don't always deserve what you get in life—*"

"*—but usually you get what you deserve.* I know, Dad. You said. Like a million times. Now will you sign me out of this fucking depressing place?"

"Don't cuss. And hold your horses," he said. "Nicole's bringing you some pills."

"Hell's Nicole?"

"Nurse right over there," he said, waving at a trim brunette in pink scrubs standing outside the door. She waved back and smiled coquettishly. "Real friendly girl."

"I bet," I said. "Can we go already?"

"What's the hurry?"

"I hate hospitals," I said.

"Why?"

"I just hate hospitals is all," I told him.

"You never even been in a hospital your whole entire life."

"I've been in a hospital."

After Kat drove away with her suitcase I'd sat on her stoop twenty minutes, suddenly spent, the day having caught up with me at last. Her neighbor, the aging hippie with a graying ponytail and chapped lips, came outside braless in a purple peasant dress. Presently her corgis followed and barked. Carrying a small bag of compost she eyed me with suspicion. I said hello. She turned away. On her dress was a black ribbon.

I spent the balance of the afternoon wandering the silent narrow streets of Park Slope lined with townhouses identical except for the doors. I walked slowly, contemplatively, as though in a church labyrinth. Mostly I had no place to go, or no place I really wanted to be. I ended up inside an old man bar where I waited in the beer and cigarette fug for the *Brooklyn Daily News* to hit the sidewalk. While I waited I drank and drank for lack of any better idea and then I was thinking of Kat's face when I told her that I missed her. Just words, but the effect upon her was like an injection. I hoped they'd been true, those pretty words, not only for her sake but for my own.

COP UNION HONCHO PROTECTS GEORGINA STUNNER: JUDGE ADMITS "PERSONAL RELATIONSHIP"

Sparks flew this morning in Brooklyn when a lawyer representing a police witness in the Georgina Reed cop-murder case clashed in open court with prosecutors. William Way, Jr., an official of the Patrolmen's Benevolent Association, the police union, is refusing to obey a subpoena to testify against Reed in the grand jury investigating the case. The district attorney claims Way, 33, has "material evidence" against Reed, arguing before Justice Henry Pomeroy in Supreme Court that Reed confessed her crimes to Way.

Today's dispute will not be decided by Judge Pomeroy, however, who stunned the courtroom by admitting a "personal" relationship with Way. While he did not elaborate, Pomeroy has faced mounting criticism for his handling of the Reed case after he dismissed charges against—

The article unsettled me and the booze uncoordinated me and soon after I walked out of the bar onto the twilit avenue I tripped on a dog. When I turned onto a tree-lined side street a man in flip-flops—at first all I noticed about him—came toward me with a bichon frise on a chrome chain. As we neared, the bichon darted beneath me on hyperkinetic little legs. I skipped awkwardly over it, mumbling something between an apology and an expletive, and continued on my way, my mind full of contradictory thoughts.

"Hey—hey, you," a voice behind me called. "How about a sorry here?"

"What's that—?" I said, stopping, turning, genuinely baffled.

"A sorry would be nice."

"I said sorry—what?"

"Yeah, well, I didn't hear you." Now the bichon was barking at me with animated stupidity, looking like a stuffed toy, each yap a pistol shot on the silent street. "You kicked my dog."

"Oh, give me a—"

"Apologize, you—!" he said, and I saw he was a larger, angrier version of his dog. Each had a curly cap of white hair. Each had dark rheumy dots for eyes and yellowish streaks along their mouths. The bichon was now pulling the leash taut to have at me, sweeping left and right like a metal detector in the man's hand. The man himself was seventy at least and like Kat's neighbor certainly one of Park Slope's urban pioneers, come to Brooklyn thirty years before to stake his claim when love was free and houses cheap. They had remade Park Slope in their own image, these fading boomers, anointing themselves with patchouli and painting their brownstones pink and purple, but now everything was changing before their eyes. Now investment bankers were doing to them what they themselves had done to pipe fitters and old Italian widows, and it pissed them off.

"Apologize, you—shithead!" he said, spitting mad. He wore a black T-shirt with Dewberry's huge copyrighted face and the words JUSTICE=TRUTH in white five-inch capitals.

"Okay," I said, "I'm sorry I stepped on your dog when it ran under my foot."

"Oh, so you're a smart-ass, too, huh?"

"No."

"What do you think, you're some big honcho there in your suit and tie with the yellow ribbon on top of it?"

"Excuse me?"

"You know what you did," he said.

"What'd I do?" I answered with some apprehension, wondering what he knew about me, wondering if he was a spirit sent from the beyond.

"You kicked my dog."

"I didn't kick your dog."

"You kicked my dog, you shithead," he said.

"What'd you call me?"

"Shithead!"

"You can't say things like that."

"You kicked my dog. I saw you," he said, secure behind his certainty. People like me kicked dogs, even if we didn't. "You shithead. You don't care. You don't care about anything, all you—people—in your fancy suits—all you care about is yourselves."

"What people?"

"You with your yellow ribbons and your expensive private schools for your rich kids," he said. "Ruining the neighborhood, double-parking your Mercedes-Benzes, pushing people off the sidewalk with your strollers. People used to care about people. Now it's all fancy restaurants and sushi and grocery stores and real estate brokers and opticians. I know you. I know your type. Real estate brokers. And opticians."

"Sorry about your dog. Okay, mister?"

"Oh, sure, now you're sorry," he said, coming nearer on wary footsteps in his flip-flops. The dog was still barking. "You're not sorry. You're just ashamed of yourself is all. You know what you did."

"Okay, hold it—"

"You fascist," he said. "You know what you did. You walk right by with your yellow ribbon like a real estate broker raising rent on people and taking their parking spaces with your fancy Mercedes-Benzes like you don't even care and shooting people in the back—"

"Wait—"

"Opticians and real estate brokers and fancy restaurants and Mercedes-Benzes—"

"That's just—"

He hit me in the eye. I didn't feel a thing so much as surprise, and at once my ankle became entangled in his leash as I tried for balance. I felt the dog break under my shoe and heard it yelp, but there was nothing I could do. Off-balance I fell backward on the bluestone pavement, cracking my head so hard I saw stars and planets glitter in the faint spring green of the ginkgo tree above me, and before all went black I saw the man hustle off, bent and crabbed on flip-flops, JUSTICE=JUST US in capitals on his back, the bichon squeaking piteously in his arms.

"Hey, boy. You're in the papers again," the Avocado King said to me over his cheap half-frame reading glasses. We were eating hamburgers with all the trimmings with fries and vanilla malts on the side. He had ordered. "You and Lemons. See that?" He showed me.

"I read it."

"Sounds like trouble."

"Not really," I said.

"Hope you know what you're doing."

"I don't. But, what it is, Dad, it's just—" I started to say, but then I realized I didn't know what it was.

"Georgina, huh?" he said, reading carefully. "She's the one killed the young boy over there, right?"

"Yeah."

"Some job," he said. "You ever get tired of ugly work, you know, I got a place waiting for you at the market. Go home at night with some money in your pocket and feeling good. Make an honest living."

"I'm fine making a dishonest living, thank you."

"Well," he said, reading. "Think about it."

"I thought about it, Dad. Like fifteen years ago already."

"That was fifteen years ago," he said.

"I'm not cut out to sell avocados."

"Now, why do you have to say it like that?" he said, putting down the newspaper, almost hurt. "The produce business isn't who you are, kiddo. No business is who you are, not even being a policeman."

"I'm an American. Americans are what they do."

"Well, that's just plain silly," he said. "I meet someone nice, I don't say, 'I'm Bill Way. I wholesale fresh avocados.'"

"And I can understand why not," I said. "But who are we, then? In your opinion?"

"Who you are is what you do with what you got," he said, wiping his mouth genteelly with a napkin.

A full second elapsed before I broke into laughter. "Jesus, Dad, get that out of a fortune cookie?"

"It's true," he said, not offended, eating his hamburger, drinking his malt. "And whatever you got, you gotta do something with it, make the world a better place."

"You're full of proverbs today," I said. After a moment I relaxed a little and told him, "Truth is, Dad—the truth is I don't know if I'm making things better or worse."

He weighed that for my sake before saying, "Then you're probably making them worse."

"I just don't know. I mean the world's kind of a fucked-up place right now. Maybe not for you—"

"Why not for me?" he said. "And knock off the cussing, boy, you know I don't like it."

"All I mean is you had your fight, Dad. You knew who your enemy was. You knew you were there to win a war and—" He smiled, which was something so unexpected in the moment that I fell silent.

Then he faced me with a benevolent expression and said, "I wasn't there to win a war."

"All I meant is no one's handing out medals and ribbons in my world. I mean, sure, everyone's got a ribbon now, but not—not like yours."

"Listen, I wasn't talking about that mix-up over there in Southeast Asia, but if you think what we got here's a mess, well—" He stopped himself, as ever unwilling to speak of his war. Then he said, "Besides. I'm more proud I got sixteen people coming to work for me every morning, and they all got lives and families because of what I built. And there's a lady at a table right over there eating a salad with my produce on it. I do my best with what I got, and I keep on doing it."

"I'm not saying different, but—"

"And if I got a son takes care of his people, well, I'm proud as hell of that, too."

"Says who?"

"Well," he said, "paper here says you are, telling the DA to go fish. Him trying to get you to say something against your people."

"It's what I'm saying, Dad," I said. "I mean, you do the right thing so the wrong thing happens? Or do you do the wrong thing so the right thing happens? I don't know. I don't know what to do."

He considered that. "Maybe Henry can fix it for you. Put in the good word with somebody big. Tell them your heart's in the right place."

I nearly laughed. "Doesn't really work that way, Dad."

"He's a good man, old Lemons," he said, smiling his winning smile to himself at the recollection of the Pomeroy he once knew. "Old Lemonpuss, ha ha. How's he doing these days? Haven't seen him around the Tamaqua in a good while."

"He has white hair."

My father considered that, but all he said was Pomeroy wasn't old, which I understood him to mean that he wasn't old. He still had all his hair, my father, still the same dark blond, still sun-streaked, still perfect. "You want to talk it over?"

"I have to figure it out on my own, Dad. Besides, I think we just did."

"Well—" he started to say, then he changed his mind. "Why don't you tell me how you got that eye? Oh—reminds me. Nicole gave me this." He placed a pink pill on the tabletop. "Says here you're supposed to take this medicine with food." He was reading the label carefully through his cheap reading glasses. "These look strong. You have pain?"

"I'm numb."

"I noticed that," he said.

"She gave you her number, I suppose?"

"Only in case I had any follow-up questions," he said, snapping off his glasses.

"Follow-up questions, Dad?" I asked. "Such as, what's your sign, baby? Or, want to come up and see my etchings?"

"She was being sweet. What's a pretty little nurse gonna do with an old horse soldier like me?"

"Women are like that," I said, my mind on Kat.

"Yeah, boy," he said, smiling again, "what are women like?"

"Women don't see us how we are but how we could be."

"Who's the fortune cookie now?" he said, laughing harmlessly. "But you're wrong. Women see us exactly how we are. Sometimes find a way to live with it." He grew distant for a spell, and I ate his French fries. He absently pushed the plate over, and I knew he was thinking about my mother so I was grateful when he changed the subject. "The lady cop herself, huh?" he said, tapping the newspaper with his glasses. There was a photograph of Georgina Reed, her service portrait, wallet-sized. "Didn't realize she was a black girl."

"Didn't realize—?" I said with a full mouth, astonished. "You been living under a rock?"

"I didn't know," he answered, unperturbed. "Don't think they ever mentioned. They just say she's the policewoman who shot the boy. Maybe they think it's wrong to mention it in the papers. I don't know the rules so much these days."

"So," I said carefully, "what do you think? You think she should go to jail?"

"Jail for what?" he said.

"Murder."

"Oh, no, no—" he said. "Jail? No."

"Why not? She killed someone. Everyone says that's murder."

"Well. She's a police officer, isn't she? If she shot that boy, she must of had a good reason. She seems like a nice young lady to me. I mean, isn't she?"

"Yeah, sure. A nice young lady. A little quick on the draw maybe, but yeah. Nice. And that's what people think?—down at the marina?—over at the market?" I said, meaning, *And that's what white people think in south Brooklyn?*

"Don't think it's ever come up," he said with a shrug, and I smiled on cue, certain he was playing. Almost at once I realized he was telling the truth, however, and that there were some people yet remaining in New York City for whom Georgina Reed was not a daily obsession. I perceived that I was the anomaly, not my father, for I could no more remove Georgina from my waking life than if she were a spaceship hovering above my head.

"Then what're all the marches and protests about, in your opinion?" I asked him. "Carrying signs, looting appliance stores, burning cars. I mean, if Georgina's not a murderer, what are people so angry for?"

"They're angry. And sometimes when you're angry, all you need is someplace to put it," he said. "You gonna tell me how you got that shiner now?"

"Someone got angry," I said. "I think he mistook me for an optician. But seriously, Dad, I don't get it—why's everyone so confused and angry all of a sudden?"

"Everyone's not confused. Everyone's not angry," he stated as a matter of fact. "I'm not. World's a beautiful place. I'm glad to be here, aren't you?" He signaled the waitress for the check, and she smiled adoringly at him and came over. Her name tag read MARY. She had the face of a cat and a zaftig body that wanted to be bigger, the sort of woman who might've starred in the high school production of *Our Town*. All the Avocado King had done was order two hamburgers and she fell in love with him. I never knew whether to marvel at it or to hate him for it. He opened his wallet and counted out thirty-two singles faceup and neat. After she left, blushing, he tucked a ten-dollar bill under his plate and said to me, "If you want to know why they're out there protesting with signs, maybe the answer's as easy as reading the signs. What do they say?"

"Oh, just crazy crap."

"Such as?"

"I don't know," I said. "Give us justice, stop the violence, tell the truth—"

"I see your point," he said, smiling lightly. "Crazy."

"No, wait," I said, shifting on the slippery upholstery. "I mean it all sounds just—beautiful, right? But they don't mean any of it. They don't want justice. They want Georgina doing twenty-five to life upstate no matter what. And truth? They decided what happened before it even happened."

He said seriously, "You're angry, too."

"Maybe, but I don't have a sign," I said, recalling with a hot internal blush the cartoon monkey.

We stood, and by the door he examined me appraisingly. Close up I smelled his familiar smell. He pronounced me fit for duty and we walked over the nighttime sidewalk to his blue-black beater illegally parked on the corner, stinking of gasoline, the windows down, the doors unlocked, one wheel riding the curb, but his radio was not stolen and there was no orange parking ticket under his wiper for his life was charmed—small wonder the man loved the world. He held on to my hand after shaking it, telling me, "One thing I did learn over there, and maybe it's something to consider. If you fight long enough and hard enough, you become the enemy. Anyway, boy. Boat's in the water. Be nice to see you at home."

THIRTY

I shrugged at ADA Jacqueline Kane when she asked me what the hell. In fact my eye had gotten worse overnight and was now perfectly livid. Smiling a weak maternal smile that eased my mind about meeting her, she asked, "How's the other guy look?"

"Stepped on him."

Jackie Kane was the first to tell me my subpoena had been quashed, but she hadn't called to tell me that. "Crimmins already took an appeal, so tell Garrity not to relax just yet," she'd said. "You may still have to raise your hand, if the Appellate Division reinstates the subpoena. But there's something else."

"Tell me," I'd said.

"Not on the phone."

"Fister listening?"

"He already knows what I think," she'd said.

"So why meet?"

"I can't tell if someone's lying to my face when I can't see his face."

"You already think I'm a liar, Jacqueline."

"Don't remind me. The Promenade in thirty."

So twenty-eight minutes later I met Jackie Kane on the Brooklyn Heights Promenade, which overlooked the East River and all the pretty rectangles of lower Manhattan—a splendid location for a first date, except that we each had seen it so many times by now that all the skyline offered was a degree of privacy in the company of a hundred Ukrainian tourists, several in I♥NY T-shirts and newly purchased baseball caps too large for their heads. Jackie had news, she said. I could think of many possibilities, none good. Nevertheless the midmorning sun was cheerfully bright, and Jackie Kane wore sunglasses and pants and a sleeveless shirt that showed two fine arms freckled a little to match her strawberry-blond hair. I asked no questions at first but simply waited for her to tell me. We both knew what it meant for her to be here, but neither of us said anything about that either. We just accepted it as something necessary or at least unavoidable.

"Whitey Fister wants Pomeroy off the Georgina case, that's no secret," she said without a run-up. We were walking north over the broad walkway cantilevered off the westernmost edge of the Heights. "Thing is, Tommy Janus wants Pomeroy off too," she continued with an inaudible sigh. She stopped walking and put an elbow atop the rail. Around us people were strolling and sitting and pointing cameras over the river. I watched them, and behind her sunglasses Jackie Kane watched me. "What are they up to, Tommy and Whitey?" she asked, not rhetorically, and I understood she wanted to see how my brain was put together.

"Tommy's easy," I said. "He's afraid of what Pomeroy'll do to him."

"Which is what?"

"Give him a fair trial."

She smiled, nearly laughed. "Is that where you are now, Will Way? Or you just trying to suck up to me? What about the DA, then?"

"He's afraid of Pomeroy, too," I answered. "Only I don't get it. Fister won three elections in this town or at least stole them fair and square."

"Fister'd win the Miss Brooklyn contest if the party wanted to see him in a dress."

"How's Pomeroy figure in?"

"The people who run things around here want a new old white male," she said. "You know the talk, I'm sure. The party's shining up Pomeroy for the primary in September, but Fister won't go gently."

She waited as three blond tourists with Slavic cheekbones stood near us to take pictures. I gestured for their camera and after they'd each given my purple face a somewhat quizzical once-over I lined them up against the backdrop of Gotham and our ancient bridge. One of them wore a still-new black T-shirt reading NEW YORK FUCKING CITY over the outlined image of a .38-caliber revolver. Another had a JUSTICE=TRUTH® baseball hat, white letters on black. The third had a yellow souvenir Free Georgina! ribbon pinned to her collar. By now downtown vendors sold them on Court Street, rows and rows of ribbons in black and yellow on card tables along with souvenirs and memorabilia and incense sticks and tube socks and snow globes featuring the Statue of Liberty and the twin rectangular towers that still monopolized the horizon behind us.

When the Ukrainians left, thanking me and bowing for some reason, Jackie Kane said, "You think Pomeroy got Georgina because someone picked his name out of a hat? No, Georgina was a gift. Pomeroy got the case because the party wanted him to have it and the free advertising that went with it."

"Pomeroy's got a strange way of ingratiating himself to the voters," I said, "tossing your indictment, getting himself talked up in the newspapers as a racist."

"Pomeroy's no racist, besides—"

"How do you know?" I interrupted.

"I've known him more than ten years, maybe not as long as you," she said somewhat pointedly. "Sure, Pomeroy's a canny son of a bitch, but he's no racist. Besides, a rep as a more or less benign racist isn't going to hurt him in Brooklyn, not among voters that actually vote. Not now, with everything that's going on. People who own houses get jumpy when other people try to burn them down."

"Pomeroy on the ticket for the Brooklyn Democrats?" I said. "He's no Democrat, I can tell you that. Used to have a picture of Ronald Reagan on his desk. The two of them holding hands and wearing cowboy hats."

"No choice. Brooklyn's a one-party town."

"Beijing on the East River," I said. "Come to think of it, Pomeroy's not a small-d democrat either."

"Neither is the Brooklyn Democratic Party."

"Yeah, and the National Socialists weren't socialists," I said, "but I don't think Pomeroy'd object to a hereditary monarchy. King Henry the Ninth." Kane didn't answer, didn't even smile. A shade had come down over her. I nevertheless added, "Except he has no male heir," under the circumstances having quite forgotten the fair-haired grandson pictured with Pamela in the far corner of Pomeroy's chambers.

"Henry K. Pomeroy will be DA in the fall, unless Whitey Fister can find a way to queer that. And believe me, he wants to find a way. Which brings me to you—"

"Pomeroy wasn't looking for votes when he dismissed your indictment, Jacqueline," I said. "You stepped on a rake."

"Maybe. And stop calling me Jacqueline, for fuck's sake," Jackie Kane said. "That was Monty Crimmins's deal, and Monty's a—let's just say Monty's a zealous advocate for the people, but not necessarily for the People of the State of New York. Understand? He had other problems with his case, though sitting on that IAB transcript wasn't the biggest until Pomeroy made it the biggest. I mean Pomeroy could've let it slide—a lot of judges would—but if he could give Fister an eye like yours, well, why not?"

"So what's the score?"

"I told you. Whitey's the ghost of Brooklyn past."

"What about Betty Moon's piece about—about Pomeroy's daughter?" I asked carefully, feeling like St. Peter after the cock crowed. "And all that stuff about her black boyfriend and everything?"

I was certain she would read me, yet all at once she seemed to wander in her own head. "Where does Betty dig up this crap? Must've been a slow news day." She shrugged. "Fister's got something better on Pomeroy."

"Yeah, what?"

"You."

"Me—?" I said.

"It's Brooklyn history month, Way," she said. "Know how Pomeroy became a judge?" I didn't like her voice when she asked the question and kept silent. "He wasn't always a judge. I mean he wasn't born a judge, although you might think he was. Before Pomeroy was a judge he was just a lawyer. He was probably born a lawyer, though, maybe in one of those buildings right over there." She pointed a little dreamily across the dark expanse of water. "I've always liked the one with the green pyramid on the roof. Looks like the kind of building I might've worked in, if I didn't have to look at myself in the mirror every morning."

"Go on," I said, my gut slowly tightening as she spoke.

"But that's not enough for Pomeroy. Anyone can be a lawyer—look around, Christ, sometimes I think everyone's a lawyer—but not everyone can wear a black robe. So Pomeroy gets political."

"What's that mean?"

"The usual," she said. "Fundraisers, donations to the party's widows-and-orphans fund, all that regular sort of New York City pay-to-play bullshit. That got him into One PP as a deputy commissioner. And that might've been enough for anyone else, but Pomeroy's a very hungry caterpillar. Out of curiosity, Way, you know how much it costs, you want to be elected judge in Brooklyn?"

"I have no idea."

"Well. When you join at the hundred-thousand-dollar level, the Kings County Democratic Party will throw in a misdemeanor court judgeship along with this handsome canvas tote bag. But if you really care about all those widows and orphans and pony up half a million, well, welcome to the major leagues, Brooklyn Supreme, the big time. But Pomeroy could afford it. Man's got a yacht, I hear."

"Just tell your story."

"Hey, I don't blame him," she said. "Pomeroy's got ambition, and he's got to play by rules he didn't write. Ask me how that feels, Way. At least Pomeroy's the real deal. Most judges in Supreme are the idiot brothers in Victorian nov-els. Pomeroy's not only brilliant—he went to fucking Oxford or someplace, for chrissake—but he works his ass off. You know he almost died a year ago?"

"No—really?"

"I was on trial with him," she said. "Back-to-back murder trials. Stew Liebe was crossing one of my cops. You know Stew—total ballbreaker, but dumb as a sack of hammers. And he's asking all these head-slap questions, and Pomeroy's boiling up there, sustaining all my objections. *Sustained, sustained, sustained.* Then suddenly—whump, he just goes down, behind the bench."

"Holy Mother. I didn't know."

"Heart something, they told me," she said. "Few months later he's back. Same old Pomeroy. Haughty as a lord, mean as a snake. Except his hair's gone white, just like in a ghost movie. So, hell yeah, I like Pomeroy. A lot. And I don't want him excommunicated. That's why this is hard."

"What's hard?"

"You sure you don't know?" she asked. "You don't look like you're enjoying Brooklyn history month very much."

"You're telling me Pomeroy's getting into the DA's office with payola, aren't you?"

"No, you're not listening, Way," she said. "I'm saying Pomeroy doesn't need money for influence. Pomeroy has influence for influence. Understand the difference? Now he's got a seat at the grown-up table, but mostly he's got a really big pen and he's not afraid to use it. That's why Fister's biting his nails." Then she drew herself up. "So imagine what Fister would say if he learned that this man who wants his job, this judge who just embarrassed the crap out of him by tossing his most important indictment in years—imagine what Whitey Fister would say if he learned that shortly before all this came to pass, this same pain-in-the-ass judge just happened to meet privately with a certain high-level official of the police union—"

"Whoa, wait—"

"—advocating for the defendants in that same prosecution?"

"Jackie, come on—"

"The very same police union official," she continued unabated, "with whom this very same judge admitted a personal relationship?"

"Come on, that's all such—"

"The same police union official who certainly received the same secret tran-script that led to the same dismissal of that same indictment by the same judge?"

"Jackie—"

She continued in her closing-argument voice, "You met Pomeroy, Way—in chambers—privately—after hours. Shortly thereafter, Pomeroy dismissed the indictment and barred Karpatkin's testimony from trial and very publicly fucked Whitey in the ass."

"Okay. Okay, Jackie. Let's say I met the man—"

"Don't get cute, Way," she said. "You met the man."

"Okay, I met him. So what—?"

"Will Way, I decided you're not stupid, so don't pretend you are. You'll just make me want to smoke." I looked away, and she went on, "Look. It doesn't make a damn difference what you talked about with Pomeroy. You could've talked about your Hummel collection for all they care. You met. That's enough. Fister'll use that to say you went to chambers to make your sales pitch. He'll say you used a personal connection to the presiding judge to sell the idea—just shut up and let me finish—that your men are getting fucked over by the DA and IAB and Bumpurs and the editorial page of *The New York Times*. That's what Fister'll say, and I'm not sure he'll be wrong when he does."

"He's wrong."

"Look, Way," she said. "I know that's the name of the game—you got a hand, you play it—but the trouble is you got caught. The rules say you can't do shit like that, but mostly the rules say you can't get caught doing it. And you did. You got busted giving Pomeroy information no one else has."

"Which is what?"

"Same thing you refused to give Crimmins," she said. "Georgina's story, what she admitted to you."

"You're wrong."

"You spoke to Georgina on the night of the incident. She never made a statement to us—you made damn sure of that, didn't you? So the only person on the planet with Georgina Reed's story is Will Way. And you handed it to Pomeroy on a platter three days later. Then you take out your big convincer. *Oh, what's this?* you say. You just happen to have the transcript of IAB's interview of Kevin Karpatkin in your briefcase. *Well, how did that get in there?* You drop it on Pomeroy's desk accidentally on purpose and suggest—just suggest, because you don't want to go for the hard sell, that's not your style, Way, I can tell—that Crimmins put fugazi testimony before the grand jury. You tell Pomeroy that Karpatkin must've lied in the jury because he said different on the night of and the transcript proves it. So someone must've fixed him. And regardless of whatever version's the truth, Crimmins had an obligation to turn it over to Georgina's lawyer, so Pomeroy tells you to tell Garrity to tell Tommy to make the *Brady* motion. So Tommy does. Pomeroy grants it. Case dismissed. Done and done. How'm I doing, Way? Getting warm?"

"Ice cold."

"Fine," she said, "but that's the way Fister sees it. And I have to tell you I know at least one objective third party who sees it that way, too."

"That would be you?"

"That would be me, Will Way."

I drew a breath. It was no good. The only reason for optimism was this conversation was a conversation, that it took place in Brooklyn Heights under a sunshiny morning sky instead of inside a windowless interrogation room at 210 Joralemon Street with a two-way mirror on the wall. There were many things I wanted to say to Jackie Kane, yet while I understood she was trusting me I couldn't trust her yet in return, not entirely, so the only thing I managed to say came out like an admission. "What are you people, following me around?"

"Pomeroy recused himself on your motion to quash Monty's subpoena," she said with such dismay in her voice that it made me feel foolish. "He stated on the record that you have a—what'd he call it?—*a relationship of a personal nature*? Case like this, you don't think someone's going to ask a few questions? Christ, Way, this is what we do!" After a spell, in a matter-of-fact tone, she said, "Our detectives pulled Pomeroy's visitor log. Piece of advice, Way. Next time you try a little clandestine rendezvous, don't sign the guest book." Then she demanded, "What's your connection to Pomeroy, really?"

"Jackie—"

"Tell me now. I want to know, and you owe me that."

At length—in fact after as much as half a minute—I said, "Boat boy," the two words inaudible even to me.

"Pardon me?" She snapped off her sunglasses, and the sudden fact of her two green watercolor eyes aimed at mine threw me further out of alignment.

"His goddamn boat boy, okay?" I said. "I worked at the marina where when I was a kid I used to wax his hull and pump his bilge and—"

She began to laugh, which relaxed me at first. Then when she didn't stop I began to find it irritating. "I'm sorry," she said. "So that's it. Beautiful. Beautiful! How typical of Pomeroy. *This court will not tolerate even the appearance of impropriety!* Meanwhile you and he are—hey, does he really have a yacht?"

"Fuck you, Jackie," I said, and by now I was disgusted and just wanted to leave. I supposed that if she meant to handcuff me she would've brought along a couple bruisers with bald pates and goatees, but all I saw were joggers and tourists and fat American babies pushed by dark Jamaican nannies, slow-moving and unsinkable as battleships. I said, "Jesus Christ, what the hell is going on?"

"I just told you. Now it's your turn."

"What, are you wearing a wire?" Before my eyes she unbuttoned her blouse to the navel. No microphone, but something more feminine than you'd ever think to find in Jacqueline Kane's drawer. When I faced her again she was smiling and her eyes had an almost cruel glint. Just another way to fuck with me, I knew, because I felt fucked with. I stared at the water. *God, she was good*, and I tried not to let her know I was thinking that. Certainly she knew it already and didn't need a second opinion. Almost at once I felt myself yield to gravity, to sink, and I needed to sit. I did, on a long bench facing the harbor. She sat beside me and put her long legs out. All of lower Manhattan was before us, and in the foreground of the harbor you could see sailboats and ferries and helicopters. I watched one. "Jackie—"

"You see, Way. Everything you told Pomeroy—or not, if you want to pretend—I want you to tell me, too. No one else has Georgina's story, and I want it."

"It's not even your case anymore."

"I could say the same to you," she said. "But I want to know anyway. You see, I made some decisions—well, let's just say I need to know I was right about something. I don't want to know Montgomery Crimmins's version of the truth or Tommy Janus's version of the truth or Archbishop Bumpurs's version of the truth. I want the truth."

"Truth equals justice, Jackie?"

"Fuck justice," she said. "I want the truth."

"I talked to Georgina. Twice," I said eventually. "Once on the night of. She told me a lie, but she thought it was what I wanted to hear. And maybe I did, so I let that one go. The second time she told the truth."

"How do you know?"

"Because she had no reason to lie," I said.

"Why not?"

"Because—because, Jackie, by the time they got around to arresting Georgina she realized I couldn't do a damn thing for her."

"She admitted the gun was a plant?" Kane asked.

"Of course."

"Tell me everything."

I hesitated for a single heartbeat, then I did. "That's her story anyway," I said forty-five seconds later. "The short version."

"The shorter version is your man shit her pants."

"Georgina thought Dewberry had a gun, Jackie. As it turned out she had a fifty percent chance of being right, didn't she?" I said. "And by the way, did Odom burst into flames when you asked him to raise his hand and swear to tell the truth?"

"I already told you I didn't put Odom in the grand jury," she said, peevish.

"That's why you quit the case, isn't it?" I asked her. "You knew Odom was a wrong guy and Fister bought him anyway?"

"Yes," she said. We said nothing for a moment and she seemed lost in thought. "I just don't know, Way. I mean I get she was scared, fine. But she's a cop. And part of being a cop is knowing when to hold em and knowing when to fold em. Georgina should have been—why the hell're you smiling?"

"*You gotta know when to hold em*—Kenny Rogers, right?" I said. "You just made me think about my dad is all. He'd like you, Jackie. You're just his type."

"Yeah, what's his type?" she asked in a skeptical voice.

"Women," I said. "But here's how I see Georgina Reed. Hundred years ago New York City patrolmen were six-foot-four-inch Irish brawlers. They carried hickory sticks. They didn't carry guns. They didn't need guns."

"So—?"

"Georgina needed a gun."

"You got a problem with women in law enforcement, Way?"

"Negative," I said, "but Georgina Reed was never gonna back Dewberry down through force of will and a stern demeanor."

"So, she's no cop, you're saying."

"We'll never know," I said. "All I know is she's no murderer."

"No hero either."

"No, she's no hero cop. Not like Kevin Karpatkin," I said with more bitterness than I felt in truth. "You got me there, Jackie."

"What Karpatkin did took some balls, Way. Coming forward like that—"

"Yeah, he's such a fucking hero he would've stayed in uniform, not put his hand out for the gold shield."

"Sure, he could've stayed on patrol," she said. "And Ralph Berrigan would've dropped him down an air shaft first chance he got."

"Then all of you could wear a pink ribbon for the little—"

"Oh, fuck you," she said, actually angry. "Fucking cops. Anyone goes blue on blue you jump on him with both feet even if he tells it like it is—*especially* if he tells it like it is. I'm so sick of cops and their macho crap."

"Yeah, well. I'm a cop."

"Then be a cop, Way!" she said. "You know, I can almost swallow this band-of-brothers bullshit from cops that're out there in the jungle putting their ass on the line, but I'm not gonna take it from a cop like you."

"What am I in your opinion?"

"Garrity's boat boy."

"And what the hell are you?" I answered, now hot myself. "You want to criticize me? Well, fuck you, too, lady. You didn't do a damn thing except get out of the way."

"Maybe what I'm doing I'm doing right now."

"I don't see you doing anything at all."

"That makes two of us."

"So back the fuck off," I said. "And something else. When I went upstairs to see Pomeroy, I wasn't wearing the badge. It was just talk, that's all. I have a long history with the man, none of which is any of Whitey Fister's fucking business."

"I believe you believe that because you seem like, well, a credulous guy," she said. "But since you're so trusting, Way, trust me now. There's no such thing as a friendly chat with Justice Henry K. Pomeroy. He didn't get where he is by passing the time of day with boat boys. Wake up, Way. He used you. He used the pretext of your so-called personal relationship to get you upstairs when any sensible person in your shoes would've run screaming. You have a pure heart and an empty head, and that's the only reason I'm here, but whether you realize it or not Pomeroy wouldn't have dismissed the indictment unless you showed him it was the safe move."

"Oh, bullshit, Pomeroy doesn't need me—"

"You're saying Georgina never came up? Karpatkin never came up?"

"I—I didn't even—" I said, mumbling. "It was all just—"

"Listen to you," she said, laughing at me. "You don't know what you told the man. You don't even know what his question was. Pomeroy used you, Way. Believe me, I know how it feels to be in the same room with the man. I've tried eighty-seven murder cases to verdict, but he can still make me feel like I'm wearing a skirt." She paused and examined me and seemed almost apologetic, sorry to be the bearer of bad news. "You had Georgina's story when no one else did, and he probably wanted to know if it would bite him in the ass if he tried the case."

"I don't get it."

"A good judge will find a way to dump a prosecution that won't make anyone happy, so he doesn't look ridiculous at trial," she said. "And did I mention Pomeroy's a good judge? If Georgina beat trial, sure, the papers and everybody'd jump on the DA, but they'd go after Pomeroy for holding the door. Remember Lance Ito? Me neither. The way it went down, only Fister ends up looking stupid. Which is why I called you, Way."

"Go on."

"Detective Mark Masterson got notified to Civil Rights," she said. "Didn't look happy to be there."

"Yeah, Crimmins already tried to rattle me with that."

"Did it work?"

"Yes," I said. "What's that mean for Masterson?"

"The usual. Thumbscrews. Maybe worse down the road if Crimmins can prove he underhanded that transcript to you. Did he, by the way?"

"Yes," I said. "But I didn't lie to you about that. I never gave it to Janus. And I never gave it to Pomeroy either, not that it matters."

"So Garrity passed it along to Janus?"

"My guess, yeah," I said. "I don't want Masterson touched."

"Sure he feels the same way about you?" she said, leaving the implication hang there between us unspoken. "But who knows—Crimmins would probably rather use Masterson than fuck him."

"Isn't that usually the same thing in your line of work, Jackie?"

"No," she said. "No, in fact."

"Use Masterson how exactly?"

"Against you, silly."

When that sunk in I asked her, "How do you know that?"

"Because that's what I'd do," she said. "Remember, Way, just because I'm here consorting with the enemy or whatever the hell you are, don't ever think I want to burn the house down. I'm not Bea Katzenbach, for chrissake. You try to get over on me, you'll regret it. I promise."

I looked at her a long time. "You're a real son of a bitch, Jacqueline, aren't you?"

"Why, William—and here I was all along thinking you didn't even like me."

She stood in front of me on long legs, stretched out her bare arms, and yawned prettily. She was full of contradictions, I was thinking, at once imposing in person yet fine-featured; firm of flesh yet delicate; strong yet—then again no, Jackie Kane had none of the expected antitheses of strength. Neither was she weak, much less vulnerable. She was self-contained, perhaps, simply content to remain the solitary figure in a roomful of people, unneedy of the comforts and suspect certainties of her fellow creatures. Certainly she recognized some of that same esoteric quality in me, like a freemason knows another by a handshake, and that was what drew us together and not what I'd originally believed: that with Georgina Reed each of us had broken something, and now we had to buy it. But I knew whatever I may have believed wouldn't change a thing between us. Jackie Kane couldn't care less what I thought about her.

THIRTY-ONE

Two days later my picture appeared again next to Pomeroy's in the *Brooklyn Daily News*. The following morning my PAA, Sheila Simmons, knocked politely on my locked office door. The two events were directly connected, cause and effect. "Mr. W., there's a visitor for you in the lobby," she said in a voice that made me pay attention and stop what I was doing, 12-across, NONCOMBATANT. I let her in and sat on the edge of my desk, now oddly desolate, Garrity having reconsidered my duties in light of recent events. "Someone to see you, Mr. W."

"Sheila, what happened to your ribbons?"

"Oh, I—" she said, her sensibly manicured hand moving of its own accord to the unadorned lapel of her jacket.

"You didn't take them off because of me, did you?"

"No, no," she said in a not entirely convincing denial.

"Because sometimes I say things I don't mean," I said.

"If you don't mean it, why do you say it?"

"Sometimes it's just easier to sound stupid than to think about everything."

"I understand, Mr. W.," she said, "but I didn't stop wearing them on account of our conversation. It's—it's just I don't know what's right anymore."

"You keep wearing them, Sheila. You're the only person I know who's right about any of this," I said. "Who's in the lobby anyway?"

"Henry Pomeroy."

"*Pomeroy! Holy Mother!*" I said, aghast, standing. "What's he—?"

She reeled a little at the violence of my reaction but said, "Mr. W., this Henry Pomeroy is a young Henry Pomeroy."

I followed Sheila to the lobby, where a fair-haired boy sat watching everything large-eyed, elbows on his knees. When I entered he stood on colt legs and gave me a look I cannot describe. No more than fourteen, he nevertheless could nearly look me in the eye as people from the elevator pushed around us with subway manners. "I'm Will Way," I told him, giving him my hand.

"Yeah, I know," he said. "I mean, I recognize you. From the newspaper and everything."

"With this black eye you recognize me, ha ha?"

"Ha ha."

"Ha ha."

I didn't know what to say. I took him in, quickly, as cops do, weighing the young Henry Pomeroy up as friend or foe from a dozen details that you could never write down but nevertheless knew. A friend, of course. And yet— Also, in my mind I was trying to do the math, trying to reckon how he might be Pomeroy's son, Regine's brother, arriving on Dover Street after I'd left the scene. His unmistakable likeness to Regine, and the sudden shock of seeing her eyes look back at me after nearly fifteen years, made my chest compress uncomfortably. He read my mind, quickly saying, "Pamela's my mom? Pamela Pomeroy?" He inflected his statements like questions, like he wasn't certain of his answer. At once, and not without a nameless sort of relief, I recollected the blond boy pictured on the far wall in Pomeroy's chambers. So, his grandson, I realized.

I led him to my office and for the first time was aware how shabby it was, how small, and with such a shitty view. Instinctively I felt the same blush I felt every time I took Regine across the channel to Gerritsen Beach, winding our way through the sad little streets to my father's sad little bungalow on Melba Court. I'd always placed the Pomeroys on a different plane than my own, even when the Pomeroy in question was a teenage boy.

We sat. Henry was, I decided, not like Regine at all. In fact, as we spoke I checked off all the ways he was unlike her. Yet even more was he unlike Pamela, the older sister, as unlike Regine as a sibling could be. Pamela might charitably be described as plain. If Pamela robbed you in broad daylight the most you could tell the police would be that the perpetrator was white, thickish, probably a girl, possibly a brunette—? That Pamela Pomeroy had somehow contrived to marry much less produce a son seemed unimaginable. At seventeen I supposed Pamela a nascent nun or future nonpracticing lesbian. By then, by the zenith of REGINE-N-WILL, Pamela had already been packed off to college somewhere in the frozen Indiana hinterlands, to be seen only on holidays. When home, her eyes would follow Regine and me with an inhuman, almost scientific interest. Always she would purse her thin lips at us with dissatisfaction, and never once did she say hello to me. She was ever there, lying in wait, it seemed, seated on the living room couch in gray sweatpants, sewing placemats or whatnot, at whatever early hour I carried Regine home, stealing quietly with her through the side door off the butler's pantry, both of us smelling like popcorn or salt air or each other, our backs covered in sand or grass, our lips chapped, our clothes in disarray, in love. Pamela would perceive, and say nothing.

As the boy Henry sat before me now I tried to see his mother in him, but she was not there. Like his grandfather, like Pomeroy himself, this boy was all legs and limbs. Pomeroy and Saint Ann were a mismatched pair to be sure, and Pamela had the top-heavy apple-like figure of her mother. The image of Pamela's amorphous, dimpled ass smiling above me as she heaved herself up the swim ladder on Pomeroy's Sportfish is still attached like a bruise to my recollection of her. Regine on the other hand had her father's long legs, his biological repugnance to fat. Regine would be the last child eaten in the fairy tale. She would sit watching in the cage while the witch shoved Pamela into an oven with a hobnailed boot.

This Henry Pomeroy was hardly a Pomeroy at all, with his untended tangle of blondish hair and beaded surfer necklace almost hidden beneath his uniform shirt. He had conventional boyish good looks, so unlike the enigmatic beauty of his lost sister. Regine would not turn your head on the street until you passed her for the fifth time, at which point you would realize there was no one more beautiful in Brooklyn or the world. Nor did I see any of Saint Ann, except perhaps in the downy whorls on his pale cheeks, which you could never imagine him shaving. His shirt cuff rolled up showed Pomeroy's length of bone, however, and that fact—along with the evident ease with which he sat, reclining just a little in the wooden chair opposite—hinted at the same easy self-assurance of his grandfather, which one could easily mistake for arrogance.

So strange and out of place was the sight of this boy before me, however, that for the first minute of our conversation I felt anxious, nearly nervous. The end with Regine had laid me bare to paranoiac notions, and even after the passage of so much time I couldn't think of her without an internal wince that came and instantly went, like the burn of Chinese mustard. If required to name that feeling I suppose I'd call it guilt.

Henry Pomeroy was dressed for school, but he was not at school. He wore blue slacks and a laundered white shirt—dress code, of course, as no boy his age would willingly dress that way. "Where's school?" I asked.

"Xaverian?" he said.

"No kidding. Me, too."

"I know," he said. "I mean, my mom said."

"Okay. Sophomore?"

"Frosh," he answered. "Two more weeks, then—"

"Like it?"

"Sure, it's all right, I guess."

"Brother Blessington still there?"

"Blessington, ha ha?" He laughed, his blue eyes bright. "For real?"

"Sure. No? Anyway." An awkward silence fell and his smile lost humor then dropped away altogether. My footing was too unsure to be of much help so I didn't try. "Henry. What can I do for you?"

He hesitated then said, "My mom, that's Pamela?" I nodded. "Um, she said you knew my aunt? Regine Pomeroy—?"

"I did" is all I admitted.

"Plus I saw in the paper yesterday? You and my grandpa Henry, so—I was wondering—? Look. This is weird, I know—it's only that everyone's always so mysterious about my aunt, and right now everything is—"

"Why ask me?" I said. "Why not ask your mom? Or your grandfather?"

"She won't, she—I told you. No one will. It's like bizarre, the whole thing with her and everyone. I just want to know what happened, that's all, you know? I don't think that's stupid to want to know. I want to know."

So do I.

I said, "Let's start with what you know."

"Only that there was like an argument or something with grandpa Henry and Regine. I mean, I knew that before. I already knew that. Before there was that other article in the paper, I mean. I always knew, but it was like ancient family history and you're like not supposed to mention it or whatever and I didn't really think about it until everything started happening, you know—with the case and everything? The case with the kid that got murdered by the cops and whatever? Anyway. Suddenly it's like a big deal but no one'll talk about it and every time I go over to my grandpa's house there're reporters and people with signs. It's all related, right? I mean, I know it is, but no one will tell me anything, so it's like—I dunno."

"It's not related," I said.

"But—"

"There's no connection between Regine and all this," I insisted to him and to myself.

"But the article in the newspaper said—"

"People are just making trouble for your grandfather," I said. "Any way they can. It's politics, Henry, so everything's fair game."

"I don't care what people say. I'm just—I just want to know if it's true, what's in the paper?"

"My advice is don't even read it."

"But it's my family," he said. "Everyone at school's like, oh, your grandpa's a racist or whatever and he let a murderer out of jail. And I'm not even sure what to say. It's like, I'd punch them in the face except what if it's true, you know? I have a right to know, don't I? I mean, how'm I supposed to know how to feel—"

"Henry, I'm not really sure it's my place to—"

"Don't you understand?" he said, sounding a little desperate. "There's no one else."

"Why do you care so much?"

"Because it's my family. I told you," he said. "I mean, wouldn't you want to know, if one of your family was just—gone—and you didn't know why?"

For an instant I thought Henry was being clever with me, that perhaps Pomeroy—who likely knew more of the story of my vanished mother than even I did, for the Avocado King certainly hadn't given me much at all—had told his grandson something of me, but I quickly understood from his expression that he knew nothing but the basics about me. I was only a name to him, a clue written on a scrap of paper, nothing more. Nevertheless, I answered him truthfully, "It's better not to know."

Now almost apologetic he said, "I don't know—and I guess partly it's because I'm supposed to look like her. I don't know."

"You do." I admitted the truth after all.

"Do I?" he said. "I guess. I don't really know. It's just so fucking—sorry— it's just so weird, I mean."

"But Henry—I think you should ask your mother. Or your grandfather. This is really none of my business."

"But you know," he said. "You were there."

"I wasn't. Not really. It was all so long ago, Henry. You weren't even born when all this happened," I told him, and that fact—that a young man could grow in the years between then and now—aged me in an instant. He looked downcast, and another silence opened between us. Before it could deepen I asked him, "Hey. Don't you have class?"

"I only have a ten thirty-five on Wednesdays."

"It's almost ten now," I said. "You won't make it to Bay Ridge by train."

"I don't care."

"What are you, nuts? I'll drive you."

"It's okay," he said, still gloomy and not meeting my eye, realizing his mistake in coming to me, opening himself to a total stranger. "It's just an algebra prefinal—"

"Let's go. I have a siren."

Walking out I passed Sheila, who asked with special care when I might return. Her eyes pointedly avoided Henry. I told her I didn't know. "Mr. Garrity wants to see you, when he comes in," she said. Another reason to take a long drive, I thought, and to keep on driving. I wanted to avoid Garrity, who'd said nothing yesterday about the newspaper article, which carried the succinct headline:

COP UNION BOSS IN MIDNIGHT MEETUP
WITH GEORGINA JUDGE

By now Garrity had certainly spoken to Tommy Janus. They would've decided something about me, but it wasn't the decision that oppressed me. Rather, it was the thought that I would have to stand before Garrity's desk while he delivered it, watching him writhe in discomfort, unable to look me in the eye, his face changing colors.

The article was short and mostly accurate. I was a union boss. Pomeroy was a judge. We met, although to be precise a few hours earlier than midnight— the only liberty taken by Betty Moon, who otherwise let the implication of the meeting announce itself. A photograph of my head accompanied the article, my official service photograph, my uniformed self against a green backdrop, the kind newspapers and televisions run when a cop gets killed in the line of duty. I saw myself like that for a moment, but the moment seemed neither here nor there, just a dryly factual report of my violent death. Readers were left to fill in the blanks, which meant that Henry had already been given some information about me, I realized, likely by Pamela or perhaps even Pomeroy himself. Yes, possibly my name had come up at Dover Street yesterday, or even earlier, although there wouldn't have been much to tell the boy. My connection to the Pomeroys of Manhattan Beach was never the stuff of legend. I was a footnote, an asterisk. I was the boat boy.

Still, the fact of this new Henry Pomeroy weighed upon me as we made our way south to Shore Road in Bay Ridge, winding our way down Brooklyn's southwestern edge along the harbor where container ships colored white over black over primer red stood motionless, just visible beyond the pin oaks now in full summer green. I rolled my window down, and the air was very pleasant. Soon—in fact, in time for algebra—I pulled before Xaverian High School, boxy and beige, clean and Catholic, unchanged from that still in my mind. Hardly a word had Henry and I said since we emerged from the Brooklyn–Battery Tunnel into a tangle of highway beneath the bright midmorning summer sun, and now with the car idling curbside we both realized neither of us was particularly satisfied. He didn't open the door, and by unspoken agreement I put the car in gear and we continued south toward the blue sculpture of the Verrazzano Bridge rising above the trees where Shore Road ended.

I knew a diner on Third Avenue, and we went there, a hangout for Xaverian boys and their segregated sisters from Fontbonne Hall Academy farther south at a sort of sanitary midpoint in Bay Ridge between the two. Feeling huge and bygone in my business suit and untied tie I slid over the red vinyl cushion across from Henry. *No, he is not Regine*, I told myself for the seventh time. Even as I sized him up he was doing the same to me, waiting, hopeful yet skeptical. He thought I had answers I myself wished I had. Nor did I cut quite the figure he may have expected, not with my black eye, twelve-dollar haircut, and Moe Ginsburg suit. To him the Will Way sitting before him was not the Will Way whose name had been spoken in an undertone in the dining room at Dover Street. That Will Way knew something. This Will Way was just another Brooklyn nobody.

So that first meeting was to leave us each disappointed. The whole affair went off like a tedious blind date, both of us going politely through the motions, neither of us wanting to hurt the other's feelings, each of us waiting for the clock to tick off a decent interval of minutes before we could get out of the other's sight. And, in a conversational lull, I believe for the first time in my life I uttered the phrase, "So—Clippers gonna have a defense this year?" Henry's eyes flashed, and I regretted the question at once. He gave a vague answer of tepid rah-rah for the home team, all the while thinking that on top of everything Will Way was the sort of man who watched high school ball.

Funny that he was a Xaverian boy, though. Here now were a half dozen upperclassmen, boys Pamela would never approve, all of them standing as boys stood when I was a boy with their older brothers, or fathers, slouching against the counter on an elbow, thumbs hooked in pockets. They were the same boys I knew, updated. They were still local Italians and Irish, of course, and gone were the Sergio Valenti jeans and hundred-mile-an-hour hair, but Travolta still hung about them like Paco Rabanne and a disco backbeat yet animated their movements. I imagined the mothers of these boys encountering Pamela

Pomeroy in a hallway of lockers or in the cafeteria after hours, at bake sales or parent-teacher conferences, for instance, and shaking her doughy little mitt and introducing themselves. I imagined the polite smile on Pamela's face as she took in the hair, the fingernails. After scarcely nine months Bay Ridge was yet certainly the same uncharted world to Henry as it had been for me—an exotic place of gilt-mirror restaurants and dangling crucifixes, all of it more foreign for being a little familiar, a little like our homes farther east. Bay Ridge was another redoubt in south Brooklyn, a white neighborhood where you could say *Merry Christmas* without thinking twice, a cousin to the neighborhoods of our birth, the cousin who married Marie and worked construction. Manhattan Beach was the cousin who never sent birthday cards and was rumored to have money. And my home, Gerritsen Beach, was the cousin who lived on a boat.

On my first day at Xaverian, my father drove me the ten miles from Gerritsen Beach in his Buick Riviera with the top down. My hair, too long, was combed in a part. I wore blue trousers and a white shirt with a collar, purchased the week before at Macy's in the Kings Plaza shopping center. He stood patiently outside the changing room as I pulled on the stiff pants. I heard him laughing it up with the redheaded salesgirl who would later put in a guest appearance at Melba Court. When I emerged, self-conscious, he gave me a thumbs-up in the three-way mirror. We bought socks and shoes, too, and a cardigan sweater. All things considered, my father was a pretty good mother. Xaverian had been his high school too, and Pomeroy's, although the connection, any connection, between the two men seemed inconceivable. They were different species to me.

At the time, another freshman named Regine Pomeroy was down Shore Road at Fontbonne, our sister school, which meant they flung us together from time to time so we could stare at one another across the varnished no-man's-land of the gymnasium floor. At the first of these I saw Regine and she saw me. I was a thirteen-year-old boy already six feet tall, so I never went anywhere unnoticed. I gave an automatic wave, knowing her, and the boys with me swung around instantly. Regine put her mouth to a friend's ear. Taped music was playing, and a slow song brought two or three couples together into the void where they moved with a kind of adolescent grace. That was before REGINE-N-WILL. She was still the sylph in wooden-soled Dr. Scholl's who watched me from her deckchair at the Tamaqua Marina all summer, the girl I hardly noticed at all. She was still the daughter of. I was still the boat boy of, but we danced anyway.

At some point that May afternoon in Bay Ridge with Henry a girl crossed to us. She said hello to Henry and crossed her ankles and held her hands behind

her back as she stood by our table, and we both seemed to welcome the inter-
ruption. She spoke only to him after giving me a brief boldly accusatory glance,
likely wondering the same thing as Henry, which was *Who the hell is this guy?*
She was pretty and aware of it, darkly Italian with bangs and purple fingernails
and breasts she couldn't keep secret if she tried, and she didn't. Henry's manner
with her was offhand, however, the nonchalance of a boy accustomed to female
attention and careless with it. The poor son of a bitch, I thought. He'd never
know that fierce elation when impossible becomes maybe and then maybe
becomes yes. There's no other reason to be young except to have that feeling,
but for Henry the answer would always be yes. For Henry there would never
be a question.

She wore a Fontbonne uniform—pleated blue skirt below a white shirt
and unbuttoned cardigan initialed FHA—and the realization had a fascinating
effect on me, not nostalgia but something altogether more immediate—points
that pricked then dulled like anesthetic needles. I noticed, too, that she had
rolled the waistband of her skirt several turns, raising the otherwise modest
hemline four inches as they did when I sat where Henry sat. My hand felt the
remembered feel of the coarse blue wool, a slender pale thigh beneath—

Almost immediately after the girl flounced off I stood and gave Henry a
plausible lie, gesturing at my watch to complete the effect. We walked outside
and stood together for a moment on the avenue, and the traffic was going by
and there were people walking along the sidewalk, which dulled the urgency of
everything and made it all feel ordinary. He said something I didn't hear over
the shriek of a truck's brakes, but from his face I gathered he'd begun to tell me
something then thought better of it. I shook his hand, which was a pretty stiff
thing to do, guessing that would be the last I'd ever see of Henry. Yet as I turned
to walk away he took my arm.

"I needed to meet you," Henry said. "You probably don't understand. I
mean, why would you? It's just that all my life no one would talk about her. Like
saying her name was a sin or something. Then all of a sudden—I mean, they
still don't talk about her, but there she is. You know?"

"I know."

Henry said, "Maybe we can—I don't know—talk sometime?"

"Sure."

"One thing you said, though. You said you didn't see Regine after—after
everything happened. But—I mean, you know she died—right?"

REGINE

THIRTY-TWO

In the cellar of my father's little bungalow on Melba Court in Gerritsen Beach—under the irregular strobe of a swinging bare bulb, bikini-clad women in a Ridgid calendar looking on, among all the busted fishing tackle and desiccated paint cans and greasy marine carburetors lying in disorderly order because my father never threw anything out—I found my Technics SL-220 turntable, as good an excuse as any to come home.

There were supposed to be some snapshots down here. I recollected packing them into a shoebox along with the rest of REGINE-N-WILL when I put us into storage because I, too, kept everything. At least I kept everything about Regine, except Regine.

I wanted a picture of her—for the kid Henry, I told myself—but now that I was down in the cellar it all seemed claustrophobic with the past closing in like the living dead with outstretched arms, and I wanted out. I put the turntable under my arm and climbed the stairs. The proceeds of a summer under the sun at the market with my father, christened by me with *Candy-O*, side two, in 1980 when I was Henry's age, still impressively weighty with a silver metal chassis and flush rectangular buttons, modern in that ancient way, the turntable made me feel my age. Nothing makes you old like old technology.

After shaking hands with Henry I didn't return to the city. In answer to his question I told him, *Yes, Henry, I know*. I knew Regine was dead without knowing more than that. I knew, even if I didn't know the particulars. And I didn't want to know the particulars. Regine Pomeroy always walked the borderline between life and death, and death called for her so loudly sometimes even I could hear. I'd always supposed one afternoon she'd answered the call, and that was enough to know. The particulars would only have proven my complicity, as if I'd opened the pill bottle or handed her the razor blade, for I'd foreseen everything and done nothing. The idea that I was no better than an unindicted co-conspirator in the murder of Regine Pomeroy had been with me so long that it had become indistinguishable from the truth.

Certainly the idea of Garrity pacing his fuggy office wasn't why I stayed in Brooklyn that afternoon. I scarcely noticed Garrity anymore. Nor Georgina Reed, nor the job, nor what was for dinner, nor Monday's dishes still unwashed in the kitchen sink. I was played out. I was tired of swimming upstream, tired of being pulled backward by the irresistible current, ready to drift out to sea. I'd become an empty idea of myself, buoyant, receding from the present into the past, thinking nothing of tomorrow. I had no tense.

So after I shook hands with Henry I found myself walking not to my car but down Shore Road, drawn to a certain wooden bench that looked onto the harbor. Regine and I sat here so often that the green-painted wooden bench across from Fontbonne had become one of a hundred unlikely monuments to REGINE-N-WILL, as she had trademarked us in purple ink on the cover of a composition book she kept hidden in her desk in her bedroom in the big redbrick green-roofed house by the sea, tracing and retracing the letters until the W disappeared altogether. Here on this selfsame bench we would sit after school waiting for the bus, or just waiting.

Today I sat waiting again, waiting for some great emotion to overwhelm me, knowing it was building like a tsunami a hundred miles at sea. Instead I felt nothing but the wind off the harbor. The day was very soft. The breeze lightly blew. The wooden bench and the entire panorama were intimate to me, unseen for years and years yet too familiar ever to catalyze a recollection of Regine. Instead, above the broad blue-gray water clouds piled high into the early summer sky. The air stirred the pines and oaks and the sunlight played through them and fell in abstract dappled shapes at my feet. I felt myself willing myself to think about her, but that was all. The bench was the same bench and the view was the same and nothing had changed except she wasn't here. She wasn't anywhere.

I felt her absence, and my own. Sometime between then and now I'd gotten lost. I'd gone missing somewhere, and if I had to name a precise time and address it would be a cold evening more than four years ago in a certain two-story brick semidetached on Eldert Street in Bushwick when I worked patrol. That was when I became lost to myself, or at least when I realized it. MK had left me even before then—clearing out the rental as efficiently as the Grinch did Whoville, taking the roast beast with her as well as most of the bedsheets—so when I awoke after a fitful sleep, still in uniform, to find the naked mattress bloodstained, I was alone. She didn't know me any longer and wanted only to be alone, she said, and in leaving left me alone with myself; I didn't recognize myself either. I missed the man I used to be. And I missed the boy I'd been when I came here on schooldays, when this green-painted wooden bench was our bench, when I could not wait for the bell so I could run down Shore Road and sometimes even cut class to be with Regine. I missed waiting. I missed knowing the next minute would be better than this minute. Now all the minutes were the same.

In that instant I became aware I was thinking of Regine and not simply trying to think of her—not a memory, just a fragment of Regine on a day such as this and the feel of her blue pleated uniform skirt as she pressed my hand into her thigh. I could remember nothing more of that day except feeling that the world was safe and entire even if it was small. There was an infinity of such lost moments, of course. Pieces of Regine lay scattered in my head, disorganized, and each one forgotten was a death more destructive than death, for what is a life but a collection of such moments? If I lost them Regine Pomeroy would not simply have died, she never would have been. At once the burden of having loved her settled upon me with the realization that she'd taken me with her. We were the curators of each other, and in losing her I lost myself.

I would think about that later, I decided. For now I wanted to remain with the boy and the girl on the green-painted wooden bench. The boy is a Xaverian junior, seventeen, lanky, harmless, someone I used to know. And she is Regine Pomeroy, the third version, the version I was to love best. I was to know seven versions altogether. In version one Regine is a coltish thirteen-year-old, a nuisance of an adolescent in white tennis shorts and Dr. Scholl's who knows nothing more interesting than the sight of William Way, Jr., emerging shirtless and grease-streaked from her father's big Hatteras. In that version, the original collector's edition, she is sitting on an aluminum deckchair on the Tamaqua pier in the late summer afternoon sun. I hardly notice her at all. Once she brings me her can of Tab, already opened, mostly full. Another time she appears on deck and demands to know what I am doing exactly anyway. I tell her I'm cleaning the bilge, and she says oh and frowns but does not leave. She puts her weight on one red sandal then the other. Then without another word she walks away, the underside of her skinny legs striped like fresh burns from the nylon webbing of the deckchair. All summer she sits there, it seems to me, with a magazine and a little transistor radio playing Linda Ronstadt and Crystal Gayle and Lionel Richie. Her skin never darkens. By August she is still the same milky white.

The second version is the freshman who waves at me across the Fontbonne gymnasium floor. I wave back. She whispers in a friend's ear. Later we dance. The song is "Shayla." I have never touched her before. We dance awkwardly, like cousins, but it is the first time. On Saturday we take the bus to the Fortway

Theatre with the velour seats that smell of spent cigarettes. I wear cologne from a sample that came in the mail. We kiss for an hour and a half while Harrison Ford shoots up the screen above our heads. Then we take the bus home.

Version three is REGINE-N-WILL. Version three features the two of us in the forward cabin of the Sea Ray where the light through the translucent hatch makes everything yellow and the water slaps against the hull in an irregular heartbeat that rocks us in small syncopated movements. Her body is my body. The waterproof mats are arranged in a pointed semicircle and burn your skin when you slide too fast on them. The air inside quickly becomes sultry, and there is the boat smell and Van Halen and ELO and the Police on cassette. When I am over her, St. Christopher on a chain around my neck sometimes falls into her mouth. After, our hair is mussed and our skin tastes like suntan lotion.

Version four is Regine trying to hold me after I have already gone.

Five is a letter that begins, *My Dear William*—

Six is Worcester, Massachusetts.

Seven is Regine dead.

Upstairs my father sat at the breakfast table in the linoleum kitchen fixing an old mantel clock found discarded on some roadside probably or bought for thirteen dollars on a nearby stoop. An assortment of tools in a paint-stained avocado crate lay upon the floor and a trouble light hung from a coat stand that more regularly featured by our front door. "Hold this, boy," he said, not looking at me, and I took hold of needle-nose pliers inserted into the guts of the clock like a surgical instrument, but almost immediately the pliers slipped free and something unwound in an angry self-destructive whir.

"Sorry, Dad." I shrugged in the heavy ensuing silence.

Time was the Avocado King would have used such an occasion to predict my future. Now he just looked at me over his cheap pair of drugstore half-frame reading glasses, his eyes somehow fierce yet benign. He hadn't exactly softened with age but the edges had dulled a bit. He knew I hadn't come to Melba Court that afternoon for a turntable, but I suppose he saw something in me had broken so all he said was, "You'll need cables, you want to use that." Instantly he was on his feet, bounding down the cellar stairs. After a moment of hesitation I followed, knowing I'd become one of his Mr. Fixit projects.

In the cellar he was already going through a drawer in a government surplus green metal filing cabinet full of cables and wires he'd labeled CABELS & WIRES. He couldn't find what he wanted, and it seemed to bother him unreasonably.

"Holy Mother," he muttered, shoving the drawer in with a harsh clatter. Under the close stark light his face seemed haunted. He moved to the other end of the cellar through a low labyrinth of wooden pallets with an assortment of whatever was stacked on them. I followed, ducking my head under cobwebs and exposed low joists. He was lifting things from a crate and setting them gently aside, and one of these was a shoebox.

After another five interminable, fruitless minutes he said by way of apology he'd make a pot of coffee. He took the stairs two at a time, as he always did, supposing I'd follow. I remained. Feeling light, as strangely light as the blue Adidas shoebox in my hands, I placed it on the workbench next to a metal tray of parts of something else long since dismantled and forgotten. Inside the box were many folded pieces of spiral notebook paper and cards and letters organized in chronological order. Now the airless cellar smelled of Regine, of the familiar perfume that lingered still on her letters and notes. I took one envelope out, the very last. *My Dear William*—the letter began.

My Dear William told me of Stephan. *My Dear William* was not news, in other words—it wasn't even the end of REGINE-N-WILL, which was over in my mind even before she mailed it. The handwriting is hardly Regine's at all but small and precise, absurdly and intentionally womanly, none of her usual loops and flying descenders nor her more familiar tendency to drift upward on the page. The anodyne handwriting tells me more clearly than her words that we are done. Her mother might have written the damn letter in the placid clock-ticking quiet of her upstairs room with the dried eucalyptus branches stinking in a terra-cotta pot and her stash of turquoise tablets of diazepam dwindling—dwindling, because by now Saint Ann certainly knows about Stephan too.

I already know, even if I don't know everything. *My Dear William* is like learning there's a diagnosis for your condition. Even so, Stephan is not the disease. I don't even blame him, the friend I bring to Manhattan Beach one spring afternoon some weeks before *My Dear William* arrives in the mail. After practice Stephan comes with me from Bay Ridge by bus, walking from the stop to the big redbrick green-roofed house by the sea. None of the neighbors call the police nor stare too openly from their windows and lawn mowers as we walk down Dover Street in our numbered jerseys, blue on gold. Nor does Saint Ann acknowledge his skin except by being more attentively kind than usual, lingering, asking polite questions, offering Cokes and Triscuits.

By then Stephan Morton is no longer black to me nor at least black like we think of black. He is almost taller and certainly smarter, and with him I am ever the salutatorian. He does the *Times* crossword puzzle on the bus to away games and reads Sartre in French. He has early admission to Williams and is wait-listed at Yale. He has something of a part in his hair that he wears otherwise free of attention, adding to his genially professorial affect. He lives alone with an orthodontist father in a Fort Greene brownstone, but we never talk about that; our differences don't divide us, so there's never a need to pretend we're alike. When I bring him to Dover Street he seems unfazed by the mahogany magnificence of Regine's home, whereas I confront my own presumption every time I cross the threshold. He is clever that afternoon with Regine, who has something to prove. They end up laughing on the couch. He stretches his legs out, already at home, while I drift away. I cast a backward glance at them, and she is still watching me. No, Stephan is not to blame. He's just a knotted bedsheet thrown from her second-story bedroom window.

Sometime after *My Dear William*, the Avocado King comes by a sixth-hand 1969 Impala from a neighbor who smokes like a fireman. "For my Samaritan!" my father says, touchingly proud. We scrub the seats and vacuum the carpets and shake out the ashtrays, but it's no use. The headliner is gray from Marlboro Reds, so with the windows rolled down I sometimes drive to Manhattan Beach on summer evenings, never stopping but only slowing for a brief genuflection, just because. I have not seen her since June.

Then, on a day when the late sun is yet full of malice, I'm making the turn in front of her house when I see the garage door shudder as it always does before clattering open. I drop the clutch, and the engine kicks once and dies. The tape deck keeps playing in the otherwise silent Impala. A comic moment ensues, seen in a thousand movies, as I twist the key and the starter winds and winds but does nothing. I complete the picture by pounding on the steering wheel. Now Pomeroy's powder-blue Lincoln Mark VII is in the driveway, and at last my engine churns unhappily to life. I gear into reverse and spin the wheel around, too late. Pomeroy pulls alongside and his window comes down. I can feel his air-conditioned air, which smells like leather and Pomeroy. He wears a pink-and-white-pinstriped shirt. "Afternoon, Will," he says, and I reply with something unintelligible. I am shirtless and my hair's full of seawater. "Come for Regine, I suppose?"

"Yes. Yes."

"Still off on their little constitutional in Massachusetts, I'm afraid," he says. A pause. *Massachusetts*, I think, the word a dagger. He's in sunglasses and therefore more obscure than usual, but his voice is untroubled. "With her mother and Pam, you know." Another pause. "You do know she's away, don't you?" *Away*—another word with another meaning.

"Yes," I lie.

A third pause, needlessly long. "Back soon, though," he tells me, and it seems he is prolonging the conversation to some end. "Why don't you come around the ranch for dinner one of these days?"

"Okay."

"Wednesday night," he says. "Just us bachelors. We'll eat steak." He holds his thumb and index finger a couple inches apart to indicate the sort of steak he has in mind, then he pulls away. I trail him unavoidably but at a respectful distance, uncomfortable in his rearview mirror, as if Pomeroy's movements over the public highways and byways of New York City are none of my damn business.

Wednesday is July 4, coincidentally a national holiday. True to his word, Pomeroy has the grill going when I arrive at Dover Street. The charcoal smell drifts over the eaves from the backyard even as I park the Impala on the pea-stone driveway, my membership card temporarily reactivated. I enter through the side door, the private doorway I always use without knocking as the family dog might, coming and going through a flap. The side door opens on the butler's pantry, which is what Saint Ann calls the laundry room. The butler's pantry at Dover Street is the cleanest place on earth, smelling of detergent and spray starch and lint, like the Pomeroys, like Regine. And here, on the tile floor, beneath the folding table near the washing machine, is a pair of beaded moccasins, yellow, hers.

I pass through the empty house, familiar and foreign. The only sound is television news in the living room, which underscores the desolation. The French doors in back are open to reveal the flat lawn. A salty breeze off the water stirs the curtains inward, and I walk out into a pleasant evening. Here's Pomeroy, tending grill, and filling the panorama to the horizon as ever is the sea. Overhead against the deepening afternoon sky seagulls call and wheel. Pomeroy shouts some gruff salutation, battling flames with one hand, a Tom Collins glass in the other. He wears an apron, *Kiss the Cook*. I give him my hand instead. His is cold and damp from the glass. He fixes me with his blue eyes and appraises me in a manner that makes me wonder. He then pushes his empty glass into my hand, instructing me to help myself. Dutifully I walk to the French doors, and he calls to me across the wide lawn to "bring forth the fatted calf." He's in a peculiar mood, I think, perhaps drunk. Inside, melting half-moons of white ice mingle with frayed lime quarters at the bottom of the kitchen sink. The bottle of gin on the counter is open, nearly empty. Everything is very still. Bumblebees knock their slow fat bodies against the windowpanes and make shadows on the floor. I suddenly feel lost and want to leave.

"In training?" he asks when I return to him, his fierce gaze on my can of Coke.

"I'm—I really don't, judge."

"Here's to sobriety," he tells me, raising his drink. He drops the steaks on the grill. On the surface of the ocean, passing shadows of jetliners on final for JFK are like the great submarine forms of whales swimming. We stand watching the fire with the dull fascination of cavemen. Our bodies assume the same posture automatically, and the curling smoke from the grill is hardly visible against the water.

Inside I take my usual seat, an empty chair—Regine's—between us. Blood pools beneath the meat. Pomeroy comes to the table with a plastic gallon of milk. "All aboard?" he asks. We are, so he pours us both a brimming orange glass patterned with circles and diamonds. That's dinner, milk and blood. After five minutes of the sort of conversation we usually have, I realize we've never spoken to each other for more than five minutes. Regine is no longer here to pull me to safety, nor is Saint Ann on hand to put forward politely neutral topics whenever Pomeroy turns inward as he so often does. We finish in silence, then it's time to pay for dinner.

He walks me outside to have a look around the property in the failing light. Some distance east along the esplanade the occasional roman candle flowers weakly red or green but makes no sound. With the toe of his boat shoe, sockless, Pomeroy points out a section of lawn that's begun to subside into a line of beachy sand. He catches his strong jaw in his hand and glowers furiously at it. He doesn't like the idea of his well-ordered property returning to a state of nature.

"Hell of a thing, isn't it?" he asks without explanation.

"Yes."

"The important thing is she's doing well, I'm told."

"Of course."

"One is always required to say I never saw it coming," he says, "but the simple truth is I never did. In a way, of course, I do feel a measure of responsibility. Perhaps if I—I understand there may have been an argument between you? A falling-out of sorts?"

"Argument?"

"No?" he says. "But you've spoken to her? Since?"

"Not so much, Judge. Not at all, tell the truth."

"No—? Well. She is away," he says, and I understand that Pomeroy waited until nightfall so I wouldn't see his face. I know this conversation is hard for him, and that a fundamental misunderstanding lies between us. I don't know how to ask him to explain what he believes I already know. "But you—perhaps she sent a letter, then? I'm not entirely sure what's permitted."

"Yes, Judge." *My Dear William—*

"You understand, Will, that you mean quite a lot to her," he says. "Regardless of anything she may have said or done. She's not—well, she's not entirely herself at the moment. And I do believe you mean much more to her than you may realize, possibly."

"I guess."

"I'm certain of it," he says as if he means it. "Of course you do. Notwithstanding that she took up with this—this fellow here—I nevertheless believe it would be beneficial, in a way, for you—that is, I believe she would listen to you, if you talked sense to her. Don't you believe she would listen to you? I believe she would."

With a civil look, which he may not have seen in the failing light, I say, "I beg your pardon, I believe you're mistaken."

He turns on me. "If you talked sense to her, I mean. If you gave her a sense of perspective on all this."

"Perspective?"

"You know the girl. Regine's a—I don't agree with what they say, I'll tell you that right now," he says. "They have their own notions, of course. They talk a lot of professional, high-sounding claptrap. You ask my opinion. I know better than anyone how one can hide behind a sea of words, when one doesn't know what else to say. Yes, I do. I know doctors."

"What doctors?"

"Coming in here. Dispensing their potions and nostrums. Rendering their learned opinions," he says. "And what have we to show for it after so long, hmm? Not a damn thing in all this time. In all this time. And it's positively infuriating to have conversations with these people. One feels at such a terrible disadvantage. The implication is always there."

"Implication?" I ask.

"That one might have done more. That it's one's fault for—for not looking after one's own—" he said. "And the implication is so damnable, since a father is supposed to care for his own, hmm? Else what is he? But what do they know, really? The girl's high-strung to be sure. She's—emotional. Why, anyone can see that. Regine simply feels life more deeply than most. One might think of it as a blessing, not an illness, for heaven's sake. I'll be the first to admit Regine's often—baffling. But as I say, she will listen to you."

I hear myself exhale and say, emboldened by the anonymous confessional quality of the moonless sky, "I—I'm not really sure she would, Judge. I mean, I'm probably the last person on earth she'd listen to now."

"Why do you say that?" he asks. In the dark I feel his eyes on me. "Why do you say 'now'?"

"She sent me a letter. She—"

"Well. As for that black fellow—" He snorts a scornful laugh, and for a while neither of us says a word. When he speaks next his voice has lost its edge entirely. "Regine is ill, not altogether herself. You do understand that at least? This—fellow brought all this on somehow, I'm certain. And I think we're all rather fortunate things worked out as they did, that her mother was on hand and able to get her away before—well, before things progressed further. I suppose my hope was that you—"

He seems to lose heart, and again we are quiet. Perhaps it's nothing more than the gin burning itself out, but he seems to regret having raised the subject of Regine at all. We are both left staring silently at the black ocean, each of us wishing Will Way had stayed home that day. I have no idea what he expects of me except the obvious thing, which happens to be impossible. Pomeroy certainly knows that, too, and if I were less taken with the idea of driving nails into my wrists I might have seen his unreasonable faith in me as a sign of desperation in a man I believed incapable of it.

In my defense, Regine always had doctors. Regine always needed doctors. She saw doctors in Manhattan high-rises, doctors in tweed jackets whom Saint Ann called by their first names. Neither was *Massachusetts* anything new, nor being *away*. Frequently there were missed schooldays and unexplained absences and exclamation-pointed letters postmarked from the commonwealth that was by now a proxy for the turmoil within her that I could never begin to fathom. None of this now was any cause for alarm, I believed as I stood with Pomeroy on his back lawn, for no better reason than it was all just so fucking familiar. Like the fireworks along the shoreline, Massachusetts was a pallid explosion too distant to hear.

When I walk later into the empty bungalow the Avocado King is not home, instead at large on the high seas, no doubt, at the wheel of the Sea Ray beyond the twelve-mile limit, his crew of tipsy regulars shooting bottle rockets in the direction of Spain. Inside Melba Court all the lights are doused but for a yellow forty-watt over the enamel kitchen sink, where I see an unwashed dinner plate and a pair of Bud Light empties pinched into the shape of an hourglass. On the plate are the distinctive bold brushstrokes of a piece of Italian bread dragged across a canvas of residual Chef Boyardee. In my room I close the door and put Blondie on the spindle, and I lie on my bed unmoving in the faint amber light from the amplifier dial, and when the music ends the record crackles with static before the needle lifts, and then it lifts and everything is more quiet than before. I do not know what I want, but I don't want this.

THIRTY-THREE

That same summer, the last before college, the Avocado King puts me to work. Monday after graduation he wakes me at four in the morning and does thirty-six push-ups—one for each year—on the orange shag carpeting of my bedroom. meanwhile chanting some badass 1st Cavalry nonsense in his underpants. On those summer mornings Wm. Way & Son set out together for Terminal Market before dawn breaks, when the wide-open south Brooklyn sky is the color of a bruise. He has the '73 Buick then, the boattail Riviera in Apollo Orange with velour bucket seats colored Bamboo Cream. Kenny Rogers is ever on the eight-track, or Neal Diamond, or Karen Carpenter, and the windows are always down and the air conditioner is always on and at stop signs I pass him coffee in a paper cup. *Reuben James, you still walk the furrowed fields of my mind,* he sings along in a voice that isn't bad.

Until three in the afternoon there is the avocado business. The avocado business is men in tinted eyeglasses who buy for supermarkets. The avocado business is Korean men in Toyota pickups with their address stenciled on the door. The avocado business is & Son driving a forklift over the hot blacktop. My father and I eat a lunch of deviled ham sandwiches and Cokes at ten thirty, and at three o'clock I take a city bus back to the Beach. On the bus are old ruddy-cheeked Irish women in blue plastic raincoats with crucifixes and little plaid shopping bags. As Brooklyn goes past at three miles per hour I sit with Cicero and the *Preppy Handbook* and Lord Chesterfield, learning to be what I want to be, which is somebody else. I underline passages—*Your reputation and success in the world will depend upon the degree of good breeding you are master of*—*There is likewise such a thing as a civil look, and a rude look*—*If you have occasion to contradict anybody you should say, with a civil look, I beg your pardon, I believe you're mistaken*—

That summer I flirt with self-satisfaction, as certain of my own perfectibility as a nine-year-old girl. I have a full ride to college. I'm tan from the midday sun and strong from swimming. I have my father's looks and my mother's brains, and at last I'm getting out. Pomeroy tells me Regine's in Massachusetts, and my answer is to do—nothing, to feel nothing. With Regine there have been too many doctors and too many pills, too many disappearances and too many episodes followed by too many resolutions. We're done even before she mails *My Dear William*, and Pomeroy's news that she's away simply proves I'm right. Until REGINE-N-WILL, of course, there's only Sally Joyce and Gerritsen girls and stolen cigarettes in ashtrays and potato chips ground into concrete basement floors and incense smoldering on metal plates and Boston on the turntable and Rush and Steve Miller and Meat Loaf and singing along without knowing all the words. And there are kisses and trial-and-error fumblings on stained nylon comforters thrown over mattresses, and beads hanging in doorways that make otherworldly music when you brush into them. They all have Farrah Fawcett hair and pink eye shadow and smell of Avon strawberry lip gloss and Love's Baby Soft. Their braces cut into my lips and I don't protest, but it all takes me nowhere and after a while isn't even fun anymore. The girls of my neighborhood are like the boats in the driveways and the bathtub Madonnas. They're Gerritsen Beach. They'll flypaper me to Brooklyn, I know, and even before *My Dear William* I start to think about Regine the same way.

As early as June we've not spoken in days, weeks, but if you're white Brooklyn's a small town and the social current sweeps us to the same graduation party in Bay Ridge before midnight. She's stopped eating again, I see at once. She's wearing too much mascara and a fuck-me skirt, but her legs are skinny and white beneath it. Her friends make a point of informing me repeatedly and unnecessarily that she's there. *Will, you know Gine's here—don't you?* All of them have bright makeup and pieces of lace knotted into their hair and they wear wide black leather belts and dog collars with flashing sadomasochistic chrome studs. I have the idea of them working it out beforehand by telephone and on the way, and of lipstick and eye shadow being passed back and forth in crowded bathrooms and in back seats of cars and taxis, and the thought makes me soften toward Regine because I understand the idea's not hers.

A girl, Julia, cashays over to me in the kitchen and pretends to be more drunk than she is. For three years I've known her without knowing her last name. She teeters on suicide heels and has this trick of falling into me whenever anyone pushes behind her. Somehow we end up on the sidewalk where the night air is very pleasant and clean after the closed stink of spilled beer inside. A moon entangles itself on the Verrazzano Bridge, and the music comes and goes as the door opens behind us. Soon the police will come, but at the moment we're alone. For the first time really I look at Julia and see she's no more than a little girl in makeup, freckles scattered like a field of stars across her small face, blue-black eyes gone flat as saucers. She is right there, ready, but the moment passes into history as a footnote while I stand briefly beguiled at seeing someone new under someone I know.

From the doorway, however, I'm certain the image of the pair of us in the moonlight et cetera is pornographic enough to Regine Pomeroy, who appears then disappears so quickly that at first I think she's only my conscience. I follow her inside, knowing no good will come of it. By then the night and the alcohol have entered my veins, and I sleepwalk through the house to find her, room to room, until I decide she has gone. Then "Shayla" comes on speakers somewhere remote. At first I don't notice, but when I do, I stop. We danced to it in a gymnasium once, touching for the first time, before REGINE-N-WILL, artificially entwined with bodies we no longer had, so the song—slow and longing— became ours. I find the music at last in a room where six or seven girls dance languidly together in the light of a weak red bulb, one singing along, *I am free but life is so cheap,* as another motions me wordlessly to her. I move on. I want Regine, only Regine. I end up collapsed against a wall in a bedroom at whatever small hour it is on the threshold of my new life with the old world having run down behind me when suddenly she is next to me on the floor.

Nothing memorable is said and we kiss. We kiss on the floor, and then she is taking off her clothes and mine. She pushes me back and sits across me. Her bare slender shoulders are lit white beneath the window, and then it all becomes desperate and goes on and on. She is saying things I don't understand and at last she slides deftly around so I am on top of her, the tendon along the inside of her thigh taut as a cello string as she pulls me urgently closer and holds me with a strength I don't know she has. Beneath me now, she is telling me to *go in go in go in* and when I do it hurts us both and she shudders but neither of us cares. When it is over she becomes inert beneath me, immediately small and lifeless as a doll, which leaves me this monstrous thing inside her and over her, silently crushing her into the rough carpet. I loose myself from her limbs and sit on the edge of a chair and they are knocking on the door.

I drive Regine home to Dover Street in my father's Riviera. By then it's nearly four in the morning, and we say scarcely a word during the half hour from Bay Ridge. We stand far too long by the side door outside the butler's pantry. Moths beat against the light. She is far away and shaking a little in the cool night air. We kiss goodbye dryly, and a moment comes and goes during which either of us might have said a word that would have reshaped the history of the world.

Instead I drive home with the radio very loud, singing, *Like a bat out of hell I'll be gone*— but the words hit too close, so I twist off the radio dial and drive in silence, thinking, *This is the way the world ends, not with a bang* et cetera and the phony drama is better than the thought behind it, which is *Fuck it, I don't care*—

Three days later *My Dear William* arrives in the mail.

In a swampy August, before I am to leave for college and shake the Brooklyn dust from my feet, I awake to a seagull outside my window, portentous as a crow. All I own is packed in three or four crates redolent of avocados—*monogrammed luggage*, the King calls them—and I am staring at the water-stained ceiling in the dim early morning light, lost in dissonant thoughts, not sure I want what I want, when my father barrels in wearing a checkered short-sleeve shirt and game-show-host necktie. He sees at once how it is, telling me only to get a haircut before he shuts my door. Then for the first time since June he drives alone to the market. From my bedroom, with a small dart of nostalgia that makes me smile at myself, I hear the Riviera stir to life and Kenny Rogers fade as my father makes his way down Melba Court.

I am shirtless and barefoot on the front porch in the midafternoon, reading, watching nothing go by, the only sound that of cicadas, when the telephone rings. The screen door shudders closed behind me on an elongated rusty spring as I walk to the kitchen. Regine. The conversation is short, not a conversation at all. Long ago I told her she could ask me to do anything, she reminds me, and now she is asking me to come to Massachusetts. I say okay and drive to Massachusetts. After all, some of the lies we'd sworn in blood to each other on moonlit nights were true.

I meet Regine Pomeroy, formerly of REGINE-N-WILL, in a parking lot near a white building in Massachusetts disguised rather well as nothing more than a large home of the Victorian age. The sun has not yet set. I see her at once, seated upon a bench, waiting. Her eyes go right over the Impala. She doesn't know my car. We kiss, on instinct and without forethought. Hers are desperate but chaste and taste like medicine. I hold her very close. In the failing light Regine is pale and her lips are dry. She wears no makeup or jewelry, but never have I seen her more beautiful. Even so, she feels shockingly frail, empty, a husk. We walk, holding hands our way. Hers are cold. Neither of us says anything for a long time. Then she tells me.

On the interstate to Massachusetts, counting exits, each an escape route, I know Regine is going to tell me something that'll hurt. I know she's going to tell me something she couldn't tell me on the telephone. I imagine a finite number of things she might say, so when she tells me now I'm not altogether surprised, and my answer—"*His?*"—is one of my thoughts from the highway. She starts with my name but cannot finish and the word hangs in the air between us, the familiar name of a stranger. She tries again, and when she still cannot answer I decide the answer is clear enough. She draws a jagged breath. I put my arm around her—not much, but enough for now. She leans into me and runs her fingers absently through my hair and does not cry.

We drive because she wants to get away. We don't go anywhere. She just wants to drive. We do, then I pull into a restaurant. The restaurant is disorientingly normal with oak accents and green leatherette seats. All around are people we don't know. We sit immobilized for an hour and a half, two butterflies pinned side-by-side in a case. I order breakfast because it's the first thing on the menu. Regine has a Sprite with lemon, which she sips impassively through a red straw with a flexible end. When I look I try to see her stomach, but there's no change I can discern beneath an overlarge Holyoke sweatshirt. If anything she's smaller now. I offer my plate, but she tells me they told her not to eat. "Who's they?" I ask, and that's how I find out about Worcester. There's a free clinic in Worcester, she tells me, and an appointment at six o'clock the following morning. Our eyes meet. Hers are very hard. She has no car is all she says.

There will be no more discussion on the subject. Neither of us ever suggests the alternative to Worcester is no worse than Worcester, each understanding the answer must be Worcester without either asking the question.

The Lumberjack Special at the Perkins restaurant in Stockbridge, Massachusetts, by the way, is three buttermilk pancakes, bacon, sausage, home-style potatoes, and two eggs any style. I order mine over medium, the only decision I make that night. Even so, the eggs sit mostly uneaten on the enormous oval plate. The waitress is displeased. "Everything okay—?" she asks, and for a moment I nearly laugh. All around are children sitting with their parents and children running around the place, and there are babies in high chairs eating from little jars and babies dropping spoons onto the carpeting and babies crying everywhere. My eyes keep going to them as Regine and I sit there not telling each other anything we ought to say. I've never seen so many children before.

We arrive in Worcester before midnight. I have no money for a hotel, so I park on the street in front of the clinic. There's no sign on the clinic to say what it is other than a clinic. The street is four empty lanes between an endless progression of low nondescript buildings. At this hour traffic lights change color unnecessarily, and no one's on the sidewalk. With the windows closed the Impala smells like cigarettes but Regine says nothing about that. She seems very tired. The windows fog. We hold hands, and I try to sleep. She is already asleep when at last I have a dream in which everything is in colorful motion, all sorts of swirling shapes of triangles and cylinders. I awake mixed up and I look around. There's nothing to see. An ambulance goes past without a siren.

At last morning comes and spreads its purple claws overhead. Awake to greet it, I glimpse myself in the mirror, the same ancient adolescent with the uncombed tangle of blondish hair who awoke yesterday morning in Brooklyn. There is no change, except in my expression. Now I have none. Beside me Regine is still asleep, her lips slightly parted, her skin pure as soap, under the olive-green field jacket with the 1st Cavalry horsehead on the sleeve. Her pale beauty and the warlike thing blanketing her—in which my father was shot twice—makes a jarring juxtaposition, an omen of peril or survival or both. She awakes at once when I softly press her shoulder, facing me with eyes luminous from sleep and absolutely blue. She makes a soundless stretch and looks out the window. For a very long while she looks out the window. I watch her the whole time. When she faces me again she smiles, but her smile is all wrong. Sometime during the night Regine Pomeroy left.

Inside the clinic she slips from me in a kind of trance behind a swinging door that leads to the room where I am forbidden by the nurse who takes her away. She goes without a backward look, and had I known this was to be the last I'd see her I'd have run to her, made her face me, never let her go. As it is, I have scant memory of Regine Pomeroy in that final moment. I have to settle for all the other moments.

Unable to sit, I pace back and forth, a caricature of the expectant father I may or may not be, awaiting the delivery of a child I've already seen on posters and flyers, lying in a surgical steel tray or a wastebasket, having been neatly sucked away like a corner of bloody gauze. My mind on its own keeps going to Saint Ann and her stone-faced marches and *Roe v. Wade* pamphleteering and midnight candlelit vigils with murmured renditions of "We Shall Overcome" in church basements. I suppose if you asked me what I believed the day before I stepped inside the free clinic in Worcester, Massachusetts, my answer would've been that I believed everything everyone told me to believe—and yes, I'm certain I'd have told you I'd never want any part of this. But that was because the day before Worcester my answer wouldn't have mattered.

The waiting room begins slowly to fill. They bring with them the fried-food smell of the poor. They come in pairs and do not look at anyone except in stolen glances. Only one is a man. Our eyes meet, a brief impact. He's not like me, but he probably thinks the same. An hour passes that way.

I am still standing against the wall when the nurse calls Regine's name. I raise my hand like a schoolboy with the answer, and she leads me though the same terrible swinging door into the back. She puts me alone in a room that smells like disinfectant where there is a vinyl table of hard upholstery covered with slippery paper with stirrups and instruments on a napkin on a tray arrayed like torturers' tools. I make some kind of joke because now I'm very scared. The nurse only raises a corner of her mouth. She asks me to wait for the doctor and leaves. When the doctor opens the door I know he's going to tell me about Regine and my insides are liquid, but there's no place to sit except the table. He looks at his clipboard. His hair is too long for a doctor. There's been a problem, he explains, not looking at me. Miss Pomrog is not well. She's had a kind of adverse response, he's sorry to tell me. He's seen this sort of thing once or twice before. I shouldn't worry too much. Frequently it amounts to nothing. They did their best, but in the end they called an ambulance. I ask to see her, and at last he looks me in the eye and tells me Miss Pomrog is not in this place anymore. He talks some more, but all I really understand is that Regine is alive.

The Impala won't start. I wait in silence before trying again. Around me the world is ordinary and oblivious. The car smells like Regine and cigarette smoke. I feel very alone, irrelevant. Everything I know is far away. Next I remember walking into the hospital. At the desk no one will tell me anything. They ask my relationship to the patient and I don't know how to answer. At last someone sends me to the fourth floor. He says it like a diagnosis. I wait for the elevator then take the stairs two at a time. No one tells me anything on the fourth floor either. Here it is quiet and not like a hospital. No one has a stethoscope. They write down my name and ask me to wait over there. I'm sorry, sir, but who are you to Miss Pomrog? Evidently there are procedures to follow. A form must first be filled out. Overhead I read PSYCHIATRIC ICU. I don't know if that's better or worse.

Another waiting room. I page through magazines and try to do the *People* crossword without a pen and recall my conversation with Pomeroy two months earlier. Regine would listen to me, he said. I could talk sense to her, give her a sense of perspective on all this. I steel myself and telephone Pomeroy collect from a pay phone. I tell the operator the call is from Regine so he will pick up, and when Pomeroy answers he says, "There you are, Gine, thank God," and it is very awkward for a moment. No one knew where she was, he says. She went missing. She wasn't supposed to leave, *didn't she tell you that? And Ann is positively frantic with worry. Evidently someone told police they'd seen her get into an old car that wouldn't start—do you have an old car?—why are you in Worcester of all places—?* And I tell him why I'm in Worcester. I tell him in the manner I believe he'd want to hear it—just the facts. After I tell him the line is silent. For a moment I'm afraid he hung up. Then I hear him ask if I'll stay with her until he arrives. I say yes, as if I'm doing him a favor.

Unable to remain still, I walk down the hallway in paint-stained deck shoes and stand at a window. Then I walk the floor for an hour, and all that time— even as I sit in the waiting room and walk over the linoleum and stare at gray mixed-use commercial Massachusetts and read about Phoebe Cates's valiant battle with whatever—I'm trying to send up a few prayers, always adding, *Not for me. For her. For her. Dear God, for her for her for her for her—*

"Are you Will?" I hear a woman ask. I turn and see a nurse with stern hair and oval glasses wearing a lab coat of an almost luminescent white. I nod in reply without immediately grasping the significance that she should know my name. "Miss Pomrog indicated you might—"

"Pomeroy. Her name is Pomeroy. You people keep saying something wrong."

"I wonder if I can ask—" she starts.

"Just wait—wait—is she?—will you tell me what's going on?"

"She's comfortable now," she says, pursing her thin lips. "I just have a few—"

"No one will tell me anything. I need to know."

"We're attempting to contact her family—"

"Why won't anyone fucking tell me anything?"

"Sir. Will. I understand you're upset," she says in a way that sounds like an accusation, "but there's no need to raise your—"

"I'm sorry. But you better tell me now."

"Well," she said, considering. "I suppose there's no harm in telling you Miss *Pom-roy* experienced an episode, an acute stress reaction this morning, and she—"

"Just tell me is she okay?"

"She's resting comfortably. I told you. I'm sorry I can't say anything more. I just have a few questions. Can you tell me whether Miss Pomroy is currently taking any medication or under medical care?"

"Probably. Yes. I mean, is she—?"

"Do you know what medicines Miss Pomroy is taking?" she asks, pushing her glasses up with an index finger.

"No."

"Do you know what condition or conditions Miss Pomroy is receiving medication for?"

"I—I don't know—"

"If you know," she asks, reading a form, her pencil poised, "has Miss Pomroy ever received a clinical diagnosis of—"

"I don't know, okay? I don't know. She gets sad sometimes."

"Sad?"

"You know," I say. "Depressed or whatever?—but I mean, who doesn't?"

"I'd like to ask you about that, if I may?"

"Okay."

"Just a few questions," she says. "Please just answer yes or no, if you know. You say Miss Pomroy has displayed a depressed mood?"

"Sometimes, sure."

"Mood swings?"

"Sometimes."

"Agitation?"

"Sometimes."

"Elevated or manic moods?"

"I don't know. Maybe," I say. "What do you mean?"

"Panic attacks?"

"No."

"Poor grooming?"

"No."

"Phobias?"

"June bugs, I guess," I tell her, trying to think.

"Thank you," she says to me. "Any obsessions or compulsions?"

"No."

"Anorexia?"

"I—I don't know."

"Substance abuse?"

"No."

"Grief?"

"No."

"Worthlessness?"

"No."

"Hopelessness?"

"No."

"Hallucinations?"

"No."

"Delusions?"

"No."

"Social isolation?"

"No."

"Guilt?"

"No," I say. "Stop asking me questions. You make her sound like she's—but she's not, she's fine. Okay? That's not who she is. Don't you get it? She's normal."

"Self-mutilation?"

"I told you she's fine."

"Suicidal threats?"

"She's fine. She's not like that."

"Your answer is no?"

"No."

"Suicide attempts?"

"No. Not for real, no," I said. "Look. She's fine. I know her. I've known her my whole life. Do you understand? You know—I don't know. I don't know anything about her. I can't answer your questions anymore. You should ask her mother. She's coming. I don't know really anything about her. I'm just, I—"

Later I drift into a shallow fitful sleep. I keep opening an eye, and at last I awaken to find Pomeroy and Ann sitting across from me. Pamela, standing, glowers hatefully in sweatpants and large eyeglasses that reflect the cold fluorescent light. The same nurse is seated with them, and when I stir she, too, shoots me a scornful look, suggesting that something she suspected has now been confirmed. Pomeroy motions to me and together we walk down the hall. I meekly obey, feeling as ever that my connection to his daughter is a kind of larceny to be perpetrated only when and where he cannot witness.

We sit. He thanks me. Of all the many things he might have said at that moment, a simple thank-you is the last I expect. *I gave her a sense of perspective on all this*, I suppose Pomeroy is thinking. *Regine listened to me*, and as for the rest—well, as for the rest, we can lay all that unpleasantness at the feet of *that black fellow*, as Pomeroy had anonymized Stephan Morton, he who had been my friend, before he became her friend, before *My Dear William*. Pomeroy does not name him now either, but in shaking my hand—firmly, and with gratitude, his eyes vacant with fret—the implication is clear that Stephan is somehow the author of all this, which makes Will Way as ever the boat boy, emptying the bilges of Pomeroy's filth.

Or so I believe, for not once that day does Pomeroy pose the same question I had yesterday for Regine—*His?*—nor do I have the courage to volunteer a different answer to the question he thinks unnecessary to ask. If anything might have brought me to my senses, it ought to have been Pomeroy's paternal resolve to hang a medal on me. But of course I say nothing. I just sit on the bench in my father's jacket that now smells like her.

Saint Ann at length drifts by in the direction of the hospital chapel, first giving me a dehydrated kiss and an absent squeeze of my hand. Her prayers are certain to be different than mine, better, more articulate. She'll pray that God forgive Regine her mortal sin, of course. She'll tearfully beg that God cleanse her youngest daughter *of unrighteousness through the blood of Jesus Christ who suffered and died* et cetera. And who knows, Saint Ann may even mention me to her God, but I suspect she will pray also for her own soul, for having believed, if only for a heartbeat as she sped along the interstate to Worcester, that as bad as this may be it could've been worse—a little beige bastard at Dover Street, for example, *playing on the back lawn in a soggy diaper and miniature tracksuit, earrings in her ears, neighbors watching through their blinds, dear God*—

Pomeroy asks my plans, meaning it's time for me to go. I ask him for gas money. He opens his wallet and distractedly peels off five twenty-dollar bills, each crisp as a starched shirt, and it feels like payment for services rendered. We shake hands again, but he's not thinking about me. He's not even looking at me.

Outside the air is clean and warm after the medicinal fetor of the hospital. All I want is to go and keep going. The sun is low on the horizon, and I start toward the parking lot.

"So you let her kill her own baby."

Pamela stands smoking a cigarette by a skeletal crab apple, and the look of naked hatred upon her plain nunnish face is like a blow. I stop, stunned. The setting sun glints on her eyeglasses. She seems ready to spit on me, a baby killer in the uniform of a baby killer, Pomeroy's distinguished service ribbon around my neck, and together Pamela and I re-create in perfect miniature my father's airport homecoming fifteen years before.

"Pam—"

"You brought her to—to that place, didn't you? I know you did."

"Pam, I—"

"You did, Will," she says. "You came up here, and you drove her to—"

"It's what she wanted, Pam."

"You have no idea what she wants," she says. "You shouldn't even be here."

"She needed me."

"She needed you," Pamela says with venom. "Aren't you just the perfect hero? What, do you think you're Regine's cavalry, riding to her rescue? Please. She doesn't need you now. She needed you in June. Where were you then?"

"What happened in June?"

"Oh, nothing much," Pamela says to me in a flat tone of voice, but her eyes are moist, magnified behind her eyeglasses. "Nothing really. She just swallowed an entire bottle of doxepin is all. She emptied all the little pills into a Sprite and drank it in the kitchen. Then she sat on the floor and—" She turns away and cries for a while.

"I didn't—" I say when I can.

"Your fucking friend was there, you know. Another hero."

"He's not my friend, he—" I start.

"Where would we be without our heroes, I wonder."

"Just tell me what happened, Pam. Please."

"I just told you. Regine nearly died. Really died. And the thing is this time she wanted to," Pamela said, moving closer to me, dropping her spent cigarette to the sidewalk. "Do you understand, Will? This wasn't a cry for help or attention or whatever they want to call the other times. This time she was finished. I know. So don't tell me what she needs. You—"

"Stephan was there?"

"Oh, I don't blame him," she says. "He's—a typical idiot. He didn't know Regine. He didn't know what he was getting into with her. He thought she was just—I don't know what the hell he thought, so I can't blame him. But I can blame you, Will. And I do."

"Pam—"

"Oh, my parents think you're oh so wonderful," she says. "Such a devoted boy, coming all the way here, despite everything, to help. But I know."

"What do you know, Pam?"

"I know what it meant when you left her."

"She left me—"

"Oh, sure," Pamela says, "and saved you the trouble of doing it yourself."

"You don't know how I feel about her."

"But I do know, Will. I know everything. That's why I can blame you. We're the only ones who know Regine, really. Just you and me. You think my parents have any fucking clue? They throw medicine and doctors at Regine like it's the answer, but really it's just you and me. And you left me to clean up the mess when you ran for the door."

"Quit saying that. She ended it. Not me."

"Regine and *that fellow*?" she says, imitating her father, nearly laughing. "Oh, I'm really seeing that, aren't you? True love, just like Wendy and Peter Pan. Spare me. But she knew what you wanted. She did it for you."

"What are you saying, Pam?"

"She did it for you, fucker."

"I don't know what you mean."

She looks at me carefully before saying, "No, you probably don't. And maybe that's why I don't totally hate your guts. I mean, you probably want to do the right thing, Will, you just never know what it is. I just wonder if you could do it, if you knew."

When I arrive home at Melba Court it is nearly midnight. In my room I empty my pockets onto the dresser and my change rolls around on it, the only sound. There are some crumpled bills and the paper receipt from the restaurant yesterday. I hold the receipt and sit on the edge of my bed and cry until it is all out. I've never cried for her before, not once, but of course it's not for her.

POMEROY

THIRTY-FOUR

"So, wait—" Jackie Kane said to me. "You know Pomeroy? I mean, you know him like you really know him."

I nodded yes but more or less denied it. She considered my answer while pouring an obscene amount of cream into her coffee cup where it momentarily became a nebula spinning a hundred light-years from the café on Montague Street where we sat. I felt her eyes on me as I pretended to be fascinated by her coffee. She was being a prosecutor with me, and I imagined she'd been a prosecutor since age eleven when she realized she was faster and smarter than everyone around her and didn't like what the other little girls liked. We were in downtown Brooklyn because she wanted to see me. She didn't say why when she telephoned, and I supposed she'd get around to it now that we'd finished the pleasant part of the day's conversation, which consisted of her telling me to sit down. Now we were in the unpleasant part. Prosecutors—the good ones— have a professional interest in discomfort; like doctors they poke and probe, repeating *Does this hurt?* as if they don't already know.

She demanded, "Tell me."

Not immediately I admitted, "I just knew his daughter is all."

"Knew?"

"She's dead, Jackie."

"Dead?" she said, seemingly surprised. "Since when?"

"Since a long time ago."

"Bullshit dead," she said. "Pomeroy introduced me last year. At the criminal bar prom. She has a kid, Pomeroy's grandson."

"That's Pamela. And her son. I'm talking about Regine. She was the young- est. She—died."

"Oh, wait. In the newspaper," she said, nodding, but I couldn't tell if she was playing dumb for my sake. "Regina."

"Regine."

"So she's the one you came to see Pomeroy about."

"Hell said that?" I asked loudly, not bothering to disguise my reaction.

"Pomeroy said that."

"When?"

"You seem surprised," she told me.

"When'd he say this?"

"When Montgomery Crimmins asked him, that's when," she said, and the name was mildly uncomfortable, like a blister on your heel.

"Since when does a sitting justice have to answer to Whitey Fister's hatchet man?"

"Since the judicial oversight committee began an investigation Tuesday," she said. "They want to know what business is between the two of you, and frankly so do I."

I said to her, "So when you asked me how I knew Pomeroy a minute ago, that was a trick question."

"Something they teach you in law school," she said, drinking coffee. "When you're cross-examining a hostile witness, only ask questions when you already know the answer." She rolled her shoulders and leaned back in her chair at ease. We had the place to ourselves except for an old man who didn't care.

"So I'm a hostile witness now?"

"Feels like."

"I'm not, Jackie. You don't trust me is all."

"Not as much as I distrust most people," she said. "Listen, Way. Pomeroy told Crimmins you came to see him in March, right after Georgina hit, but not to talk about Georgina—not to put the fix in, not to tell him what Georgina told you or what Karpatkin told IAB. In other words, Pomeroy swore under oath you came up to discuss a subject that was entirely harmless."

"Regine Pomeroy is not harmless as a subject."

"Is it true?"

Rather than answer, I asked, "Isn't this Crimmins's job?"

"He already decided Pomeroy's full of shit."

"So you're—"

"Nosey," she said. "But if it makes you feel better, why don't we say none of this is about you. Let's just say I'm not certain about Pomeroy anymore, and I want to know if his pants are on fire." I didn't respond, and she continued, "As in liar, liar—?"

"I was five once."

She shook her reddish head at me. "Will Way, what am I to do with you?" she said mockingly but meaning it. "You'd be very easy to walk away from. And

I wouldn't lose much sleep if I let Crimmins wreck you. What I'm saying is you already gave me a good reason to believe you and Pomeroy are in bed together on some seriously fucked-up shit."

"Which is?"

"Last time I asked you about Pomeroy you left out the part where you were banging his daughter—"

"Jackie—please," I said.

"—who I'm guessing meant more to you than his yacht."

"Regine's got nothing to do with this. I keep saying."

"Not my question." Jackie Kane had her teeth in me. She was taking her time, not letting go. She lit a cigarette with a book match and smoked it while I watched. "You see? When I ask simple questions and get complicated answers— or answers to questions I haven't asked? Makes me want to smoke cigarettes. Fucking hate that." Only her arm moved up and down with the cigarette in it. She said, "You're wrong anyway. His daughter has something to do with this. Pomeroy said so. I'm waiting for you to tell me Pomeroy's a liar."

"How about you stop playing around?"

She gave me a hard look but said nothing. She was creating an uncomfortable silence for me to fill with hasty, ill-considered answers and I knew it. Yet she relented with a soundless sigh and, giving her cigarette a quick tap, softened and asked, "Tell me about her—what was her name again? Regina?"

"Regine."

"What's the story?" she asked. "When'd she die?"

"I—a long time ago. I don't know. I wasn't there."

"Don't worry, Way. I'm not planning on indicting you."

"I meant we were over by then," I said, extraordinarily uncomfortable. "This happened after I knew her. I wasn't around. I didn't find out until later. There was an accident. She was sick."

"Was there an accident or was she sick?"

"Jackie, I told you I don't know."

"No, you told me there was an accident," she said. "Then you told me she was sick. Which was it?"

"Just do me a favor and fuck off—okay, Jackie? It's not funny and—"

"Am I laughing?"

"—and it's got nothing to do with her anyway."

She bided her time then said, "The thing is, William Way—and I'll tell you this is exactly what Crimmins is thinking—"

"You think I give a fuck what he—"

"You should," she said, nearly angry. "You should, because you're in the middle of this thing now, if you don't know it already. There are dangerous men all around you, and none of them could give a damn that you're the antihero of your own sad little bildungsroman, okay? If you're in their way, they'll move you. If they can use you, they'll use you. And if they have to step on you, you're getting stepped on. Simple as that."

Eventually I asked her, "What's your interest in me, Jackie? I don't get it."

"I'm your fairy godmother."

"You're a little late."

"Sick passenger on the R train," she said. "But you better listen up, Way, because I'm telling you the judicial oversight committee won't buy Pomeroy's tale about the pair of you having a fireside chat about his kid. And I'm going to tell you something else. Someone—and it's not going to be me—is going to ask you questions very soon, and if you back Pomeroy you'll get buried alive."

"What's your suggestion?"

"I hear Cuba's lovely this time of year."

"Some fairy godmother," I said. "Let's say for the sake of argument her name never came up. Just what am I supposed to do with that information?"

"Use your brain, Scarecrow!"

"You want me to rat Pomeroy? To save my own ass?" I said. "You really think I'm capable of something like that, Jackie?"

"Okay, Tin Man. Use your heart." She examined me uncritically for a long time, it seemed. She stood to leave. "I'll see you around, William Way."

I remained, yet before she reached the door I bolted from my seat and went to her. I took her wrist and she did not like it, but I was in no mood to care what Jackie Kane liked. The old man sitting alone looked over, and the waitress, but I didn't care about them either. "I should probably save my breath," I said with heat, "but I'm going to tell you anyway. No, we didn't talk about Regine. But I didn't put the fix in for Georgina Reed either. You want to know what we talked about? Well, I want to know, too. I've never had any idea what Pomeroy wants from me."

I let go and after a moment she asked me, "Do you trust him?"

The question took me aback. "Trust him?" I said.

"Pomeroy had to ask himself that same question about you before he gave his answer to Crimmins and the committee," she said. "So, do you trust him?"

I said, "It really isn't a question I can answer."

"I guess there's your answer, then," she said. I shook my head to let her know I didn't understand, but all she said was, "I might not be able to talk to you again, Will. That's just how it is. I'll do what I can, but it won't be enough."

I didn't understand that either.

The detective who arrested me was Maria from *Sesame Street* with the nine-millimeter semiautomatic brassiere. She and another rousted me from Fulton Street without a courtesy call beforehand, handcuffing me in the middle of 43-across and perp-walking me out the door as Sheila Simmons stared, angry tears filling the corners of her eyes. That, and the television cameras already waiting in front of headquarters, had the effect of pissing off a lot of people, most of them cops.

Not that anyone gave a damn about me, really, but in the ongoing aftermath of the Georgina situation patrolmen were simply tired of taking it up the ass from every self-appointed proctologist in New York City. I felt none of the shame I felt according to Shawn Garrity, who worked himself into a perfect lather on several channels and not a few newspapers in my defense. To Garrity I was one of his men once again. Now he could back me all the way. The truth was I felt nothing. The law says you cannot libel a dead man, and that's how I felt for thirty-six hours after Sheila first appeared in my office doorway with a look of hollow-eyed apprehension to say someone was here to see me. For a moment I hoped it was the kid Henry—I had a couple Polaroids to give him—but nearly at once the detectives pushed around Sheila and did their thing. They rear-cuffed me, which was all I really minded. It hurt. I had obediently extended my wrists with something like a smile, supposing we were just going to go through the motions, but when they instead twisted my arms behind my back I realized they meant business.

Nor did they haul me down to the seventh floor of the DA's office to give Montgomery Crimmins the opportunity to ask me if I wished to reconsider my negotiating position. That was where I thought this train was heading, but I never saw him. He wasn't negotiating. Instead they took me to central booking, bringing me into Brooklyn Supreme through the back door on State Street like any other mope, depositing me in the shit-and-Clorox stink of the pens to await my thirty seconds before the judge. There were a couple dozen of us standing around or talking to lawyers through the bars or just sitting disconsolately like sad primates in a sad zoo. I was the only one in a suit and the only white guy except for a heroin junkie coming down hard, talking to his imaginary friend

Dave. Dinner was a school cafeteria lunch, peanut butter on white with apple juice in a miniature carton. No utensils, of course. Nothing happened. I passed the balance of that day and most of the night in a kind of elliptical daze, but when I awoke at dawn on a concrete mattress everything made absolute sense. After all, I'd been expecting them for nearly five years.

Cut now to the deceptively placid image of Wm. Way & Son adrift on the Atlantic Ocean. Bottles of Bud Light cool on ice in the stern cubby where the fish are supposed to go. The idea is that we'll drink beer to make room for fish, but there are no fish. We're not fishing very well. By now our lines have crossed and have no bait and trail behind us like metaphors. We're in the Sea Ray, of course, where Regine Pomeroy and I once had been little adults, learning what certain things do when you do certain things with them. For that reason perhaps I don't go to sea much anymore.

Nevertheless we're doing a passable impersonation of father ampersand son. Someone who didn't know better would think this is a credit card commercial. Here is the handsome square-jawed father in khaki shorts and tanned legs powerful with muscle. And here is the son—well, for the son use your imagination, but don't get too close, else you might notice the dull, harrowed look on his face, the empty beer bottles rolling lazily on the deck boards, the black plastic Glock 17 in his tackle box among the lures and spools of monofilament. And behind the Avocado King's aviators you might notice, what?—concern? No, not concern exactly. He's just waiting for his son. He knows something's on his mind, because he always knows. But everything is all right. Everything's fine. This is just a fishing trip, after all, and everything's just how it should be. Just don't get too close is all I'm saying.

"Dad," I say at length.

Nothing for a moment. I take the semiautomatic pistol from the tackle box, consider it a moment, noting its weight, its brutal heft, then I drop it over the gunwale into the gray-green ocean where it sinks. I feel no different afterward. It was only a pointless gesture, I realize, a prayer, a sacrament, a sacrifice, a penance, an exorcism, an act of contrition, something we do down here for anyone who may be watching up there. My father is bent over an open hatch, oblivious to this, instead looking at the fuel line, probably, wondering why the engine is making that sound. Engines and fuel lines and carburetors are things he knows, and other things, things I give him credit for knowing, and one of the other things he knows is what I want to know.

"Dad—?" I say once more.

And this time my father turns but I cannot see his eyes and there is no expression on his face. When I speak my voice is thick from drinking and my movements are dull and deliberate, yet my mind is agile enough that I know I should not ask this question but I want the answer so I ask it nonetheless.

I say, "You killed some people. I mean—right?"

You never ask a soldier that question. And if you have to ask, you don't ask it like that. The casual manner of my question, coming as it does after a half-dozen bottles of beer and an hour of silence on the silent sea, catches him off guard, like a sucker punch, and I can only watch as his face changes before my eyes, darkening when he thinks I am being light about something I know nothing about, then lightening when he realizes maybe I know something about it after all. At last my father removes his sunglasses, and he and I see each other face to face, eye to eye, for the first time that day, perhaps ever.

After a moment during which there is only the sound of salt water slapping against the fiberglass hull, he says, "You had some trouble out there on the street?"

Now consider a second scene, four nights earlier, a scene that is not a credit card commercial, which is instead an ugly scene you could never mistake for anything other. Yet at first glance it is no uglier than any of the thousand other scenes like it that have played out in your ten years as a patrolman. Brooklyn is creative, however, and it can toss off a surprise now and then, just to keep you interested and awake inside your sector car at three o'clock in the morning. There is for instance a certain two-story brick semidetached on Eldert Street in Bushwick. An okay block, you may think, an okay house, but you never can tell. Everything about working patrol is that way. Either/or, neither/nor. You never know what it is until you know. Patrol is the human heart.

The job on Eldert Street comes over central radio. You take it. A domestic. *A domestic*, you think. *Another fucking domestic.* Domestic calls are no good. Nobody hates like people in love. Your partner is Mark Masterson. You work well together. You like Masterson because you're the same in different ways. You like Masterson though he's a cop all day long. Some cops are cops all day long; some cops are never cops; then there're cops who're cops the way Peter Parker is Spider-Man. You're that kind, and when you take the superhero suit off at the end of your tour and throw it in a plastic garbage bag you're whatever you were before you put it on—*right?* You want to think the job doesn't change you when you're not on the job, that you're still the same man, no matter what MK says.

You roll up on Eldert Street without lights, slowly, in no great hurry to serve and protect. You've been here before, you think. Everything about the place is familiar. Or maybe it was a block over? Somewhere on Covert or Halsey Street maybe? But who gives a fuck because it's all the same anyway—if you haven't been here then you've been close enough to picture the scene before you step out of your car: she is standing red-eyed in the greasy light of her kitchen with her arms crossed, a welt the size of a continent rising along the side of her face. You listen to her for ten minutes, but when you try to do something official she changes on you, just like that—she tells you to go *fuck off because she ain't signing no paper and ain't pressing no charges neither so get the fuck out of my house you fascist motherfuckers why ain't you come when I need you 'cause you can't do nothing about nothing anyway.* You do what you can, but usually you wind up thinking the collar had a reason even if he didn't have an excuse. All this crosses your mind and you start thinking MK may be right.

MK didn't ask for any of this. There was nothing about this on the form she signed in Borough Hall to make you man and wife. Besides, the job was supposed to be temporary. The job was supposed to be something to do instead of selling avocados, something to do until you did something else, like move to New Jersey, have kids, have neighbors, barbecue on weekends and wash the car. That's what she tells you whenever you come home stinking drunk or just stinking, whenever you argue about nonsense, whenever you tell her what you think or, worse, when you don't. And maybe that's on your mind when the domestic job comes over the air. You are a domestic call, you realize. You're at the end of it with MK and soon there'll be new forms to sign and maybe you'll think about her sometime when you pass that place on Coney Island Avenue where you had dinner once or when you hear that song on the radio but by then you'll wonder what did she expect really? Did she think she was going to fix you, like a toaster? And the memory of what she was when you were still strangers makes you soften to her now that you're not. She was good for you, for so long, but you can only tread water until you're spent. Then you sink.

MK left me are your exact words to Masterson in a quiet moment lit only by the dashboard lights when he asks what the hell's been up with you lately. Why not tell him, you decide. You're not a failure. You have nothing to be ashamed of. You simply didn't become what you wanted to be when you were eighteen and wanted to be someone else. Few do. After all, there are only winners because there are losers. You're doing a service for somebody on the other side, you think. You're providing contrast.

"MK left me," you tell Masterson.

"Fuck me, no."

"She wants to be alone, she says."

"Bullshit, she wants to be alone," McMaster says. "Women never want to be alone."

"Yeah, that much I figured out. I'm not the man she married, evidently," you tell him. "Which—and I've been thinking about it, Mark—does that mean I'm not that guy, or am I that guy and she thought I was a different guy, or—" then the domestic on Eldert Street comes over central, and it's a relief to let motion substitute for thought, to think of problems other than your own.

A low cyclone fence surrounds the front yard, a slab of poured concrete, and you look instinctively for dogs snarling at the end of a taut length of chain. Up the stoop in heavy boots, and Masterson knocks with the blunt end of his flashlight and says police. No answer. You go inside, hoping the perp's gone, out for a smoke. No luck. Here he is on an armchair. This one is slim, with a weak chin and a receding hairline that give him the profile of a dolphin. His shirt is yellow except for a long smear across the front that may or may not be human blood. He is watching a *Full House* rerun without watching it, just facing in the direction of the television set in the dark living room while the blue light washes over him. When you stand beside him the man's head turns slowly and he gives Masterson a dead-eyed stare but seems to miss you. "Fuck're you?" he asks, not really caring about the answer.

"What's the trouble, boss?" Masterson asks him.

"Bitch upstairs," he says before turning his attention once again to the television. You can't see his hands, which you don't like. You tell him to stand up, show his hands, and Masterson moves to the stairs. The man doesn't stand and you tell him again. There's something in his right hand, you're sure of it, but you can't see. The only light is from the television set.

"Let's go," you tell him. "Up."

"You 'resting me?"

"Let's go," you say. His head lolls abruptly one way and he tries to fix you with unfocused eyes. You can't decide if he's gone on crack or just gone, but he starts to understand. He begins to form inaudible curses yet remains slumped in the armchair, enervated, thin legs projecting in a wide vee, hands still hidden.

"Stand up, bro, come on," you say to the man, but you know you're talking to him from the other end of a long tunnel.

From upstairs now comes a short cry—Masterson saying your name in a voice that's unlike his—and the man in the armchair bolts suddenly, moving unnaturally fast toward the door. You grab at him and get only his shirt, but it's enough. He twists in his clothing and swings wildly at you but you put him down. You put him down hard. You press his face against the rug, your hand on the back of his neck and your knee in his spine. You've gotten very strong on the job and efficient with your body. You know how to make a man stop moving. The man beneath you feels small, with a rib cage like a bird's, bones under flesh, and all the air comes out of him. His dolphin mouth is working. You bring one of his arms back and wrench it to hurt so he'll quiet down. You hook one wrist and are groping for the other when your hand falls upon a sticky damp wad at the end of his arm. You pull it back and, twined in his fingers, you see a hank of hair, a bloody blond braid, six inches long. There's no use telling him to let go, so you close the ratchet and leave him on the floor like that, still gasping.

Upstairs she is on the bed upright, somehow. You've seen worse but it's still bad. Masterson is asking her what happened and says he's sorry but he has to ask because it's the law and he can't do anything unless she tells him. When she speaks she has an accent, maybe Russian. She looks Russian to you, but it's hard to be certain because of what he did to her mouth. She tells you Pie did it, which makes no sense, but when Masterson asks her again you tell him it's enough because the guy's going under no matter what. You make the call for a bus on your radio and tell the woman help is coming and you sit holding her cold hand.

She can walk so you take her downstairs with your partner when the ambulance arrives, step-by-step. The man is still on the floor. You can see his eyes reflecting television light, and he is just watching. You talk to her and it seems to help. Now the EMT men come and carefully place her on a gurney and one of them is looking in her pale blue eyes with a light. There is a set expression on her face you sometimes see on a woman like this, a look of apology for having been beaten, for having brought you involuntarily into her private world of shit. Her skin is ashen white, sickly, etiolated, like skin under a bandage when you pull it off. You notice for the first time lipstick on her mouth. Blood is still spreading behind her ear where he ripped her open.

Now the man Pie spins a little on the floor, his hands still pinned behind him. He begins to curse as they take her out the front door and down the stoop where another patrol car is parked and the turret lights on the ambulance illuminate the night in intermittent red and white. When the bus pulls away, Sergeant Ralph Berrigan, adjusting his age-worn equipment belt, asks you, "Whadaya got?" All three of you are now standing over the man Pie on the floor, and he is rolling his eyes up to look at you, the white showing. You ignore him. He's unimportant, just a stain on the carpet.

"Fleury," Masterson answers, reading from his memo book, where he has it all written down neat and clear like a cop. "First name Jean-Pierre. Age thirty-six. He's a player, Sarge, looks like. Four arrests for promoting, two convictions. Got a parole warrant."

"You make a habit of the gorilla stuff?" Berrigan asks the man.

"I ain't be 'rested two years, man," he speaks, his accent gutter French.

"Guess it's just a onetime deal, then," Berrigan says to Masterson.

"Bad day at the office," Masterson plays along.

"Have yourself a bad day, Jean-Pierre?" Berrigan asks the guy. "Needed someone to take it out on?"

"Bitch come that way," Pie says.

"With that face she took the train?" Berrigan tells him, nearly laughing. "Come on, seriously, Jean-Pierre?" The man begins to writhe on the floor. Berrigan puts a boot across the man's throat, and he stops. "Hey, hey. Be nice. Why don't you tell me what that's about?"

"Tole you already," the man Pie manages to say. "Ain't with me. Just some trick bitch. I ain't sell that shit, man. Bitch a junkie, man. Look at her."

"Don't look like a junkie," Berrigan says, not laughing. "Looks like a speed bag." The man on the floor is writhing again, clawing ineffectually at Berrigan's boot. You're just watching. After a moment the sergeant backs off. "What'm I gonna find upstairs, Jean-Pierre?"

"What you mean?" the man Pie gets out.

"What'm I gonna find upstairs I can arrest you with?"

"Wha—?"

"I gotta arrest you, brother," Berrigan says. "That's the name of the game. But if you tell me you didn't touch the girl, I mean—then I gotta arrest you for something else, right? Makes sense, right? So I'm asking you what d'you got I can arrest you with?"

"Why you 'rest me, man? Bitch come home that way. I dunno."

"Home?" says Berrigan. "Telling me she lives here?" Berrigan asks the question with a voice of almost fierce disbelief. Masterson turns on the lights.

The room lit up is both garish and sordid—a wide leather couch and new television among baskets of laundry and takeout wrappers. You see paraphernalia on the glass coffee table and a travel brochure for someplace. Berrigan takes his boot off Pie's neck and tells you to follow him upstairs to toss the place. He really wants to nail the guy all of a sudden, you can tell.

"Nothing up there, Sarge."

"Always something, Way," Berrigan tells you, "under the bed, in a shoebox, wrapped in a sock—in plain view, just like the Constitution says."

On the second floor you tramp around looking for something to hang on the guy. Berrigan walks to the bedroom and you look in the hall closet without much interest.

"Look at this shithole," you hear Berrigan say. "Fucking popcorn pimp, that guy. Player my ass." The closet smells like mothballs and cigarettes. You can hear Berrigan opening drawers, moving things. "I don't get it," he says behind you, sounding almost angry. "Fuck's that prick eggplant doing with a girl like that anyway."

"She a pross."

"She ain't no pross," he says, which makes no sense to you because she is. "She ain't no junkie anyway. Pretty."

"Okay."

"Got her statement, Way?" the sergeant says, coming over. "Say she knows the guy or what'd she say?"

"Yeah."

"Knows him like he's her daddy or what?" he asks you.

"I dunno, Sarge."

"You never got your eyes open, Way, that's the matter with you." Berrigan looks at you critically. He says, "Either she's his trick or he's tricking her. Home. Bullshit, home. No way. Girl like her ain't having that in the real world, no way."

"Think she lives here, Sarge. Got clothes in the closet there."

"Fuck that," he says unhappily, looking at the dresses and blouses and shoes. He closes the closet door and stumps off. After a while, in a sardonic voice, you hear him say from another room, "Fuck her. Girls like them, never the ones you'd ever touch anyways. Always got big fat titties hanging out or knocked up and smoking Kool cigarettes with something fucked in her fucking head, like there ain't no decent man left in the whole world that'd touch her so she ain't got no choice. You never notice that, Way?"

"No."

"And not for nothing, girl gets turned out like that, then fuck it. Once she takes that big mandingo pecker, ain't no one decent's ever gonna wanna—"

"I'm gonna look in here now, Sarge," you say, turning away. His words are like iron spikes. You move to the bathroom, heart pounding, flush with inarticulable rage, and in the hall Berrigan is laughing humorlessly to himself, at you, and then you hear his boots on the stairs going down. You see yourself in the bathroom mirror and all at once you're thinking of Regine and you're ashamed because that has nothing to do with this. You look around to kill time, but all you find is further evidence of the life the man had with the woman whose name you've now forgotten. Her cosmetics are arranged haphazardly on the toilet tank cover. The shower head drips in a slow regular tempo, and you notice an uncapped lipstick, dark red, the color on her lips when they took her away.

You're done. You go downstairs. Berrigan is on the radio. His driver is smoking a cigarette on the stoop. Masterson has the guy on his feet now and is holding him by the upper arm. He's small, maybe five and a half feet with a high slim waist. You're at the kitchen table writing in your memo book, getting things squared away on paper, yet through the familiar mechanics of the routine of an arrest you feel the sickness well up inside you. There's nothing new about any of this, of course. You've been here a thousand times, but this time you're thinking that the woman tried to pretty herself up with lipstick, after.

"Nothing?" Masterson asks you with a nod upstairs.

"Clean."

"Hey, cop," the man Pie says. You're still sitting at his table, writing in your book. "Hey, cop. You like her, ain't you?" He is talking to you, you realize. He seems to sense the turmoil in your head, and on his dolphin face is a private smile for you. "You wanna tap that ass, cop? Ain't you?" You're writing in your indecipherable scrawl, pretending not to hear. "You like that ass, ain't you, cop, ha ha? I seen you looking at that shit. I seen you talking to my bitch. You want it, man, you can have it. You can have that ass, cop. I ain't mind. You take it. It ain't that good, though. All worn out and tired and shit. Ain't no one wants that shit no more. Junkie bitch." You ignore him. You close your memo book and stand. When you pass by the guy he spits. You feel it on your face, on your neck and ear, and a gob slides under your shirt, under your Kevlar vest, and onto your bare skin where you can't get at it—

Ten minutes later you are driving the guy to Brookdale. He's unmoving in the back seat of your sector car, lying still rear-cuffed on his side and moaning. Masterson is at the wheel, not saying anything, not looking at you. The white headlights come at you. In the back the guy starts making faint animal sounds in his throat and a stink rises like he crapped his pants. Masterson at a stop light gives him a quick look over his right shoulder, and for a moment you think he might hit the lights and siren. You don't look at your partner or at the guy. Your knuckles are split and bleeding through the dish towel but do not ache yet. You're not thinking about Pie but the look of astonishment on Berrigan's face when Masterson pulled you off the guy. "That's enough, Way," Masterson said to you when he did. "I said that's enough." Then, a moment later, after you and Masterson carried the unconscious man into the back seat of your RMP—his body obscenely light—Berrigan said to you, almost laughing, "Jesus Christ, Way—fuck did that come from, you old pussycat?"

Brookdale Hospital is where they took the girl. You walk off to find her but they're still working on her and won't let you inside. You don't like hospitals and don't want to be here, but you come back around to the emergency room, where Masterson is waiting on a plastic seat under the hard fluorescent lights, hands between his knees. He is looking at you now with a cautious expression that could mean anything. He says nothing about what just happened on Eldert Street, and Pie is unmoving on a gurney in the hallway nearby. The whole place stinks of him now. You can see him there. His nose is flat, his face swollen and discolored grotesquely where you broke it. A nurse comes to you with a clipboard. She sees the blood covering your hands, your uniform, but she says nothing about that. There's a form she needs to fill out. She is asking you questions. Her pen is poised. She wants to know what happened. You say he fell down the stairs.

THIRTY-FIVE

I took three days lost time after that. Berrigan authorized it. In fact, Berrigan wrote it up for me, telling me to go home and sleep. Sleep is good for you, he said. You need it, he said, so I went home. I didn't sleep much. I figured IAB would come for me, so I stayed home, ready to surrender. My badge and gun were already in a plastic D'Agostino grocery bag by the door. I had no plans to fight it out Alamo-like or take hostages. I was ready to surrender meekly. I deserved it, whatever it was. But nothing happened. The house remained empty and quiet. MK was gone. After three days I went fishing with my father and dropped my pistol in the ocean. Then I went to see Pomeroy.

I wore the same white dress shirt I'd bought at Kings Plaza ten years earlier when I sold avocados for six months. It no longer fit. Now it was tight around the neck. On the Sea Ray the day before I'd sat bare-chested with my father, and offhand he said I could kick his ass now. I doubted it. Cutting mullet for bait with a Ka-Bar, the empty bottles of Bud Light rolling on the deck, my father was shirtless himself. Pushing fifty he was yet fearsome to behold. Seeing the marks of war on his dark powerful frame gave me the misbegotten notion that now we had something in common, that I was no longer the kid pouring bourbon highballs in the kitchen for his brothers-in-arms, no longer the boy who always forgot to turn out the light. I saw on the right side of his lower back the distinctive wound like a cigar burn where a large-caliber bullet had exited his body, which my mind absurdly equated with my knuckles, still ragged and painful from fracturing a handcuffed prisoner's zygomatic arch as well as shattering the lateral and anterior walls of his left maxillary sinus, which I had memorized from his hospital chart. Until he disproved me without even meaning to, I believed my father and I at last shared a grave inexpressible secret, something about man's instinct to violence or whatever, which of course was absurd. I don't know what I expected him to say when I'd emptied enough beer bottles to ask him about the men he killed. He answered only that he'd taken no pleasure in it, nor had he lost any sleep over it. In other words, we didn't even have that in common.

The following morning I examined my suddenly unfamiliar face, a fresh shaving nick on a stranger's chin. I tried to fasten the collar of the white dress shirt around my neck, and at last I went without a tie. I rode the train downtown and felt very aware of myself, but of course no one noticed. No one ever really sees us as we are, much less as we think we are. On the subway no one sees us at all.

Pomeroy was presiding over a murder trial, his clerk told me. I said I'd wait. When she asked my business I told her it was personal, and she eyed me full of doubt. I gave her my name, twice, and she wrote it on a pink slip of paper. I sat in an uncomfortable chair and after an hour Pomeroy came in, two lawyers leaping at his heels like terriers. Pomeroy unzipped his robe and ignored them. The clerk at the desk said something about "this gentleman here," whereupon Pomeroy wheeled on me with a stern imperious cast to his expression. I hadn't seen him since he gave me a hundred bucks for twelve dollars' worth of gas in a hospital waiting room in Worcester, Massachusetts. Perhaps for that reason there passed an interminable moment during which I felt as if I might have to introduce myself.

"Will Way—good Lord—hello," he said at last. Pomeroy examined me but otherwise seemed at a complete loss for a short moment, uncharacteristically nonplussed, and I believed that behind the pleasant expression his eyes showed something perhaps not altogether pleasant, something like discomfort or worse. "Hello, indeed."

Meanwhile, the lawyers with him watched me like the new kid in class. No one said anything for a spell, but the atmosphere felt all wrong, and I regretted at once my mostly impulsive and certainly desperate decision to seek him out.

"Sit a moment, will you?" he ordered me before stepping into chambers. For twenty minutes there was the sound of them behind the closed door marked private. I could make out only a few words now and then. Pomeroy's voice was never the loudest, but when he spoke the other two did not. When the door opened the lawyers walked past me. One wasn't happy. I stood and said something about that to Pomeroy when he followed them out. "These kids Whitey Fister sends to prosecute his indictments don't know shit from Shinola. You can literally get away with murder in this town. Hungry?" He had exactly forty minutes and glanced at his wristwatch to prove it.

We walked to a restaurant nearby where everyone knew him. With all the hellos and handshakes it took ten minutes to reach a reserved table beneath a

burning display of gaslight chandeliers. A martini came unbidden to his outstretched hand and was down the hatch before we opened our menus. "Just
what the doctor ordered," he told me with a conspiratorial look. "My kind of
doctor, too. An anesthetist, ha ha. And you, Will—still abstemiously unlubri-
cated as ever?"

"Pardon me?"

"Still don't touch the old firewater, chief?"

"Only to excess," I answered truthfully, but he took it as a joke, laughing
politely as he waved for another martini, which momentarily appeared. Apart
from his hair, by that point liberally streaked a senatorial gray, Pomeroy was
Pomeroy. His blue eyes were sharp and could still be unintentionally cruel
when he looked at you, which he did now in short inquisitive glances. I did the
same. We were each wondering about the other. Presently a cheap-suited man
came over, and while they spoke companionably about something involving
someone and laughed I looked at my menu and felt twelve years old. Alone
again with me, his eyes resumed the same dark cast they'd had in chambers
when I'd dropped unannounced into the middle of his midday after an entire
decade of middays in which I had not. Neither had I gotten over the sense I'd
made an awful mistake or that I cut a faintly ridiculous figure in my ill-fitting
shirt and size 17 neck. On a mirrored wall opposite I met my own eyes staring
back over Pomeroy's distinguished head with a shock of recognition. Seeing
the two of us paired that way I realized there could be consequences for him,
were I disgraced.

Perhaps he sensed the turmoil in me, for his expression remained mostly
genial, almost expectant. Surely he wanted to know why I was here. I tried
to remember myself, waiting for a moment, realizing the clock was ticking.
Meanwhile we made small talk, very small, and he asked after my father—*Billy*
he called him, which always seemed to my ear both foreign and fitting. At last
over a plate of clam bellies with a red napkin tucked under his chin, Pomeroy
asked and I told him that I was a cop.

"A patrolman—?" he said, not bothering to hide his surprise, looking at me
intently and dashing the napkin quickly over his lips. "Well, I'll be goddamned.
How on earth did that come about?"

"You know, I—"

"I'd always imagined you were in business with Billy. His trucks are
everywhere now, aren't they? Saw one just this morning. And son, I'm certain
they read."

"My father and I—we never—"

"He's a rather impressive figure, isn't he?" he said, smiling kindly, eating. "Turned that little produce concern of his into something of a far-flung enter-prise, ha ha. Good for him."

"Well."

"And an authentic war hero to boot," he continued with a distant, wistful expression courtesy of four or five ounces of gin. I squirmed uncomfortably as I always did on this topic, a favorite of those men who knew my father; I got more of the Avocado King's résumé from his acquaintances than I ever got from the man himself. "I can tell you in perfect candor every one of us at Xaverian envied Billy Way. Every one of us. A hell of a sportsman was your father. Film-star handsome, and always much caressed by the young ladies of Fontbonne, ha ha—and that was before Dick Nixon hung a ribbon around his—"

"The thing is, Judge," I interrupted. "The thing is—I think I may have a problem."

"Problem?"

"With the job, I mean. And I wanted—your advice."

"Oh—?" he said, darkening, and I gave him the abridged version. He lis-tened, finishing his lunch while he listened, but listening nonetheless, showing no reaction one way or another. When I was done he asked, "He's dead, your *Monsieur Fleury le souteneur*?" He put a proper Sixteenth Arrondissement accent on it.

"No, I—"

"So, this man's raising a holy stink about it, I suppose?"

"No," I said in surprise, thinking he missed the point, that I hadn't been sufficiently clear. I felt a blush of embarrassment rise on my face, it all seeming now a waste of Pomeroy's valuable forty minutes to have bothered him about a Haitian pimp who didn't even have the courtesy to be dead. "No, I mean—no."

"Where is this fellow now?"

"I don't know. Home probably."

"He's not on Rikers?" he said, his brow constricted with thought.

"We—under the circumstances my sergeant voided the arrest."

"Who has it at IAB?" Pomeroy asked. "Do you have a name?"

"No—"

"This fellow's lawyer's not spreading the story around?" he said, and he wiped his lips primly on the napkin. "Your command kept it in house? No referral yet?" When I told him no he didn't bother to hide his surprise. He opened his palms. "Are you telling me there's no investigation at all, Will?" I began to understand we were discussing two different things. He went silent with thought. I was just silent. The ice settled in his water glass and that was the only sound at our table. Around us was the low undercurrent of talk. Pomeroy was looking down now and seemed more irritated than anything else. Then he faced me and said, "Just what do you expect me to do with this information?"

"I don't know," I said apologetically because all at once I wondered the same thing, and I began to cast about for a better reason to have interrupted his lunchtime. "I—I mean—sometimes out there. On patrol. Sometimes I just don't know anymore. I thought the job was going to be different."

"How do you mean 'different'?"

"Policing, you know," I said. "I thought maybe it would be obvious. And I would just have to do it."

"What would be obvious?"

"The right thing," I said. "Justice."

"Ah, so you want to dispense justice, do you?" he said with a lightness belied by the gravity of his expression. "You think that's your job?"

"Yeah," I said. "I mean, I'm a cop."

"I'm a judge, and I'd shudder to think I ever had the obligation to grasp what justice is, much less to mete it out. Thankfully that's neither my job nor yours, Will."

"What's the job, then?"

"Mine, to apply the law," he said. "Yours to enforce it."

"They should be the same, law and justice."

"I rather like to think the law's as close as we can come, down here," he said, crossing himself with mock piety.

"It's just—I don't know. It's been ten years, Judge, ten years on patrol, and—" I told him. "I guess I'm not making a lot of sense, am I?"

"You're making absolute sense," he said. "You're a bright young man. You're tired of walking your feet flat—"

"No, it's not that exactly."

"Please." He shook his noble head. "You know I feel a certain responsibility for you, Will. You're not exactly a stranger to me, are you? You've put your time in. Now you want to get into the squad, I bet. Swap that white shield for gold. Start using that brain of yours, hmm?"

And I fell for it. So help me God, I fell for it. "No, no, to tell you the truth—" I said in mealymouthed protest. I had no idea what I wanted, but I couldn't disappoint him further by leaving him no favor to do me. By now his forty-minute clock had run.

"You know," he said with a gesture toward the waiter, "your union's having one of their tiresome, self-congratulatory affairs tomorrow evening in the city. I suppose Ann and I'll have to attend, which means she'll be able to extort some reciprocal favor from me. I foresee another chintz settee in my immediate future, ha ha." He faced me so I could smile on cue. I did. "Right," he continued, "I'll have a word with Mr. Garrity on your behalf. You do know him, I suppose?"

"No, we've never—"

An admonitory hand came up, silencing me. "I'll put a word in his ear."

We pushed back from the linen tablecloth, Pomeroy and I, and there followed the long walk to the door with goodbyes and more handshakes and much extending of his ring to kiss. To me it seemed absurd, Pomeroy among these low-rent Brooklyn politicos and fixers and aides with their sallow indoor complexions and uneven sideburns, all of them looking about with pouchy eyes for a hand to shake or favor to ask or bestow. And even as we stepped again into the welcome clean light of day I wondered if I'd made a mistake in coming to Pomeroy or if the restaurant had simply been wrong for it. I'd wanted a confessional or a courthouse, but what I got was a whorehouse.

THIRTY-SIX

In a downtown Manhattan lobby done in pink and blue and silver, the colors of a Miami nightmare, OUELLETTE & KATZENBACH, LLP was written above the reception desk in letters large enough to remind me I was deep behind enemy lines. I waited, unarmed, thumbing absently through thick glossy magazines making me envy people I didn't like and want things I'd never use.

"Ms. Katzenbach will see you now, Officer Way," said the receptionist, a fair-skinned black woman with delicate movements. When I gave her my name earlier she smiled politely, mechanically, but the newspapers were on her desk, folded, read, and behind her dark distant eyes she was certainly thinking, *Oh, shit, this is the cop that messed up that guy—*

Beatrix B. Katzenbach filled a swivel chair that complained when she shifted her bulk to take my hand without spending the effort to rise. Her office smelled like baby powder and raw meat. Her smooth putty-colored fingers were in mine, and our eyes met in mutual embarrassment and interest.

"Gonna ask if I did it?" I said when I sat across from her.

She said nothing immediately. I hadn't seen Bea Katzenbach since she handed me my conscience on a cafeteria tray at BABE Cathedral last spring with an expression suggesting it was the decapitated head of John the Baptist—*You asked for it, now here it is.* The newspaper had made me a topic, but public opinion remained divided. Some saw my arrest as better late than never. Others thought it all a put-up job by the Brooklyn DA, vengeance for pissing in his fireplace. My headline in the *Brooklyn Daily News* was page three, next to an advertisement promising prompt and effective bedbug extermination:

GEORGINA ALLY IN BRUTALITY BUST
SOME CRY FOUL

The story was the first in days on the case. By then the Georgina situation had nearly reached its sell-by date. At my arraignment only Betty Moon had bothered to show. CNN was busy elsewhere and no yellowy orange school buses wheezed diesel in front of Brooklyn Supreme. There were no protests, nor counterprotests, nor ribbons of any color. Even the prosecutor was not Montgomery Crimmins but some junior line assistant who had twenty-seven other bullshit cases on the calendar to run through before she got around to arraigning me. When she asked the judge to set bail there was no malice in her voice. I was just case number eighteen.

Garrity had dispatched Irving Meltzer, Esq., to court as a sort of goody bag on my way out the door along with the unsurprising message from headquarters that I'd been placed on modified duty for the duration. "One PP assigned ya out to Queens out to the auto impound lot in College Point there just until this whole thing gets squared away not that no one at Fulton Street believes ya tuned up some shithead a million years ago that no one even knows where he is no more," the lawyer said-shouted in my ear. "It's just policy ya know and by the way ya gotta go over to IAB after."

"Why IAB?" I asked.

"Turn over your gun and shield and make your statement you know that's policy too ya know that right nothing personal," Meltzer told me. We were sitting in the back row of the courtroom, waiting to hear my case called.

"I don't have a gun."

"Where's your gun you're a cop?"

"Dropped it in the ocean," I told him.

"What are ya nuts? Why'd ya drop it in the ocean for you can't do that?"

"Bad juju. I dunno."

"Okay so you're superstitious me too sometimes but did ya get better luck after?"

"I dunno, counselor, how's it look so far?"

I sat with Meltzer, waiting, feeling nothing, thinking nothing, listening for my number to come up like I was in a deli holding a ticket. Now serving customer one hundred four. I was succumbing to the long slow torpor of the circumstances when I felt a strong hand on my shoulder. I looked up into the face of my father. He winked unsmilingly at me with his sniper eye then sat on the worn wooden bench with Meltzer and me. At once there was the familiar, comforting solidity of him. When the judge set bail an hour and twenty minutes later, the Avocado King posted me out, putting up Melba Court against the bond. He'd been my one phone call.

Then we left, but as we passed together through the courtroom gallery, past all of weary downtrodden Brooklyn, lost in its own worries, I realized there were no cops. But there were always supposed to be cops. Cops always came for cops. They came freshly shaved, wearing dress blues, sitting in the gallery with stern unsmiling expressions and crossed arms, leaving a scent of Desenex when they walked away in silent disgust when the day's legal proceedings were over. They came because that's what cops do when one of them sits at the defense table in his Sunday suit and Father's Day necktie. They came whether they know the guy or not because knowing him isn't the point. Cops came because cops never get a fair shake—not out there, not before a jury of their peers. *Fuck that,* they say behind their folded arms. *You're not their peers, you don't know what it is like to stand outside a door and wonder what's on the other side of it. You don't know what it is like, so who're you to say we crossed the line? Fuck you, we made that line.* They came to show whoever might be watching that they're watching too. But Police Officer William Way, Jr., had nobody.

Bea Katzenbach telephoned me the following morning, stirring me from the thick end of a night of desultory sleep to tell me I needed a lawyer.

"I have a lawyer," I told her.

"I wouldn't let Irving Meltzer stand up for me. Hell, I wouldn't let Irving Meltzer walk my dead dachshund. Be here by ten, Way, if you know what's good for you," she said, but I came to see her anyway. *Gonna ask if I did it?* I'd said to her, for old times' sake trying to come off as nonchalant, as the world-weary fascist I played to her bleeding heart once upon a time. It was always an act, of course, but now it was just an act of an act. I didn't feel world-weary. I didn't feel a thing. Or rather I felt everything, but at a distance. Walking through the streets of New York from the subway to her office in lower Manhattan I felt as much a part of this world as a comet. All around me people moved with industry and purpose, but I just arced along an independent course described for me from time immemorial, sometimes bringing me close to the light but more often sending me hurtling away alone into dark unreachable places.

Eventually she said, not bothering to play along, "That's a question I never ask. It's irrelevant."

"The truth is irrelevant, Bea?"

"In a courtroom, yes," she said. "A criminal trial isn't about truth and justice, popular opinion notwithstanding. A criminal trial is about what the DA can prove. And if the DA can prove you did it, then you did it. Even if you didn't."

"And if I did it?"

"If the DA can't prove it, you go home," she answered. "But tell me anyway—did you do it?"

I laughed on cue. She didn't. Then, after an uncomfortable silence I told her yes, yes I did. Then I told her everything else. She let me talk for ten minutes, saying nothing. She spoke only when I'd nearly finished, when I told her I'd gone to see Pomeroy afterward.

"Pomeroy—?" she asked with a note of doubt in her voice.

"We have a relationship of a personal nature."

"I read," she said, "but why'd you think he'd ever stick his nose out to help you?"

"I didn't," I told her.

"And he didn't."

"No, he did," I said. "He fixed it for me."

"How do you know, Will?" she asked. "Did he tell you?"

"No, but—I know because I know," I said, resorting to kid logic. "No shit fell on me, on the job. I took a promotion, even. He got me into the union with Garrity."

"That may be," she said, very seriously, "but did Judge Pomeroy ever tell you he'd thrown off an Internal Affairs investigation? Complaint board? DA? Anything—?"

"No, but—"

"Then why do you believe he did?" she asked.

"I mean, I—"

"Pomeroy did nothing for you because there was nothing to do," she said. "There was never an investigation because—I'll go out on a very short limb here—this guy Fleury never complained. He kept this thing hushed up, probably because someone told him to keep it hushed up. Fleury was never charged for the assault on the female, right?"

"Berrigan voided his arrest," I admitted.

"Of course. Now everyone's friends."

"How'd you know IAB had nothing going on me?"

"I have a telephone," she said in a voice both kind and annoyed. "This is what I do. Look, Will. Judge Pomeroy may have patted you on the head, made you feel better, but he didn't fix a damn thing because nothing was broken. Until now. Now someone dug up this Fleury mishigas and away we go." I said nothing and she stood, which was a slow, disjointed process for her. I watched as she moved to the window and stuck a finger in the blinds to look at the sunlit city. "The thing is I'm not feeling Whitey Fister's heart's in this prosecution, not to suggest he has one. A heart, I mean. In fact, I'm willing to bet the DA's damned unhappy about it."

"He arrested me, didn't he?"

"No choice," she told me. "Once Betty Moon broke the story, Whitey couldn't sit on the allegation without coming across like he's protecting his witness."

"I'm not Whitey's witness."

"Not yet."

"That ship has sailed, Bea," I said. "I told Crimmins already. And the court quashed my subpoena besides. They can't force me to testify against Georgina—"

"I said you're a witness, Will. I didn't say you're a witness against Georgina."

"Fuck's Betty Moon got to do with all this anyway?" I asked angrily, still one step behind.

"Someone tipped her," she said. "Someone wanted you dirty, to queer the DA's play with you. And don't deny Fister or Crimmins or somebody on Joralemon Street made a play for you. You have something they want, don't you? They need you, so you better tell me now."

"Let's say the DA needs me—"

She held up a hand. "I charge by the hour, Way," she said, "so it's in your financial interest to get to the point."

I looked away. "Crimmins wants me to rat Georgina in the grand jury."

"Oh, that's yesterday's news," she said with a gesture to match her voice. "I told you I'm not talking about Georgina here. But since you mention, what'd Crimmins want from you anyway?"

"The truth," I said. "Or something close enough to make everyone happy."

"No," she said. "Monty wouldn't object to a few lies in the service of the truth. Out of curiosity, what'd he offer you for your testimony?"

"Nothing."

"Bullshit nothing," she said with a snort. "Crimmins would either hand you something or beat you with something. That's how these people work. So, which? Carrot or stick?"

"Make me this week's hero, I guess," I said. "He also made some noise about going after a—just somebody I used to know. Somebody on the job."

"Berrigan?" she said out of the blue.

"No—why'd you say Berrigan?"

"He fits the description—isn't that what you cops say when you want to fuck with somebody on the street?" she told me in a neutral voice. "Who're you talking about then if not him?"

"Does it matter, Bea?" I said. "He's just a friend who used to help me out on this and that, throw me a few bread crumbs time to time. Crimmins knew about him and threatened to lean on him if I didn't sign a co-op agreement. I mean, he didn't come right out and say it, but I got the message. I'm not stupid."

"Really?"

"Fuck off, Bea. Give me a break."

"And did he? Did Crimmins put heat on your friend?"

"I don't—" I said. "I mean, I really don't know for sure."

"Guess you're not too close, then. Not friends like you're friends."

"No. I mean not anymore, no," I said, and the recollection of Mark Masterson still throbbed. "I'm sure he thinks I— Anyway, what I'm saying is that's why Fister cuffed me on this new thing, this Fleury thing, because I wouldn't play ball on Georgina and—"

"What do you mean?"

"Crimmins needs me to testify against Georgina," I said. "I'm the only way the DA can make out a case against her. So the DA arrested me. The DA's trying to leverage me into court to give testimony that Georgina told—"

"Leverage you?" she said, astonished. "By arresting you?"

"Exactly."

"No, my God," she laughed, "that'd be like shooting your hostages then asking for ransom." She laughed some more, then she stopped. "You can't testify against Georgina now. If you cop a plea deal and testify, jury'll know the DA bought you out. No one'd believe you. Janus wouldn't break a sweat making you out as a government whore. You're burned, Way. All I want to know is who lit the match."

"You just said Betty Moon," I said after taking a moment to understand.

"Betty only answered the phone. I'm wondering who dimed you out to Betty in the first place, gave her a name and told her to start nosing around. And when I say I'm wondering who was on the other end of the phone, Way, I'm not wondering. It was Pomeroy."

"Oh, get out of—"

"Had to be," she said. "You just told me you sat down with him after. He knew the whole story about the guy Fleury."

"No, Bea, you're wrong."

"Am I?"

"I mean, why the hell would he?" I asked violently. "What's Pomeroy get out of it? Fuck's he care if Georgina walks?"

"I've been telling you this isn't about Georgina. The DA doesn't need you as a witness against Georgina. The DA needs you as a witness against Pomeroy."

"Against Pomeroy—!"

"This is bigger than Georgina," she said in a kind tone. "Always has been. And sorry, my old friend, but that means it's bigger than you, too. Georgina's just a rook in the big game and you're—well, a pawn. Pomeroy's pawn. Now Fister want to make you his pawn. Understand?"

"No, he—"

"Ask yourself two questions, Will. Who knew about Fleury, and who benefits from your arrest? Pomeroy and Pomeroy."

"What's he get?" I asked, sounding like I felt. "Nothing."

"You're between Whitey and Pomeroy. Both of them are big dogs fighting over the same bone. Pomeroy wants to be DA, and Whitey doesn't want to be former DA. So, round one, Judge Pomeroy tosses Whitey's indictment and makes his office look like a clown car. Now the score is one zip. Next Whitey fires back, raising hell with the judicial oversight committee because of this— this secret midnight meeting between you and Pomeroy."

"It wasn't midnight already. Christ."

"Pomeroy went on record saying the two of you were just talking over old times in chambers, about his daughter, but no one believes that bullshit. Not even you, do you?" She waited for my answer. I didn't have one. "Will, you need to understand how it looks—how it looks from the outside."

"So how's it look, Bea?"

"Like a headline," she said. "Like the cop union's in cahoots with the presiding judge to fuck the DA and—"

"That's not how it—"

"Doesn't matter!" she said. "Just tell me Judge Pomeroy told the truth and nothing but to the oversight committee. Tell me all the two of you discussed was his kid, whatever the hell her name is." Again I answered by not answering, and she went on. "You see? If you were subpoenaed before the committee, you could sink Pomeroy's battleship. So he sank yours first."

"Why would I want to?"

"Crimmins was going to subpoena you to the committee, wasn't he?"

"I have no idea," I said truthfully.

"Anyway, Pomeroy thought so," she answered. "And he knows people say all sorts of things under subpoena. Sometimes they even tell the truth."

I considered that a long time. Neither of us said a word. Through her window came the sounds of lower Manhattan, dully, as if a mile away. "No—" I said at last, brightening unreasonably, having convinced myself the twenty-three on my lottery ticket was really a twenty-eight. "No, Bea, if I'm the only one who can tell the committee Pomeroy committed perjury, I'm the only one who can say he didn't. I'm the only one who can back his story that all we talked about was—her."

"So you'd lie for him. Okay. You better call Meltzer then because I—"

"No, I—"

"But that's irrelevant anyway. Because why in hell would Pomeroy believe you'd ever lie for him?" she told me. "I mean, he's not your daddy. You're nothing to him—what'd you say you were? His boat boy? You think Pomeroy'd ever bet his life and career and reputation that his fucking boat boy would ever step up and cavalry his ass? No way. No fucking way."

"Maybe I would have, Bea. You don't know."

"Anyway, it's too late," she said. "I told you. You're burned. You're an indicted felon. Your testimony's worth dogshit. No one's ever gonna believe a witness under an open indictment. They'll think you're just trying to get a deal, even if there's not one on the table. Don't you get it? I mean, Jesus Christ, that's why Pomeroy gave you up! The judicial committee's never putting an indicted felon in the witness box. Never."

"He wouldn't do that to me," I offered weakly at last, speaking mostly to myself.

"Look—" she began apologetically. "I can see you're upset. I'm not saying this is what happened here, but—"

"He wouldn't do that, Bea," I said louder.

"—but this is my read of the situation. There's no one else but Judge Pomeroy—no one that knows about this thing with the guy out in Bushwick—and more important, no one else who's got a good reason to let you hang for it."

"No."

"Look, Will, I'm sure Pomeroy's sorry as hell you got between him and the DA. But you are between them, right between them, so you need to ask yourself—what's the shortest distance between two points?"

THE AVOCADO KING

THIRTY-SEVEN

On the way out of Bea's office I got tangled with Charles Ouellette coming in. In the door we did an Alphonse and Gaston routine until we recognized each other. Then he started to laugh at the absurdity of it and at everything, shaking his handsome head. He wore a charcoal-gray-pinstripe suit you could cut yourself on and a white carnation on his lapel. When he laughed his David Niven mustache raised on one side, but the whole time his eyes remained humorless and flat. He gave me some unsolicited advice I immediately forgot and as I moved toward the elevator bank he called, "Welcome aboard, Officer!" I didn't like it when he said it, and later when I thought about it I still didn't like it.

I walked onto sunlit Broadway and into the general up-and-down rush of the city, faster here than in Brooklyn, faster than anywhere, flowing around me and around graffitied mailboxes and around immobile Wisconsin families on street corners hunched over subway maps or craning their heads to make out skyscraper tops. New Yorkers never look at maps, or up. We already know where we're going and usually we're late. I'd been benched long enough that the sudden onrush of humanity was disorienting, nearly frightening. Part of me felt I might be noticed, carried away by the mob on a rail, or tarred and feathered, but of course no one gave a damn. No one even said excuse me.

Waiting for the train, I stood thinking of what Bea told me about Pomeroy, my stomach in a knot. Of course she was wrong. *Fuck does she know, she doesn't know Pomeroy. Beatrice B. Katzenbach's just an unreconstructed radical who believes dark and powerful men control everything, so of course she thinks it's Pomeroy,* I said to myself as my hand felt automatically for the pill bottle in my pocket. I held it up appraisingly to the diffuse light of a subway grate overhead and shook it like a maraca. Only a couple dozen left, maybe. No refills. I wondered if the Avocado King still had the telephone number for my nurse. Hell was her name? He'd know. He would certainly know. I snapped a single pink painkiller in half, but it lodged in my dry throat and I gagged. Someone turned, disgusted, and when our eyes met I mistook his reaction for recognition and moved farther down the platform, hawking and gagging, dispersing all in my path.

Alone I waited for the downtown R and for the warm narcotic to wash over me like a security blanket. I'd gotten accustomed to the sensation lately and liked it. For a moment I even considered going back up the concrete staircase and braving daylight to find an anonymous saloon for a kicker. I had booze at the apartment, of course, but often it's better to drink alone in the company of a dozen strangers. Immediately I thought better of it. Not even noon, for chrissake, I said with an accusatory glance at my watch, and besides I needed to lay off. I'd gotten fat. Kat would deny it, but she loved me, possibly yet. On the other hand I'd fallen out of love with myself and could see myself clearly as I was. And I wanted out. I wanted a trial separation from myself. I would sign the papers in Borough Hall, *nolo contendere*. I could take anything I wanted on my way out the door—the couch, the stereo—just get the fuck out, please, and leave me alone, whoever you are. *Welcome aboard!* How'd I end up here, I wondered—a cop you would read about and shake your head, paddling Charles Ouellette's boat? Somehow the promise had been rescinded, the one I'd believed since third grade when I realized I was different from those around me. The promise was simple—in exchange for being different, I would be different. I'd get out of Gerritsen Beach, for starters. I wouldn't become a cop or a fireman, and I'd never sell an avocado. Was the promise canceled, or had I simply misread the fine print? Like the Cumaean Sibyl—granted eternal life but not eternal youth, doomed to live out her long years as dust in a jar—had I been given the exact thing foretold, cursed to live in interesting times?

Even after Worcester I still believed strongly enough in the promise to continue moving forward in the same direction. That autumn at Georgetown I tried on my new self like a suit I needed to grow into. My undeclared major was Classics. I made new sorts of friends and got a different haircut, yet throughout everything Regine pulled on me like the gravity of Saturn. I'd not seen her since she walked behind the swinging door in the clinic that August. Before I left for Washington I called Dover Street, hanging up whenever Saint Ann answered. In September I tried Holyoke, but they had no record. I wrote Regine a long letter with careful penmanship full of truth and regret. There was no reply. In October I wrote another, not nearly so long nor so carefully written. Then another. By Christmas break I'd still heard not a word, and when I arrived at Melba Court after six hours in the Impala there was no mail. My father, however, was waiting on the flowery couch and instantly awake, a trick he learned in the jungle. A few days later he hauled me off to Jim's Inn for the advertised feast, wearing a jacket for the occasion and his "holiday tie," candy canes patterned over a field of polyester blue. We walked together over the darkening streets in the muffled quiet of that place I knew better than any other place, yet it seemed so abruptly funereal and bygone after four months on a bright campus full of overachievers in alligator shirts and khaki pants. The men inside Jim's came over in their slow, gut-forward way to give obeisance to the Avocado King and administer to me several obligatory fake sucker punches and smacks on the back. The waitress mussed my new haircut and said I was "cute." After, I drove to Dover Street, intending merely to pass by the big redbrick green-roofed house by the sea or maybe park for a while until I'd gotten it out of my system. Instead—overcome by a sudden need to know—I killed the engine and rang the front bell. Within, all seemed unnaturally quiet and obscure. There was no tree in the window nor the more familiar colored lights hanging along the eaves as usual. I had nearly turned to leave when her mother opened the door, and that was how I found out. The expression on her saintly face suggested Regine had done us all a favor.

I emerged from underground in Park Slope, still silently cursing Bea Katzenbach, and walked under the oppressive sunlight to my home that was not home. Frederick the doorman now ignored me, pretending to be busy polishing brass or sorting mail whenever I came through his doors. I had stopped first at the bodega on the corner and after thirty minutes of vacant contemplation bought seven cans of condensed milk and a Kit Kat—I think the pink painkiller was affecting me, to be honest—and when I passed Frederick in the lobby he said nothing, nor did he even look at me. He'd seen the newspapers, of course. Neither did Kaseem open his door when I opened mine, but I could hear him behind it.

Inside the apartment I took another shower then unpacked my groceries and wondered what the fuck. Then I turned on the television. Then I turned it off. I was out on bail. Out on bail is not what you think. Out on bail is life with the pause button pressed. Out on bail is being in familiar places that no longer seem so. Out on bail is seeing strangers in grocery stores and drugstores and knowing their lives will be the same in a year but yours won't. Out on bail is lying in bed at two in the afternoon or sitting at the kitchen table reading the newspaper, afraid you'll see yourself looking back. Out on bail is the serpent in the garden. Out on bail is original sin.

Two days later Bea Katzenbach called to give me the date for my felony arraignment in Brooklyn Supreme. I wrote it on my calendar. I could fit it in. When the telephone rang my heart lifted momentarily, supposing it was Kat. The conversation we'd had ending everything a week earlier had been succinct. She asked if I was okay. Then she asked if it was true. At first I didn't understand—*is it true that I'm okay?*—then I realized she was asking if it was true. I had the idea of her mother seeing my name in the newspaper, and her friends at drop-off. I said yes, Kat, it's true, everything's true. I didn't bother to explain that truth is irrelevant because I knew she'd disagree. She answered, "Oh, Will—" Then in a final act of kindness I excised myself like a tumor from her life. I said something inarticulate to that effect, then goodbye, goodbye, be well, and I hung up. I didn't answer her phone calls. To the messages Kat left I made no reply, but listening to them was often the high point of any given day. The rest of my time was filled with Wild Turkey and the occasional pink pill and arranging my few things into cardboard packing boxes. My rent money had gone by wire to Ouellette & Katzenbach, LLP, and after my arrest the job put me on unpaid leave. Soon Frederick would appear with a politely worded letter from management. He would deliver it with an unreadable expression on his face; he'd always been very particular about having the right sort of tenant in his building.

What I needed was a rest. And I supposed I'd get one soon enough—a three-to-six-year rest, maybe less if Katzenbach did her job, with time off for good behavior. The idea was not unpleasant. State prison seemed like a kind of stoic retreat, something you'd pay for in California. I'd be able to finish Cicero finally then circle the yard in contemplation wearing slippers. They'd give me shoes without laces because I'd be on suicide watch, but I knew I'd be just fine. Prison would be more of a lateral move than a fall from grace and I'd probably know a few people, having sent them there. There'd be no hard feelings and we could play checkers maybe.

In the meantime my father gently offered my old bedroom on Melba Court. The Avocado King, of course, had been trying to lure me back into the fold since the day I left for college. After Regine's mother gave me the news on the doorstep, I said nothing to him about it but instead spent the balance of Christmas break moving around the empty bungalow and watching Bob Barker and *It's a Wonderful Life* on endless rerun and Gilligan and Steve McGarrett and *Creature Features* and Captain Kirk and Garden Weasels and Pocket Fishermans and Hits of the Seventies and Veg-O-Matics and Boxcar Willie and Slim Whitman and Conway Twitty and Bamboo Steamers and Buttoneers and Salad Shooters and Commemorative Plates and all of it can be yours for twenty-nine-dollars-but-if-you-act-now-nineteen-dollars and everything will be here in four-to-six weeks but none of it is available in stores. When I tell my father as a matter of fact I won't be going back to college in January there's an unpleasant discussion, but the following morning he wakes me before dawn and does one more push-up than he did the previous summer. I have no reaction when he tells me to throw on some clothes and come with him. Just like old times, he says.

"No."

"Tomorrow, then," he says.

"No."

"William Way and Son. What d'you say?"

"No."

"Well, why the hell not?" he says, but at once he understands me, and understanding hits him like shrapnel. He rises from the floor in a single movement and without a word leaves for the market. The windows are still black rectangles as I wander around the bungalow, which smells numbingly like home, like mildew and mastic and steam banging the radiators. I pour some cereal—his brand—into a bowl and eat automatically. Here is a black-and-brass General Electric desk fan, circa 1937, disassembled on the kitchen table. *What fun*, I think. *What fun it is to be back in the Beach again with the Avocado King and one of his Mr. Fixit projects and all his hopes and dynastic dreams*. I pull on jeans and throw a jacket over my pajama top and walk out into the tender morning light. *Always after me Lucky Charms*, I say to myself as I walk to the Impala dusted lightly with snow under a streetlight in front of the house and of course it won't start. I sit all alone in the cigarette stink where I touched Regine the last time without knowing it was the last time, and my white breath circulates around me and my resolve seeps slowly away. I am alone. I clamber onto the road and slam the door. I would have gone to Dover Street, I know. As it is, I move around the old neighborhood, silent as the graveyard, walking over all the old streets, all part of me. And yes, if the Impala had cooperated I'd have gone to Dover Street. I do not know yet what it means to me that she is dead except that somehow I am to blame.

When the Avocado King comes home late that night—at the end of one year and the beginning of the next—he is drunk with colorful confetti scattered in his perfect hair. He smells like Sinatra, like booze and cigarettes and lipstick. You would never know he's drunk, but I know. I am still awake, lying on my bed with the lights low and my headphones on when he comes into my room without knocking and sits on a chair. After a long silent lull that quickly becomes unpleasant I ask him what he wants. Still he says nothing, nor do I say anything more. For some reason I'm the first to say anything meaningful. I tell him Regine is dead. I don't know why I tell him, nor am I surprised when he says he knows. Once he'd said that in the jungle a man would sometimes develop the feel of death to him and soon thereafter he'd be gone, and I ask him now if that's how he knew. The answer is simpler.

"Pomeroy," he says.

"You never said."

"At the marina," he says. "Tonight. We had a few. He wasn't himself. I drove him home." Pomeroy told him little beyond that, he says, and I'm ready to let the subject go when he asks with his usual indifference to the fact of death, "Pulled her own plug, I guess?"

"I don't know," I say quickly, defensively, ashamed to believe I know the answer without knowing. I brace myself, waiting for him to say something cheerful or worse, dreading he will, preparing myself to become furious on cue when he does and to tell him he doesn't know a thing about it, but he says nothing more. We remain silent together, and somehow the workings of his mind take him to my mother. Again I feel myself rankle, supposing he intends to draw some parallel or life lesson for my benefit. And again he does not. He tells me only that he misses her often. His strong hands are clasped, fingernails trimmed so close no white shows.

"Why didn't you come home, then?" I say in a different voice. "It's what she wanted. Right?"

"Of course."

"You could've come home, Dad," I tell him. "You didn't have to re-up."

"There was a war."

"She was waiting," I say.

"My men needed me."

"She needed you."

"They needed me more," he says, believing it.

"That's why she left?"

"No," he says.

"Then—?" I start. Everything closes in and the world seems to shrink around our little bungalow on Melba Court as I wait, for now is the time when all will be laid bare, I think, when at last I will know. I wait, supposing her reason was the same reason MK would offer me years later, when it came to be my turn—that my father was no longer the man she knew, that she wanted to be alone—and when I can't wait anymore I say, "Why'd she leave you, Dad?"

"She left us both."

After I was indicted on felony assault charges in Brooklyn Supreme the press got interested in me again, but not very. I made bad copy because no one knew quite what to do with me. No editorial board could decide what color ribbon to give me. Depending who you asked, Will Way, Jr., was a fascist or a political prisoner or—as some deluded bastards thought—a vigilante for abused women everywhere. As with Georgina Reed, how you saw me depended on where you stood to begin with. If anyone had bothered to ask I'd have told him I was (d) in this multiple-choice test, none of the above, but no one asked. I was irrelevant. I had only a walk-on role in the made-for-TV adaptation of the unauthorized biography of my life.

HERO COP PAYS STEEP PRICE FOR LOYALTY

The Brooklyn cop who the DA tried to force to the witness stand in the Georgina Reed case today learned the cost of standing behind his sister officer: a pair of silver handcuffs. After a series of embarrassing legal blunders forced DA Weldon Fister to all but abandon his election-year public relations stunt to jail rookie Georgina Reed, who shot a vicious career criminal in self-defense last March, Fister devised an unlikely new strategy.

Rather than rely on now-discredited testimony of two supposed "eye-witnesses" to the attack on Reed on a Brooklyn street corner, Fister sought to force Police Officer William Way, Jr., 33, a decorated NYPD veteran, to the stand to reveal Reed's so-called "confession" made during routine departmental questioning. When Officer Way rebuffed Fister's hardball tactics, Fister ordered his arrest on brutality charges that many legal experts consider unsupported and politically motivated.

Beatrice B. Katzenbach, Way's lawyer, called his arrest "retaliation, plain and simple" in light of her client's refusal to play ball with prosecutors. "When cops don't back cops, cops die," said Shawn Garrity, president of the police union, speaking yesterday at a rally supporting Way that brought scores of police officers to the steps of Brooklyn Supreme Court. "These trumped-up charges against a fine officer are the Gestapo tactics of a fascist organization," Garrity told officers who chanted "Free Will!" and held aloft placards and signs depicting the black-and-white whale symbolizing their cause.

Outside court, police clashed with several young men in hoods. Carrying pink azaleas and chanting "No violence, no peace!" members of the self-styled militant wing of the Brooklyn African-Baptist-Episcopalian Cathedral looted appliance stores along Court St. and hurled bouquets at officers, one of whom

was reported in stable condition after being struck by what appeared to be
a microwave oven.

    The allegations against Officer Way stem from his arrest four years ago
of Jean-Pierre Fleury on several counts of assault and promoting prostitution,
charges that were later dropped when the complainant refused to cooperate.
Fleury, who has a long criminal history, suffered scrapes and bruises while
resisting arrest and is reportedly refusing to cooperate with prosecutors. Last
week he filed a civil claim for $258 million against the city. His attorney,
Herman Wrublewicz of Hicksville, said in court filings that Way threw Fleury
down a flight of stairs without sufficient provocation.

    Left in doubt is Fister's high-profile prosecution of Georgina Reed, who
some accuse of using "excessive force" in defending herself against Laquan
Dewberry, a repeat violent felon offender who later died in undetermined
circumstances. The case has taken on greater urgency this year as Fister
hopes to fend off a primary challenge by Henry Pomeroy, the Brooklyn judge
overseeing the case.

    Both men publicly tangled over Fister's explosive allegation that Pomeroy
colluded with police officials to dismiss charges against Reed. As reported
yesterday, a judicial oversight committee in Brooklyn found the charge wholly
unsubstantiated, exonerating Pomeroy and clearing his way to—

I read about myself with decreasing interest, eating painkillers just in case
while the world around me became less familiar, more hallucinatory, the past
intruding on the present, the present succumbing silently to the past, the truth
of things irrelevant and indiscernible, and I thought maybe I needed more sleep
until I remembered all I did was sleep and watch *It's a Wonderful Life*, which is
the saddest movie ever made. Perhaps I'm dreaming, I told myself hopefully
one early afternoon before I realized in a moment of narcotic clarity that something was missing from the news—not once in these accounts did I read the
name Mark Masterson. Masterson, my regular partner. Masterson, who'd been
with me at a certain two-story brick semidetached on Eldert Street four years
ago. Masterson, who surely now hated my guts, believing I'd put his thumbs in
Montgomery Crimmins's screws.

    So, with the giddy realization that it was Masterson who tipped Betty
Moon, Masterson who threw me under a yellowy orange school bus, I picked
up my telephone. With an elation that might be considered obscene I dialed
IAB headquarters, unclear in my own head even what I wanted to tell him.

As it happened, Detective Mark Masterson was not in. He was "in the field," as detectives say when they're eating doughnuts elsewhere, but the PAA who answered his phone was happy to take a message.

Which told me something, I reasoned out carefully at the kitchen table, like calculus homework—

If Masterson was in the field, he was still assigned to Internal Affairs.

If Masterson was still at IAB, he was not at College Point.

If Masterson was not impounding towed cars, he was in the clear.

And if Masterson was in the clear, then he—

Oh, fuck it, I said to myself. I couldn't think. I washed down a pink pill with a swallow from a mostly empty handle of Wild Turkey, and for an hour I walked in a tight circle in my kitchen until the phone rang. "Mark," I said instead of hello. In a cool voice that gave nothing away he said, "Hullo, Way." We said nothing more than strictly necessary to arrange a meeting in an hour, the usual spot, but after I hung up I felt cold sweat drip inside my shirt. Even with my frowsy brain I knew it was a mistake. I knew Masterson had nothing to say I didn't already know. At the same time I needed to see him, to shake his hand maybe or give him a kiss, for with the realization that he was missing from the news—that it was Masterson who gave me up, either for vengeance or simple self-preservation—came another realization, necessarily and logically proceeding from the first, that was like an anvil lifted from my chest, bringing relief more profound than I might ever have believed: Bea Katzenbach had been wrong. It wasn't Pomeroy.

THIRTY-EIGHT

I shaved and dressed and moved about my apartment whistling "Reuben James" with an odd levity of spirit, strangely elated, readying for my appointment for a fistfight with Detective Mark Masterson as if it was a first date. At one point, however, I had to sit. The room was moving in several directions all at once and I wondered if I should take another painkiller. I had no pain, so—they must be working? As I sat, one wall moved one way, then another wall moved the other way. I swallowed a pill with a pull of bourbon and presently all resumed its natural order. Off I went in a state of perfect chemical equipoise.

"Going out, Mr. Will?"

Kaseem silently cracked his door the moment I stepped whistling into the hall, not even bothering to lock my door. No thumping beat, no ganja bloomed forth, only the smell of curry and onions, reminding me I hadn't eaten in memory. Never mind. I wasn't even hungry. Kaseem remained inside, the door still chained, and he regarded me through a six-inch slit, motionless, shirtless, backlit by a broad beam of daylight from a far window so bright that I couldn't read the expression on his face, and even the colors of the beads around his neck were unknowable.

"Thought so!" I said, somewhat warily. My neighbor had kept a safe distance from me, it seemed, since news broke of my arrest days before.

"Y'all be careful out there," he said slowly, and a dog's moist nose appeared below him in the door frame.

"Thanks!"

"These are dangerous times, Mr. Will."

"Don't I know it!"

"Y'all never know who gonna step in your way."

"No, you don't!"

In the lobby Frederick came toward me in a terrific hurry. I averted my eyes and kept moving to the front door. He seemed genuinely concerned. "You don't want that door today, Mr. Way," he said, and I wasn't sure what his game was. "Those people are back again."

"What people, Frederick?"

"Those people, Mr. Way. Those troublemakers." Almost roughly he pushed me through the lobby to a private door that opened onto the garage some distance from the main entrance. "There they are, the rascals," Frederick said, nearly spitting, and indeed by the front doors, filling the sidewalk and spilling into the street, were several of Bumpurs's gray-haired congregants, many familiar faces, old friends from the plaza in front of Brooklyn Supreme. They held signs and placards and some had umbrellas, for it had come on to rain and the sky was complex. Uniformed police officers from the 78 precinct were setting up blue parade barricades, and directing traffic. There in the street, too, idled an enormous coach bus with huge tinted windows, gleamingly new and a pure brilliant white against the overcast. On its side, in florid purple letters:

B'KLYN AFRI.-BAPT.-EPISC. CATH'L

EST'D 1972 A.D.

ARCH-B. B. BUMPURS, B.A., M.DIV., PASTOR

REV. 3:16

Only a week earlier *Raquan Dewberry and Marlon Odom, Plaintiffs v. City of New York and Patrolmen's Benevolent Association, et al., Defendants,* had been settled out of court for an undisclosed eight-figure sum. "Are we happy?" I asked Bea Katzenbach when she told me in an embarrassed, offhand tone of voice, but she only shrugged and didn't answer. It was just money, after all.

"Revelation chapter three," I said. "How's your New Testament these days, Frederick?"

"Not so good anymore, Mr. Way. I've been away from home too long, I'm afraid."

"Me, too," I said.

"These are godless times to be sure."

"Depends what god you're talking about, Frederick," I said. "But I don't suppose that passage says turn the other cheek?"

"I don't think so, Mr. Way. That was the other fellow. Jesus, I believe."

"*So then because thou art lukewarm, and neither cold nor hot, I will spew thee out of my mouth.*" Frederick and I turned, and there stood Kaseem, shirtless, illustrated, holding a single dog on a leash. "My moms says the archbishop always be saying that."

"What's it mean, do you suppose?" Frederick said.

"Ask me," Kaseem said before walking off, "better to be on the wrong side than not on no side at all. Else all you is is God's vomit."

Frederick and I watched as Kaseem passed into the roiling congregants and placards and umbrellas, where he was swallowed without a hiccup. "What a peculiar young man," Frederick said, as if to himself, then he took my arm again and ushered me roughly away.

"I wonder how those rascals found me?" I asked.

"I couldn't say, Mr. Way. Certainly I didn't tell them."

"What do they want?"

"They want to destroy your body," he told me gravely. "Some people just don't know you like we do, Mr. Way. Better go now, before someone spots you. And attacks you." His face showed concern not only for me, I thought, but for his glass windows and his pristine sidewalk and his bright blue canvas awning over his front doors, the brass uprights of which he polished daily with affection. Even so I stood transfixed, feeling like a ghost at my own wake.

The signs Bumpurs's congregants held today had undergone a subtle alteration from the more familiar, and there were now younger men among them wearing black hoods chanting and carrying household appliances. As I watched, the growing throng began slowly swirling counterclockwise like a hurricane on a weather map. The young men in hoods began a warlike chant and climbed onto parked cars, and they threw bouquets of pink azaleas and some held microwave ovens above their heads among placards and banners that read:

JUSTICE=ANGER

NO VIOLENCE NO PEACE

FUCK THE TRUTH

Now from the enormous white coach bus stepped Archbishop Bumpurs nattily attired in a black guayabera and Wayfarer sunglasses, his great shaven head blazing in the sun. A great cheer went up whereupon he pumped a fist in the air, a gold ring on his pinkie. Meanwhile, without my noticing, up the block another group had massed by the Suds Bucket laundromat, and they, too, carried signs and umbrellas, and their signs, too, bore threats and profanities. They were mostly serious women with Goldman Sachs hairdos from the mothers' chapter of the lower school wearing yellow ribbons and shirts without bras that read FIGHT THE POWER. As I looked for Kat they overturned a taco truck and set it ablaze. "Oh, God," Frederick said under his breath. "There's going to be some bad trouble now, that's for certain. Come, Mr. Way, follow Frederick. Have a care. It's not safe for you anymore."

I followed dutifully but lost him as the factions fell upon one another in the street with a violent crash. Mayhem was general. I stepped around the body of a woman who landed at my feet, her skull cracking loudly against the granite curb. As she lay stunned and mostly unmoving another woman in a Sunday hat who might have been her nanny unemotionally thrust the point of a furled umbrella into her eye socket. Around me microwave ovens dropped like mortar shells, but I walked through the fray wholly unscathed. Above the tumult I caught the eye of Bumpurs contentedly surveying the scene from the steps of his new coach bus, arms crossed, and he smiled at me. *Welcome aboard, Officer!* he said, and I gave him the bird. Overhead a piñata in the form of an orca burst into flames and ripe avocados fell out of it. Betty Moon was there taking photographs with a pack of Marlboros and an unoccupied police car drove by without lights or siren. I hailed a taxicab to the safety of lower Manhattan, and for a moment on the bridge I would've sworn none of it had happened.

"Mark!" I said when he came through the door at Carmine's. I stood at the table, and my water glass fell to the tile floor and shattered. Masterson walked over and you could hear his shoes grind on the glass. "Mark, old boy, old boy, old Building and Loan pal," I said. "Sit down."

"Jesus, Mary, and—you're drunk as a skunk."

"No, I am drunk," I told him, indignant. "Very glad made it. Dangerous times, Mr. Mark. Have a care. Almost died twice."

"Hell you talking about?"

"Big riot in Brooklyn. Bigger'n the last one even."

"Nothing's happening in Brooklyn," he said. "No one gives a shit about Georgina anymore. Let's get out of here."

Masterson threw some money on the table and I felt his hand on me and then I was outside where the sky was gray and the air felt gray and we walked along the river that was gray and beneath a gray steel upright beneath the gray FDR overpass I knelt by the curb, and the only color was the pink-orange of the clams I spewed lukewarm into the gutter. I didn't care. Everything was happening to someone else. Things now a little clearer, I faced Masterson, who stood with hands in his pockets. There would be no fistfight, I saw. His expression was all wrong for that. His face showed only disgust and concern, mostly concern.

"So—?" I asked him. "What can I do for you, Mark?"

"You called me."

"That's right, that's right," I said, and then my mind went away. A full minute passed that way, or an hour.

"What's on your mind?" he said finally, sounding like an exasperated father.

"No, no," I said, knuckling my head as though I had fleas. "On my mind? No—I was just thinking about that shithead Pie what's-his-name. The guy, you know."

"What about him?"

"Ah—nothing, just—shit." I stretched and yawned.

"You okay, partner?" he said, looking into my eyes like a doctor. "Hell, you're not drunk. Are you? Jesus, Way, you're rolling on something."

"Wanted to tell you. Mark. You probably think I jammed you up with the DA. Maybe I did. Not on purpose. I know you think I did. I know that's why you went to Betty—and tipped her—and that's okay, but—I just wanted to tell you—"

"Why don't I get you a car, Way? You're in no shape to be—"

"No, listen—" I said with unexpected vehemence, and he stepped back. "Have to say something. Karpatkin transcript. I didn't give it Tommy. I didn't. So if the DA told you I—"

"Oh, yeah, yeah, that—" He brightened a little with understanding and smiled, something rare and a little frightening. "Sure, the DA tried to throw a scare into me with that. I told him to go scratch his ass. I don't bow down to the Brooklyn DA. I don't bow down to no one but IAB Inspector Sheldon Danilov. And far as I know Shelly hasn't spanked me for passing that transcript to you. Which come to think of it would be damn peculiar of him, since he told me to pass it to you in the first place."

The information took a moment to arrive. "Danilov—?"

Mark Masterson laughed his cheerless laugh, his little blue eyes brightening ever so slightly, his red hair ablaze. "Jesus and all the saints, you're a mess. Hell are you on anyway?"

"I have a prescription," I said somewhat defensively, producing the vial from my pocket.

Masterson read the label. Then he gave me a hard look. Then he over-handed the vial into the East River, where it floated away downstream unseen. "I just changed your prescription," he said.

I had no reaction. I was still thinking about what he'd said, trying to understand. "You and Danilov?"

"Sure, you think Shelly don't know about you and me? Hell, I make him pay the lunch tab when you're cheap. Shelly knows the deal. I give you what I got, you give me what you got, and between us maybe things move a little in the right direction."

My mind momentarily cleared, like a rift in the gray overcast, yet all I could manage to say was "But—?"

"No one at headquarters wants Georgina Reed nailed to the cross. Not on a murder beef. She took a bad shot. Shoulda never have been out there in the first place, ask me, but times are what they are, so hey. Back in the day this clusterfuck woulda been cleaned up inside the job all nice and neat, get Georgina a desk somewhere and let her paint her nails. Instead the bosses put her up front, where she shouldn't be, and when she proves it they act shocked and blame her. It's all fuckin politics."

"So you—?"

"Sure, Shelly and me," he said. "No one else's thinking clear, on account of they don't know what justice is. Or forgot. Or don't care. What're we supposed to leave it to the lawyers and the newspapers and all them out there with the signs? Fuck no. They don't know what it is."

"What what is?"

"Justice. You still stoned, Way?"

"What's justice, you think?"

"It's not on no sign, I'll tell you that," he said. "Justice ain't words. It ain't in no book, and it sure as hell ain't in a courtroom, not over there in Brooklyn Supreme."

"What is it, then?"

Masterson drew out one of his thin cigars from an inner pocket and lit it, thinking. "The old man always said there's more justice at the end of a patrolman's nightstick than in all the courtrooms in the world," he said at last. "Only people know what justice are those that hand it out. And that's us, Way."

He smoked. I said nothing. Then I said, "You still didn't answer my question."

"Only thing is it worked too good." He laughed to himself, perhaps not hearing me. "Georgina's gonna be back in uniform in three months. Six tops. Tell me that don't make you lose sleep. She ain't no cop."

"No."

"And not for anything she flaked a gun on a dead guy," he said, disgust in his voice. "She fucking flaked a gun on a fucking dead guy. How raw is that?

That don't sit with me, partner. It don't. I mean, I get why she done it, but the fact is she done it. There's gotta be a reckoning for that. Nobody should get a free ride." He spat a grain of tobacco from his tongue, then his voice softened again. "Ah, hell, listen to me. I'm starting to sound like the old man."

"It was Berrigan," I said, telling him what I believed. "Berrigan planted the gun, or the idea."

"For a fact?" he asked.

"No one said. But it fits."

"Sounds like Bear," Masterson said without apparent concern. "He's old school—maybe too old, but so what if he did? He was watching her ass, not his own. It's his job to back his men, right? But this was Georgina's mess, start to finish. She wants a cop job, then she shoulda stood up like a cop. She never. And not for nothing a kid's dead on top of it. There's gotta be a reckoning, Way. Justice demands payment."

"I'm going in, Mark," I told him at length.

"Only if you put yourself in," he said, squinting at me. "You ain't gonna have no trial, Way. And if there is, Bear and me'll tell the jury how it went down."

"He fell down the stairs?"

"Shithead asked for it, and he got it," he said and meant it. "You asked me before what justice is, so there's your answer. Justice is you get what you ask for. You gave him justice, Way."

"I wonder, Mark, I wonder if I wanted to back Georgina because of what I—because I—because of the situation with the guy Fleury, I mean, because it's the same—"

"No," he said. "No, it's not the same."

"It is, though. Georgina and I—we're not cops, Mark."

"And that's why you ain't, Way," he said gently. "You never know who the bad guys are."

After Masterson left, the stink of his cigar remained with me as long as I stood there, which was a long time. The clouds had closed again inside my head and at length I put up my hand and let a yellow cab take me back to Brooklyn.

Outside my building there was no evidence of the earlier massacre, and Frederick gave me a face full of concern but pretended to know nothing when I asked. I slandered him silently in the elevator. *Trying to make me think I'm nuts. I'm not nuts.* On the eleventh floor a grandmother got on and looked surprised after the door closed. "Oh," she said to me, or to her dog, "we're going up?" I could see her scalp, pallid between strands of thinning gray dyed black, and it turned my stomach. She was feeding her dog potato chips from a can, and it turned my stomach. And the smell of potato chips and her grandmother perfume turned my stomach. On my floor she got all tangled in her leash moving out of my way and the door closed in my face. "Sorry, did we get in your way?" she said sweetly, and I smiled and was trying to seem complaisant but really my insides were getting ready to let go, yet I made it all the way back down then all the way back up and even then I made it as far as a packing box of folded shirts in my living room. Then I went to sleep on the rug.

When I awoke the sun was already low and the light had turned beautiful in a sky clearing fast in the west. I stood at the window and felt nothing whatsoever, and my hand automatically slapped my pocket for the pill bottle that by now had floated out to sea. I cleaned everything on hands and knees, filling a plastic garbage bag with ruined shirts and paper towels. Then I took off my suit and stuffed it into the garbage bag and started barefoot down the hall to the chute when Kaseem's door opened. "Oh, snap!" he said, and I stopped. "Go, go! It's safe. I got your back yo, anyone comes out."

I continued to the garbage chute, mostly upright, doing pretty well, but Kaseem followed closely with a pizza box lid, held low. "Hell you doing—?" I asked him.

"They's kids on this floor, yo. And women. You ain't decent, bro." I realized the truth of it, without effect. "Yo, man," he said, laughing, "why y'all always be walking around in your draws?"

He was himself shoeless, shirtless, and wearing longish denim shorts elaborately embroidered but overlarge so they sagged well off his narrow hips, revealing Tommy Hilfiger boxers, cherry red with a blue band. I said, "I can see five inches of your ass from where I stand."

"But I'm wearing pants and y'all ain't."

"Distinction without a difference."

"Say what—?"

"We're the same, I'm saying."

"Yo, maybe we be the same, but we ain't," he said. "That's just how it is. I know you know that, Mr. Will, and y'all just be fucking with me. Man, y'all ain't look right. You high, bro?"

"I think I need a pill."

"I think y'all had too many pills, yo," he said. "Gimme your key."

"It's in my pants."

"Where y'all's pants?" he asked, and I pointed at the garbage chute apologetically. "I'm a call Freddy. Don't go nowhere."

"I got nowhere to go."

"I'm a call Freddy get you in."

"No, don't," I said, and I sat gingerly on the hallway floor, the carpet scratchy and rough on the back of my bare legs. "Don't call Freddy. He's trying to gaslight me. Thinks he's so smart."

"Freddy in the lobby—?"

"He's reading my mail, too."

"Nah, man, Freddy cool, Freddy cool," Kaseem said, laying the pizza box lid discreetly over my groin. "He likes y'all, too."

From his open apartment a dog skulked morosely into the hall and took me in. I said, "Hi, Shooshka. Don't pee on me."

"That's Shiny, Mr. Will," Kaseem said. "We had to put Shooshka to sleep. Ain't we, Shiny? Shiny's bummin, yo."

"What happened to Shooshka?"

"She was a good dog," he said, "but she was old. It was her time."

"She didn't look old."

"You know, man, with dogs you ain't never can tell—" he said, but he broke off to key the intercom. He spoke lowly into it, somewhat urgently, but I didn't hear what he said. "They only look old right before they die."

"Not calling the cops, are you?"

"Nah, just Freddy, man," he said. Shiny lay beside me, paws forward, like a sphinx, and my hand absently stroked her. She felt half the size of Magdalene, but the recollection it brought was immediate and tangible. More than anything it was her cold upward-seeking nose against my palm that nearly broke me in two. "Reminds me," Kaseem said. "Seen you in the papers. I ain't never believe you was no cop, yo."

"Nice of you to say. What'd you think I was?"

"Salesman maybe, I dunno," he said, and I felt like he was talking just to keep me talking, as if he was a hostage negotiator and I had a gun to my own head. "Sell bananas or some shit like that. Your name be on all them trucks, so—yo, man, I ain't know y'all got a son neither."

"What—?"

"On your trucks. Say it's y'all and your son, ain't it? But yo, what I wanted to say is we's all behind you. Freddy and me. What y'all do, I mean."

"What'd I do?"

"You know, man," he said. "Thing in the paper? With that dude you put down, the one messed up his shorty, yo? And I just wanna tell you confidential on the down low, my dad? He would beat on my moms too. Real bad, sometimes. So, I ain't saying what y'all done is cool, like technically legally or whatever? Police brutality and shit? I ain't condone that shit, nah saying? Shit's messed up. All I'm saying is I understand why y'all done it."

"Understand what?"

"Understand why y'all put some heat on the brother's ass!" he said, with a gesture to illustrate. "I mean I ain't condone it, 'cause you a cop, but was you just a regular nigga like me? Sold bananas or whatever and whatever? Then fuck yeah. Catch that dude smack his shorty I'm a seriously fuck that nigga up. But I ain't in no uniform, nah saying? So it ain't brutality when I do it."

"What is it when you do it?"

"Justice, yo!"

His words were coming at me, beading up and rolling off like raindrops on a raincoat. I heard them, but none got through. The walls were getting bigger and smaller. Somewhere a dog yelped. "Yo, man, I don't think Shiny likes that," he said, and in fact the dog was now writhing in my hand, which had taken hold of her perhaps too hard. Kaseem picked her up but my hand remained fixed. The dog was yelping, far away. Down the hall a door opened and a disapproving face appeared. "Come on, Mr. Will. Let her go."

"Sorry," I said.

"Dang!" he said, pulling the dog away. "Anyway. I'm just saying I understand why y'all done it."

"What?"

"I said I understand, Mr. Will."

"You understand," I said. "I'm not asking you to understand. Because you can't. You have no idea who I am. I have no idea who you are. You just said. We're the same, but we're not. I'm nothing like you."

"Wait—"

"I mean, what's the point? I understand you, you understand me. Just us? So what? That makes us the same? Like we're brothers? Like we're one big happy family?"

"Whoa, man. Y'all's taking it the wrong—"

"We're not the same. Look at you. You're a fucking mess. You're nothing like me. We're not the same even if we are. You got no job. You'll never get a job. You got nothing. You do nothing. Probably going to prison—"

"Wow."

"You're a fucking failure. Look at you. Pants hanging down—on drugs—killed your dog—no education—no job—no wife—no children—no future. You'll never be anything. You're nothing. You're shit. You're shit. You're—"

At that moment I realized I was weeping beyond all control, my head on the floor. Then there were powerful arms lifting me. "Come along now, Mr. Way," Frederick was saying, and then we were in my apartment, and then in my bedroom, and the last thing I saw was Frederick's dignified, anxious face peering down at me. I was saying something horrible. "You don't mean none of that now, do you?" Frederick was telling me. "You're just upset. Maybe you had too much whiskey, I think. You've had a rough patch, I know, I know."

Still I was speaking, my voice so low even I couldn't hear.

"What's he saying?" I heard Frederick ask.

"Don't make no sense, man," came Kaseem's voice. "What's pom-roy?"

"No, he said it was palm oil."

"Palm oil—?"

"*It was palm oil,*" Frederick repeated. "What the devil does that mean, do you suppose?"

THIRTY-NINE

I awakened as if electrocuted, heart thundering in my chest, eyes trying to comprehend the blank unfamiliarity of my own bedroom. What few frames there'd been now packed into cardboard boxes, the white unadorned walls lit by the harsh light of the midday sun seemed starkly institutional and gave me a cold presentiment of a future hurtling toward me. I lay still awhile, my body unfamiliar, waiting to know how bad I felt. At length I rose on rheumatic legs, stood endlessly under a shower, dressed, and walked out the door.

Then I went to Dover Street. No one stopped me. In my mind I never weighed going. I just went. I hailed a gypsy cab because I no longer had a car. All the way to Manhattan Beach the guy kept looking at me in the mirror, saying nothing. Later he'd tell his friends he drove the criminal or hero or whatever. I didn't tip him. I didn't have to.

Outside the big redbrick green-roofed house by the sea I waited a moment by the front door. I didn't use the side door off the butler's pantry. That was another house. I rang the bell and the trimmed shrubbery shivered in the breeze that smelled like salt water and dry grass and the stand of cedar trees nearby. All around was the noise of cicadas and the ocean and—very faint—a piano. Henry answered the door in a Xaverian jersey, and for an instant it was like gazing into a mirror. I realized from his reaction that he'd told his grandfather nothing, and the idea that we shared a secret affected me in an indescribable way. Seeing the boy also made me aware it would have consequences, what I needed to do here today.

As he stood aside to let me enter I saw movement behind him, and there was Pamela. She saw me too. Then she recognized me. "Oh—" she said.

Pamela was not so very different. Her face was perhaps sterner, her figure more imposingly solid, and if she hadn't become her mother exactly she'd at least become motherly. She was carrying four china dinner plates, and inside the house it smelled as it always smelled when I was a regular on Sunday afternoons for the traditional roast beef and baked potatoes wrapped in aluminum foil and cucumber salad and milk from tall orange glasses patterned with circles and diamonds. The effect on me nearly made me walk out. Still, I said, "Hullo, Pam."

"Will—hello—what, what do you—?" she said, more from astonishment than bad manners. We hadn't spoken since Worcester.

"Just business, Pam," I lied with a shrug, but after that neither of us seemed to know what to do. We weren't friends, Pam and I. There were no good old days to reminisce about. There were only bad old days. In the uncomfortable silence she darted a meaningful glance at Henry, who stood downcast to one side. He'd let me in because I was no stranger, and I saw Pam's eyes alter with the realization. Now I was no longer a mere curiosity that might require a brief discussion before dinner. Instead I was a danger, I knew, for what I'd seen in her eyes was fear.

A little breathlessly she said, "Henry, take these to the table, and I'll show Will—"

"Don't bother, Pam," I said. "I've been here before."

I left them, walking surefooted as a somnambulist through the house. There were differences, of course, all of which I noted in some remote corner of my mind. The couch used to be there, now it was here. The wallpaper had been blue, now it was yellow. The music room was still the same, however, still a Brooklyn version of a Paris salon. Pomeroy was at the black grand when I came upon him, pounding out something brooding and Russian and appropriate. He continued playing, doing nothing to acknowledge me but to incline his great white head absently in my direction. I was expected, in other words.

While I waited in that room, where Regine had done scales while I'd done algebra, I was relieved there'd be no preliminary round of allegation and denial, that it would be unnecessary for me to start throwing Saint Ann's collected bric-a-brac until Pomeroy acknowledged at last that, yes, he'd sacrificed me to preserve everything around him from the bonfire. And seeing it all again—this room, this house, this home that was no longer a faded memory but instead a tangible thing—could I blame him? What was one boat boy more or less against all this? I might even have left at that moment, for there was nothing more to say. Yet I waited, and when he finished the piece of music he sat unmoving until the final minor chord faded slowly on the air, then died. When he stood Pomeroy drew himself to his full height before me and asked, "Shall we go outside?" He didn't want it in his home.

We paced in no hurry across the broad flat square of lawn between the house and the sea. There was little surf, for Manhattan Beach fell under the lee of the jutting thumb of Breezy Point. Here on this very patch of grass I'd stood on appointed midnights while Regine looked down from her bedroom window and we enacted scenes starring our star-crossed selves after curfew before I bicycled home. Now here with her father I glanced to that selfsame window and believed I saw the curtain move and a face momentarily appear. Not a phantom, no, but Henry watching from her bedroom, believing he was the reason for my visit. How like a teenaged boy to think your cares are the only cares in the entire world.

"In case it's weighing on your mind, Will, I should say I never—" Pomeroy began, hesitating on a difficult word like a piece of gristle. "That is, when the judicial committee inquired about our conversation in chambers, I told them the truth."

"It's not weighing on my mind."

"I'm telling you anyway because you should know," he said. "You're caught up in this unfortunate business for better or for worse."

"For worse."

"And I am sorry for that, truly," he said with a sincerity that I almost believed. "It was never my intention to involve you—"

"Don't make me laugh."

"It was never my intention to make you laugh either," he said sharply.

"You told them it was about Regine," I said. "It wasn't about her. It was never about her. It was about Georgina. It was about politics. It was about you getting one up on Whitey Fister, and then it was about you saving your ass."

"You're wrong," he said, turning away. "I wanted to see you—well, because we hadn't spoken in some years and there was something I wished to—after my own fashion I was attempting to—"

"You wanted something from me."

"Yes," he admittedly wearily, "but not that. The case, Will—that was the farthest thing from my mind when we spoke. I wanted nothing from you regarding Georgina Reed, no matter what the newspapers may choose to say."

"You wanted me to give you what Georgina told—"

"I wouldn't give a farthing for anything Georgina Reed said," he told me, meaning it. "I knew all I needed to know about her and the whole awful business from the moment I heard her name, not least because we've heard it all so many times before."

I laughed. "So you know what happened?"

"I'm saying I don't care what happened."

"Don't care—?"

"The case is interesting, Will, only insofar as we choose to interest ourselves with it," he said. "The case is a mirror. When we look at it, all we see is ourselves staring back." I didn't understand and I wasn't trying to understand, nor did he bother to explain. He grew contemplative for a spell before saying, almost to himself, "Such a brief and inconsequential thing, that moment when she pulled the trigger—a thought, barely that—and yet look at all that's flowed from it? Riot and discord and further division in our already divided city. Oh, it would have been better if Georgina Reed were a Klansman, then we would all know what to think, then we could all hold hands and sing 'We Shall Overcome.' But the ambiguity of it subverts our better selves and exposes what we are at the root—tribal and insular and ready to hate. That's the truth of the case, no matter what the facts may be. That's why I had no need for you to tell me, Will. I already knew."

I gave no answer. He was wearing boat shoes and worn red trousers and a blue candy-stripe shirt, the upturned cuffs on his suntanned forearms the only concession to the season. The ocean spread out flat and wide behind him. Very distant to the south and west you could see tankers and cargo ships awaiting pilots to steer them into the harbor. The breeze played along the hedge line, and he shifted on his feet and faced the water again. I was looking at the sun on the ocean and how it broke into a thousand pieces on the water and ceased to be the sun but something altogether more beautiful.

"I don't understand," I heard my own voice say. I sounded defeated. Somewhere between Prokofiev and the afternoon sun my moment had slipped quietly away.

"And yet you do understand," he said. "Or you will, if you give it some thought. You were always the smart one of the lot."

"But you're a judge. How can you—"

"It's because I'm a judge that I know this to be so," he said. "A verdict for or against Georgina Reed would change no minds, nor why should it? A jury isn't an oracle divining the word of God. A jury's nothing more exalted than a collection of twelve hapless souls who can't come up with some plausible reason to be excused from duty. Then we show them carefully curated bits of information we have the temerity to call evidence. We spoon-feed it to them under arcane rules designed to make it all as opaque as possible. Witnesses appear swearing to tell the truth then proceed to lie without qualm. Lawyers rant and bloviate and meanwhile the jurors can do nothing but sit meek and mute, unable to pose but a single question, wallowing in their own stupefaction with glazed eyeballs. And at the end of this masquerade I instruct them solemnly with an hour of incantatory mumbo-jumbo they cannot grasp, instead furtively picking their noses and napping in the jury box. From this stew of confusion we expect them to fashion up a verdict, the very word meaning to speak the truth. We exhort them to tell us, please, ladies and gentlemen of the jury, *please tell us what happened, please give us the holy truth.* And when at last they render their verdict we treat it as if Moses had brought it down from Horeb and—"

"Why'd you want to see me?" I interrupted. I had stopped listening.

"I beg your pardon—?"

"In chambers last March," I said, my voice cool. "You just said you wanted to see me, so I'm asking what'd you want?"

He shifted his stand. "Why, as to that, well—Regine's never far from my mind, especially where you're concerned. So when I asked to see you, I suppose I wanted to—"

"I don't have any answers for you."

"I don't have any questions for you," he said gently. "I'm at peace with her memory. It's taken a very long time, but now I seem—"

"Henry came to see me." I awaited his reaction, but he merely stiffened somewhat and faced forward, chin up, ready. "You may not have any questions, but he does. So if you have all the answers, I think you should give him some."

Eventually, he said, "What did he say to you, if I might ask?"

"You can probably guess. But I told him I didn't know anything. I don't have the truth—Holy Mother, I don't even have the facts. I didn't tell him anything because I don't know anything, so if that's what you wanted to ask me in March, there's your answer. I don't know, okay? I didn't see Regine after—after Massachusetts—so I don't know why—"

"Why?"

"Why—why she did it."

"Why she did what?" he said, turning his face to me, puzzled, old.

"Why she—you know—why she—"

He exhaled and spoke quietly. "Regine didn't end her own life, Will. I'm pleased to relieve you on that score, and I'm sorry if I—"

"Then how—?" I said, too astonished at the moment to feel any release brought by his words.

"She was rather precarious, as you well know," he said uncertainly, "both physically and of course—"

"Just tell me."

He hesitated and drew a breath. "Please understand it was Regine's wish—indeed it was her last wish that I not—"

"Tell me, goddamn it. Tell me. If I don't have a right to know then who does?"

He considered that before continuing, persuaded I was correct yet still unable to give a straight answer. "Regine had a—after all that unpleasantness in Massachusetts, she—there were some medical complications, you see, and—"

"No, I—wait—wait," I told him, for in that instant my need to know precisely how she died existed in perfect balance with my need to leave the fact unspoken. I was so delicate, so very tender in spirit that I thought I might not bear to hear it aloud. At last the balance tipped with no more than the weight of a single grain of sand, and I asked him for the answer.

He told me, "Regine died in Coney Island Hospital. On December the fourteenth to be exact. She managed to make it nearly all the way, you see, and we were all rather optimistic that she would. But I'm afraid shortly before eight months she—"

"She was pregnant again?" I said, incredulous.

"No, Will," he said. "Not again."

"Then, my God, she—in Worcester—at the clinic—?" I began as his words reached me, my understanding now like the sun rising, brightening irresistibly until I could no longer look.

He shook his head and told me, "No—and I'm aware you believed differently, but—"

"And Henry—" I began as the truth of it came upon me.

"Yes. Yes."

"Why didn't you tell me?" I said eventually.

"It was her wish, Will. She didn't want you to know of it," he told me in a judicial voice. "And I respected her wishes."

"Then why tell me now?"

"Because—because I believe you have a right to know nonetheless," he said, still uncertain of his words. "As you say."

"So does Henry."

After the slightest hesitation imaginable he agreed, "Of course." Again I fell silent. I supposed he was waiting for me, but when I said nothing he continued, "And that's what I wished to tell you when we met in March. But ultimately, quite obviously, I lacked the—lacked the, well, the courage, really. I suppose

I'm not a courageous man, Will, which is perhaps why I've always admired your father. I admire courage in a man, courage to do the right thing and to hell with the consequences. But you see I'm rather attached to my grandson, and I'm afraid—I'm afraid of losing him, not merely by his absence but by a loss of his trust, his faith in me. I suppose he believes I'm something I'm not. Or not entirely. And I'm not sure I could bear it if he realized the truth—but he has a right to know, of course—of course he has a right to know—he's already begun to ask questions, hasn't he?—he's a bright boy, and—and I admit that you— and he—you each have a right—and I—I'm sorry that I lacked the—" He grew more distant and tongue-tied until he gave up and fell silent.

Seconds passed, or an age of the world. Glaciers moved. Mountains fell. I was watching the ocean. Still I said nothing, felt nothing.

"Tell me how she died," I asked.

"Died?" Pomeroy said, returned from a distant reverie. "Yes. There's a medical term that I've forgotten, I'm afraid—and her doctors thought it advisable to perform the delivery early, by section—I'm sure you understand—which was entirely successful, and yet—she died, you see. Quite unavoidably. She died. They told us. She simply—she simply didn't wake up on the table. And that was that, don't you see?"

As he spoke I kept my gaze on the ocean, which had the comforting familiarity of an old flannel shirt. I hadn't seen it for years up close like this, not since I had dropped my pistol into its gray folds. "Why didn't anyone tell me?" I said to no one, not an accusation but a lament. "Everything would have been different. Everything."

"She wanted this kept within the family."

"I am the family," I said violently, facing him.

"What I meant to say is—" he answered, and he faltered and stepped away from the heat of my gaze when I turned on him. "It was her wish that you—"

"I don't believe it," I said as anger now came—anger hot and brutal. "Stop saying that. I don't believe it. She loved me. She would never want—"

"It's because she loved you that she didn't want you to—"

"Fuck you," I said. "She didn't want me to know? She didn't want you to know. You were the one she was afraid of—"

"What on earth do you mean?"

"She was afraid of you, afraid of what you would do, especially if—if it was his," I said.

"No, you're—"

"And that's what you wanted from me, too, wasn't it? We were standing here, right here, and you asked me—what did you say? To give her *a sense of perspective on all this*? Because the truth's all just a matter of perspective, right?"

"I'm afraid I don't follow you."

"Only you didn't need to tell me—I wanted the same thing—I mean, what if it's his?" I said, the raw emotion of it heavy on me now so that I could barely understand my own words. Nor did I seem to form them, rather they poured out like blood from a self-inflicted wound. "I mean, oh, fuck, what if it's—"

"My God, no. That's—please understand, I—"

"Funny, right?" I laughed and cried. "We're a pair of racists, aren't we?"

"No, Will—" he told me with a barbed kindness when at last I fell quiet. "All along she knew the child was yours, that it could only be yours. Don't you see that's why she—"

"Then why would she let me take her there, to that place?"

"Truly?"

"It doesn't make any sense."

"I rather expect she left it to you, Will, hoping you'd say no," he told me. "Instead you said yes. So you can understand why she wanted Henry kept from—"

"I don't—"

"I'm astonished you don't see it," he said, his voice now deadly yet deadened, like a silenced pistol shot. I turned automatically at the force of it and beheld his face, pale and damp and very old, yet his blue eyes remained fierce and wholly without remorse for anything he may have caused me to feel at that moment. He was accusing me, blaming me with the blame I'd so frequently put on my own head for Regine, yet some other part of me saw that while I may have been acquitted of that crime I was guilty of another without even knowing what I'd done until he read my verdict. "Every choice Regine made, up until the end of her days, she made for you. For you, Will, so—"

"How do you know?"

"Because I was there," he said with a sudden flare of heat in his expression, and he let the implication come upon me before stating it in so many words. "You weren't. I may have failed her as a father, not understood her or her illness, but God help me I did my best. She loved you so very much, yet you set up your own prejudices and petty jealousies as an excuse to wash your hands of an inconvenient burden and get on with your life. Which ironically is precisely what Regine wanted for you."

"What do you mean?"

"She understood more than anyone that she was a—"

He stopped—and for a moment I supposed he was simply overcome with feeling.

"Judge—?"

"Perhaps you should go now, Will," he said. "All at once I feel very—"

He collapsed, as if his long bones had dissolved within him, and at once I dropped beside him on the grass, facing him, and so it was that in his last moment I caught how his blue eyes flashed with surprise, perhaps even with indignance, before they rolled back and disappeared with him.

FORTY

They had the Mass in Manhattan Beach. Everyone came, of course—Mayor Desmond and Archbishop Bumpurs, Commissioner Gilbert and Shawn Garrity, even Whitey Fister paid his respects, his caricature of a face suitably blank for the occasion. I sat in the back. I hadn't seen the inside of a church in fifteen years, not even to get married, so everything felt off-center to me, known yet unknown, familiar yet foreign, as when you see a thing the morning after you've dreamt about it. There was the remembered smell of candlewax and incense, and on the varnished pews were the same hat clips that I'd absently stick a finger in when I sat here with Regine once upon a time, allowing my fingertip to turn purple until she stopped me. I was doing that very thing when Ann Pomeroy came down the aisle wearing a little black hat that threw off a wispy twist of lace like a smoke signal. Behind her followed Pamela, then Henry. I considered whether it mattered, that I knew. I decided no, Henry was just a fact, and I didn't know yet what truth to make of it.

The Mass ended up being the expected. Everyone endured it. There were no public displays. The Pomeroys of Manhattan Beach were not that way. The priest was a clear-complected young man with neatly arranged jet-black hair and pastoral eyes. Father What-a-Waste, Fontbonne juniors would've called him. He wore a simple white surplice and didn't aim very high in his sermon. Untimely death is embarrassing—it's hard to explain as a servant of God, for it makes friction at the point where faith touches the world. He delivered his words of benign comfort from the foot of the altar for there was no pulpit in St. Margaret Mary, more a chapel than a church, almost quaint with a pitched roof and wooden beams, an easy walk from Dover Street. Regine and I had come here often enough when Mass was an obligatory thing for us like brushing your teeth before bed. Regine always prayed privately but with intent, closing her eyelids tight and kneeling here on these vinyl pads. My faith even then had waned toward skepticism, and now I wasn't sure where things stood. I suppose I was trying to be the sole atheist in the foxhole.

Well into the Mass, in fact during the communion procession, as the few Christians who knew the lyrics intoned a listless rendition of "I Will Raise You Up" to the accompaniment of a six-string guitar—which Pomeroy never in life would have countenanced—the Avocado King materialized at the end of our pew. He came as ever unseen, unnoticed until all at once he was upon you, as if stealing up on a machine-gun nest, fragmentation grenade in his hand, Ka-Bar between his teeth. Heads and mildly disapproving faces turned, and we all scooted over one place to make room. He sat beside Kat and gave me the old trademark unsmiling wink. Suit and stoop-sale tie, I saw, but clean-shaven with no obvious nicks. I returned a short nod, supposing he'd heard the news at the marina or that Kat had telephoned him. I had not. Here now were the two of us, father and son, sitting like profane bookends with Phillip and Kat miniature between us. Soon her hand was in his, or rather her small white hand lay buried chastely beneath his strong brown hand, his fingernails glinting like watch crystals in the amber stained-glass church light.

Afterward there was a silent orderly progression through the narrow doors that opened onto the concrete sidewalk where rice and confetti collected in the cracks. The street dead-ended against the ocean, so there was no traffic. Overhead airplanes described great parabolic chalk lines, and the leaves on the trees seemed new in the late summer daylight. A fine day for a baptism, in other words, not this. Everyone stood on the sidewalk. There must have been a hundred people gathering into pairs and small factions. We stood to the side, Kat and I, while my father strolled to his car, parked in front of the church between NO PARKING ANYTIME and TOWAWAY ZONE. There was only his ancient rig and the black hearse idling under the dense shade of a beech tree. He hadn't even bothered to switch on his hazard lights as any other self-respecting lawbreaking New Yorker might have done, yet naturally there was no orange parking ticket folded under his wiper. He always walked on water, my dad.

What car did he have that year? He had a weakness for General Motors, for velour bench seats and big block engines that bled oil. All I remember is that it was a sun-faded blue-black two-door with a white vinyl roof. One bald tire rode the curb. The windows were down, the doors unlocked. The Avocado King slipped off his jacket and tie and bundled them unceremoniously inside and, hands in pockets, now leaned against the front quarter panel in sunglasses. His hair was perfect, like a London werewolf's. Seeing his crate by the curb and his larrikin posture against it I considered getting angry, yet I lacked the energy today for a losing battle. Also I'd begun lately to wonder if Kat were right and I was too hard on the old man. Here he was, after all, doing his earnest best, which is all anyone can ever ask. And in his defense he was inured to death, even his own. *Stick a bone in my ass and have the dog drag me away* were his only instructions on his final resting place.

There was to be a reception at the big redbrick green-roofed house by the sea, and Kat insisted we attend. She wanted to see Dover Street, which she knew was the belly button of REGINE-N-WILL. She'd made me tell her everything three nights ago when I showed up perfectly sober on her stoop at three in the morning and we stayed up until daybreak. I rang the bell and she let me inside, and then she let me in. My father was right, of course. Kat saw me exactly as I was.

I knew what awaited me at Dover Street and didn't want to go: a hundred strangers moving stiffly, trampling the flower beds of my memory while I watched, small and impotent, from some familiar corner. Surely some would have brought salads and casseroles covered in aluminum foil and the stink of strangers' food would fill the familiar rooms and hallways, and no one would have the faintest idea that where they now sat I'd once kissed a girl, and watched MTV, and fallen asleep, and seen Pomeroy in his boxer shorts when he thought no one was home, and eaten Chinese takeout and appended "in bed" to all the fortunes, and played Scrabble on the coffee table where their glasses of cabernet now made rings.

Already people were leaving, walking off in that direction. So while Kat packed Phillip into the back seat of my father's car, the Avocado King put his heavy hands on my shoulders and inclined his forehead to mine, showing me his eyes over his sunglasses. "What got him, d'you know?" he asked. "Stroke?"

"Heart, the guy said."

"Heart. No kidding?"

"He had a condition," I said, recalling now what Jackie Kane had told me.

"Well, I'll be goddamned," he said, smiling.

"Hell's so funny, Dad?"

"Oh, no, nothing. It's just we never believed—" he said, lost momentarily in his own recollections of a Pomeroy I never knew. Absently he lifted his hands off my shoulders. Such a weight, those two hands. "Old Lemons was—" he said, considering his eulogy and shaking his beautiful head, searching for the right words for Pomeroy. He couldn't find them, but to be polite he said, "He was okay. Old Henry, he was all right." He then kissed Kat goodbye on the cheek, as usual taking just a little too long to do so, whispering in her ear and making her laugh. He then called to me, "Bluefish're biting, boy. Come by Wednesday and we'll get our fair share. That is, if you're not too busy sitting around on your patookus counting your blessings all day long."

He had to shut his door twice before it caught, then he keyed the ignition and executed a graceless three-point turn while the steering column screamed. He narrowly missed two mourners and almost tore the front bumper off the Cadillac hearse before disappearing momentarily as he reversed into his own plume of purple-gray exhaust. Kat and I stood watching from the relative safety of the sidewalk as Phillip's pale face appeared in the window. "Seat belt!" Kat cried, then they were off for whatever awaited them on Melba Court. A waving hand shot from a window and they were gone, "Cracklin' Rosie" hanging on the air for days, it seemed.

Kat said, "He'll have fun. Won't he? It's good for a boy to get some country air."

"Country air—? Gerritsen Beach is the city, Kat."

"Sort of."

"My dad's probably going to make the kid scrape moss from the bricks with a butter knife. That's what he had me do for fun."

She patted my cheek. "Such a Dickensian youth. How did you ever survive?"

"What did he say just now that made you laugh?"

"Ha ha, all he said was that you were going to ask what he said," she told me. "He knows you so well."

"He has no idea who I am."

"You're wrong. You're just like him," she said, "only you don't see it."

"Hell do you say that?"

"Don't be angry, Will. It's true."

"He's the Avocado King. I'm—the court jester."

"No, the only difference really is you act like you have something to prove," she said. "He doesn't."

"Yeah, what do I have to prove, Kat?"

"That you're his son mostly."

"Then why've I spent my whole life trying to prove I'm not?"

All at once Kat and I were alone in front of St. Margaret Mary's. By now slow-moving, well-dressed men and women could be seen turning in the direction of Dover Street. Nearby beech trees creaked in the easy ocean breeze and overhead seagulls wheeled and cried but otherwise the world waited for us and was still. Here was the Cadillac. The driver sat at the wheel reading the racing form with his cap off, revealing a skull like a tulip bulb. A private burial was planned, just family, so this was it. One last look, then goodbye.

Kat and I set out. We walked hand-in-hand along the boulevard to the sidewalk that led to the end of Dover Street, where New York City fell without too much drama into the sea. I recalled every house, every tree. Neat strips of green grass lay alongside the street like a coded message of dots and dashes. Already Russian millionaires had begun to encroach from Brighton Beach. One had torn down a handsome Queen Ann mid-block to erect instead a stucco mausoleum, canary yellow with two huge circular windows like a staring face with a gated driveway as a tongue. I imagined Pomeroy averting his eyes every morning, roaring past in his Lincoln, muttering the same oath. Along Dover Street were scores of parked cars, some idling with blackout windows and radio antennas, others looking similarly governmental with special license plates and official placards in the windows. Near the house Kat and I stepped off the curb into the street, walking over a perpendicular fissure in the blacktop that once served as an improvised net in several matches of not very competitive tennis. Such mementos were everywhere. I tried to take them all in, knowing it was the last time.

As we drew near the open front door I stopped. "No," I said to Kat and pulled her away, so abruptly and forcefully she nearly stumbled. Certainly she knew there was no point discussing it and wordlessly relented. Instead we moved to the backyard, where the broad green swath of lawn abutted the ocean, and on the grass I could make out the parallel impressions an ambulance had made three days before. Here now a table of glasses and bottles had been arranged under a canopy of brilliant white where a uniformed man tended bar. There were groups of men and women all around drinking gin and tonic, some smoking, most looking seaward where the water lay wide and bright under the September sun. So beautiful was the day and the scene that you might have thought it a wedding reception except for the restrained expressions and the deep quiet. All you heard was the lap of the water and the low murmur of voices and the faint clink of ice cubes on glass.

Kat and I stood apart from the others saying little of any consequence until an incongruous explosion of quickly suppressed laughter shattered the peace. I looked instinctively and there was Shawn Garrity, standing with four or five men I recognized as local politicians and departmental brass hats. Garrity seemed to have been aware of me, for when I turned he bounded over at once, full of forced bonhomie. He flicked a half-smoked cigarette into the ebbing tide and offered his hand. His was cold and damp. I made the introductions and Kat gave him a glacial smile, bristling next to me, for she still harbored doubts about Shawn Garrity I'd not entirely dismissed myself.

Garrity said the expected things about Pomeroy. Then he said the expected things about my case. Then to keep the mostly one-sided conversation moving he told me my PAA, Sheila Simmons, had taken the police officer's entrance exam, and he said the expected things about her, too. Everything Garrity told me was G-rated, but I knew there was more. I supposed he was hoping Kat might get the idea and drift away, but she remained, speaking not a word, her dark brown eyes fixed on him with such intensity that he could meet her gaze only in squinted darts like a man glimpsing an eclipse. He produced a pack of cigarettes and fingered it absently.

"Didn't know you smoked, Shawn," I said.

"Ah—you know," he said, taking the opportunity to attempt another smile. "Don't tell no one. Specially the wife, ha ha."

"You're full of secrets, aren't you, Mr. Garrity?" Kat said, speaking for the first time, and still smiling Garrity faced her hopefully, ready to smile some more. Her tone was light and nontoxic, but her expression was shockingly accusive and Garrity at once fell sober and silent beneath it. "I wonder what other secrets you have," she said.

Garrity's huge face instantly reddened from neck to hairline and he forced himself to laugh only a few seconds too late. Then he started to laugh and cough, like an Agatha Christie villain whose dastardly deed has been exposed by the vicar in the drawing room before the assembled guests. *Why, Mr. Garrity!* And he couldn't stop coughing. People were now staring with expressions of concern and annoyance. Soon Garrity would lunge for a fireplace poker—

Of course Shawn Garrity had known about the domestic call to a certain two-story brick semidetached on Eldert Street when I worked patrol in Bushwick. After all, that call had taken me to Pomeroy, and Pomeroy had taken me to Garrity. No doubt fascinated by such an unlikely association between a patrolman and a sitting judge in Brooklyn Supreme, Garrity naturally had asked me about it one slow evening on Fulton Street when Pomeroy's name had arisen in a separate context. At the time the question made me mildly uncomfortable but I supposed it was meant innocently enough, and perhaps it was nothing more than mere curiosity that had prompted him to ask. Even so, Garrity noted my answer with special interest and I knew he'd remembered it. Like most men whose trade was the handshake and telephone call, Garrity valued information. He stored it all up like nuts for the winter.

Only that morning Kat reminded me Garrity had known. His name was on the short list of suspects, which had grown only shorter after I crossed off Masterson and then Pomeroy. For my part I didn't want to play any longer. I'd lost interest the moment I realized it hadn't been Pomeroy. Kat had not. "That means it has to be Garrity, Will," she had told me before Mass. "Or that scary old sergeant guy." We were seated at a diner in Bay Ridge in our dark funeral clothes, the same diner where I'd sat with young Henry Pomeroy, and Phillip—in a miniature suit and clip-on tie—was constructing something elaborate out of drinking straws and decorative orange slices. "They're the only ones left who knew—"

"Why do you care, Kat? Please. It's done."

"Because I do," she said, meaning it, a face like a lioness, which meant she considered me one of her cubs, and in fact I was seated next to Phillip on the bench seat, the pair of us facing her, each of us put on edge by the unwonted ferocity of her tone.

"Well, it wasn't Berrigan," I offered mildly, unable to meet her eyes. "I'll tell you that."

"How can you be sure?"

"Not his style. Berrigan wouldn't go sneaking around on the sly to Betty Moon. If Berrigan wanted to shut me up, he'd have thrown me down an air shaft."

"What's an air shaft?" Phillip asked.

"Then it was Garrity," she said, certain of it, furious yet at the same time immensely satisfied, knowing she was right. As I watched her drink black coffee in a white diner mug I recollected Masterson's verdict on why I'd never been a cop. Was it truly that I never knew the bad guys? Or was it simply that I refused to point a finger at anyone, especially myself?

"No, Kat. It wasn't Garrity."

"It was totally Garrity, stupid."

"It could have been the guy—"

"What guy?" she said.

"Pie—Fleury, whatever."

"Oh, it wasn't him," she said flatly. "Your lawyer said he's not even cooperating with the DA's office anymore. And his lawyer's lying to the newspaper about what happened."

"Maybe, but only to tell the truth."

"That doesn't even make sense, Will," she said. "Anyway, that—that pimp person was never near that staircase and besides he can't testify at trial because he's suing the city. Bea said so. That's why she's going to have your case dismissed."

"What's a pimp person?" Phillip asked.

"They're not dismissing my case, Kat. Bea just made a motion is all. And it wasn't Garrity who ratted me, so stop saying it."

"Why're you so sure about him?" she asked.

"Garrity stands behind his men."

"But, Will, don't you see?" she said simply. "You're not one of his men."

After Garrity lurched off, still coughing, Kat and I walked from the backyard onto Dover Street and there, by the front door, stood Pamela and Henry as a few departing mourners filed sedately past. Pamela's eyes briefly touched mine, then she returned to shaking hands. She wore makeup inartfully applied and a flat expression beneath it, and her unremarkable black pantsuit did nothing to flatter her sturdy matronly hips. Henry towered over her in a blue blazer and striped tie and black penny loafers. He was dressed very naturally, as I'd tried to dress at Georgetown, like somebody I wasn't. He was dressed like Pomeroy.

Immediately I felt a void open. Our bond now separated us. We were no longer co-conspirators blasting through the Brooklyn–Battery Tunnel with lights ablaze and sirens blaring to get to algebra on time. Yet neither were we the thing implied by the words that described the sociobiological circumstances of our newfound relationship. *Father and son*—the words signify both intimacy and hierarchy, and as Henry and I were no better than strangers only the paternal reserve remained. Seeing him in the doorway with a mother who wasn't, awkward and rangy yet now the Henry Pomeroy of the big redbrick green-roofed house by the sea, I wondered not for the first time whether my own father ever saw me that way—part yet apart, all the more alien for being his blood.

"Go in the house," Pamela said to Henry as a last elderly mourner walked delicately down the driveway, where Pomeroy's powder-blue Lincoln was parked like a monument. Kat grasped the situation at once, and as she walked away she held on to my hand until it was beyond her reach, as if I'd slipped below the surface of the cold ocean and was gone.

"How's he doing?" I asked Pamela when I came to her. We were alone.

"Upset. They were very close," she said, then immediately she asked, "What did you tell him?"

"I never knew, Pam, so no—if that's what you're asking—no, I didn't tell Henry," I said. "Your father told me, right before—"

"My father told you."

"Yes."

"And it killed him," she said.

"Pam—"

"You've spoken to Henry. I know you have. Haven't you?"

"He came to me," I said.

"Why in the world would he come to you?"

"He suspects the truth."

"And what's the truth, in your opinion?" She spat the word as if it were poison sucked from a snakebite.

"Regine—"

"I'm his mother," she said the moment the name was on my lips, so ready was she to hear me speak it aloud. "I am. That's the only truth. The truth is the life I've made for Henry, not anything else. He doesn't need to know your truth."

"You know what I meant was—"

"What did Henry say to you? Tell me what he said. I want to know."

"Only that he sees a—a resemblance, I suppose. I don't know."

"Oh, yes," she returned bitterly. "Of course! A resemblance! Henry's so tall and good-looking. And so popular and athletic and—cool! So unlike Pamela. And the implication is always so clear, isn't it? I mean, look at me—!"

"Pam."

"I was always so—" she began, shaking her head as if in disbelief. "The two of you. Such a beautiful couple! Regine and Will! So perfect. So in love. But I knew the truth. She kept a book, you know. *Regine and Will,* it said on the cover, like it was one word, or the title of something wonderful. And she put everything in it. So I knew everything. I knew even more than she knew, because my head was clear. I could see everything even if she couldn't. I knew you were dancing on the edge of a cliff. I knew someday she'd fall. And take you with her."

"Pam."

"And you knew that, too, didn't you?" she said, not able to meet my eyes. "That's why you got out."

"Pam, don't. I don't want to—"

"And you know something else I knew?" she said. "I knew I'd still be there when she fell. I knew that. And I am."

"Pam—"

"Oh, yes, I saw it. I knew. My beautiful sister. So fragile, so sensitive, like a spirit from another world. Even when she was sick. Especially when she was sick! Everyone on tiptoes. Everyone whispering, so concerned, my God. Tell me, what did she ever have to be sick about? Do you know, because I never did. Isn't that funny, ha ha. I knew everything, except that. What reason did Regine have to be sick, to want to throw it all away, when she had everything, and everything to live for, while I—"

"Pam, please—"

"But she didn't have everything, did she? I had something she never had. Do you know what I could do that Regine couldn't do? Do you know what that is, Will?"

"No."

"I could live!" she said. "I could endure. I could endure—everything. That's what I could do that Regine couldn't. And I have."

"Pam, we need to—"

"What are you going to do?" Her tone was belligerent, almost a dare, but her eyes were moist and vulnerable. She was frightened, and she frightened me.

"What do you mean, Pam?"

"Are you going to tell him? Are you going to—?" She stopped herself. "You can't. There's no need. You can't tell him. Why would you? You already have a son. I saw him. And a wife."

"She's not my wife," I said. "He's not my son."

"Well, neither is Henry!" she said, and now the tears came. "That's the truth. Whatever you think you are to him you're not. You're nobody. You can't think you can just step in and—"

"No," I said. "No, I don't, Pam. But he should know."

"Why should he know? What difference does it make?"

"He should know the facts of—"

"What do facts matter? What matters is the truth."

"He should know," I said. "If he doesn't already know."

"Ha ha, what should he know?"

"I'm his father, Pam," I said, but the words turned to dust on my tongue and I felt ridiculous for pretending.

She laughed in my face without mercy. "Father, ha ha. What sort of father are you?" she spat between tears of anger and fear of what I might do. "You're not his father. You know who you are? You're the man who tried to kill him. Before he was even born, you tried to kill him, so—"

"Pamela, Jesus Christ—"

"—so don't tell me. What sort of father tries to kill his son? Tell me that? Are you going to tell him that truth, too?" she said, and there was a tremor in her voice as in the earth before a landslide.

"He deserves to know," I said. "And goddamn it, so did I. Someone should have told me, Pam. You should have told me. Why the hell didn't you?"

"I couldn't," she said simply, flatly. Then she said, laughing in a lunatic way that made me uncomfortable, "I couldn't tell you. She made me swear, don't you see? She knew what it would mean, if you knew. Then you couldn't have what you wanted. And you wanted out. You wanted out of Brooklyn, didn't you? Oh, you wanted to go far in the world, I know. You wanted to be somebody. A great philosopher-king or who the hell knows what you wanted once upon a time. You probably don't even remember yourself. I mean, isn't it so perfect?"

"What?"

"Remember what you said to Regine? Oh, of course she wrote it in her book. In her famous book. I still have it, you know. My fucking God, how I hated you. You told her—you shit—you told her, *He travels farthest who travels alone.*"

"I never meant—"

"She knew," she said, laughing in her awful way. "And look at you now. Philosopher-king! You're not even an avocado king. Look how far you've come without her! You've gone so far, Will, and done so much without Regine to hold you back! You wanted to show the world who you are, and you did. Now we all know who you are—"

I could hear her still laughing as I walked away, but at some point it stopped being laughter.

& SON

FORTY-ONE

On a certain morning as fall closed in and trees growing from concrete in Brooklyn began to change color my case came up on the court calendar. My father drove me in his blue-black car with the white vinyl roof. Like old times, but he saw at once I was in no mood for Kenny Rogers and when he dropped me downtown in front of Brooklyn Supreme he shook my hand and gave me a significant look. "Suppose you're gonna do what you're gonna do," he said, "just like always." I'd told him nothing, but there was no need. He always read my mind.

Upstairs I sat with Bea Katzenbach alone at the far end of the long hallway. The light was coming through the windows and I was looking at the floor. She told me how it was going to go. I gave her one-word answers. *Good. Sure. Okay.* We stood and before we went into the courtroom she told me again I was an idiot. She was very angry at me. "You're an idiot," she said.

"You said."

"You can't take this back, once you do it," she told me.

"I know."

"Once it's done it's done."

"Let's go."

Maybe twelve people were seated inside. Bea sat up front with the lawyers. I sat alone in the back row. Kat was home. I'd made her stay, knowing everything was worse for her than it was for me. This whole thing, starting with this place, was outside her experience. When a doctor gets cancer he knows what it is, the traditional enemy, like Prussia, but for Kat it was all unknown and unknowable. All she knew of felonies and guilty pleas and prison she knew from television, which meant she didn't know. I knew and it helped a little. At night, in the dark, when we were alone, things were better between us than in the unforgiving daylight, when we could see each other and mostly each other's eyes. Last week, for instance, she'd had a dream, and in bed, unable to sleep, she told me.

"About what?" I'd asked.

"I can't remember."

"Good."

"Why good?" she asked, sitting up.

"People read too much into dreams."

"You don't?"

"Not particularly," I said. "For instance, the other night I dreamed I was this bird in a birdcage, right? And—"

"Cut it out," she said.

"And on the other side of the door was—"

"I said cut it out, Will. It's not funny."

"No," I said.

"I mean it's really not funny, baby," she said, but in a while she asked, "What was on the other side?"

"Side of what?" I asked.

"Of the door. You said on the other side—"

"Nobody," I said. "Nothing. I was making it up."

"You sure?"

"Maybe it was me," I said. "Is that what I'm supposed to say, so the dream makes sense? Maybe I was inside and I was outside, too, holding a key, and I wouldn't let myself out. Is that what I should say?"

"I just wish you wouldn't make fun of me," she said. "I'm really scared."

"It'll be all right, Kat."

"No, it won't."

"You'll be all right, anyway," I told her. "You're stronger than me. Women are stronger than men."

"I just don't understand."

"Understand what?" I said.

"Any of it. Why you're doing this."

"I told you why."

"I know," she said. "But I don't understand."

"I do."

My case came up before lunchtime. The clerk called, "Number twenty-seven on the part twelve calendar. *People of the State of New York against William Way Junior.* Your appearances, please." A little swinging gate separated the gallery from the well, and the sergeant held it for me when I walked through. He was a giant with forearms like calves and a stomach that strained the buttons of his white uniform shirt. I said, "Thanks, Sarge," when he held the gate. He said no problem and he looked at me in a way that made me look at him again.

The judge gave me a skeptical once-over before telling the lawyers to step up to the bench. The stenographer took her hands off the machine and picked up a magazine. The judge was talking to the lawyers. I couldn't hear what they were saying. I turned around in my wooden chair at the defense table, involuntarily hoping for a friendly face. By now a couple dozen uniformed cops were entering the courtroom and quietly filling the gallery. Court officers were moving civilians out of the way so the cops could sit. I recognized none of them. They wore dress blues and faced me with airtight faces. One gave an unsmiling nod.

The huge sergeant came over at that moment. "Goin okay here, my friend?" he asked me. I nodded and said it was going all right. Another court officer came over. "That's some fucked-up shit they got on you, huh?" the sergeant was saying to me. "Yeah, bullshit," the other officer was saying. He was younger and had wiry black hair cut into a flattop. His uniform was pressed. He was very neat and fit compared to his sergeant, who had gone to pot. They were both standing there nodding and crossing their arms. They had wanted to tell me it was bullshit, and now that they had said it they didn't know what else to say. "Fuckin DA's just trying to push you around, my friend," one said at last. "Yeah," said the other.

I shrugged in my wooden chair and told them, "Fuckin politics, you know."

"Fuckin politics is right," the one said, nodding.

"Fuckin politics," the other echoed.

We all nodded and no one said anything else. There's nothing more to say after you say it's all fuckin politics. It's all fuckin politics is what you say after you've been working the job a couple years and think you've seen it all and all of it's bad but the worst is what you call fuckin politics. It's all fuckin politics is what happens when the suits and newspapers get involved. Fuckin politics is when things enter a whole other Alice in Wonderland plane of bullshit where nothing makes sense no more. Fuckin politics is when you do the right thing but get fucked anyway because at the end of the day it's all fuckin politics and there ain't nothing you can do about it anyway except bend over and take it or quit and blow your pension and maybe end up doing freelance night security at a strip mall on Long Island, who knows. The two court officers were looking at me and nodding their heads, arms crossed. Later they'd say they'd seen me in court and that I was an all-right guy. And their crowd would say it was a shame I got fucked but I should've seen it coming because it's all fuckin politics—

"On the record," the judge said. The stenographer put down her magazine and Bea made her plodding way back over to me.

"Ready?" she asked, and I nodded.

"Counsel," said the court, "you have an application?"

"Yes, your honor," Bea said. "At this time my client authorizes me to withdraw his previously entered plea of not guilty and enter a plea of guilty to the—"

Pleading guilty was easy. Pleading guilty was like going to confession. The judge even looked like a priest with a tonsure of dishwater-brown hair and wounded eyes. He promised me a one-to-three-year bid in upstate prison and told me to say an act of contrition and three Hail Marys *and to avoid this sin in the future, my son, and fall thee not into temptation, in the name of the Father and the Son and the Holy—*

I followed Bea out of the well. The sergeant held the gate for us, and I saw the gallery was all blue. The civilians were gone. Now there were just cops, only cops, maybe a hundred. They were all looking at me expressionlessly but when I passed through their midst to the courtroom door one of them began to clap. Then another. Then all, slowly and solemnly. And they stood. The judge was calling for order but they ignored him and kept clapping. They were all looking at me, but I left. Walking down the hallway to the elevator I could still hear them. It was ridiculous and absurdly touching and I had to get out of there.

In the open plaza before the courthouse steps there were no signs or banners today nor protestors of any color ribbon but only the ebb and flow of lawyers and litigants, and nearby were carts and stands where you could buy apples and eggs and bouquets of fresh flowers beneath tents, and there were private school skateboarders and dark women pushing strollers and Chinese deliverymen speeding on bicycles with plastic bags of takeout hanging from their handlebars. To the side while ordinary life resumed around us as it had in Hiroshima after the bomb and in London after the fire I stood alone with Bea Katzenbach. She was still angry.

"Cops—" she said, shaking her head. "Always standing up for the wrong reasons. I suppose they think you put yourself in to keep Georgina out, don't they? I suppose they all think you're a regular hero now, the dumb bastards. But I know the truth, Way. I know what you're doing."

"What's the truth, Bea?"

"That you got what you asked for, some misplaced sense of street justice. Cop justice—"

"Didn't I?"

"Oh, you're just another dumb bastard," she said. "That building's Brooklyn Supreme—it's not a cathedral. Didn't I tell you already what goes on in there's not truth, justice, and mom and apple pie and the American way? It's only what the DA can prove. If the DA can prove it, then it's a fact. And the fact is they got nothing on you. I told you the guy Fleury's out of the picture already and—"

"Got himself a fat check, I read."

"Wrublewicz settled for seven point five million on Fleury's civil suit against the city," she said. "Not bad, but now there's no way the DA can use him at trial."

"Why not?"

"Don't you ever listen?" she said. "I told you, Way, he can't testify now because it looks like he was just in it for the payday. I'd eat him up on cross, and Whitey knows it. The DA needs his witness clean, without some million-dollar side deal, else he'll come over to the jury like a lying opportunistic sack of shit."

"Even if he's telling the truth?"

"No, you never listen, do you?" she said. "It's not about—"

"Yeah, Bea, I heard you the first thousand times. I get that none of this is about the truth, but—"

"There is no but."

"—but sometimes it's about the truth anyway, Bea."

She looked right at me. "Idiot. You got ten days until you go upstate. Until then my advice is eat steak and lobster. Every night. And take a lot of showers by yourself. And—oh, I don't understand any of this—"

"It's okay, Bea."

"No, I—"

"No, really, it's okay," I told her. "I mean, my whole life I've been waiting to get out of Brooklyn."

She still didn't understand but her expression softened to a half-smile. Then from nowhere she began to cry, which was very awkward. Her eyes were squinted shut and the tears seemed to originate from everywhere. Her big soft face was suddenly glistening under the sun. That was Bea Katzenbach, lumbering off toward the subway entrance, patting her eyes with a tissue.

After she disappeared from view I bought a pink azalea from a vendor and placed it on my lapel.

Then I telephoned Montgomery Crimmins.

From that moment everything happened very quickly. I suppose he wanted to get it all down before I changed my mind, but I wasn't going to change my mind. While I waited for Crimmins I sat on a bench in the brilliant daylight. I put on sunglasses and turned my face to the sky, and soon I found myself thinking of another bench in another place at another time when I waited in the sun for a girl. Regine had not freed me, despite her wish. She remained what she'd always been, which was with me, part of me, for we had formed each other when the clay was soft, each of us pressing into the other. I was born with her as I was lost with her, and in finding her again I found myself.

"I can't do a thing for you, Officer," Crimmins said, dropping next to me on the bench, breathless from the short jog from Joralemon Street. "You know that."

"I know."

"You just pleaded guilty," he said.

"I know."

"You're going upstate, Officer."

"I know," I said. "And stop calling me 'Officer.'"

"It's out of my hands now. I can't give you a plea deal," he said with a credible expression of concern. "We could've worked something out. I mean, the hell were you thinking? No one in my office wants to see you in state prison, for chrissake. You know this whole thing, it's—it's all just fuckin politics."

I smiled. Everyone was angry at me for pleading guilty. "It's better this way, counsel."

"Better how?"

"They'd think I'd say whatever you wanted, you gave me a deal," I said. "This way you're not buying me. I'm free of charge."

"Of course, but—" He nodded in agreement, but he was smart enough to know I was leaving something out. "I don't get it. Why the change of heart?"

"No change of heart, counsel. I still won't lie for you."

"Oh, please," he said. "But tell me. Everyone wants something. Nothing's ever free."

"That's not true."

"Maybe, but—just tell me what you're getting out of this."

"I still want the same thing I always did, counsel," I told him. "The same thing everyone wants."

"Which is what?"

"Justice for Georgina."

He smiled weakly. "Bullshit. Come on, really?" he asked despite himself, not wanting my answer but nevertheless too professionally suspicious to leave it alone.

"Let's just say I always wanted to be a cop."

"I don't understand, Way."

"No, I suppose you don't," I told him. "But some people are funny about how they see themselves. I mean, you would not believe what I've done to avoid selling avocados for a living."

Together inside Brooklyn Supreme we found a door marked GRAND JURY FOUR and in front of a stenographer and twenty-some civilians Assistant District Attorney Montgomery Crimmins asked me questions and I gave him answers. I swore under oath to tell him the truth and I gave him the facts. When I was done, when I'd told the jury how Police Officer Georgina Reed had admitted her crime to me, I waited for Crimmins to take the bait.

And, after a moment of hesitation, he did.

> MR. CRIMMINS: Thank you. One last thing, Mr. Way.
>
> MR. WAY: Yes, sir.
>
> MR. CRIMMINS: Mr. Way, you just described a meeting you had with Police Officer Georgina Reed at the police auto impound lot at which she admitted to you that she planted a firearm on or near the body of Laquan Dewberry--
>
> MR. WAY: Raquan.
>
> MR. CRIMMINS: --to make it appear that Mr. Dewberry was armed during the incident you testified about.
>
> MR. WAY: I assume that's why she did it, counsel. She didn't say.
>
> MR. CRIMMINS: Fair enough. But she admitted she put the gun there.
>
> MR. WAY: She didn't say she did. She said we did.
>
> MR. CRIMMINS: Okay. She or someone else did. In her presence.
>
> MR. WAY: Correct. It wasn't Dewberry's gun anyway.
>
> MR. CRIMMINS: I understand.
>
> MR. WAY: It was the co-defendant's. Odom. I forgot his first name, I'm sorry.
>
> MR. CRIMMINS: Me, too. But what I wanted to ask you is at any time subsequent to that meeting with Officer Reed did you share her admission of criminal conduct with anyone?

MR. WAY: Subsequent?

MR. CRIMMINS: Yes.

MR. WAY: I mean, I don't think I could have shared it with anyone before meeting her in College Point, counsel.

MR. CRIMMINS: No, Officer, Mr. Way. But let me ask it more directly, then. Did you ever share this admission by Officer Reed with any justice of the Kings County Supreme Court?

His dark brown eyes snapped mischievously at me although his affect remained bland and lawyerly, and behind him the grand jurors listened. I nearly smiled. Had I, he certainly would have smiled back, for in that moment Montgomery Crimmins at last knew what I wanted.

MR. WAY: No, sir, I did not.

MR. CRIMMINS: You did not?

MR. WAY: No, sir.

MR. CRIMMINS: I'm going to ask you, Mr. Way, whether in March of this year you met privately with Justice Henry K. Pomeroy? A judge of this court, now deceased?

MR. WAY: Yes, sir. I did.

MR. CRIMMINS: I see. You admit you met with Justice Pomeroy?

MR. WAY: I did.

MR. CRIMMINS: And where was this meeting with Justice Pomeroy?

MR. WAY: In chambers. Brooklyn Supreme Court.

MR. CRIMMINS: And you were then personally acquainted with Justice Pomeroy, were you not?

MR. WAY: Yes, sir.

MR. CRIMMINS: How? How did you know him?

MR. WAY: Well, I'd known him for some time.

MR. CRIMMINS: And can you say how you knew Justice Pomeroy?

MR. WAY: We had a relationship of a personal nature.

MR. CRIMMINS: I'm sorry?

MR. WAY: I was his-- When I was younger you could say
I provided maritime services.

MR. CRIMMINS: Can you be more specific?

MR. WAY: No.

MR. CRIMMINS: I see. And in this meeting in chambers
with Justice Pomeroy in March, you say you did not
discuss this investigation or any admission to you by
Officer Reed?

MR. WAY: No, sir.

MR. CRIMMINS: Did you ever disclose to Justice
Pomeroy that Officer Reed had admitted to you that she or
someone with her knowledge had planted false evidence at
a crime scene?

MR. WAY: No, sir, I did not.

MR. CRIMMINS: No?

MR. WAY: No, sir, that would have been improper.

MR. CRIMMINS: Yes. I agree. But I'm guessing you did
talk about something with Justice Pomeroy, did you not?

MR. WAY: Yes, sir, we did.

We watched one another with fierce interest. The grand jurors waited, understanding nothing. The stenographer's fingers were poised, ready for me to answer. Crimmins was a prosecutor once again, and he was no longer ready to smile. He knew I was lying, that my truth was no longer his truth, that my truth was no longer a fact, but it made no difference to me. There was nothing he or anyone could do to me any longer. Besides, I figured he'd get over it.

MR. CRIMMINS: Mr. Way, what did you discuss with
Justice Pomeroy?

MR. WAY: His daughter.

In the end, of course, I went upstate. I was on Rikers for a month before they shipped me off to Butler. Butler was not so bad. The food reminded me of the high school cafeteria and my cell had a view of nothing and seemed like a shitty motel on an interstate somewhere. I checked out after seventeen months and the entire episode seems like a movie I saw a long time ago. I have no nightmares

about it, and at the moment my business card informs me that I am *Gen'l M'ger Wm. Way & Son NY's Largest* et cetera.

The Butler Correctional Facility, by the way, is located just outside Red Creek, New York. While it will never be a place we take the kids on summer vacation, Red Creek is as far from Brooklyn as I've gotten in the world.